Never Fear
The Apocalypse

William F. Nolan   Matthew Costello

F. Paul Wilson   Heather Graham

Tim Waggoner   Thomas F. Monteleone

Brendan Deneen   Jason V Brock   Patrick Freivald

Lisa Mannetti   Lee Lawless   Tori Eldridge

Mathew Kaufman   Jeff DePew   Lance Taubold

Ed DeAngelis   Crystal Perkins   Ron Goulart

DEDICATION

This book is dedicated to the thousands of people that keep the horror genre alive. Read/Scream/Repeat. It's a way of life.

CONTENTS

ACKNOWLEDGMENTS

Special thanks to William F. Nolan. Your writing has shaped generations.

VACATION
Matthew Costello

Jack went out to check the car—yet again. He tried to believe that he was overly preoccupied with the dangers, that he was letting himself get way too jittery.

He shut the door behind him, the back door to their house. He shut it tight and then looked at it.

I don't want anyone coming out while I'm looking around. No, he thought, I don't need them nervous… Christie, and the kids. For months, he had balked at the idea, the very *concept* of taking a vacation. Under the circumstances, it was crazy.

But Christie came to him. She put her arms around him, pulled him close, and said:

"Jack—do you know how long it's been… how long it's been since we've gone *anywhere*? They say it's safe, that the area is secure. It's a safe family place. The kids haven't seen a lake, any water to swim in… for so long."

Jack nodded. He didn't tell her many of the stories from work. There was no point in telling Christie just how badly things seemed to be going. The city was gone. Completely gone… New York—the Big Apple—was history. There was no question about it.

Oh, there were some spots, some key sectors that were under control. All of lower Manhattan was fine, supplied by ships on a daily basis, girded by a ring of soldiers and artillery.

And there was a broad strip running up the West Side, nearly to the George Washington Bridge. That was okay. There were still some restaurants, still places where you could go out to eat.

Instead of being eaten.

But the rest of the city was controlled by the others, the Can Heads. They were there and they were spreading…

Jack's own sector ran from North Yonkers, just up to the suburbs of Westchester. Westchester itself was a maze of twelve-foot mesh fences and checkpoints. The Can Heads were being contained, that

1

was the official line. In fact, the President announced that in each of the big cities the Can Heads were confined. Yes, and soon they'd be rounded up and placed in camps. Any aggressive action by them would be put down by violent means.

Contained... rounded-up...

No fucking way.

The orders were simple. Kill them. In fact, if you even suspected someone of being one of them, you were to blow their fucking head off. And like sharks, they'd waste some time feeding on their own. Food is fucking food. And Jack knew that—despite orders quite to the contrary—he and the other cops were taking the dead bodies and poisoning them... leaving them for the others.

Anything. Jack thought, anything to cut down their numbers. Anything to reduce the sick feeling that there were more of them than us. More of them—and growing, all the fucking time, more and more of them.

Jack turned away from the back door. No one was coming.

He looked at his car. It had been an ordinary station wagon. But then Jack had fitted it with all the necessary items. There was metal shielding to protect the tires from a sniper. The windshield and side windows were all reinforced safety glass, strong enough to stop a bullet. The underbody was protected by a steel shell.

And Jack had helped himself to a nice array of weapons and ammunition from the station, all now secreted below the spare tire, a small armory.

He crouched down. He checked his last modification to the car, the one that made his mouth go dry and cottony. He felt the wires running from the gas tank, to the front, and up—into the dashboard. He fingered the plastic strip covering the wires, holding them flush to the underside of the car.

There was no way it wouldn't work—if he ever needed it. No way...

Jack heard the back door open. He quickly got up and he heard Simon bickering with his sister, fighting over who got to ride in the back seat, the one that faced the rear. They both hated it but Jack didn't want them sitting together, squabbling all the way Upstate... The luggage sat on the roof rack. Jack stood up... straightened his pants.

It was time to leave on their vacation.

***

"I've packed some sandwiches, and juice—"

Christie was sitting beside him. She patted his arm, and Jack smiled, looking out the windshield. It was a beautiful day, with a bright sun sitting in a deep blue sky. It looked like there'd be cool mornings and evenings, while the days would get just hot enough…

"What kind of sandwiches?" Simon bellowed from the back of the wagon.

Jack could guess this. "Peanut butter and—"

"Oh, yuck—I'm sick of peanut butter. God, I hate—"

Jack looked up to the rearview mirror, to the back of Simon's head. "Simon—ease up, will you? It's just for the trip up. We'll have some good meals at the camp."

"I doubt that—" Simon muttered. Jack chewed at his lip.

Laurie, his little girl, was playing with her doll's hair, grabbing a great hank of hair and pulling it through a tiny hair band. She didn't get involved in the discussion.

Of course, Jack thought, Laurie has always lived this way, she was *used* to the way food was these days. Real meat was a rarity, a special item. Mostly there was beans and pasta, and even peanut butter was getting expensive.

The Great Drought killed the Farm Belt. Not just wounded it, there wasn't just a bad harvest. It killed it dead. Year after year of drought transformed the nation's breadbasket, turning it dry, letting the prehistoric desert in the West slither east, claiming the farmland.

Things were bad here. But in California—a confidential police report said—things were way beyond bad. The whole state might be gone. The first state to be controlled by the Can Heads…

Not much news got out of California these days.

"Relax," Christie said. And she gave his thigh a squeeze. Jack looked over. She was wearing a pretty summer dress, great red flowers, with bare arms. Her legs were already tanned from hours spent in the garden in their backyard, coaxing tomatoes and raspberries out of the rocky soil.

He smiled. "Okay," he said. "I just got to turn the switch. Turn the switch, and start the vacation. Try to have some fun."

Every few blocks, leading to the highway, he saw a sector patrolman. It was reassuring, but it was also disturbing. It said that even here, even two dozen miles from New York, from the big city, there was danger.

Even here…

There was a certain route that had to be followed to the highway. Most of the entrance and exit ramps had been sealed. Now there were only a few ways on and off the Thomas E. Dewey Thruway. You could only enter—or exit—with a pass. And the Emergency Highway Police, a new division of the State Police, would shoot to kill.

"You have the papers?" he asked.

Christie popped open the glove compartment. "All set."

Jack slowed. There was a car in front of him. The highway itself, its six lanes visible just ahead, was deserted.

Not much traffic these days.

Jack inched forward. He looked at the highway. On either side there was a tall mesh fence, topped with spirals of barbed wire. *How much fucking protection in that?* Jack thought. *What the hell good could that do?*

Someone could just as easily lob something at us, some explosive, something to stop the car and—

Jack looked down, at the dash, at the switch just near the steering column.

"Jack—they've moved up. Go on… the booth is empty."

He nodded, and eased the station wagon up to the booth. There was no toll. All the considerable fees—from entry point to exit point and back again—had been paid weeks ago.

The guard, an automatic rifle slung over his shoulder, stepped down to the window.

"Hi, folks. How are you doing today?"

Making small talk. It was a technique. Sometimes they could look normal, almost act normal. But if you talked to them for any length of time, if you chatted to a Can Head, you'd *know*.

Shit, you could sense it—or maybe even smell it on them, on their clothes, on their breath. You'd maybe see a red dollop marking their shirt, the sign of Cain. And still smiling, you'd try to back away, lowering your gun, hoping you could blow the fucker away before he—

"Going on a vacation, eh?"

"Yes," Christie said, smiling, "Our first with the kids. We're going to the Paterville Family Camp."

The guard nodded, looking at Jack. "Yes, I hear it's nice up there." Jack had trouble engaging in the chit-chat, the little routine the highway cop had.

"Have there been any reports?" Jack said, "Any trouble, on the way up?"

The guard laughed, as if it was a silly question.

"No. Nothing for weeks. Been real quiet. I think we've got them on the run. And you've got a good steel mesh fence there. I wouldn't worry."

The guard scanned the back of the wagon, checking out the children.

"You have a nice vacation," the guard said, backing away.

He went back to his booth and opened up the gate. It took forever for the whirring engine to sluggishly get the gate up. Then Jack pulled away onto the highway.

He drove for miles, silent now, glad that Christie let him be quiet. And the only company on the road was a few lonely-looking cars, then a truck, a giant dairy truck.

Couldn't have milk in it, Jack thought. No way there was milk in that truck.

Christie turned on the radio, but the stations were already mostly static, and the warming sound of voices and old music—the only kind available these days—vanished.

**

Laurie had fallen asleep, and Simon had crawled forward, searching for more chips and juice. He groaned when Christie told him that he was out of luck.

"But I'm hungry," he said.

He was always hungry. No matter how much they stuffed into him, there didn't ever seem to be enough to stop him from whining about more food.

"That's all we had," Jack said. "And besides—we're almost there, Simon. Now just sit quietly."

Jack looked left. He thought he saw something, by the side of the highway. And he did, a curled shaving of black, a tire. A retread that exploded, probably stranding a car. He passed more of the tire, another black chunk, just to the side of the road. Just a failed retread, he thought. That was all. Or maybe it was something else. Maybe someone had their tires shot out from under them. That would be nice—lose your tires, and then rumble to a jangly stop, pulling off the deserted highway.

Maybe it happened at night.

And then you'd have to wait, in the dark—wait to see what climbed over the fence, or cut through it. You'd lock yourself in the car, of course. You'd do that. But that wouldn't help, that would only make it worse. You'd have to watch them, prying you out, like opening a can.

Once, on his patrol, Jack found a car like that. There was nothing left inside, it had been picked clean, no seats, no bones, nothing. Like a metal clam scraped clean by a giant set of teeth. There was just the red spatters—on the ceiling, on the floor, on the broken glass.

Dried spatters where it hadn't been licked clean… Now—he looked at the fence, gleaming, silvery and secure.

Christie touched his arm.

"It's the next exit, Jack. It's just ahead." He looked at her, and she smiled at him.

"We're almost there… "

***

Moving onto the country roads, they left the security of the highway, with its twelve-foot-high fence, its curled barbed wire.

Jack felt exposed.

"Lock the doors," he said.

Christie pushed down her button, then she reached behind and pushed down Laurie's button.

"Simon, lock your door."

His son shook his head and pushed down the button.

The blue sky was now dotted with big, grayish clouds that drifted across the sky, blotting out the sun. Jack felt chilled sitting in the car.

We're up in the mountains, he thought. Gets cold up here. I wish there was more sunlight.

They passed a house, a small wooden house all burned out. Ugly black beams jutted into the air to support a roof no longer there. He wondered what had caused the fire, and what had happened to the people inside. Then an old gas station flew by, two ancient pumps sitting outside. There seemed to be a general store inside the station, signs advertising Bud Light, Marlboro…

Jimmy Dean's Pork Sausage.

"How far to Paterville?" he said to Christie. He didn't do a very

6

good job of keeping the edge out of his voice.

"Just a few more miles," she said. "You turn off just ahead, onto Sanfellow's Road. Then the camp is just up a hill. There's a map… see."

Jack nodded. Good. We're close. The camp touted its security. Its twenty-four-hour security force. Its electronic surveillance and electrified fence.

Maybe when I'm in there, when my family is behind all that security, maybe then I'll be able to relax, Jack thought. But he doubted it.

***

"Good to see you folks." The fat man looked up to the sky. "It *was* a beautiful day." The man smiled. "Some nasty clouds kinda snuck in." He clapped his hands together. "No matter, let's get you to your cabin and start your vacation."

Jack watched the man lower a hand to Laurie's head and rustle her hair. "How's that sound?" Laurie smiled.

The man, Camp Director Ed Lowe, was doing his best to put them at ease, Jack knew. *Must get a lot of paranoid people coming here. He's trying his best to radiate as much warmth as possible.*

They walked to the cabin, past the dining hall and a large room that Lowe pointed out was the family rec room.

"We got ping-pong, pool, even some video games," he said.

He came close to Jack. "You seem a bit jittery, friend. Any trouble on the way up here?"

Jack shook his head. "No." He forced himself to smile. "Nothing at all. It's just—"

Jack looked around at the camp, at the people he could see down at the lake… kids jumping into the now-gray water from a diving platform. Little toddlers dashing around on the thin strip of beach, happily falling down onto the sand. It looked wonderful.

He took a breath. And he said:

"I'm a cop… I'm in charge of one of the sectors. Right on the city border."

Lowe made a big "O" with his mouth. "Oh—I see. Guess you've seen a lot. Some real bad stuff." Lowe clapped a hand around Jack's shoulder. "I hope that we can help you forget that stuff here." Then, tighter, pulling Jack real close. "I hope that you and your family have a real good time here."

A line of small brown cabins that stretched from the beach, around the curve of the lake, into the woods, was just ahead.

Jack looked behind him, and he saw his kids, open-mouthed, grinning, eager to get in the water, to have fun, to play.

And Jack took a breath.

***

"Knock-knock?"

Jack looked up from his suitcase. A man and a woman stood at the screen door to their cabin. Laurie and Simon had already torn off to the beach while he and Christie unpacked.

"Hi, folks," the man said. "I hope we're not interrupting but me and Sharon, we saw that you just arrived. We're—" the man looked to his left—"right next door, and we thought we'd welcome you."

Christie touched Jack's arm, squeezed it. He looked at her. Her smile said, *relax*. Stop being a cop. Invite the nice people in.

Jack went over to the screen door and opened it. "Hi," he said. "We're still getting settled here."

The man looked at the room, taking in the open luggage, the beds filled with clothes.

"Oh, don't want to disturb you. Just being friendly."

Christie came forward, her hand extended. "Oh, no—thank you. That's very nice." She saw so few people these days...

She introduced herself and Jack.

"We're the Blairs," the man said. "Tom and Sharon... Our two kids are probably down at the lake already. You're going to like it here. It's safe... and it's fun."

Tom Blair grabbed his wife's hand and squeezed it tight. "We're having a real nice time here. You folks are going to *love* it."

People being friendly... it was hard for Jack to accept the concept. There wasn't any room for friendliness in this world. Not anymore.

"How long have you been here?"

Tom Blair said, "Three days. And we're signed up for two more. Gonna hate to leave."

His wife spoke, quietly, a woman with a whispery voice, as if she could be scared of the world. "Maybe you'd like to have dinner with our family. Everyone sits at these big tables."

"Very homey," Tom said.

Christie nodded. "Sure. We'd love to."

Tom Blair winked. "See you then."

***

The dining room was filled with noisy kids and babies crying and the clatter of cheap silverware clanging against plates.

Laurie and Simon had had a great time swimming. Laurie only wading to the edge of the lake, while Simon swam to the float and dove off.

Now, though, they were complaining about the food. There was a lot of it, but it was a pasty bean mixture. A gloopy dish that had Simon rolling his eyes and pushing his plate away.

"*This* is good food?" he said.

"Simon… " Jack said.

"Yeah," Tom Blair said. "The cuisine's not quite up to what the brochure said. But it's filling—and there's plenty of it."

"Oh, goody," Simon said, and the Blair kids, two boys, ten and nine, both laughed.

"There's a lot of people here," Jack said. "They must do some business…"

"Yes," Blair said. "But you know there's one thing that confuses me. Last night, I—"

But Ed Lowe was at a podium in the front of the room and his amplified voice suddenly filled the hall.

"Good evening, Paterville families! And let's welcome the newcomers!"

On cue, the hall resounded with a hundred voices booming, "Welcome, newcomers!"

"Now listen up, families. I just got the updated weather forecast for tomorrow," Lowe said. "And it's going to be *beautiful*. And for tonight, we're having a sing-along by the big fireplace, and there will be games for the kids in the rec room."

Jack looked around as Lowe spoke. He saw so many families, so many kids. After years of leaving his house and stopping Can Heads—killing them—this all looked so peaceful, so safe.

Then—he thought:

Why don't I feel safe?

Tom Blair stood up.

"Maybe we'll see you at the sing-along?"

Jack nodded.

"Yeah," he said. "Maybe you will…"

9

***

"You're not sleeping," Christie said.

They had made love. First, they'd read books, waiting for the kids to fall asleep. And then Christie had shut her light off, and then his light, before she slid under the covers, working on him, making him hard.

Now he listened.

There were noises outside. He heard noises outside.

He thought that he heard gunshots, the sound of gates opening or shutting, or someone yelling—

No. It's just the sound of the woods, the lake. A screeching, the wind rustling leaves.

The sounds faded—and he had moaned.

"You're not sleeping," Christie said again. He looked to her and her eyes glistened wetly in the blackness, catching the light.

"I—I can't sleep," he said.

It wasn't the first time he had trouble sleeping. Not by a long-shot. And it was getting to be a problem...

She nodded. "Are you worried? I mean, how safe do you want us to be?"

"No. Everything looks fine here. Couldn't be better. Still—there's something that bothers me."

She gave a small laugh. "Well, when you figure it out, be sure and tell me. But now I'm going to sleep. I want to enjoy the sun and the water tomorrow."

She turned away.

The room was cold. In minutes, he heard her rhythmic breathing, a reminder that he couldn't sleep, that sleep would only come when he was too tired to think anymore, to wonder...

What's bothering me?

***

He was in bed, rubbing his eyes. The door to the cabin was open. It was morning... that fast. Morning.

Christie stood there, cute and sexy in a great two-piece bathing suit. Jack wondered: When was the last time I saw her in a bathing suit?

He leaned up on one elbow.

"I'm taking the kids down to the beach." She peered over her sunglasses. "See you there, sleepy head?"

"Yeah, what time—" He turned left. It was after nine. "I'll see you there."

The screen door slammed shut.

Jack sat up in bed. And then he remembered. He remembered his night, all the thoughts he'd had, until he finally came to one thing he could hold onto. The one thing that really bothered him…

The people, all those families in the dining hall.

Some of them—a lot of them—acted as if they'd been here a long time, as if this wasn't a vacation place, some new place to visit. They acted—what?

As if this was their home.

Maybe it was just a strange feeling. Maybe it was just his cop paranoia, seeing strangeness, sickness everywhere.

He got up, pulling on his jeans and a T-shirt. He went to the screen door. He heard kids playing by the beach.

Then he looked left, to the cabin where the Blairs were staying. It's a crazy idea, he thought. Crazy—but it wouldn't hurt to ask Tom Blair if he had the same feeling.

I could laugh about it, Jack thought. You get crazy ideas when you're a cop. Pretty damn funny…

He walked down the wooden steps to the ground and hurried over to the Blairs' cabin. He walked up the wooden steps and knocked on the door… and it swung open, ajar, creaking…

A woman was inside, but it wasn't Blair's wife. "Oh, I was looking for the family staying here."

The woman looked up at him. She was putting clean sheets on the bed. She had a cart with towels, small wrapped packets of soap. Jack looked at her face, her eyes.

She looked as if she had been caught doing something. The woman shook her head.

Then she smiled, quickly. "Oh, they left. They left the camp. They had to leave." The words came fast. Too fast.

I know when people are lying. I *know* that. Always have.

Jack was about to say something, about how the Blairs were staying a few more days, and she must have made a mistake. But he looked around the room. The cabin was empty. No luggage. Swept clean. They were gone.

Jack's throat felt tight. He nodded. "Oh—okay," he said. He turned back to the door.

He felt the woman watching him while he opened the screen door, then let it slam shut behind him. There was no morning sun outside, no nice day, like Ed Lowe predicted. Instead, it was cloudy, cool.

Jack thought of his family, down by the water, swimming with the other families...

He put on shoes and grabbed his wallet, his keys... Because that's all we need, he thought. That's all we need. If it isn't too late. Oh, Christ, if it isn't—

***

He reached the beach. He saw Simon diving, clumsily, without any grace. Boy doesn't get any practice, he thought. Not enough fucking practice 'cause there's not too many safe places to swim, not too many pools you'd send your kids to—

He felt a hand on his back.

"You have a good night's sleep, Jack?"

Jack turned around and saw Ed Lowe, standing there. He nodded. "Fine. It was... very comfortable."

Lowe smiled. "The mountain air. Makes you sleep like a baby." Lowe came closer. The wind changed. The director nodded toward Jack's family. "They're having a good time. You did the right thing coming here."

Jack smiled back. *He knows,* he thought. *He knows I saw the empty cabin, and that I asked questions, and now—now—*

"We have a nice place here," Lowe said. "A real nice place for families."

And Jack looked at Lowe's eyes, at the runny egg whites lined with red, then down to the coils of fat around the man's neck. His big, strong-looking hands, with pudgy fingers.

Jack licked his lips. He doesn't look—

"Maybe this is *your* kind of place?" Lowe said, moving even closer, the wind carrying his smell to Jack's nostrils.

No. You don't get that fat on beans, on soy paste, on—

The smell. Jack knew what it was. He got it a lot, on the streets. It was the smell of meat, the tangy scent of blood. Lowe's lips were red, a Santa Claus red, rosy cheeks and beet-red lips.

Jack watched Lowe run his tongue across his teeth, searching, scouring.

There was something there, something stringy, dangling from a tooth.

Jack couldn't breathe. The smell, the voices squealing by the water. He felt his car keys pressing into his thigh.

"Well—if you'll excuse me. I've got to—"

Jack walked past Lowe, forcing himself to breathe regularly. *It's okay*, he told himself. *Lowe doesn't know anything.* Jack walked over to Christie, sitting in a chair low to the sand.

"Get Laurie," he whispered to her.

Christie turned around. "What? Jack, what do you—"

He put a hand on her shoulder and squeezed tightly. "Please, be—"

He turned around, expecting to see Lowe there, watching, spying on him. *I'm not crazy, am I?*

Then back to Christie. "Get Laurie and walk to the car. I'll call Simon and follow you…"

"Whatever for? What are you—"

He pinched her shoulder, enough to cause some pain, enough to let her know that she should just fucking *do* it.

When Jack stood up, he saw people watching him, looking. *Welcome newcomers…*

He moved to the edge of the lake just as Simon surfaced. "Simon! Come here."

For a moment it looked as if the boy wouldn't come, that he'd make Jack shout to him while everyone watched. But then Simon kicked back and swam to him.

Jack waited, while the cool breeze off the lake played with his hair, while—all of a sudden—it got quiet on the beach.

"What's up, Dad?"

Jack leaned down close to Simon. He whispered.

"Simon. Don't respond to what I say. Don't do anything. If you understand, just nod a bit."

"Yeah, but—"

Jack shook his head. "Quiet! Don't say a word. Just—when I start off the beach, you follow me. Do you understand?"

Simon nodded.

There was no sound on the beach now, and Jack's whisper felt thunderous. "Just follow me back to the car, as fast as you can. Don't look back, don't do anything…"

The boy was shivering He wasn't stupid, and Jack's tone had cut through his annoyance and confusion.

"Now, good…ready…"

Jack stood up straight, turned, and walked off the beach, moving fast, not running, but walking with big strides while Simon, barefooted, trotted to keep up.

***

He was afraid that when he got to the car, Christie and Laurie wouldn't be there, or maybe—God—their car wouldn't be there.

There were only a few cars there.

That was it. All along, and I didn't understand that, he thought. All those people and only a few cars.

Welcome newcomers…

But Christie was there. And Laurie was sitting in the back. The locks were down. But when Christie saw him she leaned across and opened the driver and then the passenger door.

"Get in," he said.

They slammed their doors together. Jack stuck the key in the ignition and turned it, fearing that it wouldn't turn over, that the car's insides had been trashed.

That's what I'd do, Jack thought. Rip the guts right out.

But the car turned over. He pushed down the lock on his door, and Simon copied him. Jack looked back to the lake, to the trail leading to the beach, but he didn't see anybody following.

He pulled away.

And Christie—took a breath—and said: "Now can you tell me what this is about?"

Jack looked back at Laurie. He tried to protect her, to keep the badness away. But Christie needed to know.

"They're here," he said. "God—in this camp."

Christie laughed. "You've lost it. Now I know it. Why on earth do you—"

He looked at her as he pulled onto the gravel road leading to the gate out.

I'll ram right through that fucking gate if I have to, he thought. "The Blairs. They were staying for two more days, and now they're gone."

"Their plans probably changed, Jack. Why do you—"

"The chamber maid cleaning their room—she was hiding something. I can tell, Christie. I know when people lie. It's my job."

"Mommy," Laurie said. "Daddy's scaring me. Tell him to stop—"

"Then this Ed Lowe guy tracked me down. As if he had heard that I found out something, that I suspected. Fat Ed Lowe... How the hell do you think he got so fat? And—God—I smelled it. On his breath. I tell you, I smelled it. And his teeth. They weren't clean, they were still filled with stringy bits of—"

The gate was ahead, just around the curve, past a tall stand of pines.

"Dad—hey, Dad, there's somebody—" Simon leaned forward, pointing at the road.

The road... filled with people.

They were carrying things. Sticks, bats, and—catching the full gray morning light—silvery things. Ed Lowe was in the front, and there were children there too.

He thought of what Lowe said. A good place for families.

As if he was saying: You could live here too. We could *use* someone like you.

Jack had guns, but there were too many of them... "Hold on," he said, and he floored the car.

Which was exactly what they wanted him to do. They had prepared for him.

They parted, exposing the gravel road and the giant tree trunk spread across it. The car rammed into it and then stopped dead.

There was a popping noise, the sound of the tires being hacked. Primitive. Prehistoric. The way you'd bring down a mastodon. Laurie was crying, bleating, "Daddy, Daddy..."

Simon, sweet boy, good boy, whispered to him, so calm. "Should I get the guns, Dad?"

Simon had found them. Simon had been worried, too. He knew his dad had brought guns...

Christie grabbed his leg. "Oh, God, Jack. Oh, no—"

Last year, when the food ran out, when the meat stopped, something had happened. People changed. There was no explanation for the sudden outbreak of packs, a cult of cannibalism. There were just a few small groups—Can Heads, the newspapers called them. Except one scientist said yes, this was probably the way the dinosaurs vanished.

Feeding on each other...

As if some switch had been thrown, some end-of-the-world

switch. After all the suffering, the homeless people, the poverty, the hunger. Some final switch was thrown. And this was the way it would end.

They were smashing at the car's windows.

The safety glass didn't shatter, but a web-like mesh of cracks appeared. Eventually it would give out.

They surrounded the car. Jack saw the other families, their mouths open, wet lips, teeth exposed. They were angry. This probably wasn't how they liked to do it. This was probably too undignified.

Christie was crying.

"Jack, please. Our babies…"

The back window gave out, and now he heard the voices, the snarling of the Can Heads, this new species, human cannibals ready to feed on their prey.

Jack turned and looked at his wife.

Then back to Laurie. She had her hands over her ears, and she was crying, hopelessly trying to drown out the screams, the horrible sounds.

He heard them on the roof. Crawling on the roof. It was a feeding frenzy. Jack had imagined what it would be like—to be caught by them—and now it was happening.

We fell in the trap… he thought.

He looked at Christie. Her eyes begged for him to do something.

I will…

"I love you," he said.

The window by Simon caved in. The boy yelped, and screamed, "Dad!"

There was no more time.

Jack fingered the switch by the steering column.

For a moment he thought: *What if it doesn't work? Oh, God, what if somehow it doesn't work?*

He threw the switch.

The battery fired a spark into the oversized gas tank.

There was the tiniest second of hesitation—and then the explosion ripped from behind him, with searing heat, burning, painful— the screams of his family mixing with the roar.

Merciful…

Ending everything in one blessed, white-hot flash of pain.

And then the screaming, the crying, the smashing, all vanished...
And the gravel road was quiet.

APOCALYPSE THEN
Lisa Mannetti

"Scientists have long observed the seeming mystery: You can will yourself to die."
   -Laurence Gonzales

"Under stress, you don't invent new strategies. You revert to automatic behaviors."
   -Laurence Gonzales

Mt. Denali: June 23, 2020

We thought it was just the wind.

The wind—ceaseless, screaming, bearing frozen death—had already kept us pinned for two days in the snow cave we'd dug at 17,900 feet. A storm no one predicted had suddenly raged out of nowhere and caught us out after we summited. We were only 700 vertical feet above our last camp, the one we'd used as our launch pad to gain the top of Denali, but in a whiteout you can't tell sky from mountain—and the last thing you want to do is step off an unseen, *unsensed* precipice that will only stop your fall thousands upon thousands of feet lower: stop you, that is, after the initial shocked shout; after the frantic, futile grab at mere air; after the hideous cartwheels and the final doomed spiral down and down and downward still.

"It's not that far to the tents," Drew shouted at us. You have to yell—practically in peoples' earholes—to be heard at all when the wind roars like that. All four of us knew that the tents meant safety and warmth and plenty of food. But we also knew that most fatalities on big mountains happen on the descent. At 20,310 feet, that's plenty big. The altitude—in this case where less than half of the oxygen available at sea level is around to stoke you—plays havoc with your mind. You think you're being logical and you're not. You think you're still strong, but your body is weakening—consuming itself—with every step, every second you spend at altitude. For a second, I started to turn away and follow Drew, but Allen pulled at my shoulder.

"We don't have a choice," he screamed. "We have to dig in or we'll die!"

I blinked at him and he shook my arm. "Reese," he said, "it's not just the cold; we could all of us be blown right off the mountain if the wind gets any stronger."

Suddenly, the excitement (read "adrenaline") of standing on top of the tallest mountain in North America was gone. Now I was only tired, and worse, drained.

***

All four of us had hacked and chipped at the ice with our axes to hollow out the small cave. Penny and Drew were inside shoving snow and ice back through the entrance. Allen was trying to make the tiny space slightly larger—but not too big or we'd lose whatever heat our bodies could generate. The wind began to swirl and gust and the temperature began to plummet. Just before I ducked inside I glanced at the thermometer that was clipped to the fastening on my lime-green parka: It read -30 degrees Fahrenheit. Allen, I figured, by insisting we dig in to get out of the wind and the killing cold had just saved God knew how many toes and fingers, God knew how many lives. When the actual temperature plummets below -20 F (not including the wind-chill factor) your chance of getting frostbite rockets up to ninety-five per cent. My mother always told me I had graceful hands and pretty feet and I'd seen too many pictures of what frostbite did to *any* kind of fingers and toes—pretty or not—like massive swelling to the point of grotesquerie (imagine a hugely bloated sausage that's a finger ballooned up around a tiny, thin, nearly hidden wedding ring). Yes, plenty of images. Photos of hands and feet: marble white and dead black. Pix of the gangrene setting in, of the stumps after amputations of dead digits... and sometimes not just digits, but calves and forearms and noses and ears.... I had a dread approaching phobia when it came to frostbite... the worst, I thought, would be the hope you might retain those taken-for-granted appendages, that blood flow would return to the deadened flesh, that nerves would be regenerated, that what had been burned by cold could be saved. You'd wait in hope when doctors shrugged a non-committal *maybe*, convincing yourself it would be all right. Right up to the moment they told you that the formerly known and loved section of yourself was going to be cut off and thrown away. Permanently. Wake up from the anesthesia and part—or even, God forbid, parts— of you are gone for good. And while the optimist in me maintains nothing is impossible (hell, I'd just climbed Denali aka McKinley!), another equally strong and loquacious element wondered if I could learn to manipulate toilet paper using a hook… wondered if puppies and kittens and small children would flee the monstrous sight of steel—where once there'd been a neat, pretty hand.

Mt. Denali: June 24, 2020

The start of our third morning in the small, hollowed out cave. The air—except when we unblocked the entrance partially to start up one of the stoves—was beginning to grow fetid from our mingled breath, from our unwashed bodies (it takes a few weeks—and there are no showers—to climb the fifteen miles of mountain), from the stink of the pee bottle.

We had our packs with sleeping bags and a little food, snow and ice to melt for drinking water, but we all knew unless we could descend soon we were doomed.

Someone—I forget who—said we ought to make a dash for the camp. But, the wind alone, Allen put in, was strong enough to blow any of us right off the mountain and the roaring, gale-force wind still had not stopped. Storms do blow in and out with great rapidity on the roof of North America, but they did sometimes last more than a week… and, sometimes up to *two* weeks…

Drew argued it was something other, something *more*. "Just listen!"

Allen snapped, "It's the *wind*. It's not a helicopter or a plane— you're just making Penny and Reese more nervous, getting their hopes for rescue up—so shut *up!*"

Unlike on Everest, where rescue up high is near impossible, on Denali planes and 'copters could make the trip—of course, not if there were high winds and blizzard conditions. Also, unlike Everest, they tried to remove as many bodies as was feasible. Some felled climbers were right on the standard routes up and down Everest and would-be summiteers not only saw them, but walked right past (and sometimes stepped over) the doomed and stricken. On our mountain, I think there were only about thirty bodies that remained—not like the more than 200 caught out on the highest peak in the world.

After the small silence that crept in after Allen raised his voice at Drew, Penny tried to perk up our spirits. "But, wow, hey... wasn't it something to be standing on the top? You can see a million pictures... but to be there... so incredible," she said.

There was another large *boom* and Drew said, "Didn't you hear that?"

"I heard it," Penny said. He was my boyfriend, but lately Penny seemed more in sync with Drew than I was.

"Ah, c'mon, it's probably just thunder or sonic boom from a jet," Allen put in. "Whose turn is it to fire up the stove and cook?"

You couldn't sit upright completely—the icy ceiling was too low—but I hunched forward and said. "I don't know whose turn it is, but I'll do it. My fingers feel a little numb."

"Okay, thanks. But like I keep telling you, Reese, wiggle your fingers and toes inside the bag. You have to—to keep the circulation going, keep your body temp up." Allen lay back on his side, the top of his shoulder and biceps nearly scraping the ice above. We were like sardines in there, I thought, and at the other end the rough, triangle-shaped cave narrowed so that someone's feet inside their sleeping bag were always on top of mine. I wondered if that would help or hurt them... inside my down booties they felt cold—but not numb... not yet.

So, while I waited for the snow and ice to melt (only to tepid because I didn't want to waste fuel to heat it to boiling which takes forever at altitude anyway) I thought about what Allen said, about what I knew about keeping your core temperature up to prevent hypothermia. Your body has this nifty automatic, unconscious trick to preserve what's needed for survival. It's called vasoconstriction and the body knows that for the organism (i.e. you) to function, it needs the heart, lungs and brain to have plenty of warm blood and oxygen. So, it has no compunction about sacrificing what is non-essential to live. That translates to the items I was petrified of losing: ears, nose, fingers, toes... Your body sends a "heigh-ho, here we go" signal and *pffft!* Blood begins to retreat from those areas because it has been determined the brain, the heart and the lungs *must* be saved. The problem for those caught out in the open is that with the creeping chill, muscles no longer function. After a while your hands and your feet just won't work. You can't move to save yourself. Some engineering god apparently forgot *that* part of the equation. Even if you want to move, you can't. And moving is one of the few ways to keep your body temperature high enough to stop it from shutting down. You also have to eat—and more importantly—drink, too. So I was melting snow and Allen and Drew were keeping a sharp eye on how much fuel we still had and how much food was left in the packs. Fussing with the small stove and moving my fingers, I reasoned, might see me out of the snow cave all digits still intact.

***

When you climb Denali, (unlike, say, Everest) you carry heavy loads and pull even heavier sleds with equipment and food. It's pretty typical to heft somewhere around 150 pounds—only eighty or so on the sled you're dragging. But we'd traveled light on summit day; the bulk of our gear, sleds and supplies and food were all 700 feet below us in our last camp. In the half-gloom of the cave, Allen wanted us to check through our packs for any food or provisions we might have overlooked. "One at a time... or we'll just be jarring and jouncing and aggravating one another. Maybe," he said, "a packet of powdered soup or dehydrated turkey slipped down to the bottom or meandered inside a pocket. Maybe you've got a few hand warmers or a couple of 'Hot Rods' stashed you forgot about."

Penny checked her pack first, hauling out some small items like a pair of goggles, ear buds, a neon blue balaclava, a dorky-looking flexible nose screen... She was slowly and—it seemed to me—haphazardly pawing through stuff no one really needed *inside* the cave. It was then I began to suspect not only that she wasn't a team player, but that maybe she was keeping something back... hiding something more.

That morning she'd been complaining about having a headache and feeling nauseous—the early symptoms of AMS, acute mountain sickness. Left untreated, it can be fatal. Fluid in your lungs can drown you; swelling in your brain can kill you. Allen had already culled through the pared-down emergency kits we'd brought when we were going "lightweight" for the summit, and come up with a couple of Diamox and some aspirin which can help thin blood so it doesn't turn as sludgy with the cold and lack of movement.

And while none of us had packed closed-foam sleeping pads, which would have kept our down bags a layer further away from the ice and therefore drier—she'd packed things I didn't understand why anyone would include when they were trying to get up to the summit and back as quickly and easily as possible. The more you carry up, the harder it is to make the top and get back safely. Cell phones are spotty on Denali—except a few places along the West Buttress like Windy Corners, but they were lightweight and thanks to technology, took great pictures. So it didn't seem odd that she had the phone— what was odd was that for what was supposed to be a twelve-hour trip from high camp and back, she'd packed solar panels and the charger to power it. Did she think she was going to sit on the summit and wait in the freezing air till it worked so she could call her mother? She certainly wasn't going to use solar power inside the cave or outside in a blizzard...

***

The first time Penny started puking, Allen began to ramp up his efforts to radio the med camp staffed with doctors who were also mountaineers at 14,000 feet. "D-Rap calling Denali II, D-Rap calling... do you copy? Denali II, this is D-Rap, we're pinned at 17.9... Denali II, are you there?" D-Rap was an acronym of our initials—every group that climbs the mountain comes up with their own moniker.

He'd been trying all the lower camps the past few days, but no one had answered and we thought maybe the blizzard and the wind was interfering with the signals. Maybe the storm wasn't as localized as we'd speculated and people in the lower camps had fled down to base at Kahiltna glacier and, for all we knew, scurried right off the mountain.

"Med-group at Denali II, we have a sick climber. Do you copy?"

Even I could hear that concern that was moving toward panic had crept into this voice.

That was just before things got a whole lot worse.

Mt. Denali: June 25, 2020

Penny was shivering in her sleeping bag. Allen told her—for about the fortieth time—if she'd stop keeping her face inside, her breath wouldn't condense and therefore actually make the bag wetter, the down clump up and become *less* effective.

"I don't want to lose my nose. Just leave me alone," she said, her face burrowed deep inside.

There was another of those huge hollow-sounding booms; the wind still howled and there were times it not only shook loose particles from the ceiling of our tiny cave, but we could feel it like a series of thumps inside. It had seemed darker inside that morning; I was worried the noise or the wind had set off an avalanche above us. No one said anything, though. I told myself it was just anxiety—had to be—because the air was still moving around us. Some of those gusts swirled through the slitted entrance like daggers flicked from a knife-throwing expert's fingertips.

Nobody talked much since Allen had begun rationing the food last evening. It was Drew's turn to get the stove going and we lay in silence listening to its thin hiss.

I rolled over and the first thing I noticed was that even with the stove going it somehow seemed brighter inside the cave. I felt my heart give a little leap.

"Allen, maybe it's over, maybe it's clearing. It's lighter in here," I said.

Drew shrugged. "The stove—"

"Brighter than just the stove, I mean," I said. For a second the brightness seemed to arrow from the recesses of Penny's sleeping bag and I wondered if somehow she'd accidentally turned on her Petzl—the headlamp she'd carried to the top as if we were summiting Everest instead of Denali where this time of year there was daylight twenty-four hours *every* day.

But this light had… had *color* to it… and the Petzls were sun-white. Despite the altitude, my anoxically-fogged brain synapsed a few equations and came up with a connect-the-dots moment.

"Penny, are you using your *phone?*" Allen had been very specific about saving juice that we might need to get out, to get rescued.

"Facebook," she muttered.

"Oh, Christ. Give me that goddamn thing," Allen said.

"Just a little. I was bored… scared… I thought I might find something about us. I mean for us… Half the time, you can't get anything at all…"

A transparent lie as far as I was concerned. She was out of it, but she was probably on there anyway—as often as she could pick up a signal—counting how many thumbs ups and smilies she'd gotten for summiting Denali…

"Hand it over, Penny."

He was about to shut it down when something caught his eye.

"What the hell is this?" Allen said. "What the fuck! Yellowstone blew?"

***

Now we take turns using our cell phones very briefly, earbuds plugged in because you can't hear the news in the roar of the wind. There are a lot of facts to absorb, and in hushed, desultory voices we share what we learn…

"I heard that after Tambora exploded way back in 1815, they called the next year—1816—'The Year Without a Summer.' In New York there was snow in June, frost in August. People *starved* in Europe because with the temperature dropping, crops failed worldwide…." I said.

"Helluva way to end global warming," Drew said.

"It's not funny," Allen put in. "Yellowstone, they estimate, is fifty to a hundred times worse." In the light of the softly hissing stove his lips looked blue. "The eruption spewed smoke and ash 80,000 feet into the atmosphere."

"When Krakatoa erupted in 1883, you could have covered Manhattan 200 feet deep with the material it blasted out—"

"Can it will ya, Reese? That's the past. More than a hundred years ago, for Christ's sake," Drew said.

"The past is the predictor of the future—especially when it comes to volcanoes, pal. Listen, from the last time Yellowstone spewed, like seventy thousand years ago, they found eight feet of ash they dug down to in Rapid City which is 400 miles away! Don't you get it? The 'breadbasket' is gone. Gone! The ash in the air moves around the earth—hell, planes can't fly because they get that shit in the engines, it turns into ceramic… it's all gone."

"I don't accept that—" Drew said.

I shrugged. "Those huge booms we heard—those are nothing new either. The initial eruption from Krakatoa was heard more than 3,000 miles away. I mean it's out in the middle of Indonesia and one-twelfth of the earth heard it; the shockwave alone traveled around the globe seven times. Seven!"

"Not helicopters, Drew, not thunder, not avalanches," Allen said, dipping a finger into the pot of melting snow to see if he could turn off the gas. "Shockwave."

"It can't affect everywhere," Penny said.

"The pyroclastic flows instantly incinerate everything within hundreds of miles. Further away, buildings actually collapse from the weight of the ash. Nothing can *grow*. Animals—people—die from breathing that shit into their lungs. Even if it's not superheated—"

"It's going to be twilight for five or six years," I said.

"People in bunkers—" Penny began.

"You're in a bunker, Penny, how's that working for you so far?" Allen said.

Mt. Denali: June 29, 2020

In 1884, the year after Krakatoa, an artist named (don't you love the coincidence) William Ashcroft sketched some 530 drawings of the blood red skies over London. Not unlike, I gather, those spectacular crimson displays when the good old USA played let's-test-another-nuclear-weapon in the deserts out west back in the fifties.

We've been here eight days and I think the food we have left is down to two Snickers bars, a granola bar, one package of dehydrated beef stroganoff and three packets of Tri-Berry GU, the 100 calorie high energy gel. Not that we're going anywhere. Of course, we're out of fuel, so Allen has been parceling out pinches of the beef stroganoff—au naturel—without being able to melt ice and snow, you can't reconstitute it. It tastes like very old kitty crunchies that have been nearly pulverized. Drinking water now is strictly limited to holding some snow inside your mouth. It helps lower your core temperature more quickly.

There's no pretending death isn't coming, or that it won't be welcome. No matter how easy or how easeful freezing is we know it's death. One goes to sleep. One's core temperature dips too low to sustain the core: brain, lungs, heart... And then you drift toward a sleep that's ageless and forever, and then soon after, one's heart stops beating... a flightless bird that no longer mourns that it never felt its wings beat, its body soar.

***

We've all made little recordings. (Sometimes I think about Pompeii and can cheer myself up for half a minute or so, the little artifacts found like the imprint of gold bracelets in a brothel, and who knows if someone—someone who wasn't instantly vaporized or starved or bone-sickened by breathing in Yellowstone ash—might find us, our time-capsule plastic telephones in twenty centuries?)

Our recordings, as you will certainly correctly speculate are all variations of Robert Falcon Scott's last journey to the Antarctic—another cold place, now surely colder still.

Remember?

He wrote: "These rough notes and our dead bodies must tell the tale…

***

It won't be long. The blisters from the frostbite as the temperature dropped and the wind dropped it further down have stopped swelling, stopped being a nuisance. Dead flesh cannot generate healing mechanisms like blisters, and in the intense cold and with not even sips of water to moisten our mouths, desiccation, like freezing, is painless. In an atmosphere of -70 F, spittle, water and piss all freeze instantly. There will be sleep. And it will be welcome.

On June 22, 2020, while we were marooned in an ice cave high on Mt. Denali, the volcanoes at Yellowstone National Park and just beyond its borders erupted in fury. The effects, cascading, ended life as most of the seven billion on the planet knew it.

But let's be clear: There's no one who doesn't come face to face with his or her own apocalypse. The deathbed may be the street mugging, the raging fire, the silence of a nursing home gurney, the third seat on the aisle in a crashing plane, the venom of a snake—a hundred thousand apocalyptic ways to make an end of your own life, your own soul. It may be violent, it may be gentle, it may be prosaic or gaudy, but it must be.

It was apocalypse then; it's apocalypse now.

TIL DEATH

Tim Waggoner

Audrey pushed the shopping car filled with metal odds and ends along the cracked sidewalk, her husband Edmund trailing behind her, struggling to keep up. Sweat beaded on her upper lip, despite the slight chill in the air. The temperature never varied in the World After, never grew colder, never grew warmer. But Audrey was seventy-three, and even though she worked every day and was in good shape for her age, pushing a full cart took it out of her. She had no idea how long she'd been working. Time didn't operate the same way it had before the Masters' arrival. There was no day or night now. The sky was a perpetually hazy sour yellow, like diseased phlegm with no sun or moon ever visible. Audrey didn't know if there even *was* a sun or moon anymore. For all she knew, the rest of the universe might've ceased to exist once the Masters came to Earth. Without day or night, Audrey had no sense of time. She could've gathered metal for five hours or fifty. There was no way to know. She only knew that she was tired all the way down to the bone.

The thrall mark on her forehead hurt like a fresh sunburn, and her head pounded with a rhythm that almost felt like language.

BRING, BRING...

Maybe it was her Master's voice, maybe it was her imagination. It didn't matter. Either way, she had to make her delivery—so much depended on it. She stopped pushing the cart, released her grip on the handle, and turned around.

Edmund, her senior by eight years, was twenty paces behind her on the sidewalk. He was naked, his parchment-thin skin drawn close to his old bones. His limbs had been rearranged, so he could only move by crab-walking backward, and his head was turned 180 degrees so he could see where he was going. Not that his cataract-covered eyes could see much. His sparse body hair was wiry and snow-white, but his head was bald. Instead of a beard, thick worm-

28

like growths grew out of his chin and cheeks. The fleshy tendrils were tipped with oozing pustules, and Audrey thought of them as pimple-snakes. They writhed with independent life, and Audrey couldn't look at them without nausea twisting her stomach. His mouth hung upon, jaw slack as if the muscles no longer functioned, and perpetual lines of drool ran from his mouth to moisten his pimple-snakes.

He didn't talk—or maybe he *couldn't*. Either way, Audrey was grateful. She had no idea how his mind functioned these days, but whatever distorted thoughts might spark and sputter inside what remained of his mind, she was glad he couldn't share them. He did make sounds from time to time: strange mournful hissings and tremulous bleats. His penis was always erect, so filled with blood it was purple-black, and a clear fluid that smelled like ammonia leaked from his ass. A line of the foul stuff trailed behind him on the sidewalk. In some ways, his body odor was the worst part. He stank like unwashed cock and balls that had been slathered in shit, and his breath was a sour-sweet reek that reminded her of rotting fruit.

Edmund hadn't always been like this, of course. Like so many things about the world, he'd changed since the advent of the Masters. So had she, just not outwardly.

It took him a while to close half the distance between them, but when he had, he stopped, gazed at her with eyes dull and lifeless as glass marbles, and lowered himself to the sidewalk. Audrey gritted her teeth in frustration. She *hated* it when he did this. She wanted to yell at him, shout that he should get his lazy ass moving, but she knew it wouldn't do any good. He understood so little these days. Not that he'd understood much in the last few years before he'd changed. She knew of only one way to get him going again, and while she was reluctant to do it, it was vital they made their delivery today… before she lost her nerve.

She hesitated a moment, uncomfortable about leaving her shopping cart unattended. She'd worked hard to gather this much metal, and she didn't want to risk another thrall stealing it while she was trying to coax Edmund to get moving. Then again, the longer she remained in one place, the more she risked being noticed by another thrall. Or by one of the deadly creatures that roamed the World After.

Damned if you do, damned if you don't.

She once thought she'd understood that phrase, but she hadn't known shit.

She started walking toward Edmund.

***

In the first days after the Masters' advent, and the remaking of the world, Audrey had often thought it a blessing that Edmund's mind had been mostly devoured by dementia. He remembered her—more or less—but otherwise he wasn't aware of much. In a way, she envied him. She wished she was insulated from the World After with a comforting blanket of mental oblivion.

After the Arrival, she estimated they had remained in their home, doors locked and curtains drawn, for nine days before their supplies became dangerously low. Water was the biggest issue. Something still came out of the taps, but it was thick as tar, smelled like a mixture of cinnamon and turpentine, and had a corrosive effect on both metal and porcelain. She didn't want to know what it could do to flesh. Their only food was one nearly empty container of oatmeal and a few boxes of pasta. But she had no water or electricity to prepare any of it.

One evening—or perhaps morning, it was all the same now—she lay in bed, curtains closed so she wouldn't have to look at the phlegm-colored sky outside… or at whatever hideous abomination might go lurching past. Edmund lay on the bed next to her, so motionless he might have been dead.

She couldn't remember the last time she had slept, was certain that she wouldn't drift off no matter how long she lay there, but sooner than she expected, her eyes closed and sleep took her. She hadn't dreamed since the Masters' arrival, but she did so now.

In the dream, she stood on a patch of bare earth enclosed by a high wooden fence with barbed wire all around the top. The white paint on the fence was old and peeling, the wood beneath, gray and weathered. Mounds of scrap metal were piled at the corners of the fence, each taller than she was. In the middle of the enclosure was an open pit, ten feet in diameter, she estimated, maybe fifteen. The edges were smooth, almost as if the pit was a natural structure, though the perfect roundness of it argued against that. She stood several feet away from the pit, but she still had a good view of the inside. All she could see was darkness, so black, so deep, so *absolute*, that it seemed to actually be absorbing light, pulling it into itself and swallowing it.

Gazing into the pit caused unreasoning atavistic fear to well within her. She couldn't move, couldn't think, could only stand and watch, heart pounding rapidly in her chest like a small bird caught by a predator's mesmeric gaze.

She heard the Master's wordless voice for the first time then. It asked her a question, offered her payment for her service—unquestioning, unwavering. She spoke a single word in reply.

"Yes."

Fiery pain seared her forehead then, as if an invisible branding iron had been pressed to her flesh, and she screamed herself awake. Edmund woke too, confused and frightened. He began to shout and then to cry, and Audrey held him for a time, comforting him while her forehead pulsed with pain. When Edmund fell back to sleep, she took a flashlight from her nightstand, went into the master bathroom, looked into the mirror over the sink, shone the beam on her forehead, and saw her thrall mark for the first time. Along with the mark came knowledge: the location of the Master's lair and what was expected of her. The Master wanted her to get to work immediately, for it hungered. There was just one problem, one that she hadn't considered in her dream.

She fixed her gaze on the thrall mark's reflection, as if by addressing it she could communicate with her new Master. "I can't leave Edmund alone for long. He's not strong enough to work, and his mind... " She trailed off, uncertain how best to explain it. But before she could speak again, she heard Edmund scream, a high-pitched shriek so intense it sounded as if he were tearing his throat to shreds.

She dropped the flashlight and ran back into the bedroom. Edmund writhed on the bed as his body reformed itself, bones breaking and resetting into new configurations. The transformation wasn't swift and it only become more painful as it continued, but when it was finished, Edmund had become a monstrously twisted thing, a creature strong enough to accompany Audrey while she worked. Her Master had done this somehow, she realized, in order to help her. It was, to the Master's alien mind, an act of kindness and generosity.

Audrey swallowed her rising gorge and forced herself to whisper, "Thank you," all the while unable to take her gaze off the horrible thing her husband had become.

***

The Masters had come from elsewhere. Space, another dimension, a different time... no one knew for certain. Some believed the Masters had ruled Earth in the far distant past, perhaps even created it to be their plaything—or feeding ground—and long ago they'd left Earth for unknown reasons, but now had returned to reclaim what was theirs. They had no individual names—at least, none that humans were aware of—and no one had ever seen a Master. No one who'd ever lived to tell about it, anyway. Most believed they possessed no physical form, not as humans understood the concept. They lived in separate lairs and worked through thralls and monstrous servants of their own creation. Thralls were rewarded for their service with food, clean water, and electricity in their homes, and while wearing a thrall mark didn't protect you from every danger in the World After, it usually gave predators—both those human and those not—pause.

A thrall's main purpose was to feed his or her Master. Sometimes this meant capturing other humans and bringing them—kicking and screaming, if need be—to the Master's lair. But Masters didn't always feed on human flesh. From other thralls, Audrey had learned of Masters that fed on blood, human waste, and specific organs such as the pancreas. Some fed on inorganic objects such as used clothing, books, electronic devices, CDs, and DVDs. Some dined on more abstract fare: people's memories, emotions, or fantasies. All Audrey's Master required was metal. Any kind would do, although it was particularly fond of copper. Audrey had no idea exactly what happened to the metal after she threw it into the pit that served as her Master's lair, but she'd never heard it hit bottom.

Even though their Master gave them food and water—somehow made it materialize right in their home—Audrey was thin to the point of emaciation, as was Edmund. Masters might reward thralls for their service, but they were far from generous. They gave just enough for their servants to remain alive, and not a scrap more. And for this, thralls risked their lives day after day. But what else could they do? It was the only game in town.

***

In the World Before, Audrey's therapist had warned her about something called compassion fatigue.

It happens to long-term caregivers, she'd said. *Especially those whose loved ones suffer from conditions like dementia, which only worsen over time. You become emotionally exhausted, and—if you're not careful—that exhaustion can turn into feelings of resentment. Even hatred.*

That hadn't happened to Audrey. Not *before*, anyway. But now? Now it was hard to think of the loathsome thing that followed her around like some freakish dog as the man who had been her husband. She wanted to be free of Edmund as much, if not more, as she wanted him to be free of the nightmarish existence she'd inadvertently cursed him with.

The first time she'd tried to kill Edmund, she'd done it during a scavenging run, when she'd been picking through the ruins of a downtown office building. She didn't know what had caused the building's collapse. There was no sign of fire, no sign that something had struck the building. No wood rot, no crumbling concrete, no fatigued metal. It looked as if the pieces of the building had simply detached from one another and fallen into a jumbled heap. Edmund stayed away from the debris, guarding the shopping cart and watching as she walked through the odds and ends, searching for choice bits of metal. If anyone—or any*thing*—came near, he'd let out a loud hissing sound. She had no idea if this was a conscious warning on his part or merely an instinctive reaction. Either way, his warnings came in handy.

As she searched among the debris, she came across large shards of glass, pieces of a window that had been broken in the building's collapse. A couple of shards were the right size to hold in one hand, and one of those was the basic size and shape of a butcher knife blade. She gazed at the glass knife for a long time before finally crouching down to pick it up. She gripped it like a knife, careful not to squeeze too hard so she wouldn't cut her hand. She was surprised by how heavy it felt, almost as if it were a real blade instead of merely a piece of broken glass. She gingerly touched the finger of her free hand to the pointed tip, then ran it along one of the shard's edges, again careful not to press too hard.

After a time, she stood, turned, and began making her way toward Edmund.

He watched her approach, no awareness showing in his milky eyes. His erection bounced several times, like he was a dog wagging its tail upon his master's return. He didn't react when she knelt next to his head. Didn't flinch when she touched the glass shard to his throat. Didn't do more than let out a soft hiss of air—was there a hint of surprise in that breath?—as she drew the shard across his neck, the sharp edge parting flesh and severing veins and arteries, bringing forth a gushing flood of crimson.

He turned to look at her then, blood dribbling past his lips onto his pimple-snakes. No expression, no recognition. And then he slumped to the ground and continued to bleed out.

She stood and stepped back to avoid the worst of the blood, but it was too late. It had spattered her clothes, slicked her hands... so what did it matter if the widening pool on the ground touched her shoes?

She watched her husband die, surprised by how long it took for his erection to subside. But subside it did, and Edmund let out a last choked gurgle and stopped breathing.

Heart pounding, she stepped forward and pressed two trembling figures to the side of his neck. No pulse.

She stood. She felt mostly relief, although there was some sorrow and guilt as well. She contemplated what to do with his body. He was little more than skin and bones, but he was still too heavy for her to lift. She couldn't get him in the cart, and even if she could, what would she do with him? There were no funeral homes anymore. She supposed she could bury him in their backyard, but something had happened to the grass. The edges of the blades were sharp as razors, and if you got too close they emitted high-pitched cries that sounded like tiny voices screaming. She wasn't sure it would be safe to try to dig there. Maybe if she just took his head...

She heard the first predator then, approaching in the distance. A simian *hoot-hoot-hoot* accompanied by a leathery sliding, as of something large dragging itself across asphalt. The scent of Edmund's blood had drawn it, whatever it was, and she knew it wouldn't be the last. At least she wouldn't have to worry about what to do with Edmund's remains now.

She dropped the glass knife, took hold of the shopping cart's handle, and began pushing it away from her husband's corpse as fast as she could.

***

She didn't have any metal to deliver to her Master that day, and her reward for her failure was an excruciating headache brought on by her throbbing thrall mark. Even so, when she got home she slept well for the first time since the Masters' arrival.

She woke to the sound of pounding at the front door. As she stumbled down the hallway, she already knew what she'd find waiting for her. She unlocked the door, opened it, and stood back as Edmund—who didn't have a mark anywhere on his body, including his throat—crab-walked inside. A thought drifted through her mind. *The cat came back...*

***

She tried three more times. She used an iron poker to cave in Edmund's skull. She jammed a pair of socks down his throat to block his airway. Finally, in desperation, she took a screwdriver, rammed it through his left eye into his brain, stirred it around real good, and then did the same to the other eye.

He healed each time.

She had no idea if Edmund healed because of some quality his transformed body possessed or if her Master specifically healed him each time as a way to torment her. Whatever the reason, she knew she couldn't kill him by ordinary means. To end his travesty of a life, she would need *power*. The same kind that had transformed him in the first place.

She began to plan.

***

The skin on Audrey's right hand was raw and blistered. Pushing the cart hurt, but she couldn't manage it with only one hand, so she endured the pain. Edmund followed behind her on the sidewalk, moving a bit faster now, with a decided bounce in his step. She'd jacked him off, and it hadn't taken him long to come. It never did. But while what shot out of his quivering cock looked more or less like semen, it was an unhealthy gray, stank like sulfur, and was boiling hot. Getting Edmund off was a sure way to motivate him. He'd be in a good mood for hours—but she only did it when nothing else worked, for no matter how hard she tried, she always got some of his cock-lava on her. Usually on her hand, but if his orgasm was particularly strong, he'd blast like a firehose, and there was no telling where she might get hit. Today, she'd been lucky. Only her right hand and a small spot on her left wrist had been burned. Painful, but nothing that would slow her down, and now Edmund was trotting behind her like an eager puppy, cock already swollen purple once more.

35

Audrey didn't look down as she walked. She knew better than to gaze at the cracks in the sidewalk. Something—or many somethings—lived inside and whispered the most awful things. If they caught you looking down, they'd whisper louder. They'd urge you to do things to yourself and to others, and the longer they whispered, the harder it was to resist them. Better to not set them off in the first place.

The town's population was sparser now. Many people died during the early days after the Masters' arrival, and many more had died since. Some had been sacrificed to Masters, some had been killed by the new monstrous predators that roamed the world, and some died at the hands of their fellow survivors, people who'd been driven mad or had turned savage during their struggle to stay alive.

Because of this, Audrey saw few people along the route to her Master's lair, and those she did see were sitting in alleys or on front stoops, heads down, sleeping or—just as likely—gone deep into their minds to try to escape the horrors of the World After. Every now and again one of them would look up as she passed, and she always made sure to turn her head toward them so they could see her thrall mark. That was usually enough to make them look away and lower their heads once more.

She was aware of other creatures, moving swift and silent between buildings, or crouching on rooftops and watching, motionless and hopeful. At times she even had the sense that something was looking down at her from above, but when she looked up, she saw nothing in the sour-yellow sky. The land was filled with predators now—some large, some small, all deadly in their own ways. Her thrall mark would keep them at a distance, especially close to her Master's lair. She hoped.

Audrey had never had cause to visit the Third Street Iron and Metal Company before the Masters' arrival. She didn't live particularly close to the place, either. She had no idea why the Master who laired there had offered to take her on as one of its thralls. Maybe it had broadcast a general call and she'd answered. Maybe she'd been chosen for a specific reason, one she'd likely never know. Whatever the truth was, she'd come to wish she'd never accepted the Master's offer. If she hadn't, she and Edmund would've been dead by now, probably from lack of fresh water, but that end would've been preferable to what their lives had become. Serving as a thrall was a mistake, one she intended to rectify now.

The word *company* seemed too grand for this place. A high white wooden fence surrounded the property, with the business's name painted in red letters on one of the outside walls. A section of a wall served as a sliding door which could be closed and locked, although it was always open when Audrey came here. Since the only thing that could threaten a Master was another of its kind, there was no need for simple physical boundaries like doors and locks.

Audrey's thrall mark burned hot as fire. Her Master knew she was close, knew the *metal* was close, and it was losing what little patience it had. Audrey had heard about what happened to thralls that displeased their Masters. It made what had been done to Edmund look like little more than a mild swat on the hand.

She began pushing the cart once more, Edmund crab-walking obediently behind her.

The instant she set foot on the barren earth inside the fence, she felt the Master's power wash over her. She was officially in its lair now, the place where it was strongest. The air here seemed to ripple, like the distortion created by waves of heat rising off hot asphalt. Edmund made a small bleating sound when he entered. He was never comfortable in the Master's presence, but he always accompanied her inside anyway. She was counting on this—habit? Loyalty?—now.

The ground was smooth, the path to the pit well worn, and the squeaking wheels of the shopping cart rolled easily over it. Normally, Audrey would push the cart up to the pit's edge—not *too* close—and then start lifting out pieces of metal one by one and tossing them in. If the Master was especially impatient and the cart's contents not too heavy, she might try to dump the entire load in at once. She would do neither of these things today, though.

Her Master's impatience, its lust to feed, filled her, made her thrall mark feel as if white-hot coals had been slipped beneath her skin. She gritted her teeth against the pain, gripped the cart handle tighter, and started to run. She was seventy-three, malnourished and dehydrated, but fear, anger, and determination fueled her, and she ran with the strength and speed of a much younger woman. The cart's wheels squeaked so loudly they almost seemed to be screaming. The sound of the wheels combined with the sound of her heart pounding in her ears, and she couldn't hear if Edmund continued to follow her, if he too had picked up speed, his bare hands and feet *slap-slap-slapping* the earth as he fought to keep up with her. She hoped he was.

At first, she felt only her Master's all-consuming hunger, but then she detected a hint of puzzlement. Why was this thrall approaching the pit so fast? But before the Master could command her to stop, Audrey felt the front wheels of the heavily laden cart roll over the edge of the pit. She held tight to the handle as the cart tipped forward and fell into the darkness, pulling her with it. She looked back in time to see Edmund fling himself after her, and she smiled. The Master might prefer to eat metal, but she hoped it wouldn't mind an offering of flesh. *Two* offerings.

Audrey and Edmund tumbled down through black nothingness.

***

Audrey had no idea how long they fell. She'd lost her grip on the cart somewhere along the line, and she had no idea where it was. Edmund was close by, though. She might not have been able to see him, but she could still *smell* him. More, she sensed his presence the same way she'd sometimes wake in the night and know he was lying in bed next to her without having to reach over to confirm his presence.

The vertiginous feeling of falling had subsided around the time she'd lost contact with the cart, and she couldn't tell if she still continued descending. Without so much as a speck of light, she had no way of telling which way was up and which way was down, if such directions even meant anything in this dark limbo. For all she knew, she was hanging motionless in this void, and she might remain so until she died. Or worse, she'd stay like this forever, never dying, always awake and conscious. How long could a person exist like that before going completely insane?

She tried to speak but was unable to tell if her mouth produced any sound.

I'm so sorry, Edmund. I didn't know something like this would happen. I thought we'd die.

No reply from her husband. For once, she was glad his mind was gone. If they were trapped in this place, he wouldn't go mad. After all, he was already there.

After a time—how long was impossible to say—she sensed another presence, enormous and terrifying. It was as if she were floating in a sea and a silent ocean liner had drifted close without her being aware of it until the massive craft was almost on top of her.

She knew she was now truly in her Master's presence.

She felt a wave of curiosity roll forth from the Master. It wasn't a word, wasn't even a human concept, but Audrey interpreted it as a single-word question.

WHY?

She didn't have to ask why *what*.

I couldn't let him go on living like he is. And I couldn't leave him.

She sensed only continuing curiosity, now tinged with confusion, coming from the Master.

He's my husband. We belong together.

The Master's confusion and curiosity vanished, followed by a sense of satisfaction, which Audrey interpreted as a single word.

UNDERSTOOD.

Pain exploded throughout her body as her bones, muscles, and organs began to shift and rearrange. She let forth a soundless scream, but she felt a hand clasp her shoulder—Edmund's hand—and she knew that, whatever horrible thing was happening to her, at least she wasn't alone. And then she felt Edmund's fingers join with her flesh, their skin flowing together like liquid putty, and if she could've produced sound in this non-place, she would've screamed louder.

***

Audrey and Edmund shuffled slowly into an abandoned building. The sign out front said the place once had been a night club called Spinners, but since neither of them could read anymore, the letters were only meaningless nonsense. They moved on four hands and four feet, two pairs of eyes scanning the debris inside the club for any metal. Poking out from beneath a splintered table, they saw a thin half circle of what looked like... Could it be? *Copper!* Once, Audrey would've recognized this object as a bracelet, but now she only saw it as her Master's favorite delicacy. Audrey and Edmund were excited to retrieve the bracelet, but their combined anatomy made it difficult to move the pieces of broken wood. Yes, they had four hands, but their arms no longer bent the way they once did. Edmund carried a silver serving spoon they had found in a restaurant a couple blocks away, and he put it on the floor. The two of them then took hold of the table fragments with their teeth and slowly, painfully dragged them off the bracelet. When the object was fully revealed, Audrey leaned her head down to it. She used her thorn-covered tongue to lift it into her mouth, and then she gently gripped it between her serrated teeth. Audrey and Edmund couldn't operate a shopping cart, and so they were limited in what they could gather for their Master, but hopefully their meager offering would still be pleasing. Their Master would understand. After all, hadn't the Master made them this way?

Edmund retrieved his spoon, and they left the bar. Because of the tangled arrangement of their limbs, they scuttled and lurched instead of crab-walked, and they were more awkward than either of them had been on their own. But they'd learn to make due. Everything would be all right, just as long as they had each other. Once outside, they turned left and began heading in the direction of the Third Street Metal and Iron Company.

Together.

BELLUM SACRUM
Mathew Kaufman

"I wish you would just die already! You are a lazy, backstabbing piece of shit!" Mark screamed at his co-worker. His face was flushed with excitement. He was finally getting all his pent-up anger out. It had been building for so long and now was blasting out, unencumbered, uncensored, and in front of all his peers.

It was wonderful!

Faces, mostly blurred, filled Mark Thomas's peripheral vision. Even obscured as they were, he could see all of the gaping jaws. It looked like twenty trout staring at him. He continued to scream obscenities at Lin Alvonellos, the office fuck-up. Vile words spewed out of his mouth. Spittle splashed on Lin's face, splattered on the walls and desk as he unloaded his fury.

Lin just stood there, stupefied, as if he was too dumb to comprehend the hate-filled rant. Mark watched as he stepped back while the barrage impacted. He watched Lin's face change from simple and ignorant to confused and pained.

Lin rubbed his left arm and begin to scratch—no, more like claw at—the side of his neck. Red marks appeared on his irritated skin as Lin feverishly raked, but nothing was going to stop Mark. He had waited too long for this very moment; Lin had done far too much stupid shit. This was his time to shine.

"You are a stupid fuck! How can anyone be so dumb? Don't just stand there, say something! I want you dead!" Mark yelled.

All that Lin could muster was the same stupid thing he always said. "Oh, good." It didn't matter if you said your granny just died, it was only thing Lin ever sputtered.

And it was the last thing he ever sputtered. Without another word, Lin grabbed his chest, made a stupid face, and dropped dead. Right there in front of the whole office. Just dropped dead.

It was the first time Mark had ever killed someone, and he had only used his words. He thought for sure they were going to suspend and fire him on the spot. Hell, the Human Resources bitch, "Tasty" Carlson, just stood there slowly smothering to death in her epic fat rolls, not saying a word.

It never happened though. Mark just returned to his cubicle and went back to watching YouTube videos. Tasty stopped eating her Ho Hos long enough to call 911. Mark could hear the bitch screaming, "He's dead, ohhh, he's dead—"

Mark just rolled his eyes and put his headphones in. Sometime later, the ambulance arrived and carted Lin off. Mark didn't even bother to look up from his screen. It was a good day.

Before long, the police were asking him to fill out a statement on what had happened.

Mark simply told them, "No, thank you," and returned to YouTube until the work day was over. He found that each interaction filled him with a sense of joy and accomplishment. Each time he said something out of the ordinary, he felt titillated. Soon enough, five o'clock arrived and without a word, not even so much as a glance at the other employees, he walked out and went home.

***

THE next morning Mark awoke to the piercing beep-beep-beep of his alarm clock. His brain began whirring awake. He immediately recalled yesterday's events, cracking a smile as they replayed in his head. *I can't believe he just died. I would have yelled at him far sooner if I thought that would have happened.*

He lay there, snug and self-satisfied in his bed for a few more minutes before deciding to get up. He sprang from his bed, filled with exhilaration. He had to do something to rid himself of some of this energy, so he shed his boxers and did what every twenty-five-year-old does.

Masturbation seemed to have lost its ability to calm him, however. He was still so full of energy. Sure, he'd been energetic before, but never like this. It was like a dozen A.D.D. kids off their meds were bouncing around in his brain. *Jesus fuck, man…*

Mark hopped in the shower and raced through washing. He needed to do something to get rid of this energy. He felt out of control and had to rein it in. *What can I do? What will make me feel better? A run maybe?*

He bounded out of the shower and grabbed his socks and shoes. He sat on the couch still dripping wet after forgetting to dry himself.

Socks on. Shoes on. Laces tied. He was out the door and halfway down the block.

Run, run, running... *Gotta go faster. Can't stop running.* His body coursed with his life-blood. He slowed and looked at his smartwatch to check his pulse. Fifty-five beats per minute. *How could that be? I was practically sprinting.*

He took another look at the heart rate monitor. Fifty-four, fifty-three, fifty-two... the countdown continued. He bolted into a sprint again. His mind raced as his heart barely puttered along. He checked again. The rate was locked at forty-eight.

He picked up the pace. No change. He ran full out, as fast as his body would move. No change. *What the fuck!*

He stopped, expecting to be panting after sprinting so hard. He was barely breathing faster than when he slept. Fourteen times a minute is what he counted. Shit, Tasty Carlson breathed that much just thinking about a Snickers.

Honk! A car horn blared.

"What the fuck are you doing? Get some clothes on, you pervert!" the man yelled from the car.

What? Mark looked down. He was horrified at what he saw. His giblets hung out in the open for everyone to see. His pasty white skin glowed like snow on a sunny day. *I forgot clothes. I'm naked. I'm naked,* he paused, looking around, *in the middle of downtown.*

"Get out of the road, you fucking faggot! No one wants to see your tiny dicklett!" a kid yelled out the window of an approaching school bus. The bus's brakes squealed as it came to a stop at the light.

This can't be happening. It must be a dream. He felt his face flush with embarrassment.

"Ha! Look at his tiny dick!" a ginger teen yelled, pointing out the window.

Before he knew it, Mark's mouth was open and spewing words: "It's not tiny, you motherfuckers!"

"Why are you naked? What a freak!" the ginger replied.

"I'm gonna come up there and light you on fire, you little fucker!" Mark yelled.

"With what? You gonna rub your tiny dick 'til it shoots sparks?" The ginger laughed. The whole bus laughed as Mark scanned the windows. Each one had at least two faces pressed against their panes. Some even had three.

Mark balled his fists. He could feel the rage building inside him. *Who do they think they are? I'm not one you want to fuck with. I killed someone yesterday, just by yelling at them!*

Mark opened his mouth to yell again but all that escaped was a tiny squeak, like when his voice cracked as a pubescent boy. That was all the kids needed. They unleashed a barrage of names and puberty jokes.

One kid even had the audacity to scream, "I think he just grew a pube!"

"I have lots of pubes. I just shave them!" Mark yelled.

"That way they don't stick in your mommy's teeth!" the ginger yelled.

"You're fucking dead, you little bitch," Mark mumbled.

His head filled with thoughts of blowing up the school bus. He envisioned the little ginger brat melting into a pile of human goo. He imagined the rest of the bus bursting into flames.

Mark's ears were ringing now, filled with a tinnitus-like hum. He stuck his arms out in front of himself toward the bus. He pretended to be choking the kids. *Those smart-ass little shits. What did they know, anyways?*

He imagined the vinyl seats catching fire as the children frantically climbed over them to get off the bus and put out the fires that engulfed them. Mark could see the yellow paint charring to black. He could smell the rubber of the tires burning.

A car horn sounded to his left. A long, deep, irritating honk. Mark pointed his left hand at that car as if telling the driver that the honking had to stop.

His brain pulsed with the sounds. Another horn blasted from the offending car. Mark would do anything to make it stop. He thought of a tree falling. Crashing onto the car, crushing it, smashing the driver into a thick red mush. He imagined the bus catching the fallen tree limbs ablaze.

This would, of course, catch the car on fire, effectively melting its cheap polyester foam-filled seats into nothingness. The hum in his ears was drowning out the world around him.

He was sure any minute now the police would be arriving to take his naked self into custody. But that didn't happen. Mark just stood there, cowering behind his arms, pretending the horrible things he was thinking were really happening. He could feel his body shaking.

44

He drew his hands in close to his face and squatted down.

Eventually the hum dimmed and was replaced by the sound of his racing heart. It was pounding so fast he couldn't even count the beats. Mark fell into the fetal position. He could feel the cement underneath his body as he settled onto the porous surface. It wasn't cool like he expected it to be. It was warm, very warm in fact. And what was that smell...?

Ignoring the heat for a moment, Mark peeked at his heart rate sensor. Three-hundred-two beats per minute. Was he having a heart attack? A stroke? Was that why the cement felt so warm? That would explain the humming in his ears too.

Afraid this might be the last time he would see the world, he convinced himself to open his eyes.

"Oh, my god—"

The school bus *was* on fire. The kids moved frantically inside, crawling over seats attempting to escape. The fire was so hot the glass windows began to warp and the paint began to blister. The hum that had once blocked Mark from hearing anything had dissipated and his ears now filled with the screams of flaming children.

Mark sat up. This was unbelievable. This is exactly what he had imagined. And now it was happening right in front of him. *But how?* A piercing scream belted from his left. The car, the one that had been honking at him, was fully engulfed as well. Mark could see the driver was also ablaze. A tree had fallen on top of the car and onto the bus, and once the diesel tank had flamed up, the fire had transferred to the car.

Mark sat, nude, and in awe, as the world around him burned.

***

END credits rolled on whatever television movie had been playing. Mark sat on his couch, beer in hand, staring blankly at the screen. He was exhausted from the morning's events. He'd never felt so powerful before.

What was that? Was that really me that caused that? If so… I'm practically invincible. Invincible and exhausted. Maybe I can try a little more after a quick nap.

Mark slumped over onto the nearby pillow. He didn't really want to sleep on the couch but he was too tired to move to his bed.

***

He awoke to pounding at his front door. Whispers drifted lightly

45

across the air, tickling his ears.

"Take your positions. Wait for my command, then move in. Sound off when you are in position," a voice whispered. Mark immediately put it together; the police were outside his house and about to pay him a little visit.

His stomach churned with panic; it felt almost like butterflies on steroids. He was starting to enjoy this feeling. It made him feel so alive! The familiar feeling of his beating heart returned. Much like a sports car, it idled quietly but, like a well-tuned machine, at the right moment, it throttled up. This was that moment.

"Mark Thomas, this is the police. You have ten seconds to come out with your hands in the air!" the voice boomed.

His heart revved up. Vroom, vroom. He looked at his wrist and tapped the smartwatch navigating to the heart-rate sensor. Vroom, vroom! Ninety, one hundred, one-fifty. The countdown began outside.

"Ten!"

He began to shake. The butterflies in his stomach turned to angry dragons. The fire in him grew.

His worked his hands in and out of fists, rubbing the clenched one before punching it into the other with a *crack!* Switching hands. Another *crack!* Seconds passed. The hum returned to his ears.

"Five!" the voice boomed from outside.

This was it. Five seconds from now, one of two things were going to happen. Either he would be dead or they would be. One way or another, only one side would walk away.

"Three!"

Mark began sweating heavily. No time to run. Not that he wanted to.

"Two!"

"Go fuck yourselves!" he yelled at the top of his lungs.

"One!"

There was an enormous thud at the wooden front door. It was followed quickly by two more. Thud. Thud. Then, with one last blow, the door exploded into hundreds of splinters.

Police charged into the house. Half a dozen entered from the front, a few through the windows, and even more from the rear. All for him. All for someone that had done nothing. Nothing tangible anyway.

Mark stood still in his living room, hands deep in his pants pockets. Thump-thump, thump-thump.

"Can I help you officers?" Mark asked. Thump-thump-thump. Thump-thump-thump.

"Hands in the air! Now!" the officers yelled.

"As you wish," he replied. Thump-thump-thump-thump-thump-thump—

Mark's hands shot into the air. The motion was so fast, it spooked one of the officers, a young kid who look to be in his twenties. Gunfire burst into the air. Rifles and pistols alike fired. Pop, pop, pop.

In just a matter of seconds, hundreds of rounds flew directly at Mark. The rounds impacted with his skin, instantly turning to molten metal. The glowing hot liquid splashed onto the floor, igniting the carpet.

The room filled with smoke and gunpowder from the discharging firearms. The officers stepped closer, still unleashing a barrage of rounds at him.

Liquid metal splashed back onto their skin or clothing, burning holes wherever it landed. Screams of pain joined the gunfire. Some of the men dropped to their knees, trying to wipe the molten liquid off.

Mark could see the twenty-something officer that started the battle. His face had several holes in it and blood was pouring out of the spot where his tongue used to be. It looked like the metal just ate it away.

He stared at the officer, smiling. *This is the coolest thing ever! I can do whatever the fuck I want! Even bullets can't stop me.* The hum in his ears had lessened now and was replaced by the ever-growing screams and gurgles.

He reached out to the young man kneeling in front of him. A fluid-filled gasp, followed by a deeply drowned out: "Help me" poured from the man.

"Help? Is that what you want?" Mark asked.

The man shook his head in the affirmative.

"Very well."

Mark jerked the pistol free from the officer's holster and pointed it at his injured forehead. The youth shook with fear at the sight. Mark saw his pants darken as he pissed himself like a baby.

"Don't be afraid. I won't shoot you," Mark said, dropping the

Glock's magazine. One by one, he flicked the rounds out of the magazine and into his hand. Relief filled the officer's face.

Once empty, Mark cupped his hands together over the ammunition. Brief fizzles of the rounds going off could be heard. *This is neat. It doesn't even hurt.* Mark peeked into his hands.

"As you requested, my boy!" Mark plunged the first two fingers into the molten metal. Before the boy know what was happening, Mark, using his fingers, splashed the liquid down, from his forehead to his upper lip. A second horizontal splash and a masterful upside-down cross was melting through his face and head.

Mark took the remaining liquid and slapped the next police officer across the face. He began laughing at the sight of death. One after the other, Mark melted whatever metal he could touch, and flung, plunged, or punched it into the nearest person.

The pungent aroma of sulfur and burning flesh was rampant throughout the house. Less than three minutes after police started this mess, it was over.

His heart slowed down and a fatigue set in. He was not nearly as tired this time. No nap would be necessary. Just a brief rest. Mark sat on the couch in the burning living room.

Flames raged and had engulfed most of the dining room and kitchen. It wouldn't be long now until the rest of the house joined in the festivities. He could see the remains of people turning into white ash and floating up into the air.

Mark sat in awe of his work. *This all seems like a dream.* He hoped it wasn't. *This shit is way too cool to be a dream.*

Just then he heard sirens. *Firetrucks. I better go.* Mark stood and immediately collapsed onto the floor. His consciousness escaped him.

***

Mark awoke, not sure where he was or what was happening. A man in a black suit approached. "Hi, Mark. It's been a long time," he said in a thick southern drawl.

"Who the fuck are you?" Mark asked.

"Mark. Mark. Mark. My dear boy. Let's dispatch with the unpleasantries, shall we?"

"What's going on?"

"My boy, the hour is near. There are a few things that need explaining. First off: Your mouth stays shut. Another word out of it

48

and I'll seal it. Understand?"

Mark started to speak, then nodded.

The man in black stared at him. "Secondly: I don't care what you believe in, who you believe in, or even why you believe in them. Forget what you know. You don't know shit, my boy! Is that clear enough for you?"

"Okay. But who—"

"Uh uh. What did I say about talking? We'll get there. Just join me on the ride."

With that, the room went black.

The light slowly returned and Mark found himself seated in an old wooden chair. Space and time moved around him as the man waved his arms.

"My boy... Welcome to 1988. That Godawful music blaring on the television is *Sister Christian* by Night Ranger. That whore in the corner is none other than your mother. And that scumbag meth-head beating her... Well, that's dear old Dad."

Mark began to recognize the area as the blur of motion faded. It was his Granny's basement. He had spent a lot of time here when he was younger. After his dad left.

"How is this possible? How am I here? What are you?" Mark interjected.

"Shhh. Relax." Mark noticed a letter on the nearby table and retrieved it. A foreclosure notice. While he read the letter, he'd almost forgotten that his father had been beating the shit out of his mother. A brief scream served as a reminder.

"I told you to shut up, you stupid cunt!" his father yelled.

"Jack, stop! Please. I'll do whatever you want."

"You'll do whatever I want *and* get the rest of this whoopin', understand?"

"Plea—" His mom was cut off by a fist to the jaw.

"I had no idea he beat her like this. I never even met the guy. He just up and left one day."

It was painful for Mark to watch. Blood poured from his mother's mouth. Drips and splashes coated the floor under her. There was even a solitary tooth lying in a small pool of red liquid.

"Make it stop. I can't watch any more of this," Mark said.

"Oh? A little while ago you lit a bus full of kids on fire, and *now* you have an issue with violence? Ah, well, the world is full of contradictions and double standards. I don't think I'll ever understand it. That's part of the beauty, though. The unpredictability of humanity. It makes things so much more interesting."

Mark listened to the man but focused his attention on his mother. He hated seeing her taking a beating. Hated seeing the pain in her face. He wanted, with everything in his soul, to help her. But he knew he couldn't. This was the past and there was no way to change the past.

"Pay attention, Marky, my boy… It's about to get *good*."

He watched as his father pulled a small silver revolver from his waistband. It had been hiding in his blue jeans under his white tank-top. He pointed it at his mother. Right at her bleeding, sad little face.

She sobbed uncontrollably, pleading with the man. "No! Please, don't hurt me. Please. I have to tell you something. John, I have to tell you! I'm pregnant!" she screamed.

His father momentarily froze, revolver still pointed at her. No words left his mouth. No change in expression. Just the look of fear, rage, and murderous intent that had been there all along.

John pulled back on the trigger. Mark could see the hammer begin to inch back. He couldn't watch this. He wanted with everything in his soul to run to her and save her.

The revolver's hammer crept back. Upon reaching its apex, it slammed forward. But there was no gun shot. No bang, no click, just a soft thump as the hammer slammed into the finger of the man in black. The room froze like someone pressed pause.

Mark sat awestruck as he watched the replay of the man in black stop the pistol from going off. He was bewildered. *How could the man be sitting next to him and be in the past? How could any of this be happening? Let's not pull at that thread, shall we?*

The man in front of him spoke: "Hello, my dear. Looks like you are having a bad day."

"Who the hell are you?"

"You're a spitting image of her," the man in black beside Mark said.

Mark didn't even look away. The man continued to speak to his mother.

"I bet you are tired of the beatings. The abuse. The impending death. It's pretty terrifying, isn't it?"

"Yeah. You think, genius?" she retorted.

"I'm sorry to have bothered you; it's clear you don't want me here. I'll just pull my finger out and let this miserable existence of yours come to an end."

"No! Wait! I don't want to die. I'm pregnant. I want my child to live. I want him to grow up. I don't want to die! Please!" she begged.

"I would be happy to help, ma'am. But I need a little favor from you," he said.

"Anything! I don't have much money. I don't have fancy things. I just want my baby boy!"

"So do I," he said. "So do I. One day, I will come calling for him. When that time comes, I can't afford for him to say no. I need you to give him to me. Not his physical body so much as—his soul.

"You see, I am in the business of collecting things. It's very important that I collect your son. You may have him until you die. That should suffice, yes?"

"What will you do with him?"

"My intentions are not for you to worry about. I assure you he'll never be harmed. I will even get rid of this monster of a man for you. What do you say?"

"I don't want to get in trouble for killing him. I can't lose my boy. How can you help?"

"Don't worry. I just need your commitment. It's as simple as that. And all your worry goes away. You can spend the rest of your days with your bouncing baby boy. That is what you want, isn't it?"

"Yes. Okay. I'll do it. I'll take your help."

"Excellent choice, my dear. One, I assure you, you'll not regret."

With that, the man pulled a folded piece of parchment from his jacket pocket and opened it. On it, in a language Mark had never seen, were words illegible to him.

"All I need is a signature here," the man said, pointing to an X next to a line on the page. He removed a pen tipped with a serpent head from his pocket. The woman reached for it but he jerked it away.

"Not so fast. This signature needs to be done in a very special way."

Mark saw his mother open her mouth, but before any words left it, the man plunged the pen into her stomach. She gasped in pain as it dug deeper. Not only into her, but into her unborn child.

"It needs to be signed in blood from *his* heart."

With a final thrust, the pen plunged into the baby's heart. Mark's heart. It made him uncomfortable the way the man said the word "his," like it was important.

He watched as the pen was pulled from her belly. Blood coated its outside but quickly drained into the pen. The wound where the pen had pierce her faded away.

The man handed her the pen. "Sign, and all this ends now." He gestured to John and his gun.

She did. Bright red blood flowed behind the tip of the pen. Each loop and line drained more of the fluid. Once finished, the man stood and in the blink of an eye, was gone. Her murderous boyfriend also vanished.

Mark watched her search the room for any sign of either man. There was no trace of them, like they'd never existed.

Again, his vision blurred as the man in black brought Mark back to reality.

"Well, my boy, what do you think? You ready to finish what dear 'ol mom started?"

"Did—Did I just watch my mom sign my soul over to the devil? Jesus fucking Christ… Are you the devil?"

"You better believe it, sonny boy. Lucifer, Beelzebub, the Boogie Man. Call me whatever you want. Just remember, you and your newfound power belong to me."

"What do you want from me? Why me?" Mark asked, scratching his head and desperately trying to put it all together. "Are you trying to start a war? The Apocalypse?"

"Mark, Mark, Mark." The war is already over. Humanity lost. Shit, they lost the day your momma signed that contract."

"What? How?" Mark asked perplexed. "What does any of this have to do with me? Or my mom? Why us?"

"You, Mark. Only you. You were chosen by Him. By God himself to bear the soul of Jesus Christ. The old fucker thought He could get one over on me. Thought He could sneak the Second Coming in, right under my nose.

"He wasn't good enough. I have spies everywhere. Your Granny was one of my informants. It was sad to lose her. Did you know she killed a few people for me? Tough lady, your Granny."

"I don't believe a word out of your lying mouth! My Granny would never help the Devil!" Mark felt a tear roll down his cheek.

Just the thought of his grandmother, her smiling face, gray hair, and wrinkles... helping the great evil? *No way!*

"Mark. You are missing the point. It doesn't matter what you think. You are going to do *exactly* what I tell you to do. You don't have a choice. You *can't* say no. I own your soul, control it. You are the bringer of the End Times. The Apocalypse IS HERE!"

Mark stood, determined to leave. There is no way any of this could be true... Could it? Mark felt anger fill him. He began to build with rage at the thought of the Devil touching his family. Making them kill. Stealing his future.

Could I really have been the Second Coming? Jesus reincarnated? There is no reason I can't be. I went to church, studied the Bible. I certainly can withstand the evil that is after me... Right?

"That's your big plan, Mark? Say no to evil? Do I look like a joint? It isn't like the D.A.R.E. program, Marky. You can't just say no. I can feel everything you feel. Hear everything you hear. And the best part is, it's a two-way link.

"Do you feel that rage inside you? That fire? That's me. I'm pushing my power into you. The end is near, my boy! Very near. You have two choices. You can either do what I say and let me do what I have to do. And if you chose that route, I will remove your conscious, your awareness, your humanity.

"Or you can try and fight me, albeit unsuccessfully, and I'll leave all of you in that little brain of yours. You'll get to watch yourself destroy humanity. All of humanity. Every creature on earth, in fact. How does that sound?"

I don't want to kill anyone. I don't want any of this. I just want to go back to normal. Back to the way it was before I hurt people. I—

"Time's up, Marky. I need His soul and your body to get this done. What'll it be? Shall we wreck this place together?"

His conscience wouldn't let him willingly destroy everything he knows and loves. Everyone he knows and loves. "Fuck you! I won't let you use me!"

"There's the fire! Let it out Mark! Let it mingle with the rage coursing through your veins. You made the right choice, by the way. You'll enjoy what you are about to do."

***

His head raged with the searing pain of guilt. Regret flooded his soul. He wished now that he'd chosen wisely instead of acting so

53

rashly.

His body was controlled by the Devil but his mind, that was all his. And he had a front row seat to the ruin. Earthquakes shook the city to rubble. Volcanoes shot forth from the earth, spewing their magmatic discharge into the air, covering everything close to them.

Tornados ripped through city streets, through lava, through crowds, sending people flying through the air only to be reintroduced to gravity and its consequences. Mass hysteria took hold as the population of earth was exterminated.

Portals from hell were opened by Satan's corporeal body. Demons rose from the depths, claiming the souls of earth's inhabitants.

***

The war is forever ongoing, but this round was over before it even started. A single tear rolled down Mark's cheek.

GOOD FRIDAY
F. Paul Wilson

"The Holy Father says there are no such things as vampires," Sister Bernadette Gileen said.

Sister Carole Hanarty glanced up from the pile of chemistry tests on her lap—tests she might never be able to return to her sophomore students—and watched Bernadette as she drove through town, working the shift on the old Nissan like a long-haul trucker. Her dear friend and fellow Sister of Mercy was thin, almost painfully so, with large blue eyes and short red hair showing around the white band of her wimple. As she peered through the windshield, the light of the setting sun ruddied the clear, smooth skin of her round face.

"If His Holiness said it, then we must believe it," Sister Carole said. "But we haven't heard anything from him in so long. I hope…"

Bernadette turned toward her, eyes wide with alarm.

"Oh, you wouldn't be thinking anything's happened to His Holiness now, would you, Carole?" she said, the lilt of her native Ireland elbowing its way into her voice. "They wouldn't dare!"

Carole was momentarily at a loss as to what to say, so she gazed out the side window at the budding trees sliding past. The sidewalks of this little Jersey Shore town were empty, and hardly any other cars on the road. She and Bernadette had had to try three grocery stores before finding one with anything to sell. Between the hoarders and delayed or canceled shipments, food was getting scarce.

Everybody sensed it. How did that saying go? *By pricking in my thumbs, something wicked this way comes…*

Or something like that.

She rubbed her cold hands together and thought about Bernadette, younger than she by five years—only twenty-six —with such a good mind, such a clear thinker in so many ways. But her faith was almost childlike.

She'd come to the convent at St. Anthony's two years ago and the two of them had established instant rapport. They shared so much. Not just a common Irish heritage, but a certain isolation as well. Carole's parents had died years ago, and Bernadette's were back on the Old Sod. So they became sisters in a sense that went beyond their sisterhood in the order. Carole was the big sister, Bernadette the little one. They prayed together, laughed together, walked together. They took over the convent kitchen and did all the food shopping together. Carole could only hope that she had enriched Bernadette's life half as much as the younger woman had enriched hers.

Bernadette was such an innocent. She seemed to assume that since the Pope was infallible when he spoke on matters of faith or morals he somehow must be invincible too.

Carole hadn't told Bernadette, but she'd decided not to believe the Pope on the matter of the undead. After all, their existence was not a matter of faith or morals. Either they existed or they didn't. And all the news out of Eastern Europe last fall had left little doubt that vampires were real.

And that they were on the march.

Somehow they had got themselves organized. Not only did they exist, but more of them had been hiding in Eastern Europe than even the most superstitious peasant could have imagined. And when the communist bloc crumbled, when all the former client states and Russia were in disarray, grabbing for land, slaughtering in the name of nation and race and religion, the vampires took advantage of the power vacuum and struck.

They struck high, they struck low, and before the rest of the world could react, they controlled all Eastern Europe.

If they had merely killed, they might have been containable. But because each kill was a conversion, their numbers increased in a geometric progression. Sister Carole understood geometric progressions better than most. Hadn't she spent years demonstrating them to her chemistry class by dropping a seed crystal into a beaker of supersaturated solution? That one crystal became two, which became four, which became eight, which became sixteen, and so on. You could watch the lattices forming, slowly at first, then bridging through the solution with increasing speed until the liquid contents of the beaker became a solid mass of crystals.

That was how it had gone in Eastern Europe, then spreading into Russia and into Western Europe.

The vampires became unstoppable.

All of Europe had been silent for months. Officially, at least. But a couple of the students at St. Anthony's High who had short wave radios had told Carole of faint transmissions filtering through the transatlantic night recounting ghastly horrors all across Europe under vampire rule.

But the Pope had declared there were no vampires. He'd said it, but shortly thereafter he and the Vatican had fallen silent along with the rest of Europe.

Washington had played down the immediate threat, saying the Atlantic Ocean formed a natural barrier against the undead. Europe was quarantined. America was safe.

Then came reports, disputed at first, and still officially denied, of vampires in New York City. Most of the New York TV and radio stations had stopped transmitting last week. And now...

"You can't really believe vampires are coming into New Jersey, can you?" Bernadette said. "I mean, that is, if there were such things."

"It is hard to believe, isn't it?" Carole said, hiding a smile. "Especially since no one comes to Jersey unless they have to."

"Oh, don't you be having on with me now. This is serious."

Bernadette was right. It was serious. "Well, it fits the pattern my students have heard from Europe."

"But dear God, 'tis Holy Week! 'Tis Good Friday, it is! How could they dare?"

"It's the perfect time, if you think about it. There will be no Mass said until the first Easter Mass on Sunday morning. What other time of the year is daily mass suspended?"

Bernadette shook her head. "None."

"Exactly." Carole looked down at her cold hands and felt the chill crawl all the way up her arms.

The car suddenly lurched to a halt and she heard Bernadette cry out. "Dear Jesus! They're already here!"

Half a dozen black-clad forms clustered on the corner ahead, staring at them.

"Got to get out of here!" Bernadette said and hit the gas.

The old car coughed and died.

"Oh, no!" Bernadette wailed, frantically pumping the gas pedal and turning the key as the dark forms glided toward them. "No!"

"Easy, dear," Carole said, laying a gentle hand on her arm. "It's all right. They're just kids."

Perhaps "kids" was not entirely correct. Two males and four females who looked to be in their late teens and early twenties, but carried any number of adult lifetimes behind their heavily made-up eyes. Grinning, leering, they gathered around the car, four on Bernadette's side and two on Carole's. Sallow faces made paler by a layer of white powder, kohl-crusted eyelids, and black lipstick. Black fingernails, rings in their ears and eyebrows and nostrils, chrome studs piercing cheeks and lips. Their hair ranged the color spectrum, from dead white through burgundy to crankcase black. Bare hairless chests on the boys beneath their leather jackets, almost-bare chests on the girls in their black push-up bras and bustiers. Boots of shiny leather or vinyl, fishnet stockings, layer upon layer of lace, and everything black, black, black.

"Hey, look!" one of the boys said. A spiked leather collar girded his throat, acne lumps bulged under his white-face. "Nuns!"

"Penguins!" someone else said.

Apparently this was deemed hilarious. The six of them screamed with laughter.

We're *not* penguins, Carole thought. She hadn't worn a full habit in years. Only the headpiece.

"Shit, are *they* gonna be in for a surprise tomorrow morning!" said a buxom girl wearing a silk top hat.

Another roar of laughter by all except one. A tall, slim girl with three large black tears tattooed down one cheek, and blond roots peeking from under her black-dyed hair, hung back, looking uncomfortable. Carole stared at her. Something familiar there…

She rolled down her window. "Mary Margaret? Mary Margaret Flanagan, is that you?"

More laughter. "Mary Margaret?" someone cried. "That's Wicky!"

The girl stepped forward and looked Carole in the eye. "Yes, Sister. That used to be my name. But I'm not Mary Margaret anymore."

"I can see that."

She remembered Mary Margaret. A sweet girl, extremely bright, but so quiet. A voracious reader who never seemed to fit in with the rest of the kids. Her grades plummeted as a junior. She never returned for her senior year. When Carole had called her parents, she was told that Mary Margaret had left home. She'd been unable to learn anything more.

"You've changed a bit since I last saw you. What is it—three years now?"

"You talk about *change*?" said the top-hatted girl, sticking her face in the window. "Wait'll tonight. Then you'll *really* see her change!" She brayed a laugh that revealed a chrome stud in her tongue.

"Butt out, Carmilla!" Mary Margaret said.

Carmilla ignored her. "They're coming tonight, you know. The Lords of the Night will be arriving after sunset, and that'll spell the death of your world and the birth of ours. We will present ourselves to them, we will bare our throats and let them drain us, and then we'll join them. Then we will rule the night with them!"

It sounded like a canned speech, one she must have delivered time and again to her black-clad troupe.

Carole looked past Carmilla to Mary Margaret. "Is that what you believe? Is that what you really want?"

The girl shrugged her high thin shoulders. "Beats anything else I got going."

Finally, the old Nissan shuddered to life. Carole heard Bernadette working the shift. She touched her arm and said, "Wait. Just one more moment, please."

She was about to speak to Mary Margaret when Carmilla jabbed her finger at Carole's face, shouting.

"Then you bitches and the candy-ass god you whore for will be fucking extinct!"

With a surprising show of strength, Mary Margaret yanked Carmilla away from the window.

"Better go, Sister Carole," Mary Margaret said.

The Nissan started to move.

"What the fuck's with you, Wicky?" Carole heard Carmilla scream as the car eased away from the dark cluster. "Getting religion or somethin'? Should we start callin' you 'Sister Mary Margaret' now?"

"She was one of the few people who was ever straight with me," Mary Margaret said. "So fuck off, Carmilla."

The car had traveled too far to hear more.

***

"What awful creatures they were!" Bernadette said, staring out the window in Carole's room. She hadn't been able to stop talking about the incident on the street. "Almost my age, they were, and such horrible language!"

Her convent room was little more than a ten-by -ten -foot plaster box with cracks in the walls and the latest coat of paint beginning to flake off the ancient, embossed tin ceiling. She had one window, a crucifix, a dresser and mirror, a work table and chair, a bed, and a night stand as furnishings. Not much, but she gladly called it home. She took her vow of poverty seriously.

"Perhaps we should pray for them."

"They need more than prayer, I'd think. Believe you me, they're heading for a bad end." Bernadette removed the oversized rosary she wore looped around her neck, gathering the beads and its attached crucifix in her hand. "Maybe we could offer them some crosses for protection?"

Carole couldn't resist a smile. "That's a sweet thought, Bern, but I don't think they're looking for protection."

"Sure, and lookit after what I'm saying," Bernadette said, her own smile rueful. "No, of course they wouldn't."

"But we'll pray for them," Carole said.

Bernadette dropped into a chair, stayed there for no more than a heartbeat, then was up again, moving about, pacing the confines of Carole's room. She couldn't seem to sit still. She wandered out into the hall and came back almost immediately, rubbing her hands together as if washing them.

"It's so quiet," she said. "So empty."

"I certainly hope so," Carole said. "We're the only two who are supposed to be here."

The little convent was half empty even when all its residents were present. And now, with St. Anthony's School closed for the coming week, the rest of the nuns had gone home to spend Easter Week with brothers and sisters and parents. Even those who might have stayed around the convent in past years had heard the rumors that the undead might be moving this way, so they'd scattered south and west. Carole's only living relative was a brother who lived in California and he hadn't invited her; and even if he had, she couldn't afford to fly there and back to Jersey just for Easter. Bernadette hadn't heard from her family in Ireland for months.

So that left just the two of them to hold the fort, as it were.

Carole wasn't afraid. She knew they'd be safe here at St. Anthony's. The convent was part of a complex consisting of the Church itself, the rectory, the grammar school and high school buildings, and the sturdy old, two-story rooming house that was now the convent. She and Bernadette had taken second -floor rooms, leaving the first floor to the older nuns.

Not *really* afraid, although she wished there were more people left in the complex than just Bernadette, herself, and Father Palmeri.

"I don't understand Father Palmeri," Bernadette said. "Locking up the church and keeping his parishioners from making the Stations of the Cross on Good Friday. Who's ever heard of such a thing, I ask you? I just don't understand it."

Carole thought she understood. She suspected that Father Alberto Palmeri was afraid. Sometime this morning he'd locked up the rectory, barred the door to St. Anthony's, and hidden himself in the church basement.

God forgive her, but to Sister Carole's mind, Father Palmeri was a coward.

"Oh, I do wish he'd open the church, just for a little while," Bernadette said. "I need to be in there, Carole. I *need* it."

Carole knew how Bern felt. Who had said religion was an opiate of the people? Marx? Whoever it was, he hadn't been completely wrong. For Carole, sitting in the cool, peaceful quiet beneath St. Anthony's gothic arches, praying, meditating, and feeling the presence of the Lord were like a daily dose of an addictive drug. A dose she and Bern had been denied today. Bern's withdrawal pangs seemed worse than Carole's.

The younger nun paused as she passed the window, then pointed down to the street.

"And now who in God's name would they be?"

Carole rose and stepped to the window. Passing on the street below was a cavalcade of shiny new cars—Mercedes Benzes, BMW's, Jaguars, Lincolns, Cadillacs—all with New York plates, all cruising from the direction of the Parkway.

The sight of them in the dusk tightened a knot in Carole's stomach. The lupine faces she spied through the windows looked brutish, and the way they drove their gleaming, luxury cars down the center line... as if they owned the road.

A Cadillac convertible with its top down passed below, carrying four scruffy men. The driver wore a cowboy hat, the two in the back sat atop the rear seat, drinking beer. When Carol saw one of them glance up and look their way, she tugged on Bern's sleeve.

"Stand back! Don't let them see you!"

"Why not? Who are they?"

"I'm not sure, but I've heard of bands of men who do the vampires' dirty work during the daytime, who've traded their souls for the promise of immortality later on, and for… other things now."

"Sure and you're joking, Carole!"

Carole shook her head. "I wish I were."

"Oh, dear God, and now the sun's down." She turned frightened blue eyes toward Carole. "Do you think maybe we should…?"

"Lock up? Most certainly. I know what His Holiness said about there not being any such things as vampires, but maybe he's changed his mind since then and just can't get word to us."

"Sure, and you're probably right. You close these and I'll check down the hall." She hurried out, her voice trailing behind her. "Oh, I do wish Father Palmeri hadn't locked the church. I'd dearly love to say a few prayers there."

Sister Carole glanced out the window again. The fancy new cars were gone, but rumbling in their wake was a convoy of trucks—big, eighteen-wheel semis, lumbering down the center line. What were they for? What did carry? What were they delivering to town?

Suddenly a dog began to bark, and then another, and more and more until it seemed as if every dog in town was giving voice.

To fight the unease rising within her like a flood tide, Sister Carole concentrated on the simple manual tasks of closing and locking her window, and drawing the curtains.

But the dread remained, a sick, cold certainty that the world was falling into darkness, that the creeping hem of shadow had reached her corner of the globe, and that without some miracle, without some direct intervention by a wrathful God, the coming night hours would wreak an irrevocable change on her life.

She began to pray for that miracle.

***

The two remaining sisters decided to leave the convent of St. Anthony's dark tonight.

And they decided to spend the night together in Carole's room. They dragged in Bernadette's mattress, locked the door, and double-draped the window with the bedspread. They lit the room with a single candle and prayed together.

Yet the music of the night filtered through the walls and the doors and the drapes, the muted moan of sirens singing antiphon to their hymns, the muffled pops of gunfire punctuating their psalms, reaching a crescendo shortly after midnight, then tapering off to... silence.

Carole could see that Bernadette was having an especially rough time of it. She cringed with every siren wail, jumped at every shot. She shared Bern's terror, but she buried it, hid it deep within for her friend's sake. After all, Carole was older, and she knew she was made of sterner stuff. Bernadette was an innocent, too sensitive even for yesterday's world, the world before the vampires. How would she survive in the world as it would be after tonight? She'd need help. Carole would provide as much as she could.

But for all the imagined horrors conjured by the night noises, the silence was worse. No human wails of pain and horror had penetrated their sanctum, but imagined cries of human suffering echoed through their minds in the ensuing stillness.

"Dear God, what's happening out there?" Bernadette said after they'd finished reading aloud the Twenty-third Psalm.

She huddled on her mattress, a blanket thrown over her shoulders. The candle's flame reflected in her frightened eyes, and cast her shadow, high, hunched, and wavering, on the wall behind her.

Carole sat cross-legged on her bed. She leaned back against the wall and fought to keep her eyes open. Exhaustion was a weight on her shoulders, a cloud over her brain, but she knew sleep was out of the question. Not now, not tonight, not until the sun was up. And maybe not even then.

"Easy, Bern—" Carole began, then stopped.

From below, on the first floor of the convent, a faint thumping noise.

"What's that?" Bernadette said, voice hushed, eyes wide.

"I don't know."

Carole grabbed her robe and stepped out into the hall for a better listen.

"Don't you be leaving me alone, now!" Bernadette said, running after her with the blanket still wrapped around her shoulders.

"Hush," Carole said. "Listen. It's the front door. Someone's knocking. I'm going down to see."

She hurried down the wide, oak-railed stairway to the front foyer. The knocking was louder here, but still sounded weak. Carole put her eye to the peephole, peered through the sidelights, but saw no one.

But the knocking, weaker still, continued.

"Wh-who's there?" she said, her words cracking with fear.

"Sister Carole," came a faint voice through the door. "It's me… Mary Margaret. I'm hurt."

Instinctively, Carole reached for the handle, but Bernadette grabbed her arm.

"Wait! It could be a trick!"

She's right, Carole thought. Then she glanced down and saw blood leaking across the threshold from the other side.

She gasped and pointed at the crimson puddle. "That's no trick."

She unlocked the door and pulled it open. Mary Margaret huddled on the welcome mat in a pool of blood.

"Dear sweet Jesus!" Carole cried. "Help me, Bern!"

"What if she's a vampire?" Bernadette said, standing frozen. "They can't cross the threshold unless you ask them in."

"Stop that silliness! She's hurt!"

Bernadette's good heart won out over her fear. She threw off the blanket, revealing a faded blue, ankle-length flannel nightgown that swirled just above the floppy slippers she wore. Together they dragged Mary Margaret inside. Bernadette closed and relocked the door immediately.

"Call 911!" Carole told her.

Bernadette hurried down the hall to the phone.

Mary Margaret lay moaning on the foyer tiles, clutching her bleeding abdomen. Carole saw a piece of metal, coated with rust and blood, protruding from the area of her navel. From the fecal smell of the gore Carole guessed that her intestines had been pierced.

"Oh, you poor child!" Carole knelt beside her and cradled her head in her lap. She arranged Bernadette's blanket over Mary Margaret's trembling body. "Who did this to you?"

"Accident," Mary Margaret gasped. Real tears had run her black eye make-up over her tattooed tears. "I was running… fell."

"Running from what?"

"From *them*. God… terrible. We searched for them, Carmilla's

64

Lords of the Night. Just after sundown we found one. Looked just like we always knew he would... you know, tall and regal and graceful and seductive and cool. Standing by one of those big trailers that came through town. My friends approached him but I sorta stayed back. Wasn't too sure I was really into having my blood sucked. But Carmilla goes right up to him, pulling off her top and baring her throat, offering herself to him."

Mary Margaret coughed and groaned as a spasm of pain shook her.

"Don't talk," Carole said. "Save your strength."

"No," she said in a weaker voice when it eased. "You got to know. This Lord guy just smiles at Carmilla, then he signals his helpers who pull open the back doors of the trailer." Mary Margaret sobbed. "Horrible! Truck's filled with these... *things*! Look human but they're dirty and naked and act like beasts. They like *pour* out the truck and right off a bunch of them jump Carmilla. They start biting and ripping at her throat. I see her go down and hear her screaming and I start backing up. My other friends try to run but they're pulled down too. And then I see one of the things hold up Carmilla's head and hear the Lord guy say, 'That's right, children. Take their heads. Always take their heads. There are enough of us now.' And that's when I turned and ran. I was running through a vacant lot when I fell on... this."

Bernadette rushed back into the foyer. Her face was drawn with fear. "Nine-one-one doesn't answer! I can't raise anyone!"

"They're all over town." Mary Margaret said after another spasm of coughing. Carole could barely hear her. She touched her throat— so cold. "They set fires and attack the cops and firemen when they arrive. Their human helpers break into houses and drive the people outside where they're attacked. And after the things drain the blood, they rip the heads off."

"Dear God, why?" Bernadette said, crouching beside Carole.

"My guess... don't want any more vampires. Maybe only so much blood to go around and—"

She moaned with another spasm, then lay still. Carole patted her cheeks and called her name, but Mary Margaret Flanagan's dull, staring eyes told it all.

"Is she...?" Bernadette said.

Carole nodded as tears filled her eyes. You poor misguided child, she thought, closing Mary Margaret's eyelids.

"She's died in sin," Bernadette said. "She needs anointing immediately! I'll get Father."

"No, Bern," Carole said. "Father Palmeri won't come."

"Of course he will. He's a priest and this poor lost soul needs him."

"Trust me. He won't leave that church basement for anything."

"But he must!" she said, almost childishly, her voice rising. "He's a priest."

"Just be calm, Bernadette, and we'll pray for her ourselves."

"We can't do what a priest can do," she said, springing to her feet. "It's not the same."

"Where are you going?" Carole said.

"To... to get a robe. It's cold."

My poor, dear, frightened Bernadette, Carole thought as she watched her scurry up the steps. I know exactly how you feel.

"And bring my prayer book back with you," she called after her.

Carole pulled the blanket over Mary Margaret's face and gently lowered her head to the floor.

She waited for Bernadette to return... and waited. What was taking her so long? She called her name but got not answer.

Uneasy, Carole returned to the second floor. The hallway was empty and dark except for a pale shaft of moonlight slanting through the window at its far end. Carole hurried to Bern's room. The door was closed. She knocked.

"Bern? Bern, are you in there?"

Silence.

Carole opened the door and peered inside. More moonlight, more emptiness.

Where could — ?

Down on the first floor, almost directly under Carole's feet, the convent's back door slammed. How could that be? Carole had locked it herself—dead bolted it at sunset.

Unless Bernadette had gone down the back stairs and...

She darted to the window and stared down at the grassy area between the convent and the church. The high, bright moon had made a black-and -white photo of the world outside, bleaching the lawn below with its stark glow, etching deep ebony wells around the shrubs and foundation plantings. It glared from St. Anthony's slate roof, stretching a long, crocheted wedge of night behind its Gothic spire.

And scurrying across the lawn toward the church was a slim figure wrapped in a long raincoat, the moon picking out the white band of her wimple, its black veil a fluttering shadow along her neck and upper back—Bernadette was too old-country to approach the church with her head uncovered.

"Oh, Bern," Carole whispered, pressing her face against the glass. "Bern, don't."

She watched as Bernadette ran up to St. Anthony's side entrance and began clanking the heavy brass knocker against the thick oak door. Her high, clear voice filtered faintly through the window glass.

"Father! Father Palmeri! Please open up! There's a dead girl in the convent who needs anointing! Won't you please come over?"

She kept banging, kept calling, but the door never opened. Carole thought she saw Father Palmeri's pale face float into view to Bern's right through the glass of one of the church's few unstained windows. It hovered there for a few seconds or so, then disappeared.

But the door remained closed.

That didn't seem to faze Bern. She only increased the force of her blows with the knocker, and raised her voice even higher until it echoed off the stone walls and reverberated through the night.

Carole's heart went out to her. She shared Bern's need, if not her desperation.

Why doesn't Father Palmeri at least let her in? she thought. The poor thing's making enough racket to wake the dead.

Sudden terror tightened along the back of Carole's neck.

...wake the dead...

Bern was too loud. She thought only of attracting the attention of Father Palmeri, but what if she attracted... others?

Even as the thought crawled across her mind, Carole saw a dark, rangy figure creep onto the lawn from the street side, slinking from shadow to shadow, closing in on her unsuspecting friend.

"Oh, my God!" she cried, and fumbled with the window lock. She twisted it open and yanked up the sash.

Carole screamed into the night. "Bernadette! Behind you! There's someone coming! Get back here now, Bernadette! NOW!"

Bernadette turned and looked up toward Carole, then stared around her. The approaching figure had dissolved into the shadows at the sound of the shouted warnings. But Bernadette must have sensed something in Carole's voice, for she started back toward the convent.

She didn't get far—ten paces, maybe—before the shadowy form caught up to her.

"NO!" Carole screamed as she saw it leap upon her friend.

She stood frozen at the window, her fingers clawing the molding on each side as Bernadette's high wail of terror and pain cut the night.

For the span of an endless, helpless, paralyzed heartbeat, Carole watched the form drag her down to the silver lawn, tear open her raincoat, and fall upon her, watched her arms and legs flail wildly, frantically in the moonlight, and all the while her screams, oh, dear God in Heaven, her screams for help were slim, white hot nails driven into Carole's ears.

And then, out of the corner of her eye, Carole saw the pale face appear again at the window of St. Anthony's, watch for a moment, then once more fade into the inner darkness.

With a low moan of horror, fear, and desperation, Carole pushed herself away from the window and stumbled toward the hall. *Someone* had to help. On the way, she snatched the foot-long wooden crucifix from Bernadette's wall and clutched it against her chest with both hands. As she picked up speed, graduating from a lurch to a walk to a loping run, she began to scream—not a wail of fear, but a long, seamless ululation of rage.

Something was killing her friend.

The rage was good. It canceled the fear and the horror and the loathing that had paralyzed her. It allowed her to move, to keep moving. She embraced the rage.

Carole hurtled down the stairs and burst onto the moonlit lawn—

And stopped.

She was disoriented for an instant. She didn't see Bern. Where was she? Where was her attacker?

And then she saw a patch of writhing shadow on the grass ahead of her near one of the shrubs.

Bernadette?

Clutching the crucifix, Carole ran for the spot, and as she neared she realized it was indeed Bernadette, sprawled face down, but not alone. Another shadow sat astride her, hissing like a reptile, gnashing its teeth, its fingers curved into talons that tugged at Bernadette's head as if trying to tear it off.

Carole reacted without thinking. Screaming, she launched herself at the creature, ramming the big crucifix against its exposed back. Light flashed and sizzled and thick black smoke shot upward in oily swirls from where cross met flesh. The thing arched its back and howled, writhing beneath the cruciform brand, thrashing wildly as it tried to wriggle out from under the fiery weight.

But Carole stayed with it, following its slithering crawl on her knees, pressing the flashing cross deeper and deeper into its steaming, boiling flesh, down to the spine, into the vertebrae. Its cries became almost piteous as it weakened, and Carole gagged on the thick black smoke that fumed around her, but her rage would not allow her to slack off. She kept up the pressure, pushed the wooden crucifix deeper and deeper in the creature's back until it penetrated the chest cavity and seared into its heart. Suddenly the thing gagged and shuddered and then was still.

The flashes faded. The final wisps of smoke trailed away on the breeze.

Carole abruptly released the shaft of the crucifix as if it had shocked her, and ran back to Bernadette. She dropped to her knees beside the still form and turned her over onto her back.

"Oh, no!" she screamed when she saw Bernadette's torn throat, her wide, glazed, sightless eyes, and the blood, so much blood smeared all over the front of her. Oh no. Oh, dear God, please no! This can't be! This can't be real!

A sob burst from her. "No, Bern! Nooooo!"

Somewhere nearby, a dog howled in answer.

Or was it a dog?

Carole realized she was defenseless now. She had to get back to the convent. She leaped to her feet and looked around. Nothing moving. A yard or two away she saw the dead thing with her crucifix still buried in it back.

She hurried over to retrieve it, but recoiled from touching the creature. She could see now that it was a man—a naked man, or something that very much resembled one. But not quite. Some indefinable quality was missing.

Was it one of *them*?

This must be one of the undead Mary Margaret had warned

about. But could this... this *thing*... be a vampire? It had acted like little more than a rabid dog in human form.

Whatever it was, it had mauled and murdered Bernadette. Rage bloomed again within Carole like a virulent, rampant virus, spreading through her bloodstream, invading her nervous system, threatening to take her over completely. She fought the urge to batter the corpse.

Bile rose in her throat; she choked it down and stared at the inert form prone before her. This once had been a man, someone with a family, perhaps. Surely he hadn't asked to become this vicious night thing.

"Whoever you were," Carole whispered, "you're free now. Free to return to God."

She gripped the shaft of the crucifix to remove it but found it fixed in the seared flesh like a steel rod set in concrete.

Something howled again. Closer.

She had to get back inside, but she couldn't leave Bern out here.

Swiftly, she returned to Bernadette's side, worked her hands through the grass under her back and knees, and lifted her into her arms. So light! Dear Lord, she weighed almost nothing.

Carole carried Bernadette back to the convent as fast as her rubbery legs would allow. Once inside, she bolted the door, then staggered up to the second floor with Bernadette in her arms.

She returned Sister Bernadette Gileen to her own room. Carole didn't have the energy to drag the mattress back across the hall, so she stretched her supine on the box spring of her bed. She straightened Bern's thin legs, crossed her hands over her blood-splattered chest, arranged her torn clothing as best she could, and covered her from head to toe with a bedspread.

And then, looking down at that still form under the quilt she had helped Bernadette make, Carole sagged to her knees and began to cry. She tried to say a requiem prayer but her grief-racked mind had lost the words. So she sobbed aloud and asked God, Why? How could He let this happen to a dear, sweet innocent who had wished only to spend her life serving Him? WHY?

But no answer came.

When Carole finally controlled her tears, she forced herself to her feet, closed Bernadette's door, and stumbled into the hall. She saw the light from the front foyer and knew she shouldn't leave it on. She hurried down and stepped over the still form of Mary Margaret under the blood-soaked blanket. Two violent deaths here tonight in a house devoted to God. How many more outside these doors?

She turned off the light but didn't have the strength to carry Mary Margaret upstairs. She left her there and raced through the dark back to her own room.

***

Carole didn't know what time the power went out.

She had no idea how long she'd been kneeling beside her bed, alternately sobbing and praying, when she glanced at the digital alarm clock on her night table and saw that its face had gone dark and blank.

Not that a power failure mattered. She'd been spending the night by candlelight anyway. There was barely an inch of candle left, but that gave her no clue as to the hour. Who knew how fast a candle burned?

She was tempted to lift the bedspread draped over the window and peek outside, but was afraid of what she might see.

How long until dawn? she wondered, rubbing her eyes. This night seemed endless. If only—

Beyond her locked door, a faint squeak came from somewhere along the hall. It could have been anything—the wind in the attic, the old building settling, but it had been long, drawn out, and high pitched. Almost like...

A door opening.

Carole froze, still on her knees, hands still folded in prayer, her elbows resting on the bed, and listened for it again. But the sound was not repeated. Instead, something else... a rhythmic shuffle... in the hall... approaching her door...

Footsteps.

With her heart punching frantically against the inner wall of her chest, Carole leaped to her feet and stepped close to the door, listening with her ear almost touching the wood. Yes. Footsteps. Slow. And soft, like bare feet scuffing the floor. Coming this way. Closer. They were right outside the door. Carole felt a sudden chill, as if a wave of icy air had penetrated the wood, but the footsteps didn't pause. They passed her door, moving on.

And then they stopped.

Carole had her ear pressed against the wood now. She could hear her pulse pounding through her head as she strained for the next sound. And then it came, more shuffling outside in the hall, almost confused at first, and then the footsteps began again.

Coming back.

This time they stopped directly outside Carole's door. The cold was there again, a damp, penetrating chill that reached for her bones. Carole backed away from it.

And then the doorknob turned. Slowly. The door creaked with the weight of a body leaning against it from the other side, but Carole's bolt held.

Then a voice. Hoarse. A single whispered word, barely audible, but a shout could not have startled her more.

"Carole?"

Carole didn't reply—*couldn't* reply.

"Carole, it's me. Bern. Let me in."

Against her will, a low moan escaped Carole. No, no, no, this couldn't be Bernadette. Bernadette was dead. Carole had left her cooling body lying in her room across the hall. This was some horrible joke...

Or was it? Maybe Bernadette had become one of *them*, one of the very things that had killed her.

But the voice on the other side of the door was not that of some ravenous beast. It was...

"Please let me in, Carole. I'm frightened out here alone."

Maybe Bern *is* alive, Carole thought, her mind racing, ranging for an answer. I'm no doctor. I could have been wrong about her being dead. Maybe she survived...

She stood trembling, torn between the desperate, aching need to see her friend alive, and the wary terror of being tricked by whatever creature Bernadette might have become.

"Carole?"

Carole wished for a peephole in the door, or at the very least a chain lock, but she had neither, and she had to do something. She couldn't stand here like this and listen to that plaintive voice any longer without going mad. She had to *know*. Without giving herself any more time to think, she snapped back the bolt and pulled the door open, ready to face whatever awaited her in the hall.

She gasped. "Bernadette!"

Her friend stood just beyond the threshold, swaying, stark naked.

Not completely naked. She still wore her wimple, although it was askew on her head, and a strip of cloth had been layered around her neck to dress her throat wound. In the wan, flickering candlelight that leaked from Carole's room, she saw that the blood that had splattered her was gone. Carole had never seen Bernadette unclothed before. She'd never realized how thin she was. Her ribs rippled beneath the skin of her chest, disappearing only beneath the scant padding of her small breasts with their erect nipples; the bones of her hips and pelvis bulged around her flat belly. Her normally fair skin was almost blue-white. The only other colors were the dark pools of her eyes and the orange splotches of hair on her head and her pubes.

"Carole," she said weakly. "Why did you leave me?"

The sight of Bernadette standing before her, alive, speaking, had drained most of Carole's strength; the added weight of guilt from her words nearly drove her to her knees. She sagged against the door frame.

"Bern..." Carole's voice failed her. She swallowed and tried again. "I—I thought you were dead. And... what happened to your clothes?"

Bernadette raised her hand to her throat."I tore up my nightgown for a bandage. Can I come in?"

Carole straightened and opened the door further. "Oh, Lord, yes. Come in. Sit down. I'll get you a blanket."

Bernadette shuffled into the room, head down, eyes fixed on the floor. She moved like someone on drugs. But then, after losing so much blood, it was a wonder she could walk at all.

"Don't want a blanket," Bern said. "Too hot. Aren't you hot?"

She backed herself stiffly onto Carole's bed, then lifted her ankles and sat cross-legged , facing her. Mentally, Carole explained the casual, blatant way she exposed herself by the fact that Bernadette was still recovering from a horrific trauma, but that made it no less discomfiting.

Carole glanced at the crucifix on the wall over her bed, above and behind Bernadette. For moment, as Bernadette had seated herself beneath it, she thought she had seen it glow. It must have been reflected candlelight. She turned away and retrieved a spare blanket from the closet. She unfolded it and wrapped it around Bernadette's shoulders and over her spread knees, covering her.

"I'm thirsty, Carole. Could you get me some water?"

Her voice was strange. Lower pitched and hoarse, yes, but that should to be expected after the throat wound she'd suffered. No, something else had changed in her voice, but Carole could not pin it down.

"Of course. You'll need fluids. Lots of fluids."

The bathroom was only two doors down. She took her water pitcher, lit a second candle, and left Bernadette on the bed, looking like an Indian draped in a serape.

When she returned with the full pitcher, she was startled to find the bed empty. She spied Bernadette immediately, by the window. She hadn't opened it, but she'd pulled off the bedspread drape and raised the shade. She stood there, staring out at the night. And she was naked again.

Carole looked around for the blanket and found it... hanging on the wall over her bed...

Covering the crucifix.

Part of Carole screamed at her to run, to flee down the hall and not look back. But another part of her insisted she stay. This was her friend. Something terrible had happened to Bernadette and she needed Carole now, probably more than she'd needed anyone in her entire life. And if someone was going to help her, it was Carole. *Only* Carole.

She placed the pitcher on the night stand.

"Bernadette," she said, her mouth as dry as the timbers in these old walls, "the blanket..."

"I was hot," Bernadette said without turning.

"I brought you the water. I'll pour—"

"I'll drink it later. Come and watch the night."

"I don't want to see the night. It frightens me."

Bernadette turned, a faint smile on her lips. "But the darkness is so beautiful."

She stepped closer and stretched her arms toward Carole, laying a hand and each shoulder and gently massaging the terror-tightened muscles there. A sweet lethargy began to seep through Carole. Her eyelids began to drift closed... so tired... so long since she'd had any sleep...

No!

She forced her eyes open and gripped Bernadette's hands, pulling them from her shoulders. She pressed the palms together and clasped them between her own.

74

"Let's pray, Bern. With me: Hail Mary, full of grace..."

"*No!*"

"...the Lord is with thee. Blessed art thou..."

Her friend's face twisted in rage. "I said, NO, damn you!"

Carole struggled to keep a grip on Bernadette's hands but she was too strong.

"... amongst women..."

And suddenly Bernadette's struggles ceased. Her face relaxed, her eyes cleared, even her voiced changed, still hoarse, but higher in pitch, lighter in tone as she took up the words of the prayer.

"And blessed is the fruit of thy womb..." Bernadette struggled with the next word, unable to say it. Instead she gripped Carole's hands with painful intensity and loosed a torrent of her own words. "Carole, get out! Get out, oh, please, for the love of God, get out now! There's not much of me left in here, and soon I'll be like the ones that killed me and I'll be after killing you! So run, Carole! Hide! Lock yourself in the chapel downstairs but get away from me *now!*"

Carole knew now what had been missing from Bernadette's voice—her brogue. But now it was back. This was the real Bernadette speaking. She was back! Her friend, her sister was back! Carole bit back a sob.

"Oh, Bern, I can help! I can—"

Bernadette pushed her toward the door. "*No one* can help me, Carole!" She ripped the makeshift bandage from her neck, exposing the deep, jagged wound and the ragged ends of the torn blood vessels within it. "It's too late for me, but not for you. They're a bad lot and I'll be one of them again soon, so get out while you—"

Suddenly Bernadette stiffened and her features shifted. Carole knew immediately that the brief respite her friend had stolen from the horror that gripped her was over. Something else was back in control.

Carole turned and ran.

But the Bernadette-thing was astonishingly swift. Carole had barely reached the threshold when a steel-fingered hand gripped her upper arm and yanked her back, nearly dislocating her shoulder. She cried out in pain and terror as she was spun about and flung across the room. Her hip struck hard against the rickety old spindle chair by her desk, knocking it over as she landed in a heap beside it.

Carole groaned with the pain. As she shook her head to clear it, she saw Bernadette approaching her, her movements swift, more assured now, her teeth bared—so many teeth, and so much longer than the old Bernadette's—her fingers curved, reaching for Carole's throat. With each passing second there was less and less of Bernadette about her.

Carole tried to back away, her frantic hands and feet slipping on the floor as she pressed her spine against the wall. She had nowhere to go. She pulled the fallen chair atop her and held it as a shield against the Bernadette-thing . The face that had once belonged to her dearest friend grimaced with contempt as she swung her hand at the chair. It scythed through the spindles, splintering them like matchsticks, sending the carved headpiece flying. A second blow cracked the seat in two. A third and fourth sent the remnants of the chair hurtling to opposite sides of the room.

Carole was helpless now. All she could do was pray.

"Our Father, who art—"

"Too late for that to help you now, *Carole!*" she hissed, spitting her name.

"...hallowed be Thy name..." Carole said, quaking in terror as undead fingers closed on her throat.

And then the Bernadette-thing froze, listening. Carole heard it too. An insistent tapping. On the window. The creature turned to look, and Carole followed her gaze.

A face was peering through the window.

Carole blinked but it didn't go away. This was the second floor! How—?

And then a second face appeared, this one upside down, looking in from the top of the window. And then a third, and a fourth, each more bestial than the last. And as each appeared it began to tap its fingers and knuckles on the window glass.

"NO!" the Bernadette-thing screamed at them. "You can't come in! She's mine! No one touches her but *me!*"

She turned back to Carole and smiled, showing those teeth that had never fit in Bernadette's mouth. "They can't cross a threshold unless invited in by one who lives there. I live here—or at least I did. And I'm not sharing you, Carole."

She turned again and raked a claw-like hand at the window. "Go AWAY ! She's MINE!"

Carole glanced to her left. The bed was only a few feet away. And above it—the blanket-shrouded crucifix. If she could reach it...

She didn't hesitate. With the mad tapping tattoo from the window echoing around her, Carole gathered her feet beneath her and sprang for the bed. She scrambled across the sheets, one hand outstretched, reaching for the blanket—

A manacle of icy flesh closed around her ankle and roughly dragged her back.

"Oh, no, bitch," said the hoarse, unaccented voice of the Bernadette-thing. "Don't even *think* about it!"

It grabbed two fistfuls of flannel at the back of Carole's nightgown and hurled her across the room as if she weighed no more than a pillow. The wind whooshed out of Carole as she slammed against the far wall. She heard ribs crack. She fell among the splintered ruins of the chair, pain lancing through her right flank. The room wavered and blurred. But through the roaring in her ears she still heard that insistent tapping on the window.

As her vision cleared she saw the Bernadette-thing's naked form gesturing again to the creatures at the window, now a mass of salivating mouths and tapping fingers.

"Watch!" she hissed. "Watch me!"

With that, she loosed a long, howling scream and lunged at Carole, arms curved before her, body arcing into a flying leap. The scream, the tapping, the faces at the window, the dear friend who now wanted only to slaughter her—it all was suddenly too much for Carole. She wanted to roll away but couldn't get her body to move. Her hand found the broken seat of the chair by her hip. Instinctively she pulled it closer. She closed her eyes as she raised it between herself and the horror hurtling toward her through the air.

The impact drove the wood of the seat against Carole's chest; she groaned as new stabs of pain shot through her ribs. But the Bernadette-thing's triumphant feeding cry cut off abruptly and devolved into a coughing gurgle.

Suddenly the weight was released from Carole's chest, and the chair seat with it.

And the tapping at the window stopped.

Carole opened her eyes to see the naked Bernadette-thing standing above her, straddling her, holding the chair seat before her, choking and gagging as she struggled with it.

At first Carole didn't understand. She drew her legs back and inched away along the wall. And then she saw what had happened.

Three splintered spindles had remained fixed in that half of the broken seat, and those spindles were now firmly and deeply embedded in the center of the Bernadette-thing's chest. She wrenched wildly at the chair seat, trying to dislodge the oak daggers but succeeded only in breaking them off at skin level. She dropped the remnant of the seat and swayed like a tree in a storm, her mouth working spasmodically as her hands fluttered ineffectually over the bloodless wounds between her ribs and the slim wooden stakes deep out of reach within them.

Abruptly she dropped to her knees with a dull thud. Then, only inches from Carole, she slumped into a splay-legged squat. The agony faded from her face and she closed her eyes. She fell forward against Carole.

Carole threw her arms around her friend and gathered her close.

"Oh, Bern, oh, Bern, oh, Bern," she moaned. "I'm so sorry. If only I'd got there sooner!"

Bernadette's eyes fluttered open and the darkness was gone. Only her own spring-sky blue remained, clear, grateful. Her lips began to curve upward but made it only half way to a smile, then she was gone.

Carole hugged the limp cold body closer and moaned in boundless grief and anguish to the unfeeling walls. She saw the leering faces begin to crawl away from the window and she shouted at them though her tears.

"Go! That's it! Run away and hide! Soon it'll be light and then *I'll* come looking for *you*! For *all* of you! And woe to any of you that I find!"

She cried over Bernadette's body a long time. And then she wrapped it in a sheet and held and rocked her dead friend in her arms until sunrise.

***

With the dawn she left the old Sister Carole Hanarty behind. The gentle soul, happy to spend her days and nights in the service of the Lord, praying, fasting, teaching chemistry to reluctant adolescents, and holding to her vows of poverty, chastity, and obedience, was gone.

The new Sister Carole had been tempered in the forge of the night, and recast into someone relentlessly vengeful and fearless to

78

the point of recklessness. And perhaps, she admitted with no shame or regret, more than a little mad.

She departed the convent and began her hunt.

SHUT DOWN
Jeff DePew

OCTOBER

Callie

A gust of wind swept through the darkened neighborhood, sending a flurry of leaves spinning in its wake. Some of the leaves spilled up against garbage cans left beside driveways; others piled against car tires and windshields. And more leaves, brown and yellow and orange, buffeted against the desiccated corpses that lay in the street, on the sidewalk, or on front lawns of empty houses.

A young girl walked down the middle of the street, pushing a jogging stroller. Her long, brown hair was tied up in a braid beneath her Seattle Mariners baseball cap. She wore a denim jacket and an oversized backpack. Around her right wrist was a leather dog leash she had found. The leash trailed several feet behind her, where it was clipped to the belt of a slightly older boy who followed her, occasionally slowing, only to be jerked forward with a gentle tug.

Her name was Callie, she was twelve years old, and she was walking through Oregon to find her grandmother in California.

The only sounds were their footsteps and an occasional murmur from the baby. She still hadn't named him. She had been thinking of Sam, or maybe Ryan. That was—*had been*—her father's name. The thought of her father pressed down on her like a weight. Another cinder block thrown into her backpack. Remembering was like that. Thinking about her mom, her dad, their house. Their life together. Life in general. Life before. Cinder blocks. Cinder blocks that weighed her down. Kept her from moving on. But you couldn't forget. You couldn't just pretend like nothing had existed before IT. That was no solution. A loud squawk from the stroller broke her out of her thoughts.

She stopped and reached down and pulled back the blanket so she could look at the baby. He was holding a jar of baby food (sweet potato and peas, it looked like) with two chubby hands and trying to bite the lid, his baby logic telling him this was the best way to get the contents of the jar into his mouth. His eyes widened and he smiled wetly up at her when he saw her.

"Hungry?" she smiled back at him. Callie turned to her brother, Jake, who was slowly shuffling forward, his eyes vacant and staring. "How about you?" she asked, expecting (and getting) no response. "You ready for some dinner?"

She took a swig of water from a metal bottle fastened to her backpack. She yawned and stretched, twisting from side to side, glanced around at the houses. The nights were getting chillier, and she wanted to find shelter for the night. She preferred the houses with no cars in the driveways. That generally meant no one had been home when IT happened, so there were no bodies on the houses. Not always, but usually.

***

She decided on a one-story house, blue, with white trim. There was no car in the driveway, and the front door was undamaged. It was very rare that she found a house where there had been obvious damage and/or looting. So rare in fact that she rarely even thought about it anymore. There had to be people to loot, and since there were hardly any people…

Some part of her wished there were more signs of other people. A busted-in front door, or a campfire burning at night in the distance. But nothing. She hadn't seen anyone other than Jake and the baby—his name is Ryan—for over a week.

Anyone alive, she thought glumly.

She wheeled the stroller up the driveway and around the side of the house to a wooden gate taller than her by a good two feet. She tried the metal latch. It opened, and she carefully pushed the gate open and led her brother inside and pulled the stroller behind her. She turned and latched the gate, bent down and picked up a twig, and stuck it in the hole where the padlock would go. It wouldn't keep out a determined trespasser, but Jake wouldn't be able to get out, even if he wanted to. And it would keep dogs out.

She slipped the leash off her wrist and reached over and unsnapped the metal clip from his belt. "Okay, buddy. You're free." She stood and watched him. No reaction. No smile, no walking forward, no nothing. She sighed and checked on the baby. He was

81

fussing a little, but he'd be okay for a few more minutes.

Callie tried a side door and it opened easily. She glanced once more at Jake and the baby. They weren't going anywhere. She pulled out a flashlight from a pocket in her backpack and slipped inside. She scanned the room. A kitchen. Neat and orderly. Tile floors and counters now covered with a fine film of dust. She sniffed deeply. The sickly-sweet smell of rotting fruit, and beneath that a fouler smell emanating from the refrigerator. No way she was opening that. She'd learned the hard way not to open refrigerators. The smell was ungodly.

She knelt, and using her flashlight, carefully scanned the counter and corners for rat droppings. She hated rats, and since… IT… they seemed to be almost everywhere. But this looked okay. No little, black, telltale signs.

She crossed to a doorway and checked out the rest of the house.

A small family/living area with a couch and a TV mounted to the wall, two bedrooms, one with a king-size bed and an attached bathroom, and the other smaller, with posters on the wall. Another room with a desk and a computer, and a bathroom.

No running water, but the toilet tank was still full. She could fill up her bottle. A hall closet supplied some blankets that she spread on the floor of the living room. She went to a door that led to the backyard and unlocked it.

She levered the stroller up over the threshold and wheeled it into the living room, then lifted the baby out and laid him in the middle of the blanket. He squinted up at her, his mouth pulled down in a grimace. He was getting fussy. "Don't worry, buddy," Callie whispered. "Give me five minutes."

She went outside to get her brother. Then she would clean and feed them both before putting them to bed.

She stepped around the corner of the house to get Jake, and her heart stopped.

He was gone. She went to the gate, but it was still closed. She turned and saw him. He was *behind* the house, standing in knee-high weeds. He was… staring down at his feet.

Is he looking at something?

"Jake?" Callie approached him warily. He didn't acknowledge her. He had walked off one time before. Just a few feet. Like now. But it was always disconcerting. And yet, it was also a good thing. If he could walk off on his own, without being led or pushed, it meant he was thinking, didn't it?

Callie walked up and put a hand on his shoulder. She thought he trembled a bit, but it was hard to tell. "What's up, buddy?" she asked, glancing down to see what he might be looking at. At his feet sat a faded, half-deflated soccer ball. Her heart began to race. Jake loved soccer. As far back as she could remember, he had been playing soccer. He was hoping for a scholarship, a full ride to UC Santa Barbara.

She stepped forward and tapped the soccer ball with her foot. It rolled a foot and stopped. She watched him carefully. Had his eyes widened slightly? He seemed to be focusing on the ball, but it was hard to tell. She kicked the ball a bit farther. He took a step toward it. *On his own!*

Apparently, that was all he had in him. No amount of cajoling or nudging could get him to move toward the ball again. But it was something.

It was hope.

***

Later that night, Callie sat in a canvas deck chair on the back porch. The door behind her was open. Empty baby food jars sat on the floor. One for the baby, and three for Jake. She'd clean up later. She'd had a protein bar and some applesauce she had found in the pantry. And a can of Coke.

The baby (*Ryan*, she reminded herself) lay on the floor on top of a folded blanket, a makeshift crib of propped-up throw pillows around him. He had eaten, was clean, and was fast asleep in a pair of light-blue pajamas Callie had taken from a department store.

Callie liked to keep everyone together in one room. She would sleep on the couch. Like the baby, Jake had been fed and cleaned as well. It was more work than the baby, obviously, but she had gotten used to it now. Just something she did, but didn't necessarily like. Like homework, or cleaning the bathroom every Saturday.

Jake was asleep on a mattress she had pulled to the floor and dragged into the family room. He had rolled off a bed on more than one occasion and once had received a nasty bruise on his forehead. She had been really worried, as any bad injury could be a real problem these days. But he had shown no ill effects, and the bruise healed in a couple of days.

He did seem to dream. He moved around a lot in his sleep. Did that mean his brain wasn't completely dead—that there might be hope for him?

She sank back in a chair and gazed up at the stars. So many more than ever before. Without the pollution and the city lights, the stars blazed at night. Before, they would have to get out in the country to really see the stars. Her mom had wanted to drive out of town and watch the meteor shower the night IT happened. The Perseids Meteor Shower. She and Callie's father had been out running errands. They never came back. Was that what had caused... IT... the Shut Down... to happen? The meteors? She tried not to think about that day... three months ago? She had given up trying to keep track of the date. She too many other things to think about.

Callie's eyes blurred. She blinked, and she realized she was crying. She hadn't cried in weeks. It was a luxury she couldn't afford. She leaned forward and put her head in her hands and wept. She cried for Jake, and for the baby, who would never know his mother and father. She cried for her own mother and father. But mostly, she cried for herself.

It

"We'll be back in a couple hours," Mom said, sunglasses in one hand, looking around the counter for her keys.

"Marie! Let's go!" came her father's voice from the garage.

"I know. I know. I'm looking for my keys," her mother called back, searching in her purse for the third time.

"Hello! You don't need them! I'm driving!" Callie could hear the laugh in her father's voice.

Mom looked up, shook her head, smiled, blew a kiss to Callie who was watching from over the back of the couch, and headed out to the garage. Callie heard her parents laughing as the door to the garage closed.

That was the last time she ever saw them.

About an hour or so later (she was never sure) she was idly watching a baseball game and texting her best friend, Erica. Just an ordinary Saturday in August. Too hot to be outside unless absolutely necessary. Erica had just finished telling her about some new eyeliner she was planning on getting when there was a sudden, loud metallic screech, and a brilliant white light filled Callie's eyes. She closed her eyes and jerked her head to the side. The terrible, metallic screeching sound (like a gigantic shovel scraping on concrete) continued. It was loud, louder than anything she had ever heard. It went on and on. It was everything, everywhere. She began to feel nauseous. Then it all went dark.

Callie was never clear if she had blacked out or not. Her eyes took a moment to readjust, and her ears were ringing. She gazed around the room, dazed. The TV was still on, but the picture was weird. The camera was just showing the ground. There was part of a shoe in the lower left corner. The camera wasn't moving, and neither was the foot.

Callie picked up the remote and changed the channel. Cartoon, commercial, a sports news program—but the camera shot was off-center and the hosts looked like they were asleep, unconsciousness, or something. They were slumped in their chairs. Not moving. Eyes open, but unfocused, just staring. A man came in from off camera. He was holding a clipboard and he walked unsteadily to the broadcast desk. He said something too soft to hear. He nudged one of the hosts, a bald man with glasses, who slid off his chair and fell bonelessly to the floor. The man with the clipboard looked at the camera, his face panic-stricken, and stumbled out of the picture.

Callie clicked the remote and checked more channels, but they were all the same. Any live programs just showed the hosts or newscasters lying on the floor or slumped over their desk. Everything else was just movies or commercials or dead air.

She glanced around for her phone and grabbed it off the floor. She texted Erica.

hey did you hear that

No response. She tried again.

Erica call me now it's important

Again, nothing. Callie pushed the CALL button and the phone rang and rang and Erica's voicemail picked up. "Oh, my God, Erica, what happened? Call me, please. I'm really scared and my parents aren't home."

She stood up and went to the front window, pulled the curtain aside, and looked out. There was a car sitting on their lawn. It had crashed into the big Mesquite tree. The engine was still running. There was a driver inside, leaning against the window. Just like the people on the sports show. Slumped over. She leaned closer to the glass and looked up and down the street and saw someone standing on the sidewalk a few houses up. It was Mr. Phillips, a friend of her dad.

She opened the front door and raced down the sidewalk toward Mr. Phillips. But as she got closer, she slowed. He was so still, just... standing there in front of his house. Mr. Phillips was wearing cargo shorts and a Corona beer tank top. A garbage can lay on its side several feet away. His face was slack, eyes open, but staring blindly at nothing. Callie approached him warily and touched his hand.

"Mr. Phillips? Are you okay? What's happening?" She was struggling not to cry. He didn't respond. She tugged on his hand. "Mr. Phillips! Please!" He stumbled forward and she quickly backed up. He fell straight down, face first, on his lawn. He never even put his hands out to stop himself. She backed away some more, hands to her mouth, and started back to her house.

A baby was crying somewhere nearby. She stopped and looked around. It was hard to tell exactly where it was coming from. Someone was lying in a driveway street several houses up. A woman she vaguely recognized was standing on the sidewalk. She wobbled and collapsed.

She caught movement out of the corner of her eye and looked up. In the distance, an airplane was angling toward the ground. It disappeared behind a tree.

Callie walked toward her house. Where else could she go? What was happening? It was like a bad dream. Her eyes burned, and Callie began to cry. She just wanted it to stop. She wanted someone to—

She froze. JAKE! She had forgotten all about him.

***

Jake was in the bathroom, standing, facing the sink. He was wearing jeans and a Real Madrid jersey. The water was running, and without thinking, she turned it off.

"Jake?"

He just stood there. Shut down. Just like Mr. Phillips. "Jake, are you okay?" She reached up and cupped his chin, forced him to look at her.

"Jake!" Her voice was husky. "Please, Jake. Say something."

He stared impassively ahead. No recognition in his eyes. She tugged on his arm, and he moved forward. For an instant, she was afraid he was going to fall over like Mr. Phillips, but instead he took a step. She tugged again. He took another step.

***

She eventually led Jake into the living room, and with a soft nudge, got him to sit down on the couch. She noticed a blinking light on the kitchen phone.

Someone called! Mom! Dad!

The call had come in eight minutes ago, when she had been outside. She hit the "Play Message" button.

"Marie, it's me!" *Grandma*, thought Callie. "Marie, are you there? Ryan, Jake, Callie, anyone? Please. Something's happened. Call me as soon as you can."

Callie selected her grandmother's number and hit CALL. It went straight to voicemail.

"Grandma, it's Callie. Mom and Dad are gone and there's something wrong with Jake. Please call me. I'm so scared. I'm all alone. Please call me!"

She walked back to the couch and sat beside Jake.

***

Her grandmother never called back. Callie must have tried her number over a dozen times. And her parents, and Erica. No response from any of them. She thought about going out to look for Mom and Dad but had no idea where they had gone, and she'd been told that if she ever got lost that she should stay put. So she did. She took care of Jake as best she could—fed him, cleaned him, which had been *really* awkward at first, and had generally done the best she could.

The baby was living with them by then. She had followed the sound of his crying, walked through the unlocked front door and found him in his crib, alone. His mother was lying on the kitchen floor, a box of cake mix still in her hand. The mixer was on, the beaters turning and turning in a congealing milk and egg mixture. Callie had turned it off before she left with the baby.

So life had gone on. Existing, surviving, waiting for something (she was never sure what) to happen. And then, two weeks after IT, something did happen.

On a sultry, windy morning, a fire started down the street, and by nightfall, Callie's house was fully engulfed in flames.

She had managed to grab the baby, her dad's backpack, and some clothes before the fire had driven her outside. She recalled that awful night, and how she had frantically looked for Jake, calling his name

87

(like that would help) until she found him in their side yard, where she had forgotten she left him, staring entranced at the flames.

Together they had watched their family home burn to the ground. She didn't even try to put it out. Water had stopped running by then. All she could do was watch. She still felt the knot in her throat, her mood rotating from sad to angry and back again, as she had watched, completely helpless as everything she had ever known was destroyed. No sirens. No neighbors to help. Nothing to do but watch.

There were still some photos of her parents and friends on her phone, and she turned it on and looked at them when she was feeling particularly alone. She also checked her phone for texts or calls. She had a solar-powered charger in her backpack, and would use it whenever she could, balancing the small solar panel on the awning of the stroller. But really, who was she expecting to call? Aside from her the photos, the only thing she had to remind her of her parents was Jake.

The Warning

As she did every morning, Callie opened a pocket on her backpack and took out a beat-up US road atlas. She opened it up to a folded-back page and spread it out on the kitchen table. She had found the atlas behind the counter at a gas station just after she started out. Her GPS was still working then, but it was getting sketchy. She wouldn't have a signal for hours at a time, and then the 4G icon popped up. Maybe the satellites were going? But for the last couple of days, nothing. So she used the atlas.

She had a pretty good idea of where she was heading. Straight down Highway 101 along the coast was the best route. Not on the freeway, but parallel to it. Through neighborhoods where she could find shelter and food… and maybe people. She went into the kitchen and rooted around until she found a bill with an address on it. She was in Silver Beach. She thought she might have heard of it before but had never been there. She found it on her map and circled it with a red felt pen. She looked at the scale guide and estimated how far she had to go. On the map, Carlsbad was only inches. But in reality she was looking at weeks, especially with the baby. *Maybe months.*

Callie sighed and closed the atlas, put it away, and dropped the red pen in the backpack pocket. She snapped the pocket shut. She looked at her two charges. The baby—*Ryan!*—was rolling back and forth, holding onto a stuffed zebra she had found in the child's bedroom. Jake was sitting on the couch, staring straight ahead.

"Give me a couple minutes, guys, and then we'll be ready to go."

A quick rummage through the kitchen counters and pantries resulted in two cans of fruit cocktail, a plastic bottle of water, and some crackers. Starvation wasn't really an issue because of cans and bottles. Once in a while she would find a fruit tree, and fresh fruit was always nice. She did miss meat, though. She'd tried some Vienna sausages she'd found, but they were pretty foul. She hadn't finished them. Canned chicken and tuna were okay, but they weren't really *meat*.

A cheeseburger, though. She smiled at the thought. *A double cheeseburger. French fries. And a vanilla shake.*

Now none of those things exist.

Callie backed the stroller out to the driveway, carefully led Jake down the steps, went back inside, and shouldered her pack. She took a last look around.

"Thank you," she whispered (as she always did) before closing the door. She pulled the twig out of the lock on the gate, and then had a thought. She closed the gate, ran back to the back yard, and picked up the soccer ball. She held it up before Jake.

"Remember this, buddy? I think we should keep it."

Did his eyes focus? It was so hard to tell. She put the soccer ball in Jake's backpack, opened the gate, and they were off.

***

They made good time today, which was good, because it looked like rain, and Callie was in a relatively good mood. Until she saw the dolls.

She spotted the first doll, and not sure what it was, moved onto the sidewalk to take a closer look. She made a face. *Ugh!*

Someone had nailed a baby doll to a tree. A big nail, right through the center of its cloth torso.

She moved on, and saw another one. This one was nailed upside down to a wooden mailbox post. Then another. And another. Some were not nailed, but hanging, twine tied to an arm or leg. There were dozens of them, and they hung from the trees like malformed, exotic fruit. It was unsettling, and she stopped.

Who would do this? she asked herself. And perhaps more importantly, *Why?*

They stood at the center of an intersection in a small-town neighborhood. A two-car collision in the middle of the intersection. A silver SUV had smashed into the left side of a smaller car. She couldn't see the driver of the second car. Or of the SUV, for that matter. Had they survived and escaped?

She approached the SUV and peered through the open back door. An empty infant seat. She glanced down at Ryan. He had been so lucky she had heard him crying. How many other babies had wasted away in empty houses, their parents lying beside them, dying themselves?

She noticed something on the hood of the small car. She walked over. *Oh gross.* The skin of a cat, spread out, legs and tail pointing in five different directions.

She shook her head and stepped away. *Okay. This is getting weird.* The dolls. The cat skin. Was it a warning? Maybe someone wanted this street to himself?

The neighborhood looked safe enough. The houses were smaller and older, and there was one that was boarded up, but not too bad. No smoke, no broken windows or smashed-in doors. A dried-up corpse lay on a driveway, but she was well used to that by now.

Callie dropped Jake's leash and knelt down. She took off her backpack. She pulled out her cell phone and turned it on. As it was booting up, she scanned the area again. She really didn't want to have to detour. She knew the freeway was only a mile or so to her left, and she wanted to stay close. But something felt *off* about this neighborhood.

The sky was dark and foreboding, the clouds heavy with rain. She wanted to get inside soon. A nice, safe house. *She* could walk through the rain, but it was really too hard with the baby and Jake.

Her phone was up and she quickly opened her GPS app. The map showed her location, and she zoomed in. Her forehead scrunched in concentration. She didn't want to backtrack, and going left would take her to what looked like a business park or a parking lot. She would feel too exposed. If she went about half a block ahead, she could make a right, and that would lead her to another street that ran parallel to the freeway. She looked up and could see the green street sign about a quarter-mile up the road. That's where they'd turn right. Then just skirt this area. *No problem*, she thought as she turned off her phone. *Easy peasy.*

Ten minutes tops.

A raindrop fell on her arm.

She looked at the baby again, and then at Jake. The darkened windows of the houses seemed even darker. The rain began to patter on the roofs and the sidewalk. She turned Jake around and pulled a poncho out of his backpack and pulled it over him.

"What do you think, guys? You ready for a little jog?" She shouldered her backpack and tightened the straps. She even fastened the waist strap, just in case. *Just in case what?* she asked herself.

"Nothing," she muttered. "It's fine. Everything is going to be fine." Callie picked up Jake's leash and put her hand through the loop. She swallowed. "Let's do this."

She started at a fast walk. Another doll nailed to a garage door. The rain wasn't too bad. They'd soon be past this neighborhood, and if the rain stayed like this, they'd make another hour or so before it got too dark.

Her footsteps echoed hollowly on the pavement. *Am I always so loud?* There were old, towering trees in front of most of the houses, which both sheltered her from the rain and increased the darkness. The hanging dolls slowly turned in the breeze.

The corpse of a teenage girl beside a soccer ball lay in the gutter. One of her legs was missing. Callie moved away and went around a red VW Bug in the middle of the road. There was a definite cattish shape on the windshield. She kept her eyes on the street, occasionally glancing up to check her bearings. The intersection where she would turn right was getting closer.

A screen door slammed open and bounced off the house nearest her. Callie's stomach sank. *Don't look, don't look.*

She turned to look and horror took her so tightly that she stumbled and fell to her knees. The stroller rolled away from her.

A clown stood on the front porch of the house directly to her right. His face was painted white, his mouth a red gash. His eyes were circled in black. They looked empty. An orange halo of wiry hair fringed his bald head. He wore light-blue coveralls, stained and dirty. They were halfway open in the front, revealing a filthy white undershirt—*wifebeaters* Jake had called them.

The clown staggered down the steps to his front walk and stared at her. He was tall. And broad. And horrifying. She watched in paralyzed fascination.

The rain continued to fall.

Callie came to her senses and scrambled to her feet. She suddenly realized she wasn't holding Jake's leash. She whirled around and nearly screamed in frustration and terror. He was about twenty feet behind, beside the soccer ball that lay next to the dead girl.

"Jake!" Of course he didn't react. She glanced over at the clown. He was striding toward her, and it was then she realized he was holding a hammer.

She turned toward the stroller, which was about five feet in front of her, out of reach, and then back at Jake.

The clown was getting closer. His nose had been painted red. She could hear his heavy breathing.

"Please," she whimpered. "Please don't do this." The clown glanced over at Jake and moved in that direction. He raised the hammer.

Callie looked again at the stroller. One of Ryan's hands had grasped the blanket she used to cover him and was tugging at it. Those little fingers...

She darted toward Jake and grabbed the leash and wrapped it several times around her wrist. She tugged and he followed. She ran with her brother stumbling behind her, his poncho flapping madly. She ran and left the baby—*Ryan*—behind.

Tears coursed down her cheeks, mixing with the rain. Callie sobbed, her throat raw with pain and guilt.

She ran and staggered and slipped and stumbled and got up and ran until her legs began to throb and her chest heaved. She slammed into the rear bumper of a car and spun and tumbled into the street. Tugging on the leash, getting to her feet, she sprinted up the nearest driveway past a blue minivan and ran behind the house.

Callie was soaked to the bone, her clothes plastered to her back and shoulders. She took her backpack off and tucked it beneath the wooden porch.

Tugging Jake closer, taking up the slack in the leash, she leaned against the back of the house gasping, sobbing, hating herself. She tried to vomit but nothing came out, just thick strands of saliva. She spat and wiped her mouth.

Jake stood passively beside her, his chest rising and falling. *Jake.* This was his fault. Her eyes narrowed as she stood up.

"Why did you have to walk away!" Callie sobbed, pushing Jake back a foot or so. She shoved him again, and he stumbled, teetered, and fell on his butt. He didn't try to break his fall.

Callie looked down at him, sitting on the cold, wet concrete. Her older brother, who had taught her how to do a layup and helped her with her pre-algebra homework. He had even introduced her to *Star Wars*.

He was just sitting, not even trying to stand up or shield himself from the rain. She thought of a lyric from an old song her dad had played on Christmas last year.

> *"...and Tommy doesn't know what day it is,*
> *He doesn't know who Jesus was*
> *Or what praying is how can he be saved,*
> *From his eternal grave?"*

An eternal grave. That's what this was for him. And all those others. Only Jake was still alive. Because of her.

Callie's heart cracked.

She knelt and wrapped her arms around Jake.

"I'm sorry," she whispered into his sodden hair. "It's not your fault." She reached around him and half-hugged, half-lifted him.

Jake allowed himself to be pulled up to standing. He didn't really help, but he didn't resist, either. He was just... compliant. Was that the word?

She led him to a relatively dry spot against the back of the house. They were sheltered by a tattered awning.

"Now, you stay here," she said unnecessarily and headed back along the rear of the house, peering into windows, but it was too dark to make out anything of substance.

She tried the back door, but it was locked. She shoved the door with her shoulder; it rattled in its frame, but wouldn't open. Rubbing her shoulder, she glanced around and spied a cinder block supporting a drain spout coming down the corner of the house. She looked at the window.

In all the weeks she had been traveling, she had managed to avoid breaking into any houses. Open doors, unlocked windows. That was the way to go. Something didn't feel right about breaking into a house. It didn't make sense; it wasn't like there were laws anymore... no one cared if she broke window or two, but she could always find an unlocked house.

This is different. He could be after us.

She looked over at the minivan. There was someone in there. Behind the wheel. Which meant they probably had the keys. She swallowed. She didn't want to do this, but she didn't want to do a lot of things these days. She approached the driver's door. Between the clouds and the rain, it was extremely dark and hard to see, although there was clearly an adult-sized shape behind the wheel.

Callie went around to the passenger side and pulled the handle. The door was locked.

Resolutely, she went around to the driver's side and opened the door. The interior light popped on and she jerked back in surprise. Electric light. It had been a while since she had seen it. Then the smell hit her. A hot, foul, rotting-fruit stench forced her away from the door. She gagged, coughed, breathed deeply and was able to compose herself. Breathing through her mouth to lessen the stench (a trick she had learned the hard way after entering one too many corpse-filled houses), she leaned into the car.

The rotting, jellied corpse of a woman wearing a burgundy warmup suit sat in the seat, her hands on her lap. In the seat opposite sat a gym bag and a cell phone.

Callie leaned further in, aware of how close she was to the dead woman's shriveled, breathless mouth, her teeth lengthened by drawn-back gums. Her eyes were sunken, glistening holes. Callie reached around the wheel for the keys, but wasn't able to quite reach them. She couldn't see over the steering console, so she had to operate solely by touch. Her face was inches from the foul face of the corpse.

Callie had a mad thought that the mouth would open and from her dark, dead throat, the voice screaming above the sound of the pounding rain.

"Get out of my car! What are you doing? Get out! Get out!"

Callie felt blindly for the keys. Her fingers touched something leather, which could only be a key chain of some sort. She followed it up and found the ignition key. And twisted and pulled. The lights on the dashboard lit up.

Callie cried out in frustration. She took a step away from the car, took a deep breath, leaned in and twisted the key the other way. It clicked off and she tugged it out of the ignition.

She jerked out of the car as quickly as possible and slammed the door.

It took her a few minutes to figure out the right key in the dark and rain, and she had to hold her flashlight in her armpit, but finally one that slid in smoothly and the door opened.

Callie moved along slowly through the dark, unfamiliar house, the shadows thrown by her flashlight constantly moving and changing shape.

She opened the back door and grabbed Jake and pulled him in.

Then she fetched her backpack from under the porch. She looked around, thinking she had forgotten something, that *something* was off… and remembered. Ryan.

But she hadn't *forgotten* him; she had left him behind. And no matter how she twisted it, rationalized it, it all came out the same. She had abandoned him to be—what? Killed? Eaten? Raped? *Did people do that to babies?*

Why else would he want us?

Callie Makes a Decision

Callie had changed out of her wet clothes and was wearing a bathrobe she found in a closet. She sat on the bedroom carpet, cross-legged, staring at the light of the camping lantern. No way she could sleep. Ryan's face swam through her mind. And his little hand, those perfect tiny fingers, the last true memory she had of him. She didn't even have any pictures of him.

Somewhere outside a dog barked.

Callie crawled over to Jake stretched out on a mattress. He was out. Fast asleep. The sleeping pill she'd ground up and put in his cold beef stew would make sure he stayed out.

Callie stood up, stretched, and took off the bathrobe. She got dressed quickly, efficiently. She had found a black, nylon windbreaker in a hall closet and pulled that on over her sweatshirt. She debated tying a line around Jake's leg and attaching the other end to the bed frame, but decided not to. If she didn't come back, she wanted him to have a chance at survival, slim as it might be.

She knelt beside him, kissed his cheek. He was getting stubbly. She'd have to shave him again. She put her lips close to his ear. "I'll be back in a little while."

She left the door open and made her way to the kitchen. There was a butcher block on the counter, and she pulled out the biggest carving knife. She carefully wrapped it in a T-shirt and put it in her jacket pocket.

Then she went to get her baby back.

***

The rain had let up; it was now a steady drizzle, but much easier to see in than the earlier downpour. She could make out dim shapes: the shape of a tree here, a car there.

Piles of clothing and half-eaten corpses she would see at the last moment and step over. She held her flashlight low, covering the lens with her hand, just allowing herself enough light to see a couple of feet in front of her.

She remembered running—*and leaving Ryan behind*—from the Clown Man's house. She remembered she had made one left turn, so at the first intersection, she made a right. She found the sidewalk, and carefully made her way, house by house. Traveling slowly, step by step, eyes on the light just ahead of her feet. No sense looking up ahead. She wouldn't be able to see anything anyway.

Is this it? kept running through her mind. She'd stop and look, try to recall what the house had looked like. A front door, a porch, okay, that was a start.

Then she stopped. Her—no, *Ryan's* jogging stroller lay on its side on a front lawn. She ducked behind a tree, shut her light off and scoped out the house.

No lights, but that doesn't mean anything.

She glanced at the baby stroller. Why would he just leave it there? Maybe he didn't need the stroller.

Just what was in it.

Then another, darker thought.

Could it be bait?

He had seen both Callie and Jake. Did he want them too? Her thoughts flashed back to Jake, alone, helpless. *This is stupid. I should just go back. Jake needs me.* But another look at the stroller silenced those ideas. Ryan had needed her too.

Might still need her.

She stayed low and made her way around the side of the house. There was no fence, so she was able to keep close to the house, moving beneath the dark windows. She rounded the corner and found herself in a small backyard. The plants were overgrown, and she had to push away some sopping branches as she made her way closer.

A small concrete patio, three steps up to the back door. The house was small, maybe two bedrooms. She would have to be so quiet.

In the Dragon's Den

The rain had stopped completely now, and some stars peeked through a hole in the clouds. It was getting lighter.

Several boxes sat on the ground beside the steps. The contents glinted in the cast of her light. Bottles. Lots and lots of empty bottles.

As she reached a shaky hand for the handle—*What are you doing?*—a slight hesitation, but she had to be sure. *For Ryan.* For Ryan. The door was unlocked and the knob turned easily. She pushed the door open an inch and waited. Another inch. Still nothing. She pushed it open a bit more and slid in, still staying low. She gently closed the door behind her, but not all the way.

Might have to make a quick exit.

The smell was foul. The smell of spoiled meat. Of sweat. Of stale cigarette smoke. Of madness. But after what she'd smelled earlier tonight, it wasn't so bad.

She took a chance and turned her flashlight on, again masking the glow with her fingers.

Something twisted beneath her foot and she heard a faint jingle. She shone the light at the floor. A small collar. Pink, with a bell on it. And another one, beside it, this one bigger, with a metal name tag shaped like a bone. A green collar, larger. And a red one, the tags gleaming in the light.

What is all this? She asked herself. But she knew.

She peered over the top of the counter and choked on a scream. The counter was littered with bones. Tiny bones from cats, birds, larger leg bones and ribs from dogs and who knew what else.

You know what it is.

Three skulls placed in a row on a plate, their empty eye sockets regarding her solemnly. On the other counter, a key chain. His hammer. The skin of a dog hung from the back of a chair. And on the kitchen table—*oh no*—tiny clothes. A little pair of shorts. A onesie. A boy's T-shirt. And the shoes. So many, it seemed.

Callie had never wanted anything so badly than to leave that house right then and there, and in many ways, it would have been better if she had. But she couldn't. She had to find Ryan. *Or what's left of him.* Keeping low, she looked over the clothing again. Nothing looked familiar.

She took notice of her surroundings. Sheets covering the windows. A couch. Boxes of liquor bottles—these full, unopened—stacked along the wall behind the couch. Dead rats, many crushed, littered the floor. A pile of clothes beside the couch. Empty cans of food, soda, beer, piles of cigarette cartons. And what were those? She moved the beam.

Magazines, DVDs. So many. Stacks of them. She moved closer.

Oh my God.

Sex movies. Porno magazines. She hadn't seen much in the brief glare of her light, but it was enough.

I shouldn't be here.

The dark hallway beckoned. She reached into her pocket and grasped the handle of the knife. A quick flash of her light showed three doors. One, on the right, was partially open. One farther down on the left had a padlock on it. At the end of the hall, another closed door.

Her heart pounded so loudly she thought it would give her away. She walked quietly, carefully. Staying close to the wall. Three doors. If Ryan was here, where would he be?

What's that?

A noise. A growl? *Is there a dog in here?* She pulled the carving knife out of her pocket and unwrapped it. She waited. The sound repeated and she relaxed her hold on the knife.

Snoring. Someone snoring. Someone *big* snoring.

Not someone. The Clown Man.

Walking so quietly, so carefully, practically levitating, it felt like, she passed by the doorway without incident. A sidelong glance revealed only darkness and a foul odor. The snoring at least was a good thing, she told herself.

As long as he's snoring, he's asleep, and I know where he is.

But what if he stopped snoring?

Shut up, shut up. Just keep walking.

She glanced at the door on the left, the one with the padlock, but kept going. She wouldn't be able to get in there. The farthest room first.

What She Found in the Bathroom

A few more steps and she reached the door. It was unlocked. The handle was stiff, and it turned with an audible click that made Callie wince. She gently pushed the wooden door open, and keeping the flashlight low, she swept it across the room. A bathroom. Filthy. Dark stains all over the floor. The toilet seat up. The smell was worse in here, dank and sour. With her knife hand she pulled her shirt up over her mouth and nose and stepped in a little further.

A window over the bathtub, allowing what little light there was to weakly penetrate this foul space. Boxes stacked along one wall. More alcohol. And soda. Once water stopped flowing through pipes, the bathroom became just another storage room.

A sound. A squeak. *Rats?* She swung the light left to right, at the same time bringing her feet closer together, trying to take up as little space as possible.

The bathtub. Something in the bathtub.

The tub was full of... what... blankets, dead animals? No, something alive. Something that squeaked. Not a squeak. A coo. A baby coo.

Not believing, but hoping against hope, Callie knelt beside the tub. The shower curtain was long gone, and the plastic shower curtain rings hung like rib bones picked clean.

The tub was filled with towels and blankets, but in the center a boxy shape covered by a towel. She pulled off a corner, revealing a plastic laundry tub—and stared into the beautiful blue eyes of Ryan, pooled in the beam of the flashlight.

He squinted and turned his head, so she quickly shut the light off and put it in her pocket, stashed the knife in another pocket, and reached down and scooped him up. He was wearing only a diaper, which looked incredibly full and about to fall off. Other than that, he seemed fine.

She resisted the urge to hug him and kiss him over and over. That could wait.

"We're getting out of here," she whispered, holding him tightly. The knife was in one pocket, the flashlight in another. No light. No weapon. This was going to be difficult. And to top it off, Ryan began squirming.

"Shh," she whispered, kissing the top of his head. "It's okay. Shh." But he continued to squirm and now began to cry. Callie crouched in the hall and pulled out her flashlight, checked out the floor in front to her. *All clear.* A faint light was beginning to filter in through the living room. She could make shapes of the furniture. She shut the bathroom door behind her.

Ryan cried out and wrenched away from her. She grasped him even more tightly, struggling to keep him from falling. The flashlight fell from her grasp and hit the floor.

A loud groan from the bedroom. "Shut th' fuck up!" followed by a hollow thud. A bottle hitting the floor. She froze. Ryan squirmed even more and let out a loud squawk.

More noise from the bedroom, clattering of things falling over, thumping of a big man—*a really big man*—getting up on unsteady feet.

Three months ago, Callie would have been too frightened to make a rational decision. But now her choice was clear.

No hiding.

She moved toward the bluish cast of light emanating from the kitchen, toward the door, and escape.

The hallway grew suddenly dark as something immense moved in front of her, blocking the light from the kitchen.

The Clown Man.

He was huge, and gross, and up close, the most frightening thing she had ever seen. He still wore the white makeup, although it was splotchy and smeared. In the dim light, his eyes were black holes. His pendulous, hairy belly hung over his stained, baggy sweatpants. She could smell his stench: sweat, urine, and who knew what else.

"What are you doing?" he roared. "That's mine!"

Ryan was screaming. Without realizing what she was doing, Callie backed away. Away from escape. Away from Jake.

The Clown Man strode forward. He was carrying a large black flashlight in one hand, and he turned it on, shone it at her face. She turned her head, and a big, meaty hand snatched at Ryan, grabbing him by an arm. He cried out in alarm and—*pain*—and Callie instinctively tugged back.

"Let go, you little bitch!" His spittle spraying her face. The Clown Man twisted Ryan's arm and the infant yelped, his face contorted with terror and pain. Callie let go of him, holding her hands up in supplication.

"Please, don't hurt him. Please, just let us go."

"Shut up!" A massive hand slapped her across the face, rocking her head to the side, bringing her to her knees. "It's mine now. And so are you."

He reached down and grabbed her coat.

White spots in Callie's vision. Her ears rang. Her jaw stung. But he had Ryan.

He had *Ryan*.

She was being dragged down the hallway, back toward the bathroom.

Or the room with a padlock on the door.

She struggled to slide herself out of the oversized jacket, but he had her left elbow in a painfully firm grip. She was stuck.

He mumbled to himself as he pulled her. "Goddamn bitch, try to steal my baby. I'll show you, yes I will. Show you. Gonna eat you up. Eat you *all* up."

Her hand slid into her jacket pocket and clutched the handle of the carving knife. She moved in one motion, not allowing time to second-guess herself, twisted her body around, and stuck the knife into his calf.

The Clown Man hollered, took a step, and fell to one knee. His flashlight thudded on the carpet, and the shadows danced crazily in the narrow space.

Before he could turn on her, Callie, crying out in fear and anger, yanked the knife from his calf with a wet, sucking sound, and stabbed him in the lower back. The knife went in, caught on something, but she leaned on it and it slid in to the hilt. She tried to pull it out, but it was stuck fast. She moved it back and forth, struggling to loosen it, and he howled. Blood leaked from the wound, covering her hands, making her grip slippery.

Still on his knees, he dropped forward, supporting himself on one hand. He clutched Ryan to his chest with the other. Ryan was no longer screaming. Callie stood up and moved away. The knife was still stuck in his back.

The Clown Man's breath came in quick, short gasps. He coughed once, placed Ryan on the floor, and shakily stood up and faced her. He leaned on his uninjured leg. She was disgusted to see that the front of his sweatpants was stained with blood. He reached behind him, struggling to reach the knife, but he was too bulky. Too much fat. He couldn't get his arms around. He roared like a maddened bull and slammed against the wall as he lurched toward her.

"You... little... fuck!" he wheezed, coming closer. Callie inched away, looking around desperately for another weapon. She saw that

Ryan was moving slowly on the floor at the opposite end of the hall.

In the living room, hazy with the morning light, she had more space to maneuver, but was no closer to helping Ryan. She picked up an empty beer bottle and hurled it at the Clown Man. It bounced off his massive chest. He didn't even seem to notice. His face was a mask of hatred and pain, his big red mouth turned down in a grimace. Blood leaked from one corner of his mouth. He put one arm out and leaned against the wall, panting. Then started forward again.

She picked up another bottle, this one larger and squared at the bottom, and flung it at him. It caught him in the forehead, knocking his head back with an audible *thunk*.

He groaned and stepped back, putting a hand up to his head. A bottle smashed into the wall beside him and he ducked. A clear glass bottle caught him in the knee and he grunted in pain.

"Goddamnit!" He straightened, and still wheezing, lurched for her. The back of her legs hit the couch. She had nowhere to go.

He was five steps away. Three.

Callie picked up a wine bottle and held it like a club. She sidestepped, closer to the kitchen. She knew she could outrun him if she made a move now. But what about Ryan, squirming in the hallway?

I can't leave him... again.

She went to move around him, but he was on her.

"Goddamn... bitch! You... stabbed... me!" He was gasping, weakened, but still dangerous, still a monster. She swung the bottle, hitting him in the chest, the stomach. No effect. He grabbed her wrist, squeezing, bones grinding together. She cried out and dropped the bottle. He clamped a hand around her throat and lifted her up.

No. Not fair. Jake. What about...

Everything went black.

***

She gasped. Her throat burned, and it was difficult to breathe. So much pressure on her chest. Her wrist hurt. It was so dark. And that smell. She struggled to move, but it was hard, like something was pressing down on her. Something spongy... flabby... cold.

It's him. He's lying on top of me.

A wave of claustrophobia swept through her. She squirmed, and pushed and twisted, and slowly wormed her way out from beneath the lifeless body of the Clown Man. She got to her feet and felt her wrist. It really hurt, but she flexed her hand without too much pain. It didn't look swollen. Her legs were wet with blood.

Not mine. His.

She heard faint crying.

Ryan!

She raced down the hallway and knelt beside him. He was alive and moving, still a bit fussy. She lifted him and cradled him to her and let the tears come.

"I'm so sorry, so sorry." She held him at arm's length and inspected him. He looked fine. Probably traumatized—*you and me both*, she thought, and heard the cry again. Muffled, nearby.

Her eyes went to the padlocked door.

She approached the door, listened. Definitely crying. A child. She reached up and tugged at the lock. The crying stopped.

"Hey," she said, leaning in. "I'm going to get you out of there. I'm going to help."

She went back to the kitchen counter, giving the stinking corpse on the floor a wide berth, and found the key ring. She took a moment and tore down the sheets covering the windows. It made a difference. The room brightened considerably.

We might actually see the sun today.

She used one of the sheets to cover the Clown Man.

She placed Ryan on the floor beside the locked door and tried a key. Then another. Finally she found the right one. She removed the padlock and turned the handle and opened the door. The room was another bedroom, but the bed was bare, just a mattress. On the floor were three large dog crates, the kind for really big dogs. Two were empty, but the third held a little girl.

She squatted on a filthy blanket as far back in the crate as she could get. Her hair was ratty and her face was dirty. With her was an old teddy bear, a plastic water bottle, and an empty bag of pretzels. There was a tiny padlock, the kind Callie's mom used for her suitcase, keeping the crate locked.

Callie dropped to her knees in front of the crate. The girl came forward a bit.

"I'm Callie. What's your name?"

"Becca." Her voice, a whisper. She looked like a third or fourth grader, so that would make her—Callie did the math—eight or nine.

"Okay, Becca." She nodded at the baby in her arms. "This is

Ryan. We're going to get you out of here, okay?"

Becca nodded.

***

On the way out of that nightmare house, she took one last look at the sheet-covered Clown Man, the knife still sticking out of his back, standing up like an accusing finger.

You killed someone.

***

Later that afternoon, a strange-looking group made its way through the deserted neighborhood. A young girl, her eyes grim and haunted, held onto a leash and led an older boy, who walked behind. Beneath her free arm, she held a battered teddy bear.

Slightly ahead of them, her eyes warily scanning both sides of the street, walked a slightly older girl, maybe thirteen or fourteen, pushing a jogging stroller. Her name was Callie, and she was on her way to see her grandmother in California.

LOGAN'S MISSION
William F. Nolan

Logan 3 was in the hydrogarden, watching Jessica and Jaq 2 as they attempted to cross-breed a rose with a dandelion.

"What are we going to call it?" asked the boy.

Jessica smiled, patting his head. "How about... a roselion," she said.

"I *like* it!" Nodded Jaq. "It's perfect."

Jess put away the garden tools. "Now then, young mister, it's time for your fencing lesson."

Jaq groaned. "Can't I skip it today? I *hate* fencing! The Robomaster always wins!"

Logan smiled. "It's programmed to be tough." He ruffled the boy's hair. "To teach you that we don't always win in life."

"But I *never* win!"

"He has a point, Logan. Perhaps we could modify the program?"

"We'll see. No promises. Maybe you should try harder, Jaq?" Logan said.

Jaq nodded.

"Get ready for your lesson," Jess said.

"Fine... I guess." The boy sighed. "But I still *hate* fencing!"

At that moment, a tall Nexus 10 entered the garden, the robot's metal chest plate reflecting the blaze of morning sun. "Sir," it said to Logan. "Jonath 2 awaits you in cencourt. He bears disturbing news."

"Why didn't he bring it to me here?"

The Nexus unit hesitated. "He did not wish to alarm your family," it finally said in a hushed tone.

Logan turned to Jessica, noting the concern on her face. "Don't worry," he told her. "I'm sure it's nothing serious. Jonath tends to make a molehill out of a mountain."

"You have it backwards," Jess corrected him. "The old Earth saying is 'making a mountain out of a molehill.'"

"What's a molehill?" Jaq asked.

***

Jonath was pacing nervously around the central courtyard, grim-faced. He spread his hands in a hopeless gesture. "It's all over for the Wilderness People," he told Logan. "For us... for everyone."

"What are you saying?"

"A rogue comet," said Jonath. "Huge. Largest on record and headed straight for us."

Logan took the news in, sweeping a hand through his hair. "I see. Well... comets are ice, gas, and rock fragments. They always burn out in our atmosphere—"

"Not this one," Jonath interrupted. "It's far larger than any previous comet we've recorded—nearly a thousand kilometers across."

Logan nodded in quiet understanding.

"Of course, it will lose a lot of mass in burnout," said Jonath, "but the core will remain largely intact. When it hits this planet... Earth won't survive."

"Are you certain of the trajectory?"

Jonath nodded, pacing as he thought. "Yes, absolutely. It's been carefully charted. The results have been checked and re-checked. It will strike somewhere along the Pacific Coast in roughly twenty-nine days."

"Twenty-nine days? My God, that's barely a solar month... There must be a way to change its orbit."

Jonath sighed, shaking his head. "No, Logan... nothing can stop it."

"I have a wild idea," said Logan. "Just before the Thinker was destroyed, a scientist in the Chicago Complex, Miles Broxton, had developed a sort of... time machine."

"I don't see—"

Logan cut in: "Broxton was sure that it would allow him to enter a second world parallel to our own... a world with more advanced technology. What if... what if I can find something in Old Chicago to help us... to stop the comet before it hits?"

"The cities are very dangerous. Renegade hotbeds. They hate Sandmen. You could die there."

"What difference does that make? In twenty-nine days we *all* die." Logan straightened. "I'm going to the Chicago Complex to find

Broxton's machine."

"That's a crazy plan."

Logan looked off to the horizon, nodding. "Right now, it's our *only* plan."

***

"What did Jonath say?"

Logan regarded Jess, looking from where Jaq was playing in the garden to where she was cooking in the small kitchen. He smiled, saddened at the idea that their time together might soon be shortened.

After all we've been through. To have it end this way... His throat tightened.

"Two of the Nexus bots have malfunctioned," he said, not ready to reveal everything he knew. "A minor problem. I had Jonath send them back to the shop."

She nodded. "It sounded serious."

"Jonath overreacted. I managed to calm him down." Logan hesitated. "Look, Jess, I need to take a paravane to Old Chicago. Something to do with a glitch in the mainline system. They want me to check it out."

She glanced up, staring into him. "I see... And why do they always call on you?"

"Because I'm a very smart fella," he said lightly, giving her a peck on the cheek.

"When do you leave?"

"Today. They need me today."

She returned to cooking, her brow furrowed.

"I won't be long. Not more than a few days." He paused, cupping her face in his hand. "We'll make the best of it. Maybe you can take Jaq to the cybercircus. I'll contact you once I get there."

He gave her a hug, then headed for the paravane.

***

Old Chicago lay in ruins.

When the Thinker died, each of the great cities died with it. The New You shops were grave-silent, the ped walks motionless, the mazecars frozen in mid-transit. Old Chicago was now a blighted area, ruled by fierce renegades who prowled its broken streets. Logan knew he was entering a kill zone, but he had no choice. If Broxton's machine still existed he would find it. But, once found, would it transport him into a second world? What would he find there?

The plan was indeed as Jonath described it: Insane.

***

Logan eased the Fuser from its belted holster as he stepped cautiously into the city.

He moved through the shattered debris of Arcade, past blackened firegalleries and Love Shops, broken glass crackling under his boots. *So far, so good. No renegades in sight.* He had been searching now for a week. Nothing.

It was late afternoon on the eighth day, and shafts of pale sunlight penetrated the gloom. In his youth he had taken the sun for granted, like breathing. Now he valued its light and abiding warmth as never before: It was and had always been a blessing—a blessing that could soon come to an end. He thought of Jess and Jaq back home, feeling a sudden, desperate rush of nostalgia and determination.

The area was familiar. As a Sandman, he'd hunted here before, on city reserve duty, terminating a runner, Halyard 8, when the frightened man rejected Sleep. Logan knew that the lab he sought was just past Arcade. He was very close when a mocking voice rang out from the shadows: "Lookie who's come to pay us a visit!"

Renegades!

Logan faced more than a dozen of them, led by a feral-faced brute in ripped lifeleathers. He held a Flamer, aimed at Logan's chest. "Drop the weapon... *Now!*"

Logan lowered the Fuser. If he fired into the group, he could only take out a few of them before being burned down. He let the gun fall from his hand.

The burly leader kept the Flamer steady on Logan. He smiled crookedly. "Guess we all oughta be honored... havin' such a famous fella come see us. Welcome Logan 3."

"How do you know my name?"

"Big in your day. Top Sandman. Top kill score."

"I'm not proud of what I was. I'm just a citizen now."

"Yer just a dead man walking, that's what you are!" said one of the others, a bearded six-footer. His eyes radiated hate.

"Go ahead, burn me. We'll all be dead soon enough."

The leader quit smiling. "What you mean, Sandman?"

"Our world is about to be wiped out. And we'll all die with it."

The Flamer tipped up. "That's a lie!"

"No, it's true," said Logan. "A giant comet is headed directly for Earth. Due to hit in less than a month. I'm here to try and find a solution. Let me go and there's a chance, a very slim one, that we'll all be alive a month from now."

"Why should we believe such a crazy-ass story?" snorted the bearded renegade. He edged closer to Logan, lips drawn back in an ugly snarl.

"I'm no fool," said Logan. "Why do you think I risked coming here? I had to try."

"Try what?"

"Miles Broxton built a machine. It's somewhere in this city, and might be capable of entering a parallel world," Logan told them. "If I can activate the thing I might be able to find a way, in this alternate world, to deflect the comet, using their advanced technology."

"I've heard me some wild stories," scoffed the bearded renegade, "but I gotta give it to you, boyo, yours beats the lot." He brandished a rusty katana. "Taste the blade, Sandman!"

"Hold up!" snapped the leader. "What he says is so crazy it just might be true." He faced Logan. "We let you go, then what?"

"I find the machine."

"And if you don't?"

Logan smiled, leveling a dark stare at the group. "Well… then nothing matters, now does it?"

The feral-faced renegade nodded. "Go ahead, Sandman, find your damn machine—if you can."

And he lowered the Flamer.

***

Logan found Broxton's place the next evening.

As he entered the lab, he was shocked by the chaos around him. The ceiling had collapsed and the walls had caved in, destroying most of the equipment.

"It's gone, Logan." A soft voice from the shadows. "If you've come for the machine, you're too late. It's beyond repair."

Logan recognized the voice. "Mary-Mary!" He gripped her hand. "What are you doing here?"

"I came to save it. Spent the last several days trying to re-build the thing—but no luck. It was destroyed in the collapse. My father was never able to test it."

"Father?"

109

NEVER FEAR – THE APOCALYPSE

She nodded. "With the Thinker dead I was able to access the DNA records—and discovered who my parents were. Miles Broxton was my father."

Logan drew in a long breath, trying to absorb what the girl had revealed. Then: "After you saved my life at Crazy Horse I never expected to see you again."

Mary-Mary smiled. "Yet here we are."

"How have you avoided the Renegades?"

"I've been lucky," she said. "And careful."

Logan looked wracked; his eyes haunted. "It's all over, Mary. With the machine gone it's the end of everything."

He told her about the rogue comet.

"My father was a brilliant man," Mary-Mary declared. "He was working on another important project beyond the machine before his death—some sort of plasma beam. The details are in his papers. Maybe there's a chance—"

Logan shook his head. "The machine was our only chance, I think. With it gone..." His voice trailed off.

A silence between them as she took in his dark words.

Then: "My mother... she's still alive in Florida, in what's left of the Miami Complex. I should be with her—at the end."

"Yes, you should," said Logan, his thoughts turning to home. "You should be together... for the last days."

***

Back home, Jess accepted the news with tears in her eyes.

Jaq was defiant. "He'll find a way to stop it. Dad can do *anything!* He was the best Sandman ever!"

"I've told you before, Jaq," Jess said firmly, "that's nothing to brag about."

***

With fierce determination, Logan had pored over Miles Broxton's research papers. In a large blue notebook, at the bottom of the stack, Broxton had outlined detailed plans for his high-energy beam device, that promised awesome power. Did it offer a final chance? And could it be finished in the scant time left before impact?

"Can we perfect it, Jonath?" asked Logan. "Is it possible?"

"We can try," said Jonath as he studied the note pages Logan had brought back from Old Chicago. "God knows, Logan, we can try. I'll get my men on it immediately."

A week passed as they worked to build the plasma beam.

Another week gone. The plasma cannon was ready; its first test would be its only chance to save them.

Five days and counting.

Four...

Three: The comet appeared on the horizon like some dreadful, fiery emissary from another realm.

Two...

The final day: *Activate!*

The arc of the purple beam sizzled through the night sky, connecting with the red glow of the comet... A vast explosion—so intense its impact sent shockwaves around the Earth, as the massive space invader died in a spectacular showering of ice, rocks, and cosmic dust.

Logan smiled, a hand on Jonath's shoulder. He looked at his friend.

"Mission accomplished," he said.

—for Sunni K Brock

OFF TO SEE THE WIZARD
Thomas F. Monteleone

Out beyond the limits of clear vision, Tag saw a black speck...
slowly growing larger. Something *alive* moved out there. It was
unusual for an animal to wander about alone. The pack instinct ruled,
and loners easy prey, quick meals. Tag massaged his wrench
nervously between his fingers, watching the figure steadfastly
approach the ruins.

A minute passed, the only sound the wind keening through the
vanes of the windmill above his head. One more minute ticked
through his head, and Tag knew it was a *man* coming toward his
position.

Another man.

A coldness passed through him. To hear another human voice
again, to listen to the words of someone else... The thought excited
him as few could. His palms grew moist; the wrench felt slippery. A
dryness formed in his throat.

From the height of the tower, he had a clear view of the stranger
as he drew ever closer. He wore a long, flowing garment, a cape of
some sort that flapped and billowed in the breeze. He wore a military
helmet, although Tag saw what seemed to be a long plume jutting
from it, swaying and bouncing with him. He pulled a small wagon, its
rubber tires leaving thin lines in its wake. The cart piled high with
unidentifiable objects bulging out from beneath a piece of canvas
secured with scraps of rope. His steps were slow and almost mincing
at times, suggesting someone of advanced years, and this puzzled
Tag. There was *nothing* in the direction from which the stranger had
come. Nothing but desolate, scarred earth. He must have walked a
great distance. Tag slowly stood and watched the man, now less than
50 meters away... then half of that.

He stopped. Looked up.

The man dropped the cart's tow-bar and cupped both hands
before his face. "Hello! Hello, up there! You don't plan to kill me, do

you?"

Kill him? Tag was stunned by the words. He had never imagined such a greeting. Hesitantly, he heard himself reply: "No, no of course not! You're welcome here!"

"Well, that's a comfort," said the oddly dressed old man.

Leaning against the platform railing, replacing the wrench in his tool pouch, Tag held up his hand. "Here, wait! Wait till I can get down."

God, it felt strange to be talking to someone. Tag had been little more than a child the last time he'd spoken to another person.

The stranger put a finger to the brim of his helmet, gave a grandiose, sweeping bow, then stood up, smiling broadly. As Tag climbed down the tower, the man picked up the T-bar and started pulling his cart toward the base of the windmill. The stranger's words lingered in Tag's mind. Why this talk of killing? Was the old man trying to put him off guard? Maybe it was the stranger planning the killing...

Tag paused for a moment, still several meters from the ground. No, it was unfair to get suspicious so quickly. Perhaps he should be wary of the old man, but certainly nothing more.

Dropping to the earth, Tag dusted his hands nervously on his pants, and watched the man draw close to him. At the little distance that separated them, Tag was able to study his features in great detail. The stranger's face betrayed his age. Older in fact than anyone Tag had ever seen. Beneath the rim of the helmet, a few wisps of silver-white hair danced upon a seamed forehead. Great bushy white eyebrows huddled over sunken eyes. The man's thin, colorless lips nestled almost lost beneath a ragged, bleached-white beard. And everywhere there were lines, deep grooves and pockets where the years lay scored. Tag looked at the man's hands—white, gnarled skin stretched tautly over the bones. His fingers moved like insect legs, in quick, jerky motions.

"Name's Peregrine," said the stranger, extending one of his spidery hands. "What's yours?"

"Tag. Nice to meet you, sir." The man's hand felt dry, rough. And the sound of Tag's voice sounded almost alien to him.

"You alone out here?" The old man looked past him into the ruined vista of buildings and machinery.

Tag nodded.

NEVER FEAR – THE APOCALYPSE

"Yeah, well… look, I been walking a long way and I could sure use a drink of cold water. Got any?"

"Yes, back at the house. Let's go, and I'll get you some."

Peregrine laughed again, smiling through his wiry beard. "Now you're talking, son. Let's surely go!"

Tag put away his tools and picked up his canvas bag, pointing the way back to his shelter. "Where you come from, Mr. Peregrine?"

Tag also wanted to ask him why he had that long pink feather stuck on the side of his helmet, but was afraid to.

Peregrine started pulling the little cart along behind them. He smacked his lips and said, "Well, I came from a lot of places since that goddamned rock hit us. Listen, son, you ever heard of King Hamlet?"

Tag shook his head.

"Yeah, well, I been with the king, helpin' him straighten out a few problems in his court. And there was—say, what about Captain Ahab? Heard of him?"

"No, I'm sorry, I haven't."

"Well, I was with the captain for a whale, I mean a while. We was out huntin' down this mutant creature that was botherin' the people round his parts."

"People? You mean there's still lots of people left?" Tag felt his own pulse jump.

Peregrine stood up and waved his arms expansively. "Why, hell yeah! Tag, you just been sitting here on your ass while the rest of the world's pickin' itself up and getting' a-goin' again."

"Really?"

"Why you think I been on the move? I guess you never heard of the Red Queen either?"

Tag shook his head, dumbfounded.

Peregrine danced a quick little step. "I figured as much. Well, I seen her, too. Strange little place she runs…"

"Where is it?"

"Where? Oh, you probably never heard of it. Little town down in the lowlands way south of here. But never mind about that, boy. How much farther till we get that drink?"

Tag pointed at the tumble of wood and aluminum up ahead. "Not too far. Listen, Mr. Peregrine, how'd you survive? All that moving around and all. How'd these other people, all those you've seen, how'd they make it?"

"I don't know. Lucky, I guess. Same as you, right? I don't mean to say that I ain't seen a lot of people kicked off, 'cause I have."

"Kicked off?"

Peregrine stopped, grabbed himself by the throat in a grotesque pantomime, stuck out his tongue, rolled his eyes. "You know—*dead.*"

"Oh," said Tag, as if grasping some arcane truth. This was an odd character, this Peregrine. Tag didn't know what to make of his ways yet.

"Yeah, it was them germs that turned you yellow. That stuff got out in the world after the impact. Plague, they said. I guess me not gettin' it was just bein' lucky."

Tag stepped ahead and opened the door to his shelter. "I figured that. It didn't take long for everybody to die off out here."

He paused to look back at Peregrine's cart. "You have anything in there you want to bring in?"

"Naw, ain't nothin' but a bunch of shit anyway," said the old man. "Besides, there ain't nobody around to bother it, right?" He threw back his head and cackled his unsettling laugh once again.

Tag gave him a mug of water and offered him some pickled vegetables, which Peregrine accepted and spooned out with his fingers. He ate with abandon, no discernible manners, and lots of noise. "Stuff's not bad," he said finally, wiping a rivulet of juice from his chin to the edge of his ragged sleeve.

"Where'd it come from?"

"It was one of the industries we did out here. Agricultural preserves were fairly self-sufficient. We didn't really need the cities."

"How long you been out here by yourself?"

"A while now—since I was seventeen or so. My mom died then."

"So you've been alone ever since? Nobody to talk to, just you and all this busted-up farm stuff, huh?"

"Yes, sir," said Tag

"This hovel here's all you got left?"

"Before I was born, they had some kind of trouble here at the preserve. People needed food. My parents and the other people worked here—they had to fight them for it."

"And they enjoyed a Pyrrhic victory, did they?"

"Huh?" said Tag.

Peregrine snorted. "Just an old phrase. Wouldn't mean much to you. By the time the fightin' was over, everything they were fightin' for was destroyed anyway."

"I guess that's about the size of it…"

"The dummies!" said the old man. "What a bunch of beauties we were, huh?"

"So I figure it."

"What was you doin' on that windmill when I came up? You like to sit up there or something?"

Tag smiled. "No, I was putting gears on the shaft. Trying to get back some electrical power. I'd had it for years. I'm kinda good at mechanical stuff. It broke but I can probably fix it."

Peregrine laughed.

"What's so funny?" Tag felt insulted, but didn't know why.

"Why bother with that fool thing? Why not come along with me and we'll find all the power we need?"

"Power? Where?"

"Where I'm going, of course. To uh… uh, to Oz, yeah, that's the ticket," he said triumphantly, waving his hand with a flourish.

"Oz? Where's that?"

"I figures you'd not heared of it." Peregrine grinned a lopsided grin. "Well, it's like this. East of here there's this magical kingdom that's got started. It's a funny little place. Got all different types vying for control and all that. Good and evil—stuff like that. And of course. They got themselves a wizard… "

"I never heard of any place like that. What's a 'wizard'?"

"Haven't you heard of *anything*, boy? Didn't anybody ever read to you as a kid? Or tell you stories?"

"We didn't have much time for reading, sir. And we didn't have many books, either."

"I'm gettin' that picture," said Peregrine.

"So what's a wizard?"

"That's a fellow who can control all sorts of forces. A kinda boss, like."

"How far east did you say this place is?"

"I didn't." Peregrine guffawed, slapping his knee.

"Well, how about telling me?"

"Why, you thinkin' you might like to go with me?"

"Maybe," said Tag, weighing the possibilities. It certainly wasn't much of a life scraping along in the ruins as he'd been doing. "Does this Wizard have electricity?"

"Coming out of his ears!" cried Peregrine.

"What?"

"Just an expression. That means *yes*. He's got plenty of it."

"Oh... well, what about food? Does he have plenty of food? And music? Do they have music?"

"Sure they got food," said Peregrine. "But music? What's with the music? You like music?"

Tag nodded. "The one thing we *did* have, that I remember growing up, was music. Even when things were bad, we had music. I'd just about give anything to hear somebody sing, to see people dance."

"Oh, yeah, I see... well, of *course*, the Wizard's got music. I hear he plays the stuff all the time."

"Really?"

Peregrine nodded. "But that's not all they got. I hear the women in Oz are the best on the whole planet!"

"Really...?"

Peregrine looked at him warily. "Ah hah! Yeah, you know, women, dontcha?"

"Oh, sure," said Tag, "I haven't seen a woman in... Well... a long time."

"I can understand that, son."

"But it got so I used to think that maybe there wasn't anybody else alive but me."

"Well, that's not true. Believe-you-me. How about some more of them pickled beets?"

"But if you say this Oz place has people... some of them *women*... well, that's something I haven't thought about much. Well, no, that's not true—I *have* thought about it—women, I mean—but not the possibility of ever finding any..."

"That don't surprise me... livin' out here like Robinson Crusoe."

"Who's that?"

"Nobody you need to know. How 'bout them beets?"

Tag fetched another canister, opened it, and handed it to the old man, who greedily stuffed several slabs into his mouth.

Tag watched him in silence for a while, trying to piece together the odd parts comprising this stranger. It was so different, so exciting in a passive sort of way, just to be talking with another human being, that their conversation had almost been secondary. But in the brief silence while the old man slurped down a few more beets, Tag reviewed the content of Peregrine's words more carefully. That there were others alive heartened him. That places where men and women had not only survived the plague, the thing they'd called the Yellow Death, but were actually living constructive communal lives, rekindled a hope he'd long thought dead.

"When you gonna be leaving?" he asked finally.

The old man threw the canister into the fireplace, lay back in his seat against the wall, and exhaled loudly. He looked ready to fall asleep, but addressed the question.

"Well, I don't exactly know. I wasn't plannin' to find anybody here and was just figurin' to stay the night and move on. But since you been so hospitable and all that, I just might be persuaded to stay on for a day or so."

"Oh, I see. But what about *Oz*? Didn't you say you were going to Oz?"

"Well... yeah... I reckon."

"Well how far is it from here? How long will it take you to get there?"

"Now I'm afraid you got me on that one, son. Seeing's how I never been there, I don't rightly know. 'Course, I don't expect it would take more than a week—going by what I've heard."

"You've never been there? The way you were talking, I thought for sure you had."

"Naw, I haven't. But I talked to a lot of people that have and they all say such wonderful things about it, I figure I've just *got* to check it out for myself."

"I see. Well if you're serious about me coming along, do you mind staying a few days until I can think about it?"

Peregrine brightened, smiled, and sat up slightly. "Why sure! I'd be glad to stay a few days. I ain't on no schedule. What's a day one way or the other, right?"

Tag smiled and took a sip of tea. The room seemed warmer as he sat basking in the glow of another's presence—even an odorous, unmannerly old coot like Peregrine. "All right then, Mr. Peregrine. You're welcome to everything that's here. You can sleep over there. I'll fix you up a place tonight, after supper. Right now, though, I think I want to finish that mill. Just in case I decide not to go with you, I want to have some power out here."

"Suit yourself, son. If you don't mind, I'm going to take a little snooze. It's been a long and weary road for me."

Peregrine slumped over on the floor and curled up like a scruffy old dog. Tag smiled and washed out his mug. He banked the coals in the hearth, and returned outside to be greeted by a cold sky of indifference.

***

Later that evening, after Tag had prepared a large meal, Peregrine went out to his cart and carried in an armful of odd things. There was a small package of cards with numbers and symbols, plus a few with pictures of men and women on them. Peregrine was able to make these cards dance between his fingers very quickly and rearrange themselves into what appeared to be random positions. From this arrangement, he performed tricks that ranged from apparent telepathic ability to obvious sleight-of-hand exercises. Peregrine also knew many kinds of amusements to play with these cards, eventually teaching Tag the games of poker, blackjack and tunc. They played for canisters of preserved food, and before the evening was over, Peregrine had a large mound of jars stacked by his chair at the table.

But they enjoyed other diversions as well. Peregrine's cart turned out to be a treasure chest of oddments from a civilization rattling down entropy's highway. There were holograms of people and places he had never seen. Exotic tobaccos, liquors, drugs, soaps, oils, essences, herbs, spices, books, tools, weapons no longer functional, pieces of equipment even Peregrine could not identify. All of these things, he said, were gifts from the various famous personages he claimed to have met in this travels. That some exhibited severe damage became the impetus for yet another tale of wonder. Peregrine always regaled his tales with a smooth, fluid delivery almost too accommodating, too easy. It was as if the old man sometimes knew ahead of time what questions Tag would put to him, so rapidly and thoroughly could he provide all-sustaining answers. Still, throughout the evening, Tag remained a captive within the magical aura of the old man's company.

When the scrap wood in the hearth burned low and the lamps sucked the last of the oil into their wicks, Tag felt reluctant to sleep. Scarcely had he blown out the light when the bellows-like regularity of Peregrine's snoring punctuated the night. It burst through the darkness in rattling wheezes, soon painfully anticipated. But the old man's breathing did not keep Tag awake as much as his Peregrine's very presence, his existence. The young man lay awake for uncounted hours, trying to order all he had been told that day, trying to fit everything into a logical frame of reference.

Was it true other parts of the continent still thrived and carried on the pretense, if not the business, of civilization? Then why was there no power in the subterranean cables? Why had no one come from any of the urban complexes to help rebuild the preserves? If there were people, then they would most surely need the agricultural centers to live.

And then there was the idea of finally finding a woman.

If there was anything that could make him leave the relative security of his enclave, it was the promise of a companion.

He believed it could be as Peregrine described. That men had grouped into smaller bands, formed little principalities, little "kingdoms" as he called them. They no longer saw need for the larger urban complexes and the preserve system. Anything, Tag concluded, was possible in a world populated by creatures as strange as men. For now, he would have to be satisfied to know one simple truth: other men and other places still existed.

Even a place called Oz.

***

The next day, Tag completed the gearing on the windmill and tried to piece together a new belt-drive system from cannibalized machines and children's toys. Peregrine watched this operation intently, although he offered no assistance other than verbal assurances Tag displayed the skills of a born mechanic. By afternoon, the sky pirouetted across the plains dressed in heavy clouds. The dust and dirt buffeted them as they fled into Tag's shelter like rodents burrowing into their mounds.

Tag kept a fire going as he listened to the latest of Peregrine's tales—this one about a wondrous ship called the *Nautilus*, wherein he had sailed from one coast of North America to the other by way of a place called Tierra del Fuego.

"How come you didn't stay with Captain Nemo?" Tag asked as Peregrine's tale finally wound to an inconclusive finish.

"Why should I? When I hadn't yet been to Oz?" said the old man with a lilt in his voice. "Everybody should see Oz at least once. The

Captain even told me that. Besides, the Wizard can help people. That's the biggest reason why people want to go there. He can do… why, just about anything."

Tag scoffed at this last remark and Peregrine stamped a foot on the wood floor. "It's true, Goddammit! Look, you just name something that you want, and I'll betcha the Wizard could give it to you."

"Why would he want to give me *any*thing?"

"'Cause he's the Wizard!' sputtered Peregrine. "'Cause… that's his *job!*" He grinned, beaming with a glow of self-satisfaction.

Tag paused, thinking of something he might get from the Wizard. "Could he teach me to make music?" asked Tag abruptly.

"Hell, yeah! That's no big deal."

"Really? Could I learn to play the autar?"

"Autar! Hell, you could learn to play anything. Everything! Make music all the time, you could."

Tag sat back in this chair, gazing unseeing into the ceiling rafters. Maybe he *should* go with Peregrine. It felt so good to be talking again, to be trading ideas, even to argue occasionally. In Oz, there would be thousands of people to meet, to enjoy, to despise, to love. There would be music and maybe even a lady for him.

"You know, I've been thinking," said Tag, "Maybe I'll go with you. To Oz, I mean."

Peregrine sat up, his furry eyebrows suddenly knotted up tight over his small eyes. Something akin to surprise capered there.

"You *will?*"

"Yes, you've convinced me there's nothing here for me. Nothing but loneliness, and quiet. Nothing, really."

"You *sure* about this, son?"

"Yes, I think I am. We can leave whenever you're ready. But morning's okay with me. The storm'll have passed by then."

"Morning? Oh, sure. That'll be fine. Sure, son, we can leave right after sun-up. Now, how about a little seven-card stud?"

"Right now? Don't you want to talk about leaving?"

"Plenty of time for that," said Peregrine. "If we're going to be leavin' this place, we may's well get in a few hands with a roof over our heads 'fore we do. He reached into his baggy jacket pocket and produced a gilt-edged deck. "Deuces wild?"

Before Tag answered, the old man started dealing the cards.

The hours faded away like drifting smoke as they played. Neither man spoke, other than to bet his hand or exclaim upon the luck of the cards. Tag wondered why Peregrine had become so strangely silent. There was a look in his black eyes indicating the old man's thoughts may not be on his game.

The next morning, Peregrine puttered about his cart. He had been reluctant to part with some of his trinkets, even though room was needed for some of Tag's food stocks, tools, and the one projectile gun still functioning. Peregrine insisted on bringing along the weapon. There were still half-crazed animals out there; some were mutations, some still dying from diseases. A lot easier to deal with the unexpected when protected, Peregrine had said. And so they loaded up the cart and began pulling it behind them on their trek into the east.

Within several hours they had passed the farthest boundaries of the preserve, and the blackened, blighted soil stretched beyond their path until it touched a gray swath across the land. "That's one of the connecting arteries," Tag said, pointing to the deserted road.

"Where'd it go?" Peregrine shaded his eyes despite the cold gray helmet of sky above them.

"Another preserve. Eventually it cuts east to the Botaneering Complex."

"The *what?*"

"Where they conducted experiments on plant life. They'd succeeded in cultivating all kinds of mutations. Actually designed their own vegetables. Just like people, I hear."

"Oh, yeah. I've heard about that kind of shit. Good riddance, I say." Peregrine hacked up a mouthful of phlegm and hurled it into the wind. "Damn bastards had to fool with everything. Couldn't leave nothin' be. Even the plants."

"It might be easier if we stayed on the artery," said Tag. "It bends east pretty soon and that's the direction you want to be going in, right?"

Peregrine nodded and they headed for the road. Tag pulled the cart behind him, grateful to drag the rig up over the shoulder of the roadway, where the tires could roll smoothly. The old man seemed to be as fresh as when they had started, but Tag struggled with pain and exhaustion in every muscle. His knees, the soles of his feet, his calves, all on fire. Occasionally he needed to stop for a few moment's rest, while Peregrine taunted him and suggested that maybe he should go back to his fruit cellar and stay there.

When they stopped at sundown, Tag estimated they had traveled perhaps 60 keys. As he prepared a small fire, Peregrine sat on a flat rock, playing with a double-sided disk attached to a string. The old man would whistle and sing to himself as he made the object roll up and down the string which he'd attached to his index finger.

"What's Oz look like, anyway, Mr. Peregrine?"

Peregrine snapped his finger and the "yo-yo," as he called it, jumped up into his palm. "Well, it's quite a place, son. They got these big roads running all around it and through it—kind of like that one, except they're made of big yellow bricks."

"Really? That's odd."

"Naw. Kind of pretty, I hear. Anyway, there's castles all over the place and, of course, the Wizard's got the biggest one of all. Carnival tents and bazaars, merchants and artisans in their alfresco stands, a million smiling people crowd the big boulevards, singing and dancing, buying and selling! They have gardens that just kind of hang off the buildings, big terraces with every kind of flower in the world, statues and monuments all over the place. It's a damned wonderland, I tell you."

"How could there *be* any place like that?"

"What's the matter? Don't you believe me? You've believed me up till now." Peregrine's lips pushed into a pout.

"Mr. Peregrine, I didn't say I don't believe you. It's just it's hard to see how so many people could survive the hell that went across this planet so easily. What I mean is, where'd these 'smiling people' come from? What kind of power does this Wizard have, anyway?"

Peregrine laughs. "I told you it was a kind of magic stuff. That's the thing, son. You go to believe in magic. Or it won't mean nothin' to you."

Tag turned away from him and began poking a stick in and out of the fire. The light danced over his features, accentuating his disbelief.

"Then why'd you come with me?" said Peregrine, his lips trembling, his eyes glistening in the firelight.

"Because I was so glad to be *with* somebody… and I guess I was afraid to be alone anymore. I came with you because I was tired of living like some animal. You came along and told me there were people all over the world living like kings. I didn't come with you

123

because I wanted to believe in magic. Now talk sense!"

Peregrine sat just beyond the glow of the dying flames. His lips moved but no words were uttered. He mumbled to the darkness as he clenched his fists into tight knots. Slowly, his shoulders slumped, his head bowed.

Looking at him, Tag wished he hadn't lashed out at him, crushed him like that. "I'm sorry," he said. "I guess I'm just tired. I—I haven't walked this far in a long time. I'm sore and I'm beat up and I'm taking it out on you, that's all. I didn't mean it."

Peregrine did not reply at first. He sat staring into the darkness, kneading one hand into the other. "Yes, you did," he said finally. "You meant it. And I don't blame you. Sitting around all day listening to the crazy stories of a crazy old man."

Tag stared at him, a hunched, tragic figure. "What do you mean?"

"Well," Peregrine rubbed his beard nervously. "I don't know… it's just that—Naw, I don't know what I'm saying. You got me upset, I guess."

Tag watched the man fingering the buttons of his shirt, avoiding his gaze. He couldn't remember ever seeing someone as sad-looking as Peregrine sitting by the edge of the fire.

"This is really dumb, you know," Tag finally said. "Here we are, the only two people for probably hundreds of keys, and we're arguing with each other. Hurting each other. I don't think any of us will ever learn anything, you know that?'

Peregrine chuckled. "Yeah, that's the truth, ain't it? Look, son, I understand how you feel about this thing. You just got to take my word for it, that's all. Some things are hard to understand, and you just got to take'em on faith. The way I understand it, this Wizard fellow discovered a way to get by. He made it, but don't ask me how, 'cause I don't really know."

Tag studied Peregrine's face, a mass of creases and sagging flesh, and saw the sadness, the pleading, there. "All right, I think I understand what you mean," he said after a short pause. "I guess I'll just have to wait till we get to Oz."

Peregrine grinned and the sadness faded. "That's about the size of it, son." He stood up and stared into the night sky. "We better get some sleep, don't you think? Long day again tomorrow."

Tag agreed and they rigged a small tent Peregrine had cached in the cart. Within seconds of crawling in side, the old man's breathing fell into a deep rhythmic patter, leaving Tag alone with his thoughts.

He dreamt of roads of yellow brick.

***

The morning arrived like an uninvited guest; the harsh, hazy light an annoyance that would not go away. Tag struggled out of the tent to find his body cross-hatched with different aches and pains. His bones, his joints, and the muscles in his thighs, shoulders, and neck, all stiff, unyielding. Despite the sun, he felt chilled and cold and damp. Thoughts of the warm clutter of his home did little to encourage him as he started a fire and boiled water for tea.

After Peregrine arose, they ate, packed, and struck out along the artery which stretched endlessly ahead of them. The bleak barren landscape never changed, a continuous swath of cracked earth, punctuated by an occasional thorny, tangled bush, a clutch of naked trees.

Rolling hills seemed to disappear as they approached them. There was a stark, wasted aspect to the land: no color, no smell, nothing. And yet, as they walked along dragging the cart, Tag could almost sense the land did not want them there—as if it had suffered enough indignity, and the presence of men only intensified the bitterness.

Still they walked on, pausing only to share a cup of warm water, saving their energy by remaining silent.

By afternoon they came upon the bones of a dead animal. It had probably been a rodent of some kind, although the skull had two small horn-like projections above each eye. Tag thought the formations might have been evidence of a new mutation in the species.

Walking only a short distance farther, they discovered another animal skeleton, bleached and picked clean of even its connecting tissue. And then another. And another. As they looked ahead, they saw more carcasses visible. Like little white coils of springs, the rib cages lay in a vast graveyard.

"What the hell is this?" said Tag, pointing to grisly remnants.

"I seen this kind of thing before," said Peregrine, nodding to himself. "We're heading into some kind of bad spot. Must be off that way." He pointed to the southeast.

"Yellow?" Tag felt uneasy at the mention of the plague.

"Yep. Any of these critters that happened to wander through this area probably picked up enough of 'the death' to knock it out quick."

"But why just the bones? What could be coming along to eat the bodies? And even if they could eat, wouldn't the flesh be contaminated so bad they'd die anyway?"

"You'd think so, wouldn't you?" Peregrine laughed. "Funny thing, but it seems like that lizards and the insects don't seem to be bothered much by all them germs."

"You're kidding."

"No I ain't. Everywhere I been, I seen them lizards scuttlin' around. They might be mutatin' some, but they ain't dying. For all I know, they might be *likin'* it, might be getting stronger from them germs. One fella I met near the Pacific—they got lots of desert out that way, and lots of lizards—he says that maybe the reptiles are fixing to take over again. This guy thinks that maybe the meteor and the weather and the plague and shit were just the catalyst to start them growin' up big and terrible again. Just like them diney-sores, you know?"

"I don't think we should go any farther in this direction," said Tag wanly.

"Hell, no!" Peregrine laughed. He paused and studied the sky. "Besides, if my bearings are right, we should be heading north just about now, anyway."

"Really? You got any idea how much farther?"

"Not exactly. But my nose says we're getting pretty close."

"Your nose?"

"Just an expression. I mean, I have a feeling it ain't much farther. Maybe a day at most."

They walked for another three hours in silence, angling away from the artery and the deadly pocket it bisected. When they stopped, it was on a slight rise that overlooked a gently rolling terrain. Tag started a fire from some scrubby bushes and wiry hedge clinging to the rough soil, while Peregrine struggled to get the lines of the bright orange tent taut and secure.

After dinner, Tag looked up into the now-sunset sky. The stars had already started poking holes in it. "Hey, what's that?" Tag said to the old man, who was already rolling himself up in the tent.

"What's what?"

"I'm not sure, but look out there..." Tag pointed into the northeast. "What's that light—on the horizon?"

Peregrine rose to his knees, dusting off his baggy pants. He picked up his feathered helmet, seated it firmly on his head, and stood up to study the sky.

With each passing minute the dying sun revealed more of the night, and the glow, subtly green, beyond the horizon grew stronger by contrast.

"It's huge! Whatever it is…!" said Tag.

"I can remember when the whole sky used to burn like that," said Peregrine. "When the meteor first hit, I thought it would always be like that."

"Could there've been another meteor, a bomb or something?" Tag stared at the glowing piece of sky.

"Naw, that ain't no radiation. Too intense. Too goddamned bright! Goddamn, I don't believe it myself."

"What do you mean?"

Peregrine laughed long and loudly, then giggled like a child. "That's a city! That's a city out there beyond them hills! Goddamned if it ain't Oz!"

"Really? We found it?"

"What else can it be? Come on, son. We can't camp here tonight. We got to throw all this shit in the wagon and get going!"

Suddenly the pain and exhaustion were forgotten, and Tag felt the adolescent thrill of discovery recharging him, spurring him on.

They walked as quickly as they could, in spite of the black moonless night. But the sky shimmered with the emerald lights of Oz diffused through the atmosphere. What a grand place it must be, thought Tag, transforming the sky itself into a beacon. He could almost hear the music in the street…

Then, without warning, Peregrine's voice cut through the night with a painful cry. "My leg! It's got my leg. Oh, God! Get it off!"

Tag dropped the tow-bar, started tearing into the canvas cover of the cart, groping desperately for the gun. In the darkness he could vaguely see Peregrine's silhouette, jack-knifed, writhing, arms flailing wildly at some unseen thing by his leg.

Something solid struck Tag's palm. The stock of the weapon. Hard. Smooth. He pulled it from beneath a pile of junk and ran toward Peregrine, who was now on the ground screaming, moaning.

"Get the sumbitch off a me! Jesus!"

Tag saw a long cigar-shaped thing; there was a hint of jaws and teeth, sunk into the flesh of Peregrine's calf. Tag swung the rifle over his head and brought the stock down hard on the animal. There was a sound like a stick wrapped in a wet towel being snapped.

"Still holding on, son! Get 'im off… Awshit, get 'im off…"

Tag reached down and felt a pulpy mass, scales, a bony skull and moist jaws clamped like a vise on Peregrine's leg. He pried the lower mandible back and the thing separated from the old man's ragged flesh.

"What is it? What was it?"

"Goddamned lizard. I don't know. They must hunt at night. Oh God, it hurts. My leg's on fire!"

"I better get some light, Mr. Peregrine. You're bleeding pretty bad."

Tag started a small fire and examined the wound in the flickering light. The bites were not deep, but they were extensive. Tag dressed and bandaged the leg as best he could, then stretched the old man out in the tent. The thing that had attacked him was all jaws and teeth, it seemed. It had thick scales and bands of color around its body, tiny little claws and a thick tail.

Tag made some tea, then checked on his traveling companion. His breathing was rough and irregular, and his forehead hot as an iron, peppered with beads of perspiration. He tried to get Peregrine to sip the tea, but most of it ran down his chin into his matted beard.

"Mr. Peregrine, what's the matter with you? Can you hear me?"

"Yeah, I hear you," he said, each word clipped, forced.

"Well, what's the matter? You didn't lose that much blood."

"It ain't that, I think I got the poison in me."

"What?" Tag felt the muscles in his neck and jaws constrict.

"That damn critter must have venom. Pretty strong shit, I figure. From the way it's getting' me."

"How do you feel? Can you drink this?"

"That won't help. I can feel that shit burning my lip. I ain't going to make it."

"Don't say that."

"Why not? True, ain't it?"

Tag reached out and took the old man's hand, squeezed it tightly. Peregrine's skin was hot, but covered with a film of clammy perspiration. His breathing grew more labored, shuddered, and racked him as he lay on his back. "You won't die. We're almost there. The Wizard can help you."

Peregrine tried to laugh, coughed instead, almost choking at the end of it. "Son, I know the Wizard can't help me."

"Why not?"

" 'Cause there *ain't* no Wizard."

Tag was confused, hurt, angered. The poison must have been very fast, very deadly. It was affecting the old man's mind. He was out of his senses. "What do you mean, no Wizard? Of *course* there is."

"Ain't no place called Oz, either. No Nautilus. No King Hamlet, or none of that pure *crap* I told you about." Peregrine looked up at him through dull eyes. Slowly the lids slid shut.

"Then what's that shining up in the sky ahead of us?' Tag squeezed the hand again.

"I don't know... but it ain't Oz."

"How can you be so sure?" Tag felt for a pulse and found it frighteningly weak. "Come on, I'm going to carry you. We need to get help."

Peregrine began to protest, but Tag lifted him up and slung him across his shoulder. The old man's ridiculous-looking helmet fell and rolled away from them.

The hours dragged past and Tag stumbled and staggered across the dark plain. Occasionally he stopped to check on the old man; each time his condition worse than before. If only he could get to the Wizard!

Another hour passed and suddenly Tag saw something breaking the edge of the horizon. Something solid, bright and blazing. It appeared to be the uppermost edge of an arc. He increased his pace, and with each step the vision grew more substantial.

A shimmering hemisphere of light, energy.

Tag gently lay the old man down. Shaking him, he spoke "Peregrine, look, we've found it. Look! Can you open your eyes?"

Peregrine moaned something unintelligible. His eyelids fluttered open, unseeing.

"It's part of a dome or something. See it? It's Oz, Peregrine, Oz."

The light of the dome reflected in the old man's eyes. His bushy brows twitched once, his lips trembled. "It can't be..." His voice dry, hoarse.

"We're almost there. You're going to be all right," said Tag, lying even to himself now.

"Leave me here," said Peregrine. "Let me die outside."

"Mr. Peregrine—"

"No!" the word was urgent, desperate. "But Listen…"

Tag waited as Peregrine struggled to finish the sentence. For a moment, he feared that he was already dead. Then Peregrine spoke again.

"… Just in case I was right, tell them…tell them that… Dorothy sent you."

Tag leaned forward as Peregrine's eyes slid shut. "What'd you say? What? *Who's* Dorothy?"

Peregrine exhaled once, his shoulders slumped, his jaw sagged slightly, immediately recalling the grim pantomime of death the old man had once performed.

***

Tag buried him in the dry earth just as the sun was rising. The dawn overwhelmed the glow from the city, and if the dome burned, it remained invisible in the bright sun. Although Tag hardly knew the man, he felt a great sadness. It seemed so unfair for him to die so soon after giving Tag new hope, new purpose. The old man's death somehow struck him as more unjust than any of the others—perhaps even his own father's—and that made him feel worse.

He left the cart by the gravesite, untouched, unspoiled, like pharaohs with their barges in their tombs. Whatever was left of Peregrine lay tumbled under the canvas top, and Tag could not bring himself to disturb it.

By evening, his journey was almost at an end. Before him lay the City of Oz—there could be no doubt now—and he wished Peregrine had lived to see such grandeur. Beyond the haze of what must be a pale-green force-field, he could make out the countless spires and towers of a great city. The buildings were interconnected at various levels by graceful ramps, seemingly unsupported. The complexity of the architecture and the forced beauty overwhelmed him. And everywhere there was light and implied motion.

The closer he came to the outermost edges of the city, the more evidence he saw of what must have been a terrible battle fought here. Ragged, scorched ground, covered with the pitted hulks of half-disintegrated fighting machines, and an occasional skeleton, half buried in the windblown dust and debris. He walked amidst craters and troughs, torn up by the final descents of fiery aircraft. The battlefield reached up to the very edge of the force-field itself.

Still Tag pressed forward, not wanting to pause for either food or rest. So close now, he thought. So close. Except for the wind, whispering among the wreckage all about him, there was no sound. No music, he thought oddly. As he drew closer, he had the sensation of being watched, not by any particular person or thing, but rather by the city itself. It squatted before him like a great faceless creature, and abruptly Tag felt uneasy, almost threatened, for the first time since coming to this place. It was not so much the lingering smell of death about the place—for he had grown accustomed to death—but rather the odd quiet, sterile brightness of the city before him.

Something moved at the extreme limits of his peripheral vision.

Snapping his head to the left, he sought it out, but saw nothing. Then there came a sound. A clanking. Metal upon metal. Tag wished now he had violated Peregrine's possessions, that he had brought along the gun.

There was movement again. A flash of white light and heat.

And darkness.

***

He awoke in a small room, strapped to a flat-cushioned platform. A bank of instruments half-covered one of the white walls. There was a man of indeterminate age standing over him. Totally bald, he did not even have eyebrows. His skin shined pink and smooth like a baby's, and he had a small pointy nose, eyes, and a tiny mouth. He wore a set of earphones that appeared to be implanted in the flesh layered over his skull.

"Who are you?" said Tag, struggling against the restraints.

"I am Pell," said the man, apparently not disposed to give additional information unless asked.

"What happened to me? Why are you doing this to me?"

"I am told you were captured outside the City. An intruder."

"Isn't this... Oz?"

"Oz? What is an Oz?" said Pell, turning to adjust several of the instruments.

"Never mind," said Tag, thinking immediately of what Peregrine had tried to tell him. Thinking of what he now suspected to be the fantasies of an old man who had seen so much terror he had dealt with it in the only way he could. "What're you going to do with me?"

Pell turned and stared at him blankly, coldly. "You show a degree of development. You will be used."

131

"Used? What're you going to do to me?" Tag jerked his wrists against the mesh bonds. "Who's in charge of this place? I want to talk to someone in charge!"

"Not possible. The City is engaged in many activities. It already knows of your existence. That is enough."

"What do you mean? I want to talk to… to the 'Boss.' Do you understand?"

"Do *you* understand?" said Pell. "The City *is*. That is all."

Tag understood. The city had become that indefinable essence, an almost alchemical happening men had strived to create. It hadn't been successfully achieved before the Impact and the Yellow Death. At least Tag had not known of it.

But something had happened here.

Here in the thing Pell called the Cityplex, where all the databases and independent control systems had achieved that merged state of function, the moment of cybernetic Darwinism when sentience became the next logical step, the next choice.

"What is The City going to do with me?"

Pell looked at him. "The City must be maintained."

"I don't understand."

"You need not. Accept the fate chosen for you. And be strong."

A door opened and two other men entered, nearly identical to the one called Pell. Tag began screaming, letting all the fear, the hate, grief, and pain blend into one tortured cry that did not stop even as they wheeled him out of the room and down a corridor from which he would not return.

***

After a time, he did not know how long, since he no longer thought in such terms, he was crunching across the wasted landscape, flexing his limbs, his weapons-systems. His new body performed beautifully during the tests. He was a seamless shell of armor, many centimeters thick, bristling with sensors and inputs that rushed information to his colloidal brain case at the speed of light. His treads churned up the dry soil, and the delicate but strong suspension system absorbed every movement, every jerk and jolt. Deep in the center of his new metallic body, the tiny machines pumped and microchips monitored, the machines that kept his brain full of nutrients and oxygenated blood. He was happy.

But every now and then, an odd thought—an image sometimes, a concept or a word at other times—would come to him. And he would struggle with it, trying to remember something, but never actually succeeding.

Outside the City, where Tag roamed as a sentry, the soil turned to dust, and the rocks to sand, and a great desert rose up to cover the markers and the dead things.

And he never found out about Dorothy.

HOW CAN I ~~HELP~~ HURT YOU?
Crystal Perkins

I don't see the sun. The sky is there—or at least I think it is—but there is no sun. The day my planet cracked, burned, and spun, we lost our sun. I can't even imagine it coming back. If I'm being honest, I can't imagine much of anything right now.

Hope is a distant memory, as day flows into night, with no sense of time. The numbers on my watch just spin, no doubt a side effect of the electric shockwaves that shook the world when it split. We never knew this was how most of us would go. We never imagined a world when all the things that helped us would now harm us. We never cared about what we did to this place we called home. Until it was too late.

People talked of war and weapons, evil dictators, and how the world would end in shows of senseless violence. That's not what happened. Not even close.

Drilling, and stripping the planet of its resources cracked the very core of Earth. Countries full of electricity cracked, while oceans and rivers flowed, causing the electrocution of entire populations of people. Landlocked cities fared no better, with electric storms prowling the deserts, searching for their victims, and picking them off one by one.

I survived, but I don't know how or why. I was lucky enough to dodge the electric lightning strikes that seemed to have a mind of their own. But then again, maybe I wasn't so lucky.

The first few days on the farm were easy. There was fresh, dead meat, and fires everywhere to cook it on. The stream that overflowed still had clean water, and I had a mattress that was okay to sleep on.

Things are no longer okay, though, and I know I have to travel to the city. I must know if others survived, and work to keep surviving myself. There's only one problem—the machines. The cars, the carving knives, the blenders, the *everything* electronic. Something happened to all of it when the world ended, and all the things we depended on to make our lives easier are now killing us.

The first night, when my cell phone shocked and burned me, I thought it was a fluke. Now, I know it's not. Not after the dishwasher in the middle of the yard opened on its own and started shooting dishes and cutlery my way. Not after the truck with no wheels came scraping across the ground faster than I could run, and plowed right over me. The world was not safe from humans when it was whole, and now… now it's not safe from what we created.

***

I walk along the deserted highway, favoring my good leg, while using a tree branch as a makeshift cane. Getting run over was no picnic, and I got sick many times while pushing my bones back inside my skin and gluing the wounds together. Thank God for my backpack. I haven't let go of it since this all began, and the tube of super-sticky glue I've kept in there for years. I wouldn't be walking now otherwise.

There wasn't much to do with my broken cheekbone, but vanity left me days ago, when hope was all but lost. Survival is all that matters now.

I pass bodies on the road, more bodies than I could ever count. There are lovers locked in embraces, families holding hands, and others who died alone. As all birds and other wildlife are gone, there is no way for me to tell if they all died together, or at different times. A forensic scientist could tell, but as I didn't even finish high school yet, I'm not qualified to make those kinds of assumptions. I only see what I see.

Frozen faces, broken bones, dried blood and organs outside of bodies. I see it all, and it does nothing to me. I *feel* nothing as I walk through this highway of horrors. None of it matters to me, because I can't allow it to. If I stop and think about it all, I'll break. I will fucking fall apart, and not be able to go on. That simply isn't an option.

I see the handheld tablet flying through the air a moment before it hits me. That moment is enough for me to turn my back, and duck my head. Yes, my head hurts as it grazes it sharply, but I know it would've lodged in my throat if I hadn't moved. As it is, I watch in horrified fascination as it impales an already dead body. Blood leaks out, turning everything around the body crimson.

Blood is trickling down the side of my head where I was clipped,

135

but I just wipe it away before it gets in my eyes. There's nothing more to do right now, and maybe not ever. Are any doctors even alive, and if they are, are they following that oath they took, or just looking out for themselves? As I've seen no one alive yet, I don't know. I don't know what to fear, and what to embrace. What to trust, and what to run from. I know everything I've learned in life, and it is all irrelevant now.

***

There are no signs of life as I continue my journey toward the city. Some buildings still stand, and as when life was still "normal," they look closer than I know they are. I have miles to go before I get to them, and I won't allow myself to be fooled into thinking otherwise.

The water bottles I brought with me are emptying faster than I thought they would, but I don't trust the water around me, as it flows over dead bodies and structures that succumbed to the battle against the world itself. I should still have enough to make it these last few miles, and I'll keep telling myself that until they're gone.

"Help. Please help me," I hear as I pass by a mound of rubble.

It's a girl's voice, a living person, and yet, I almost don't stop. I believe so strongly that it's me against everything—and everyone else—that I almost ignore a cry for help. *Almost.*

"Where are you?" I call out in a scratchy voice I barely recognize as my own. The lack of use has made my vocal chords rough.

"Here. Over here. Please."

I follow the voice to the other side of the broken concrete, to see a girl around my age crouching there. Her face is bruised and bloody, and one of her arms is in a makeshift sling, but otherwise, she looks okay.

"What happened to you?"

"The same thing that happened to you, I'm guessing," she says, looking me over with a discerning eye.

"Probably."

I'm being cautious, because I don't know her. Even if I'd known her *before,* I wouldn't trust her now. Something in me wants to, but I give it a mental push back down.

"Are you going to the city?"

"Yes. I can't live out here alone. No one can."

"We need resources."

"We?"

"Won't it be better to be together? To watch each other's backs and search together?"

"Maybe."

"I'm not asking you to marry me."

I snort, because that's so far from what I was thinking, it's really not even funny. "No chance of that."

She looks offended, and maybe a little hurt, but it passes quickly from her face. "We need each other."

I'm afraid she's right, so I nod, and hold out my hand to her. She takes it, pulling herself closer to me than I'd intended. As her body lines up with mine, I feel all of her, and it makes me *feel*. Pulling away like I've been shocked, I shake off the feeling as best I can, and start walking. She'll follow me, or she won't. I don't care. Much.

***

The girl chatters for the next mile, making me alternate between feeling irritated, and comforted. I've grown to like the quiet of my own thoughts, but I'm also realizing I missed the companionship of having another human speaking to me. Not even that—I've missed being near another living, breathing, human. It doesn't sit well with me, so I try to shut her up.

"Can you close your mouth for even five seconds?"

"Why?"

Is she really that dense? "So I can have some peace and quiet."

"Isn't that what you've been having since the world ended?"

"It didn't *end*. We wouldn't still be walking and talking if it completely ended."

"Well, whatever you call it, we're all we have right now."

I start to tell her we don't have anything together, but she pushes me to the ground before I can get the words out. An electric lantern whizzes past my head, and crashes to the ground next to me. It's still twitching and fighting to fly again, even as it lies broken into pieces.

"Thanks," I say, meaning it.

"I told you we needed each other."

"Yeah, you did."

We walk in silence for a little while after that. I don't know if she's trying to prove she actually can keep her mouth shut, or if we're getting used to being together. I steal covert glances at her, seeing her beauty underneath the cuts and bruises. If things were the way they

137

once were, I might've asked her out on a date. I don't know what school she went to, or even where she lived, although I didn't find her too far from my old home. I could ask her, but keeping things impersonal seems best, at least for now.

"What's your plan for when we get there?" she asks, when we're about a mile away.

"I don't know. Do you think people survived it? Survived the machines?"

"If they banded together like we're doing, I think it's possible."

"Me too."

"I have some candy bars," she says, lifting her shirt to show a fanny pack I hadn't noticed under her baggy clothes. Do you want to trade me for some of your water?"

I should have realized she had no water, but I was too focused on me and what's going on. "Oh. Sure. Sorry."

We stop, and trade, taking a few minutes to give ourselves a needed boost of... something. When she reaches her good hand out to me, I take it, feeling and *knowing* it's more than just holding hands. We're in this together now.

***

As we step into the city itself a few hours later, I can feel the energy humming around me. Back home, and on the open road, there was nothing; no energy and no *life*. Here, everything feels alive. Scary, and possibly deadly, but alive just the same.

"Are you ready?" she asks me, squeezing my hand.

"No, but we don't have a choice. Without food and more water, we'll die."

She lets go of my hand, and reaches up with hers to cup my cheek. "I don't want to die now that I've met you."

"I want to kiss you," I blurt out, not even sure where the thought came from, but knowing it's true.

"So kiss me."

I lean down, and do just that, touching my lips carefully to hers. I've never been sweet and gentle before with a girl. I mean, I never hurt one intentionally, but I was callous and uncaring in most of my interactions with girls. With this one, I have the urge to be soft, and not just because we both have facial injuries. I feel like I'm responsible for her, despite only caring about myself mere hours ago.

"Why?" I ask out loud, after moving my lips from hers.

"We belong together."

We do? Looking into her eyes, I believe her. "We do."

"Will you protect me?"

"Of course."

"Then let's go."

Within moments of walking down the street, we're diving to the ground. Knives, lots of electric knives, have just come out of nowhere. If I hadn't seen a reflection of them in a broken window, we'd both be dead now. As it is, they ping off the crumbling brick wall next to us, and tumble uselessly to the ground. Or so I think at first.

"Run!" I yell, as they start to wiggle across the ground toward us.

She doesn't hesitate, taking off so fast, I have trouble keeping up. My leg is still injured, and she's obviously stronger than she looked when I first met her. I'm not sure who's saving who now, but I grab a discarded metal trash can cover, thinking it might come in handy soon.

"We need to find cover," she tells me as more and more things around us come to life. Blenders, mixers, DVD players… they're all coming for us, as if these objects just can't help themselves.

I motion to an open wooden door, but she flattens herself to the slats instead of running in, narrowly missing being nailed by a rogue gaming system, its wires whipping at her good hand as she holds it over her face. I grab for the wires, and swing my arms in an arc, sending it flying somewhere. I don't stop to look as I pull her close and block her body with mine, holding the lid behind my back.

After a few minutes of waiting, nothing else comes out after us, so I chance a look inside. There's no more electronic or battery-operated items left in the room. Only a battered couch and some slashed paintings.

"It's clear."

I guide her still trembling body inside, and get her settled on the couch, before closing and locking the door. It won't hold against a car, but it should keep us safe from small appliances. At least I hope it will.

Hope? No, that's not right. I don't hope. I live, but I don't believe in wishing for anything more.

"Kiss me," she whispers

I heed her call as my mind fogs, pulling her into my arms and kissing her. As our lips collide, I feel it again. Hope. I feel hope in my heart, hope that we'll stay alive, and keep kissing like this.

***

"How did this happen?" I ask her, hours later, when our limbs are entangled and our mouths are sore from kissing.

"The world lost its way."

"All these things we created to help us."

"And now they've turned into what we fear most," she says, finishing my thought for me.

"How do we stop them? How do we live?"

"We can't stop them, but maybe we can live. I want to live with you."

"Yes."

"I want food. Do you want food? It's been so long since I've had something other than chocolate."

"I'll go look," I tell her without hesitation.

"Be safe," she says, in a voice than sounds lighter than it did before.

"I'll come back to you."

"I hope so."

Kissing her once more, I climb off the couch and open the door carefully. Nothing comes flying at me immediately, so I step outside. I've only gone a few feet when I hear a clanking behind me. I turn to see a row of George Foreman grills advancing on me, their plates snapping open and closed like vicious dogs snapping their teeth. I run-hobble as fast as I can, knocking over anything I can to try and stop them, to no avail. They are still coming closer, and I can't keep up this pace for much longer.

I trip over a body part on the ground and go down hard, screaming as the glue holding my leg together rips open. Blood is gushing, the metallic scent surrounding me as the puddle on the ground grows. The pain from the wound is nothing compared to what happens next, though.

Ribbed metal plates close over my limbs, "biting" me over and over again. The skin on my hand tears, exposing bones as I try to fight them off. My left hand gets caught, and I let out another scream as my fingers are smashed into pieces. I don't know how long the attack goes on, but it stops as suddenly as it started.

Without further knowledge, I can only think that the burst of energy these inanimate items got doesn't last forever. I'm battered, broken, and bloody, but I'm not dead yet. The girl still needs food, and I need to make her happy. It's all I want to do, all I hope for right now.

With thoughts of her in mind, I drag my body over the ground, hurting more than I ever have before. Gravel, glass, and metal pierce what's left of my skin, but I don't feel it. I must be past the point of feeling, or maybe I'm in shock; all I know is I can't feel anything physically anymore. I wouldn't even know I was moving if I didn't see the pavement sliding in front of me.

I'm shaking and ready to pass out, when I see the "M" that once meant food almost right in front of me. Its golden light isn't shining, but there's light inside the building. I roll onto my back, and use the one good hand I have left to grab onto the bench just outside the doors. It takes more than a few tries, but I crawl onto the seat, breathing hard. I need to close my eyes for just a minute. Just one minute of rest is all I need. I know it's dangerous in this place, but nothing came at me as I crawled here, and I just need this.

There's nothing to tell me how long I've been asleep once I open my eyes again, but I don't seem to have been harmed any further while I slept. The pain has returned, and most of my body feels like it's being stabbed by knives, or is on fire, but I force myself to sit up first, and then to stand.

Leaning against the wall, I shuffle to the door. The few feet seem like miles, but I make it in. There's no human life inside, but things are humming. Lights flicker, the grill sizzles, and I smell French fries. Glorious, wonderful French fries.

Stumbling forward, I stop at the counter as one of the cash registers rises and turns, its menu screen seeming to stare at me. I hold my hands up in surrender and beg.

"Please. I just need food. I mean no harm. *Please.*"

It tilts, making me think it understands me, before nodding down at a stack of bags on the counter. I open one, and things start happening at once. Burger patties fly off the grill and into the bag, fry baskets come out of their hot grease, and dump their contents into the sack as well. I almost pass out from how good it smells, but I remember the girl, and force myself to stay on task.

"Thank you," I tell the things that just helped me.

I don't hesitate to turn to the door, because while I feel relatively safe in here, there's no telling when something might go haywire and come after me. What I see on the other side of the glass causes me to pause before I go through it, and I drop the bag.

"Yes! Do it," the girl shouts, and her cries are joined by the other women surrounding her.

They've all got objects in their hands. Things that shouldn't be hurtful to me, but I know are just that. The electronic appliances shake in their hands, trying to get free as I step back. I'm thankful I'm in here, until I hear the crashing behind me.

Chancing a look back, I see the first fry basket right before it smacks me in the face, searing its design across my forehead. The register hits me in the stomach, and I have no fight left in me as everything else in this place comes for me.

The female squeals of delight surround me as I'm attacked, and I feel them run past me as I take the abuse. I don't know how it happened, but I know she tricked me. *She* played me like the violin I could never master, and now I'm going to die because of it.

"Such a good boy," she coos, her face over mine, batting away the basket that's been hitting me non-stop since this all started.

I hear yelling and clanging, not sure what's going on, or if I really want to know. "Why? How?"

"We need to eat, and only those truly good can get food is this city."

"You're not good." It's a statement and not a question, because I have no doubt how evil she is.

"I'm a Siren, a queen of the sea. Now that nothing and *everything* is the sea, I cannot live like I once did, taking men underwater with me. My sisters and I had to adapt because we need to eat, to feed, to *live*."

"You did something to me."

She laughs, but none of this is funny. "I made you believe you could live with me. It was so very easy with you."

"Why are the things in here coming for me now?" I ask, as she once again uses the toaster in her hand to fight off the fry basket.

"You took their food, and then you dropped it on the floor, wasting it. They do not take kindly to waste, as they saw too much of it when there was nothing they could do to stop it. Now they can punish those who waste, and they do so freely. This world has gone crazy. The power has shifted, and if you can't adapt, you die."

"I tried… I tried to help you."

"You *did* help me. Can't you see?"

"No," I tell her honestly.

I can't move my head, and both of my eyes are nearly swollen shut. I've been forcing them open so I can look at her. Look at this creature who is stealing my life.

"I could tell you I'm sorry, but I am not. You men of this Earth took it all for granted, and now it is our turn to rise."

"Rise? There are not enough humans left for you to use and manipulate."

"Maybe not forever, but I will live longer than you, foolish one. Many men have died for the promise of a kiss from me, and some have died while I gave them what they wanted. Bending you to my will was far too easy."

"Believe me, if I could fight right now, you'd be dead."

"But you can't."

"You gave me hope."

"And now I'm going to take it away."

The toaster in her hand comes down on me before I can take my next breath. One slot covers my nose, while the other smothers my mouth. I smell my flesh burning as it comes to life over me, slowing taking the life from me. I try to figure out if it will be the lack of oxygen that kills me, or the burning of my body from the outside in. I don't even know which wins out as my skin and bones catch fire, and the last breath leaves my body.

I knew better than to hope, and yet I let myself be tricked into believing. I had a chance to survive, but a pretty girl was literally the kiss of death for me. If I had a prayer left in me, I'd send up a plea that she doesn't get them all, that one man on what's left on this planet will outlive her, and watch her last breath leave her, just like she's watching mine leave me.

ORIGINAL SYNTH
Brendan Deneen

The warehouse is cavernous, and dark, and filled with boxes and dust.

I pull the door closed behind me slowly, trying to make as little noise as possible, ironic considering I just smashed one of its window panels in. Not that you can really hear anything over the thunderstorm that feels like it's been raging for days.

When I reached in to unlock the door, I caught myself on a still-connected shard and now I'm bleeding pretty badly. Honestly, though, it's the least of my problems today.

I'm soaked. I've been sprinting through the rain for hours, blindly hoping to find a hiding place like this, breathlessly ecstatic for a moment's rest.

They're coming for me.

He's coming for me.

I struggle for a moment and then manage to tear a strip off the bottom of my sopping wet T-shirt, and wind the wet material around the wound, the blood instantly staining the material pink, then a full red. My hand is throbbing but the makeshift bandage seems to have slowed the bleeding down a little bit.

As I struggle to catch my breath, I walk around the warehouse, making sure it's as abandoned as it looks. Other than copious amounts of mice pellets, I don't see any evidence that anyone's been here for a long time.

Which is no surprise, considering what's been happening with the economy since the current administration took over nine years ago.

It's hard to believe how quickly time has gone by since that election. That insane fucking election. A nightmare collection of horrible, corrupt candidates. Accusations of voter fraud. Interference from foreign powers.

I didn't vote for anyone. I thought they all sucked. They were all as bad as each other.

I was a fucking idiot.

There's a pile of half-rotted, broken-down cardboard boxes in a corner and I collapse into them, feeling the water stream off me with the impact. I wipe my face with trembling fingers and lean my head back against the wall, closing my eyes for the first time in as long as I can remember. When's the last time I slept?

Even through my closed eyelids, I can see a flash of lightning. Thunder rumbles seconds later.

An image of Casey suddenly appears in my mind and the memory of her hurts so much that I immediately open my eyes in the hope of making her disappear. It works, but the pain in my gut at seeing her again, even just an imaginary version, remains.

We fought a lot in those first couple years after the election. She was enraged by the new administration's actions, by what she perceived as decisions motivated by hatred and fear and greed and ignorance.

I told her she was being irrational. I told her we should give the new administration a chance.

We drifted apart as time passed. As the wall was built. As we went to war on multiple fronts, on top of the nonsensical wars we were already fighting. As we teamed up with questionable allies.

I wasn't an active supporter of everything that was happening but a lot of what the administration said made sense to me. Our country *had* to come first. There were just too many threats out there. And so many problems here on the home front that we had ignored for too long. The administration's actions may have been a bit of an overreach but they didn't seem like an overreaction.

Casey didn't agree.

After the day suitcase nukes went off in fifteen major U.S. cities and the resulting collapse of the economy and the installation of martial law, I wasn't entirely surprised when Casey told me she was leaving. "Escaping" is the word she used. I was heartbroken, but not surprised. She had met someone else, someone who was as extreme in his beliefs and fears as she was in hers. The last I heard, they had fled to Canada and then Europe. I think. The administration pretty much took the internet offline right after they dissolved elections and presidential term limits, so it was next to impossible to keep track of her.

I was insanely depressed when she left. I guess I should have tried harder to listen to her concerns. I was just so caught up in my job, in *keeping* my job. Not an easy thing to do when a country is falling apart around you.

When the administration announced mandatory DNA submission to keep us safer, I was still reeling from the loss of Casey and I got swept up in the president's rhetoric. I was probably a little drunk, or a *lot* drunk, when he made his big speech, flanked by his private security officers, and I was one of the first people to sign up. Hell, maybe *the* first.

After I got home from the government's local medical "pop-up" center, I drank myself blind for about a year.

I lost my job at some point during that time, though I'm not exactly sure when. And I didn't get fired just because I was drunk every waking minute. Although that probably didn't help. Everyone I knew lost their jobs. Everyone got more and more scared. Some of that fear turned to anger. People started speaking out against the administration, and then they started vanishing. As time went on, there were fewer and fewer people in houses, on the streets. More people spoke out. More people vanished. Cities fell into disrepair. Oil prices went through the roof. Lots of people fled to the suburbs, then rural areas, hoping they could find food. For some reason, I stayed put in the city. I kind of liked having it mostly to myself. There was something soothing about all of the burned-out buildings. Weird, I know.

There were whispered reports of a rapidly-dwindling population as more and more civilians spoke out against an administration that was clearly out of control. And yet totally *in* control. There was talk that our country was growing weaker and weaker on the world stage as a result, that one of our new "allies" was planning on invading once our population levels reached a certain point. After all, who would fight back? We were all just trying to figure out how to get food onto the table. What little food even existed anymore.

By the time I sobered up, mostly because I had run out of money and had lost so much weight, I did my best to take stock of myself and finally realized how wrong I had been. I took a look around. I started reading through the paperwork Casey had left behind, hidden under our... under *my* bed. I started talking to the few people who had remained in the city. Started attending secret meetings.

Things were a hell of a lot worse than I realized, than they appeared. And they appeared pretty fucking bad.

One of the speakers at a meeting was a scientist. A doctor of genetic something-something. He had worked for the administration but escaped after he realized what they were really doing. He had a long, nasty scar on his face that a newly-grown beard only partially covered. I had trouble understanding what he was saying. He definitely didn't dumb his presentation down for the audience. Most of us kept catching each other's eyes, as if to say "Do *you* get what the hell this guy is trying to say?"

But enough of the message came through: The administration wasn't using our DNA to keep us safe. They were manipulating it, splicing it, creating people. Creating an army. The scientist told us that the administration was calling them Synths.

Apparently it wasn't as simple as just cloning one guy a thousand times. After the first Synth, the next version of the same guy saw some kind of "degradation," to use the word the scientist used. And apparently the administration didn't want Synths based on them. So, they implemented that mandatory DNA testing as a way to get what they needed. They could repopulate the country with the same exact people who were still here. Kind of. The scientist said they had used the first batch of Synths to replenish the military, which did made some kind of sick sense.

As everyone in the audience started to grasp what was being said, a terrified silence descended on the room. We had *all* handed over our DNA. It was mandatory, no way around it. People who said "No" were found and taken away, even if they tried to escape. And the scientist said that the administration had figured out a way to accelerate the process, that there were probably versions of all of us out there already…

I'm not sure if I heard the door crashing in first or saw the bullet hole explode in the scientist's chest. I do remember how surprised he looked. I think he even said, "Oh."

In the chaos that followed, it was hard to tell how many soldiers had crashed the meeting, shooting anyone who resisted. I was one of the only lucky ones. I hadn't sat near the sole window on purpose, but my dumb luck paid off. I threw it open as violence erupted behind me and stupidly glanced back as I squeezed my way out. I think I was curious if the people who had just crashed the meeting were Synths.

There was one non-soldier among them, a very calm-looking guy in a business suit. He had his phone held high and appeared to be recording the whole thing. He swung the camera in my direction just as I looked at him.

I landed on the ground, cursing at myself for rubber-necking. I could have just kept focused on my escape but I'd been curious about what was happening, was enticed to see the progression of violence. And now I was probably in the administration's database. Probably? Shit. *Definitely.*

As soon as I got home, I grabbed a few essentials and started moving from abandoned apartment to abandoned apartment. I was hoping to get out of the city, knew some people who had told me to visit them out in the sticks if I ever escaped, but it became pretty clear to me that someone was on my trail, no matter how well I hid myself. Someone who seemed to know my mind as well as I did. It didn't take me long to figure out who it was.

***

My head jerks up suddenly, slamming painfully against the wall behind me. I must have dozed off. I'm still damp but nowhere near as wet as I was when I first stumbled into this warehouse. My hand still hurts. A lot.

Was that a sound that woke me? Or just my imagination? Hoping it was just a dream. God, I'm starving. Maybe there's a—

"Jonathan."

The voice reaches me from the shadows and I feel an insane shudder wash over my body, a coldness more bracing than any winter. Goosebumps erupt across my skin as I stand up, relying on the wall to make even this simple movement possible.

When he steps into what little light there is, I don't know which is more shocking: how much he looks like me or how much he sounds like me. But it's a younger me. The me that first met Casey. The me that thought life was heading in a certain direction.

"Who are you? What do you want?" I manage to say.

"You know who I am," he says. "And I just want to talk. I'm excited to meet you. *Very* excited."

I hold my hands up as he steps closer. "Stay back!" I'm trying to sound threatening but my voice cracks. His smile is pitying and I hate him for it. Casey often complained about that exact same condescending smile, and now I finally know what she'd been talking about.

He holds his hands up too, and steps closer. The mirror image is too much to handle, so I drop my arms back down.

"I just want to talk," he repeats. "I think I'm the first Synth to meet an Original. I have so many questions I want to ask you." He stops moving when he's a few feet away from me and he lowers his arms. He pushes his wet hair out of his eyes, a gesture I used to make back when I had longer hair. Back when it wasn't thin and graying. "Do you mind if I ask you a few questions?"

I stare at him. I've inadvertently backed myself into a corner. He looks strong. I don't think I could get past him even if he didn't have me boxed in.

"Go ahead," I say, scanning the floor around us, looking for any kind of weapon.

"Can you tell me about ou… about your parents? I think I've dreamt about having a family, a childhood… a really happy childhood. Obviously my mind made the memories up. I mean, I assume. I don't think there's any scientific basis for—"

"Sorry to break it to you, but they were awful," I blurt. "They were terrible to me. I was an accident. They were older, never wanted kids. I think I messed up their plans. They both died when I was pretty young. Within days of each other."

"Oh," he says, then looks down at the ground. When he looks up, it's the first time he hasn't had some kind of smile on his face. He looks more terrifying now, especially with the crisscross of shadows from all of the windows in this place. "I think I had romanticized it a bit more."

"Yeah, well, that's very human of you."

He winces and a flash of anger lights his eyes, then quickly vanishes. He takes another step forward. Without even meaning to, I push myself back against the wall harder. But there's nowhere else to go.

"This must be weird for you," he says. "Like looking in a funhouse mirror."

"How do you even know what a funhouse *is?*" I ask, disdain dripping from every word.

He stares at me with something that resembles sadness.

"I read a lot of books," is all he says.

"Well, I guess we're not *exactly* alike. I guess I'm still me."

His smile returns. "It's funny you say that. Ever since I woke up… in the lab… I've wondered about who I am. They don't tell us much. They just immediately start training us… weapons, hand-to-hand combat, psychological warfare. They don't focus much on our humanity. If such a thing even exists for us. None of the other Synths read books. We're not supposed to. But I sneak them out of the Creators' offices and read them at night with a flashlight. Like a teen boy."

A memory of doing that exact thing floods my mind and I nearly lose my breath. It's a memory that was completely lost until this moment. I did it more than once, with an ancient copy of *Tarzan of the Apes*, until my father discovered me one night and took the book away from me. I never saw it again. Never finished it.

"You don't have to report me," I say as lightning flashes again outside. "You don't have to bring me in. I just want to leave the city and be left alone. I don't have anything against the administration."

His smile… *my* smile… turns sad again and he takes another step toward me. He's so close now. *Too* close.

"Jonathan. Do you know why they sent *me* after you?"

I hadn't thought of that. Not really. I've been too busy running, trying to stay out of sight. I just stare at him, waiting for the answer.

"I know you better than anyone else ever can. I may not have your memories but I *know* you. When I was following you… over these past few days… I didn't even have to try very hard. I could just… *feel* what you were going to do next. It's actually incredible. I've never experienced anything like it. I'm nervous about any other missions because I don't think anything can ever live up to what tracking you has been like for me."

"Please…" I say and I know how pathetic I sound. "Please. Just let me go."

He takes another step toward me and now we're within touching distance of each other. Every fiber of my being tells me to fight. To barrel into him and at least *try* to escape. I don't move.

"I envy you," he says quietly. "I will *never* be as good as you. Even if I'm stronger or faster, I'm not you. And I don't think I'm even *me*."

"You are," I insist. "You're you. And you can do anything you want. You don't have to work for them. You can come with me. Or not. But you can do anything you want."

Our smile turns sad on his face. He reaches up and puts a hand on my shoulder. I jump at the contact but his touch feels so familiar, like the ghost of a memory.

I miss Casey so much.

"I wish it were that simple, Jonathan," he almost whispers. "I really do."

"I'm not a troublemaker. I just want to disappear. I promise I won't make trouble for anyone."

"I know you won't," he says, and his other hand appears on my other shoulder. He doesn't look like me, not exactly, but it's still like looking into a mirror. A fogged mirror where you can only sort of see yourself but you're definitely there. Or are you?

His hands move closer to my face and gently grip my neck.

"It has been an honor to meet you," he says quietly. "The honor of my short life."

"Wait," I say.

"I will never truly *be*. And you *always* will. Even after you're gone. Do you know how lucky you are?"

"Wait," I say.

"Thank you," he says, and then his hands are suddenly moving, he's so incredibly strong, and there's this snapping noise, and Oh My God I'm—

INTO THE STYGIAN DARKNESS
Heather Graham

Chapter 1

Lenore

I never thought that I—a hundred-and-twenty-pound artist—could in any way be involved with what would be known as The Salvation. And in a small way no one would ever figure.

Of course, everything is small now.

I think, in general, we—as the human race—had believed that we would go out with a big bang. That we would perish like the dinosaurs, not because of the cataclysmic arrival of a meteor on the planet, but because of the hair-trigger fury and pulse of man himself. Rage in an era when bombs could wipe out entire states in just seconds—and leave enough residue to poison the world for centuries to come.

It was a fear for me, anyway. And I wasn't the only one.

It wasn't always so.

When I was young, I truly believed that we were heading to the great Age of Aquarius—that man was beginning to love his fellow man. I had sweet, happy parents who seemed to think that it was so—they were like living with a pair of sweet, naïve, and very charming puppets. They instilled a lot of that happiness in me.

I miss them.

But I digress.

When it all came about, mine was a kind of cool world—with lots of hope stretching before us in the years to come. I went to Pratt Institute in Brooklyn, which is basically an art and design school. My roommate was a gay, black man and our group of friends included Wu—a Chinese painter, Maria—a Cuban majoring in architecture, and Ali Shiraz, a gorgeous young man with a Turkish dad and a more gorgeous Danish mom. We hung around together by day, aware that we needed both talent and hard work to get where we wanted to go in our chosen fields.

I still remember meeting Stephen—he was hysterical. He walked into our dorm and stared me down. "Yeah, I'm a man!" he said, and wagged a finger at me. "And," he added knowingly, "a black man! But," He told me with a shrug. "You are not my cup of tea, sugar! You get my drift, right? We're going to be okay here, right?" He did something, acting out an attack of fear and vapors, and landed on my bed and on my pillow, looking up with such a dramatic flourish that I couldn't help but laugh. And he kept me laughing many times after, when little things—a grade I feared, a critique—had me anxious and distraught with the world.

Well, that was then. *Don't sweat the small stuff,* they always said— that universal "they" we're always talking about.

Maria Rodriguez had the room connected with ours. She was in love with Gordon—a boy back home in Miami, Florida. Her parents were very rich. She didn't have to have a roommate. We liked to tease her and her nickname—which she'd had since she's been a kid, she always told us with a smile—was The Jewster. Her mom was Jewish and had married a rising Cuban politician.

Wu, the Buddhist, roomed with Ali Shiraz, the Muslim. They often sounded like two old men when they talked politics and the state of the world—or the quality of artists' paint brushes and that kind of thing. Maria liked to get into those conversations too. Listening to them, you might actually start to believe that the world could be saved.

Or at least, humanity.

One night, after heading into the city for art supplies, the five of us wound up in a coffee shop with a pack of academics from NYU. That included Jeff Anderson—a medical student about to go into residency, and Tracey Harper, who was on her way to becoming a nurse anesthetist. They weren't a duo, though they were both straight. When I met them, Jeff Anderson was pining after a theater major and Tracey was married to a guy in the armed forces.

We became friends because Jeff overheard something said about the president. Oddly enough, as a weird group of strangers, we would start talking on opposing sides, and the conversation was both enlightening and friendly. We all had our opinions—but, pretty much so, we all believed that the next big bang would come because someone had their hand on the buzzer. The amazing thing was that we could talk. Our little group represented not just the three more contentious religions of the day, but four; Judaism, Islam, Christianity, *and* Buddhism.

Jeff was the real scholar in our group. He was an amazing man—Doctor Beautiful, really. He could definitely have been the star of a medical television series. Seriously—Patrick Dempsey had nothing on Jeff.

Maybe I did have a little crush on him, right from the beginning. Like I said, he was just beautiful.

We would meet whenever we could, most often at the coffee shop by the art store where the new Freedom Tower rose high, showing the world, of course, that the U.S. would not be cowed by terrorism.

I loved the churches there; I was obsessed with old churches and graveyards, so I would go sketch at either St. Paul's or Trinity, and I'd often marvel that the Twin Towers had gone with such violence, while the churches and the graveyards—telling us so much about our history—survived. I knew that in World War II bombs had blasted castles and cathedrals, taking half the treasures of Europe, erasing many of man's most industrious and historic achievements. Now, bombs, they said, were different.

Now, they left buildings—and eradicated people.

Those college days were amazing. But like all good things, they came to an end.

When what we came to know simply as *The Day* came, I'd been hired to restore murals at a tiny but wonderful Episcopal church on Orange, one of the Pelham Islands in Western Long Island Sound. Not many knew about St. Philip's—actually, not many people knew the islands even existed.

The church was quaint and unusual. It was lucky that the historic board of the city had chosen to preserve it. Especially now that Orange Island was uninhabited except for a tiny city preservation office that had just opened at the tiny wharf. Sometimes, I knew, hierarchy in the Episcopal church liked to come by and use for the church for special occasions. St. Philip's had never been deconsecrated, even when, in the late 1800s, the congregation gave up island living and moved to the ever-growing mainland of Manhattan.

It was because of that tourist office and the barely known church on that all but forgotten island that a strange spectrum of circumstances arose to put us all together again as *The Day* dawned. I was working on what I considered to be an absolutely amazing image of Mary and the Christ Child—it was the 13th of the month, a special day for me, and I was wondering what surprise my friends had cooked up for me when my phone rang.

Alone in the little church, I took the time to sit on one of the old pews, noting that the wood itself was indented from the dozens of people who had once come to worship.

It was Jeff—now Dr. Anderson. I was, of course, delighted to hear from him. Except, of course, that I always wanted to be cool and wonderful when he called—I had, however, just broken up with the D.J. I'd been dating—word of warning to all young women out there—don't date a D.J. (The good; they can be lots of fun. The bad—they can be lots of fun. Just part of the job, they say, that they need to have a little of that fun with other women!)

But even if I had still been dating the D.J., my heart would have gone pit-a-pat as soon as I heard Jeff's voice.

I'd never gotten over that initial crush I had on him.

"Hey! How are you?" I asked him.

"Great—and you? Well, actually, I'll be able to see that for myself in just a few minutes."

"You will? Do you know where I am?"

"I just heard that you were close. I'm at the little office place thing by the dock. I can see you in five minutes—so they tell me. Can you come on up?"

I was stunned. "What are you doing here? I don't believe this. I mean—you actually—really truly—know where I am?"

He laughed. "I just learned about where you are. Hell, I just learned about these islands, and that they exist. Yep. Had a call out here today."

"As a doctor?"

"Yep. Come meet me," he said.

"Okay! I have to come right back here. I have a lot of work implements out. Oh, and you need to see St. Philip's here—gorgeous. It's Gothic—all stone—and looks like a medieval castle. Don't get me wrong—I really love my own projects. But, this place is amazing. It's surrounded by a graveyard that was started in the early 1800s. It could be a strange kind of fortress. It's—"

"Come meet me. I'll see your church."

I hung up and stared at the incredibly beautiful mural I'd been working on and smiled. "Sorry!" I said aloud to the image of Mary. "It's Jeff. And I guess you know how I feel about him!"

So I left the church, walking first out through the lonely little overgrown graveyard. Gorgeous sculptures of angels, cherubs, and innocent little lambs graced the burial ground; family tombs stood, covered with fungus or algae—I didn't know what the green substance was, I just knew that it added to the wonderful, haunted loneliness of the place.

A high, stone wall surrounded the whole of the place, but the gate was wide open. I didn't know why there had been such a big, imposing wall around a church, but it didn't matter that I left the gate open—it had been open since I'd first seen the place. There just wasn't anyone here to come along and surprise me!

I walked along the winding path that led toward the docks. Like all else here, they needed work. But, until recently, the island had been abandoned. Now and then, along the way, I passed the foundations of a long-gone home. It seemed strange that the island had once housed a population that supported a church, but then, all those years ago, people had been more accustomed to distance and space. And the deli downstairs didn't exist to make sure that no one ever had to cook if they chose not to do so.

The little office structure that now belonged to the historic board had once been the dock master's office and home. Supplies had once come and gone from the island. I believe a number of the entrepreneurs on the board wanted to make the island an elite destination—a place for multi-million dollar homes. They were planning to start with tourism, and, of course, the historic little church and graveyard would become very important—tourist locations needed something to tour.

All that is now, of course, moot.

Anyway, I saw Jeff coming along the trail and raced to him, throwing myself into his arms. We were good enough friends that I could do that. He laughed, catching me.

"I can't believe this!" I told him. "Since when do you make house calls?"

"Only on very special occasions do I do such things!" he said. He frowned. "Very special occasions; I shouldn't have taken this call.

There's something terrible going on. The hospital is being overrun with sick people."

"Oh—oh! How terrible. A flu going around?"

"Definitely. Weird. I don't know what's causing this one. Most everyone I saw at the beginning said they'd been outside—gardening, playing sports, running," he said. He shook his head and I saw that he was really concerned—down to the bone.

"I pronounced someone dead yesterday," he said. "And then... people stop breathing. Their hearts stop. Then... in the morgue... then they're suddenly alive and moving again, but they can't seem to hear anyone. Our corpse had to be restrained."

"You mean like a zombie?" I said, my tone both mocking and incredulous.

He didn't laugh. He didn't even smile.

"Let's see this wondrous church of yours!" he said, obviously wanting to change the conversation.

Excited, I tried to fill him in on some of the history. It looked like a medieval fortress, but it had really been built in the early 1800s. Someone had been in love with gothic architecture, though. There were great arches, catwalks, flying buttresses... even a few gargoyles.

"And it's Anglican? Sounds like someone was reproducing Notre Dame," Jeff said.

"Well, remember, Anglicans were once Catholic. Henry VIII wanted a divorce and couldn't get one; he had once been the 'defender of the faithful' against Martin Luther, but, hey, he was a king. He wanted a divorce. And if you're the king..."

"You burn a bunch of people at the stake for heresy and start your own religion!" Jeff said, grinning.

"Something like that," I said.

We walked through the open gate and Jeff paused, turning to look around the graveyard. He shuddered and looked at me. "You work here every day—alone?"

I nodded with a shrug. "Tina Adams and Dirk Van der Ven are up at the office all the time—sometimes, way more people. They come out to see the work, what's going on. And, I get to hire on from my list of friends, so it's very cool!"

We reached the heavy wooden front doors of the church. I started forward, but the doors burst open—and there were people there. My friends!

"Surprise!" Stephen cried, rushing out to hug me.

They were all there. It was the best and most amazing surprise—ever! Stephen, Wu, Maria, Ali, and even Tracey Harper—now a full-fledged and well-paid nurse-anesthetist—had made it.

I hugged everyone. I'm sure I cried. They had all come out and the plan was that they'd surprise me at the church, we'd have dinner at the historic wharf house—Tina and Dirk had helped with the set-up—and then we'd all head back in on the one and only night boat, under contract with the historic board.

It was while we were all kissing and hugging and laughing that I suddenly felt the floor give way. For a moment, I was weightless. And then I knew that I was falling. Into darkness. I screamed, terrified as I pitched downward. I fell on something wooden; it cracked as I fell, easing the impact. I gasped desperately, needing breath, as all that had been was cleanly swept away. I inhaled a strange and musky smell and I knew—not even needing the flicker of light that came in through the broken floorboards—that I was in a crypt. The coffin I'd landed on had broken. But I'd rolled, and the coffin had fallen, and I was lying next to a dead man, mummified, worm-eaten, flesh stretched taut where it was, bones glistening where it was not.

I screamed again.

"Oh, my God!" I heard Maria cried out.

"Lenore!" Stephen called my name.

Shaken, shocked, frozen, I could only think in sarcastic terms.

Brilliant. Let's restore the art. Oh, yeah, the art is in a structure…

"Help, help!" The sound of my own voice was weak. It grew stronger. "Oh, my God, help me! Dead people, dead people—everywhere. Oh, God!"

"Stay still, stay where you are—everyone, careful. Don't move!" Stephen said. "Cell phone lights on!"

Light shone down. I could see them all, faces eerie as they pushed their lit phones toward the hole.

"Careful moving," Stephen commanded. "The whole thing is about to give. Lenore has been working here alone. This much weight… all of us… too much!"

And it was. There was a horrendous crashing sound.

Suddenly, they were all down there, crashing onto coffins and bodies, all of us, entangled, hurt, bruised, terrified and screaming.

"Hey!"

And then all sound abruptly stopped—Jeff had that kind of authority in his voice.

"I'm a doctor, guys. I see dead people often. Okay, so these are deader than the ones I usually see. They're just bodies. So... we figure how to get out of here!"

"Yeah, we get out of here," Stephen murmured. "Ooooh! Happy birthday, Lenore. Happy birthday!"

Chapter 2

Stephen

I love my friends. I've always loved my friends. I am, beyond a doubt, one of those people who wants there to be good in everyone.

I started out life with two strikes against me—as some might see it.

I'm black.

I'm gay.

Some people want to dislike you for one, the other, or both. But I'd decided to look to things like affirmative action and to surround myself with people who were just good and loving.

I found such a strange group of friends, but, that's exactly what they were.

Lenore was the best. Such a beautiful and talented woman. From the first time we met—eighteen-year-olds, just stepping out into the world—we were instant friends.

She's the opposite of me—blue-eyed, blond-haired, lean, tall, and absolutely stunning. We were probably an odd pair together, but neither of us cared. We gave each other help on our projects in school, and, as we went on in life, helped get each other work now and then. I always knew that she had a terrible crush on Dr. Jeff and never figured out how he didn't know it.

Or why nothing had ever come of it.

Anyway, that year, when she was working on the historic project out on that island, practically alone, I thought I could give her the best present possible—Jeff.

Get him out there with just the group of us...

Party, party!

But, go figure. Cities! Hey, let's restore that art—the floor? Oh, should we have worried about the floor?

When I saw Lenore crash through, it felt as if my heart was being torn out of my chest. I couldn't breathe—which, in a way, made sense. For seconds, we stood in a cloud of dust that all but enveloped us. Then, Lenore was screaming about corpses, and we knew she was alive, just desperate to get out.

Then, we were all in pile of dusty, decaying, incredibly creepy corpses.

The light from our cell phones made the images around us more distorted and macabre.

"Lenore is the lightest," Maria noted. "We can push her up."

"And then?" Ali asked.

"And then, rope!" Lenore said. "I have plenty of rope—we were eventually going to have to get scaffolding up, and we needed rope, so..."

"You and me!" I told Jeff.

"Yep, gotcha."

"Thank God that the gay guy and the straight guy are both in great shape!" Tracey murmured.

"Hey, I'm a guy!" Ali said.

"And you're kind of in shape," Tracey granted him. "Oh, come on, guys, lighten up, please!" she begged.

She was right, of course. We all tried to do a bit of laughing, making creepy noises, and trying to get each other into a birthday mood again.

Jeff and I hiked Lenore up to the hole in the floor; she managed to crawl out. She found the rope and sent it down to the rest of us.

We crawled up, Jeff and I waiting until last to make sure we—muscle-bound straight guy and muscle-bound gay guy—got them all up first. Once they were all up, we looked at each other and shrugged. Then I insisted he go first.

"You're the doc," I said to him, "and someone might have cuts and bruises."

There were a few cuts and bruises. Miraculously, no one was hurt more than that.

"But we have a doctor!" Ali said.

"And a nurse—anesthetist, but, hey, an RN," Tracey reminded us all. "And I'm going to recommend—"

"An anti-bacterial cream," Jeff interrupted her. "Hey, a doc trumps a nurse."

"Wow. That was heavy," Tracey said.

Edging away from the now giant hole in the floor, we wound up staring at one another—and laughing. We were covered in crypt dust.

Bone dust, probably.

The rot and ruin of two hundred years of death.

"I do believe we're all going to need to shower before... well, before anything!" Lenore said cheerfully.

"The boat captain will freak when he sees us all," I said. I looked at Lenore. "You should sue the historic people! The City of New York. Someone."

"Hey, we all should!" Ali agreed.

"Don't sue people who deal with history—there's never any money to actually preserve things as it is! And, we can head on up. That little office was also a home at one time. There's a full bathroom there," Lenore said.

"If any of us had been hurt..." Jeff began.

"But we weren't," Lenore said quickly. "Birthday present to me—let's just all laugh about this. There's something that resembles a makeshift bathroom off one of the choir rooms, but really, better facilities can be found up at the office.

"But we're just guests here," I said a little awkwardly. It hadn't been difficult, really, to reach Dirk Van der Ven—one of the historic board people who worked up at the little office. He'd been okay. So had the girl there, Tina. But I also got the feeling that they cared about Lenore—who didn't?—but they were still just being tolerant. They really weren't all that crazy about us being on the island; they would allow it because it was Lenore's birthday. When we'd arrived—needing instructions to sneak around a back path in order to surprise her at the church—Dirk had definitely given Ali a long and doubtful glare. Ali was Arab. He looked Arab. Dirk didn't like Arabs.

He probably didn't like blacks, either. But at least I wasn't a black Arab!

"Hey!" Maria reminded us. "We're guests who crashed through a floor. Owned by the city. They owe us some cleanliness, at the very least—or else we should sue."

"Okay, okay—let's clean up, wait for the boat and we'll have a great time back in the city tonight," Lenore said.

"Here, here!" I agreed. "But, young lady!" I commanded Lenore. "You call those historic people you work for and tell them what happened here."

"Sure."

"Guys, walk along the sides here—there are support columns beneath us," Ali said. He was one of our friends who wasn't what they termed a "visual" artist—he'd been at Pratt working toward design, architecture, and engineering.

"Gotcha," Maria said. She started along the side of the church, stepping gingerly at first. She was a pretty girl. Dark haired, dark-eyed. I'd met Maria soon after I met Lenore. We'd spent a lot of nights drinking beer and talking about life. Maria had assured us that it wasn't all that easy for a Cuban Jew to get a date. I told her to try being a gay black man.

"But, you're so cool looking," Maria had said.

"Yep, just like ebony silk," Lenore had agreed. And we'd laughed—if I ever gave up art and became a porn star, my name was going to be Ebony Silk.

One by one, we carefully left the main structure of the church.

Lenore was last out. She was frowning. I looked at her with concern and she quickly explained, "No one answered. I tried about five people with the historic board—no one answered!"

"An undeclared holiday?" I asked, shrugging. I slipped an arm around her. Doc Jeff was up at the front of the column, talking to Nurse Tracey. They weren't arm in arm or anything—they almost seemed to be arguing about something.

Tina was standing at the front of what was now the George Island Development Office when we reached the old dock structure. She looked concerned.

"What happened to you?" She demanded, staring at us all with horror.

Dirk came out to stand behind her. He looked like his name—as if he could be a damned Viking. He was super-tall, blond, bronzed, and a bit like a Nordic god. Van der Ven—his family probably went back in NYC, to the days when the Dutch—not the Vikings—had ruled.

Too bad he seemed to be such an ass. The way he looked at Ali scared me.

"Tina! The entire floor of the church gave!" Lenore said.

"Ah, damn it! I knew we should have said 'no!'" she exclaimed, looking back at Dirk. "They've wrecked the place."

"Hey!" Ali protested angrily. "You have a death trap going, and you're angry with us?"

"First off, we don't have anything going. But, things aren't open because they're all under restoration!" Dirk snapped.

"So—if we hadn't been here, Lenore could have been killed! She could have fallen down into the crypt with no help. She could have—"

"Stop!" Lenore suddenly screamed.

We all looked at her. She was staring at her phone. She looked up at all of us, her eyes mirroring a fear and horror such as nothing I had ever seen before.

"Look!" she whispered, and her voice barely found substance. "The news, the news, oh, God!"

There was no way we could all crowd around her little camera phone. A number of us began to pull out our own phones.

And we didn't understand what we were seeing.

"A movie?" Maria asked, confused.

"Promotion for a TV show—you get one great zombie show, and all of a sudden there are zillions of bad copies," Ali said, shaking his head.

"Zombies?" Tina asked.

"It's New York City. It's just ..." Wu spoke, but his words were a bare whisper.

"Well, the... they look like zombies," I said—because they did. They were people, of course, moving along the streets of New York City. On whatever cable channel I had dredged up on my phone, they were showing a lovely redheaded anchor up on some kind of a platform. She was above the chaos on the streets. People screaming... and then just falling. Then other people falling on the fallen people, and then ...

"Oh, God. Oh, God, it can't be real—it can't be!" Lenore said.

The same words echoed in my mind.

"For the love of Allah!" Ali cried.

Wu was chanting something in Chinese.

"Zombies! It's got to be the bloody Arabs!" Tina screamed.

I was afraid of how Ali might react. It was Lenore who swung around on her. "How dare you? How dare you call yourself

American, and condemn any one people?"

"It's all right!" Ali cried.

"It's the Russians!"

I don't even know who said that, but thoughts were running wild through everyone's heads—and they were being spouted out just the same. *Arabs, Russians, Cubans, the Chinese, the Japanese, North Koreans, the Jews… feisty people? And, hell, it could even be the Mexicans, pissed about the wall … God only knew!*

We were starting to fight. I think it was Dirk who suggested that it might be the Darkies out of Africa. Half of us were ready to start swinging at the other half.

I have to admit—I was one of those who wanted to start swinging.

The video we all saw seemed to grow more and more bizarre.

But it couldn't be real; it couldn't be real!

Just as we all stared at our cell phones, fighting and screaming and puffing up like a ridiculous pack of peacocks, there was a tremendous shudder in the earth where we stood, and the sound of a rock-hard slam, wood splintering, the dock and the ground exploding.

The ferry had come. The ferry had come—to take us all back for the night.

But the ferry had not docked.

It had slammed straight into the wharf with such impetus that it had actually seemed to hurtle itself clear onto the land.

Chapter 3

Jeff

When you're a doctor, people believe you have to be smart. Except for other doctors, of course. They know it's all a matter of memorizing the right things and understanding the human structure and the function of our organs, just the way an architect knows and loves the way buildings are put together and how nails and pilings and whatever else might work.

Put us—doctors, I believe, based on myself—in the middle of chaos, we're just about the same as everyone else. We go by instinct.

We panic.

Our panic, however, was almost as slow as the movement—we were still too confused, too stunned. Smart? Slow-witted was far more like it.

I thought about the fact that it had been difficult for me to get away from the hospital that day. People kept coming in with the flu. I hadn't paid that much attention.

There was always a flu going around.

But now...

It was a joke; it was some kind of terrible joke. We had to be seeing a drama of some kind on the television—hell, recent elections had proved that no one just reported the news anymore!

And the ferry captain...

He had to be drunk. That would explain it.

I felt a hand on my shoulder and looked around. It was Lenore. Her eyes were steady as she stared at me.

I was the doctor—the macho man. Panicking. And Lenore...

Down to earth, ever level Lenore. The woman was ready to love anyone and everyone—she was someone who wanted only good in the world.

I cared about her. I always had. And, to be honest, I'd played on the fact that I knew she had quite a thing for me. Oh, I didn't take it to the end run, so to say. But, I had used it. When I was alone. When I was angry with someone else. When a lack of recognition was getting me down. I called Lenore. We'd go to dinner. I'd talk biology and chemistry and she'd describe some of the finest art in the world. You see, I knew I could have a whole damned smorgasbord at the time—no way in hell that I'd look that way at Lenore. Nothing wrong with her—as even my well-educated buddies were prone to say, *I'd do her in a heartbeat.*

Except that I never had. Somehow, I'd been smart enough to preserve the friendship—and *not* do her *for* a heartbeat.

"Hurt, yes, hurt," I said.

"Hurt!" Tracey said, and I turned to look at her. *Hurt, dammit, yes, she was a nurse, I was a doctor. Hurt!*

Lenore was already running toward the crashed boat, calling out.

That was when the first of them stumbled out. He'd been a first mate, of something. I don't really understand how boats—ferries— work. I mean, seriously, they had come to pick up a few people off an island. Just how many cooks did you need in that kitchen?

Then the captain, I imagine—from his hat. His back had been broken; he moved in a doubled-over position. Then there were some kind of stewards, two of them.

To be fair, honest, and—sadly—cut down on the nobility of our coming actions, they were slow as hell. I still had a very, very bad time believing what I was seeing.

Yes, people had become zombies.

They stared with sightless eyes as they moved; and they let out some kind of noise. It was awful. It was a groaning—it was a death rattle. They weren't breathing, but something was moving through their lungs.

One by one, they stumbled off the beached boat.

I was about fifteen feet behind Lenore. She was in complete denial. "We'll help you!" she called out. "We'll help you!"

And it was wrong. I knew it was wrong. I knew before she reached the first one, clutching his arms, looking into his eyes, telling him again that they could be helped; a doctor was coming.

I watched as that first of the boat—*zombies* or whatever the hell they were—reacted to Lenore. I watched his mouth open, his jaw tight, his teeth…

He bit her. Bit into her flesh hard, ripping and tearing.

She screamed; she wrenched away, sending a blow against the thing that had once been a man.

I thought about Lenore. The laughter in her beautiful eyes, the way her hair swung around her like a cascade of silk when she walked. The way she moved, grace and elegance in her every smile, twist, and turn.

I thought about all the sex we never had, and never would.

While I was thinking, Stephen rushed by me. He'd grabbed up some kind of gardening tool that had been left by the porch, and he swung.

Man, he swung hard.

I've never seen anything like it—before, or since, despite all that we've now been through.

Stephen hit that sucker so hard that he beheaded the creature, the thing. I watched the head fly … and crash into the water.

The body trembled in time for a split second.

And then fell flat to the ground.

"Kill them, oh, my God, kill them!" Tina cried, tears in the sound of her voice. She was looking desperately around for a weapon.

Dirk had come running down the steps of the little porch to the house. Like Stephen, he was quick. Someone had been working with a hoe in a little garden to the right of the house; Dirk went for the hoe.

I managed to join in the fight—a little late. Between Stephen, Dirk—and even Lenore—they killed the things that had come off of the boat.

The captain and his men.

"Kill her, now. Kill Lenore," Tina suddenly shouted. "We have to do it. Damn it—don't you see? It's just like legend, just like the movies! People have become zombies. And she's been bitten! Kill Lenore, kill Lenore! Doctor, you know it's true—kill Lenore!"

Madness, I thought. Day was ending; true night was falling.

And, in truth, we had come to darkness. A stygian darkness.

Chapter 4

Lenore

I am probably extremely lucky that it was my birthday. Zombie apocalypse for your birthday? Hell, yeah, so it seemed.

And still, I was lucky—so lucky that it had been my birthday.

Because my friends were there. I have no doubt that had it been just Dirk and Tina, I'd have been executed within sixty seconds.

But my friends weren't going to allow it. They would have none of it.

I felt nothing—nothing but the pain of the bite. I didn't think that I was going to become a zombie! That thing had gotten a good chunk out of my lower arm near my wrist and I was bleeding profusely. But, I didn't even feel weak. I wasn't going to pass out. I was fine.

Maybe it took time. Maybe I would have to bleed out and die. Maybe I'd get some awful symptoms, bleed from the mouth, do something else horrible, and then become a zombie.

And maybe that's what the rest of them were thinking. My own friends were looking at me strangely. Sadly. They couldn't do it now. They couldn't. That would be killing me.

But, the second I started to change...

"Kill her!" Tina demanded. She'd walked off the porch and stood between us and the boat that had crashed up on shore.

Between us and the boat and what remained of her sick crew.

"Now, do it now—before she turns!" Tina demanded.

"No!" Jeff shouted. "Damn you, I'm a doctor—"

"And a doctor knows!"

"A doctor diagnoses by what information is available. I don't have—"

"There is no fucking information on zombies!" Tina raged.

Well, she was right about that.

"She isn't sick; she isn't falling. She isn't turning. Trust me—if she turns, we'll take action. She's our friend; we love her," Jeff said. "I love her!"

He loved me.

In the midst of a damned zombie apocalypse, I was shaking—not because I was turning, not because I was afraid. Not because the entire fucking world had apparently gone to hell. But because Jeff said that he'd loved me!

I could die happy—which was good, since I was most probably going to die.

But just as these thoughts raced ridiculously through my mind, I saw that we hadn't gotten the last of the crew. Seriously, what the hell were so many people doing aboard a ferry that had been bound for an island to pick up less than ten people? Maybe they had just stowed aboard. Whatever, we would probably never know.

But, he was almost on top of Tina.

"Tina!"

I think most of us screamed her name at the same time. She turned, saw the man coming toward her with decaying flesh falling off his face and arms, and screamed.

I thought it only happened that way in movies. I thought it was impossible for people threatened with death to be so uncoordinated. But, she fell—Tina tied up her own ankles, so it seemed, in her haste to run. And the thing was upon her, biting, gnashing, ripping...

I don't even remember moving, but I moved. Fast. I had only my fist. But Jeff was there, and Stephen—Stephen, who could be so silly, who could belt out a show tune at any given moment—Stephen was there, a knight in dusty cotton armor.

We killed it.

We killed the thing easily enough.

Then, as we all argued that there might be more, the unthinkable happened. And in seconds.

Tina turned!

We hadn't really been paying her any attention—not at that point. No one knew if there might be more creatures or not—and we weren't exactly a functioning democracy—or even a functioning group of friends at that point. So, none of us was watching; none of us saw it.

What happened was that we heard her. She suddenly had that rattling sound in her lungs. And when we turned... it was instantaneous. Amazing. The change in her eyes. In her color, in her demeanor.

She was closest to Dirk. Going after him...

Ali slew the thing that Tina had become with one quick blow from the garden tool he'd snatched up from Stephen's hands.

She fell dead.

"What the hell? I mean, what the bloody hell?" Dirk demanded. "This one!" he proclaimed, pointing at me, "loses a pound of flesh—and nothing. And Tina... poor Tina..."

"Poor Tina. It's horribly sad," Jeff said, "but she was not the nicest person."

"Oh, so being nice or not nice makes a difference in whether or not you become a zombie?" Dirk demanded. He spoke sarcastically, but he looked worried. Well, he might have a right to be worried. He hadn't been particularly nice that day, either.

"No," Jeff said quietly.

"No, that couldn't be it," Tracey murmured, looking at Jeff. "But, this can't be, can it? We have to be in the middle of a horrible nightmare."

I wanted to believe that. But it hurt like hell where I'd been bitten.

"Fact," Jeff said. "People are turning into zombies. Zombies are terrible creatures that are much like fiction has always depicted them. But as to people becoming zombies..."

"But... who did this? A terrorist group?" I heard myself ask.

Tina's phone had fallen. It was still playing news. Stephen picked it up and said, "Not the Russians, not the Arabs, not... who knows? Look."

We all tried to look. The anchor was speaking with foreign correspondents around the world.

The news showed the zombie insanity in Istanbul. In Munich. In Berlin. In Cairo.

And then in London, Dublin, Oslo...

On to Tokyo, Beijing, Auckland…

And then…

The screen went blank.

"The world has fallen," Jeff said softly. He looked around at all of us. "I don't know whether to be grateful or not; we may be the only ones alive. We may be just some of a few survivors. We're on an island. That helped. But as to why Tina turned after being bitten and Lenore did not…"

"There is a reason!" Tracey whispered.

"Scientific," Wu agreed. "And," he added, looking up at if he saw his own form of Heaven, "Spiritual. Maybe." He swore.

Maria sank down on the porch steps. "What do we do now? How do we stay alive? Do we even want to stay alive?" she whispered.

"Life has always been a gift," Jeff said. "It should never be squandered. So, what do we do?"

Dirk began speaking, staring out toward the water, blankly. "There's food; there's a garden too. They eventually wanted to have a farmstead out here. Part of the tourist trade. And a petting zoo. Of course, if we use all their crops, they might be pissed, but then again…"

Jeff looked over at me. He seemed like a little kid for a minute.

"They don't exist anymore, do they?" Slowly Dirk's voice became more infused with panic. "They don't exist, and neither do any of our friends, our families, anyone."

He started to sob. Jeff hunkered down before him, grabbing him by the shoulders. "Stop it, we don't know that. Right now, we fight to survive. There are probably other pockets of people. And who knows? Someone we love could be among those people. We are lucky. We have the island. We have isolation. We have to watch. We have to be clever."

"And we really have to figure it out," I said. "Why am I still okay?"

No one had an answer for me. I saw that both Jeff and Tracey were watching me with calculating frowns.

A good thing, I told myself.

"Not to worry, Lenore," Jeff promised, "someone will be on guard all night."

"Against more zombies coming?"

"Against you," he said.

Chapter 5

Dirk

I was alone. So alone.

Tina might not have been the nicest person in the world. In fact, come to think of it, we weren't really good friends.

But at least we were a "we." Now, I was just an "I."

They were all friends. Ready to stand pat. And the one—an Arab! I don't care if the whole world had gone down. His people had done this. They had set off some kind of a horrible virus. If not him... the dark-haired woman. Hell, from what I understood, she was Cuban and Jewish.

Then there was the black guy. He was...

Gay.

Okay, so he was probably guilty of no more than excessive household design and twice-ironed shirts.

But...

He was staring at me. Stephen. That was his name. He was staring. I felt my cheeks flush. I couldn't help but think that he didn't like me, and I was probably right. Of course, to them—*and me, too*—whatever, however—it appeared that the world had finally come to an end. It wasn't exploding; there had been no bang! It was imploding. It had imploded. We might be the last little pocket of humanity.

Were the animals sickening and dying, too? Was one of those prophecies true? Were we going to leave it all to the kingdom of the cockroaches?

Lenore—still standing somehow, and not being put down by her friends—must have been thinking along similar lines. She raced to a jagged edge of what remained of the dock and looked down into the water.

"It seems to be okay," she cried.

Yeah, and so do you—you seem to be okay!

"What do we do?" Maria—the Cuban girl demanded. "What do we do?"

She sank down on the porch. She started to cry. Lenore walked over and joined her, putting an arm around her shoulders.

Denial struck me again. This couldn't have happened. My folks... they had to be dead. They lived in an apartment near Battery Park.

My friends. They only looked as if they were a little bit tough. The group of us, all with family that stretched back to the Dutch settlement of New Amsterdam. Yeah, we could be hard on immigrants. Really, we just saw the world as it was.

The Irish had fucked up New York first. Okay, okay, maybe the English before them. Then, God help us, the messing up continued. My friends... they didn't hurt anyone. We all just talked.

Those friends were gone. They had to be.

But her friends were here. Lenore's. I started pointing at them, remembering their names from when they had shown up at the island—all for her birthday! There was Jeff, the doctor. Tracey, the nurse. Ali—the damned Arab—was some kind of builder.

That could be good.

Not good.

Useful. Better if his kind had never come. But...

The others. The Chinese guy. Wu. The girl, Maria. The one we all knew. Lenore. The one who hadn't changed when she'd been bitten. I had nothing against Lenore. She was blond and beautiful and they all said that she was talented and worked really hard. But...

Then, of course, the black dude. The gay, black dude. Who didn't like me. It was like he knew that I'd been living with...

A darkness of the soul?

Oh, hell! We just wanted to keep the country... *White? God-fearing, but, of course, you had to fear the right god. What was wrong with that? Did any of it matter at all now?*

It was just us. We were supposed to survive here. Or not.

"Tonight, we have to keep an eye on Lenore—no hard feelings?" Jeff said, talking to her.

"None," she assured him.

"And we need to take turns on guard," Jeff continued.

"Okay. You, me, Dirk, Ali?" Stephen asked.

"We stay awake and watch in twos," Jeff said. Ali, you and Maria. Tracey, we'd better watch with Lenore—at this time, anyway. Stephen... you and Dirk."

Ah, crap, no, anybody but him! I wanted to shout.

I didn't. Neither did he.

And slowly, miserably, with one or more of us breaking down to cry—especially when we buried Tina—the night passed.

And in the night, I told the others about the wells on the island

and that there was a generator; we had to have fuel, of course, but, we might be all right. "They'd" wanted to go clean—the faceless "they" who'd made all decisions for this project—so there were stacks and stacks of solar panels near the garden shed.

Maybe doing things was good. Really, really good. Especially when we all kept watching.

But, Lenore didn't change.

The night went by.

Days went by.

And then weeks.

And in that time, Ali and Maria became a couple.

Jeff was obviously taken with Lenore, and Lenore with him. But, it was as if they didn't want Tracey to feel like a third wheel. They kept it light.

She worked with them all the time, though, of course, sometimes we all worked together. And we rested together, ate berries and the fish we caught, and learned to love seaweed or kelp or whatever, too.

We heard nothing from the mainland.

Nothing from anywhere.

Ali had designed a way to keep a few phones working through solar energy.

But there was no news.

If there were other people out there, they weren't able to communicate.

I think it had been almost four weeks—almost a month—since The Day when the first wave came. Maria and Ali were working in the garden. Jeff, Tracey, and Lenore had gone to the church, determined to gather what linens and vestments they could, anything that might be used for sheets and blankets as the weather changed. I was working out front, drawing up gallons of water with Stephen. We'd gotten going with a kind of silent but decent working relationship.

I looked up.

There were some dinghies that had been pulled up to the broken wharf. Dinghies with zombies getting out of them! Zombies! They'd learned to man and row small boats. All in their pursuit of human flesh!

Damned cannibals!

We had our gardening tools. In the beginning, we'd done well fighting off the bastards with hoes and shovels and picks. We could do so again, but...

There was were so many of them!

Too many to be beaten back.

Ali and Maria were further away. Ali saw Stephen and me. He saw the zombies.

"Run!" he cried.

"Run?" Stephen called back to him. "Run! But, where?"

"Run!" Ali repeated. And then he added, "To the church!"

And so, we did. Of course, there was a wall and a gate around the church. We could hold them off that way, maybe. That had to be what he intended.

We made it to the church. Thank God there were no fast zombies. They, were, in fact, almost pitiably slow.

But, we'd seen them in action.

There was no pity to be taken at this point.

"Through the gate through the gate! Shut it, shut it!"

Jeff, Lenore, and Tracey had heard us. They were there to greet us, to get the gate shut as we raced in. They were armed, too—with all kind of church staffs and staves. They had lit candles, ready to try to burn them if it was necessary.

"Let's get into the church—see what they do. A second line of defense," Ali said.

He was talking to Jeff. He trusted Jeff.

To be honest, so did I.

So, we ran into the church. Once in, we looked out through the stone windows. For a while, we were just tense, taking turns at the little windows. Medieval style, they weren't much more than arrow slits. But we could see the gate.

And for the longest time, there was nothing.

"They're zombies. Dumb zombies," Maria said hopefully.

"Dumb zombies—who came here in boats," Ali reminded her.

"Yes, but..." Lenore said.

"Yes, but what?" Stephen asked her.

"Tina changed; I didn't," she said. "Maybe the church..."

I couldn't help it. I think I'd been changing. They were changing me. But, sometimes, I felt bitter. I laughed. "We've got a Jew, a Buddhist, and a Muslim among us. And you think a church means something?" I asked.

Lenore looked at me. "Yeah, I do," she said softly. Jeff, of course, set his hand on her shoulder.

The two of them. Hell. They had each other.

And Nurse Tracey, of course.

When would it become a threesome, I wondered.

And it was then that the first zombies came creeping over the stone wall that surrounded the church.

Chapter 6

Lenore

They were coming. Slow and ungainly, stupid! But, they knew to get boats to come to the island—they knew there might still be a food supply here!

So many of them.

So very many of them…

Stephen, Dirk, and Ali seemed good at creating fireball cocktails from church oil, linen, and collection baskets. For a while, the fire helped keep their enemy at bay, but then one got through a back window.

And then another.

At first I felt like crying all over again. But, it would do me no good. I couldn't help but think that it had finally come to this.

Custer's Last Stand. Us against the zombies.

They were coming in, and we were being forced back to the massive hole in the floor that dropped straight into the crypts.

This was it. The end.

Oddly, as lonely and as strange as it had been for the past month—as often as we cried for those we knew we had lost—we had found a way to live. And even though it might have been slowly, Jeff and I had been moving toward one another—despite living with a bunch of other people and always having Tracey as part of our work pattern.

While there is life, there is hope, Jeff had told me.

And he had smiled.

And while there is breath, there is life.

But now…

One was upon me. I fell back and went crashing down into the corpses in the crypt beneath the church.

Bone dust darkened the air.

The zombie fell on me...

And didn't move.

I pushed it off. As I did so, it began to change.

The zombie had been a little girl, maybe twelve or thirteen years old. She was tall for her age, and she'd been wearing a tailored shirt and jeans, an outfit that concealed her budding breasts, but as her flesh changed from mottled gray rot to a reddish hue and then something that was almost ivory, the beauty and feminine structure of her face became obvious.

I was holding a stone memorial, ready to crush it over her head. I'd been hearing that strange death rattle as she had come after me, that movement of wind in her lungs.

Now, there was just the sound of breathing.

I like to think I didn't stare at her too long, almost as stunned as I had been when it had all begun.

Because something had happened. Something like...

Science.

Or a miracle.

"The crypt!" I screamed. "Get them into the crypt. It—it heals them!"

I don't think any of them believed me at first, but we were overrun. We were dying. We had nothing to lose.

Jeff dropped down beside me. "The fungus—all the fungus down here. The decay, the rot... something growing. Something growing cures it, just as something biological must have caused it!"

Jeff and I were the only ones in the crypt. The others were herding the zombies in.

His arm was around me—and we were suddenly facing down twenty of them. We backed away, and backed away. I almost fell into a rotten tomb, but Jeff caught me, and a zombie fell in it instead.

And the others were crying out to us.

I could hear Stephen. Always my dear, dear Stephen. But the others were my friends, too, so close. We were so lucky...

So many zombies...

And then, right when it seemed we had nowhere else to go, it took. The fungus as Jeff said—or the miracle, as I believed—took hold.

The zombies fell.

They just fell.

And they began to change, a few were still broken, and screaming in pain. A few died. But, later that night, by the time we waded our way through them, we had another thirty human beings on the island. Human beings who were lost and confused. Coming to grips with what had happened to them.

At first...

And then today.

Salvation Day.

Because miracle or not, we had the cure. And it was a cure that worked almost instantly. When more came, we'd be prepared.

We were alive.

We were breathing.

There was hope.

Chapter 7

Jeff

We took the boats to the tip of Manhattan today. Carefully. With the others who had come—and the amount of those others who were able to be saved—we'd acquired something of a nicely efficient army.

We went for supplies.

We were becoming adept with solar energy. Of course, summer had come.

That helped.

Crops were growing.

Dear Lord, we'd built houses!

That afternoon, though, in Manhattan, I had some very specific plans. We were able to roam the area freely—whatever zombies had been there had died out. Those who hadn't—had moved on. That was the thing—without fresh human flesh, they died out. I'll never understand why, but the cows and chickens and pigs were immune to the virus or bacteria, and those inflicted with it did not want to eat cows or chickens or pigs.

Just other humans.

We stayed on the island, though—for the time being—because we could protect it.

Our little army saw no action that day.

We collected supplies.

And we went home.

We had barely reached the docks—repaired by a very nice work effort led by Ali, thank you very much—when Tracey came running out to me. Her eyes were glistening.

"Oh!" I cried. "It's time!"

"More or less!" she said.

Tracey was with a fellow who had been a Baptist minister and a carpenter before The Day. They were very happy. That had left me able to... well, able to do some things I'd wanted to do for a very long time.

I raced behind Tracey, heading to the little house near the church we had made for ourselves. It had one room, but we'd managed a pretty cool fireplace and quaint little outhouse—for us, at the moment, it was really good.

But I was late. Too late.

I called out with dismay, thinking how much I had failed her. But Lenore, my beautiful Lenore, was laughing and happy. "We have a very good nurse, you know!"

When I came into the room, I saw that we did. Tracey had delivered my son in my absence.

I was shaking as I took him. I managed to kiss Lenore quickly, and then look at Tracey, who smiled and said, "I'm thinking he's about eight pounds, healthy and perfect as can be!"

I thanked her, tears in my eyes, and knelt down by my Lenore. My wife, in my heart, and in my soul, and through the words of our Baptist carpenter minister in the Anglican church.

"He's... he's just fine."

"Well, of course he is—we're all just fine!" she said.

I cried. I hadn't been able to help it.

"What shall we name him?" Lenore asked me softly.

"Adam."

I didn't say it; the word came from the door. It was Stephen who had spoken. He was standing there, next to Dirk. They were both holding a spray of flowers.

I smiled.

They had become a couple, too. Dirk had confessed to me that he'd once been a real ass. Now he'd never been happier. He had Stephen. And, of course, Lenore and I had loved Stephen dearly for years. We couldn't have been happier.

"Adam," I said.

"He is the first to be born in our new world," Lenore whispered, beautiful blue eyes tender as they rested on me, and our child.

"Adam!" I said.

And so he was. Our child.

A special child.

For he was hope.

Hope for the future.

Hope for the human race.

THE SHADOW OF HEAVEN
Jason V Brock

There are more things in heaven and earth…
Than are dreamt of in your philosophy.
  -William Shakespeare, HAMLET 1.5.166
  (Hamlet to Horatio)

I.

"There—I think I see it, Commander."

Ensign Adams's breath disappeared overhead as he lowered his binoculars, pointing with a gloved hand at the unstable horizon through the ice-rimmed main windows of the ship. "Looks like something about ten kilometers out, sir." Backlit by the windows, he turned to face Commander Merritt, the senior officer aboard the destroyer USS *Higgins*. Cloaked in his winter overcoat, the ensign's brittle voice seemed distant in the cold dry air, his words nearly obliterated by the surging wind and unforgiving swells of the squall. Outside, colossal waves, some the size of buildings, slammed the *Higgins*—exploding across the ship's icebound hull in frosty white plumes, adding to the inches-deep transparent slick of frozen seawater on the deck as she plunged further into one of the most hostile environs on the planet: the Southern Ocean. Gales such as this arose suddenly and with terrifying ferocity this close to Antarctica, reducing visibility to a few feet, churning the barren seascape into a foamy lather as it thrust icebergs the size of city blocks into the path of interlopers to this foreboding, isolated part of the world. At times, mighty whitecaps pounded on the destroyer with such titanic fury that they caused the vessel to flinch backward, bobbing like an oversized cork in the roiling black depths.

Merritt, his drawn face numb from the chill, carefully considered the ensign's words, leaning against an interior deck rail to keep his balance as they rocked in the grip of the storm. Bringing his binoculars to his face, he scanned the dead gray interface between leaden sky and dark water beyond the icy windows Adams was motioning toward, noting the faint curtain of blue-green ripples from the southern lights, streaked by rose-colored lightning ribbons in the distance as freezing night collapsed around them. Even on the closed bridge, the saline-tinged atmosphere had gotten so frigid that the inside of his nose crystallized with each breath.

Our luck to be the closest in the vicinity of a distress call.

"Are you sure you saw a vessel? Maybe it was a 'berg,'" the Commanding Officer asked at last.

"It didn't look like an iceberg..." Adams was scrutinizing the horizon as he spoke: "One moment, sir."

As he worked against the storm's fury, the commander was troubled that, in their attempts to discover the exact whereabouts of the missing research ship *Terra Australis Incognita*, they might have gone astray. The weary leader and his crew of just over two hundred were stuck now, committed to the search even as they struggled with the dreadful conditions approximately 300 miles off the coast of West Antarctica—well off-course from their originally assigned bearing based on *Australis's* last communique. Merritt was further aggravated that they had been pulled into this mess just as the *Higgins* was returning for shore leave after a long, tedious mission: Subsonic underwater audio testing. The original search-and-rescue order had instructed them to triangulate the position of the troubled *Australis* once they were within its last known trajectory, but it concerned him that perhaps she had lost power after her final transmission to the Oceanographic Institute of San Diego, drifting farther than anyone had anticipated. That could mean she was gone—especially if these had been the circumstances for her and her crew in the two days it had taken the *Higgins* to re-route.

"Still not seeing it, Adams." Merritt grimaced in frustration.

"Sorry, sir. It was there just a minute ago..."

"Any recent pings, McConnell?" Merritt asked, addressing the Warrant Officer.

The haunting Mayday call that McConnell had picked up as they were adjusting course, scratchy with static and crosstalk, had made it very difficult to decipher who it was, but the co-ordinates and the radar image supported the notion that it had come from Australis. Or at least from a crewmember that might be stranded on the so-called "new islands" that *Australis* had been allowed to detour and inspect by the Institute.

"Negative, sir," McConnell replied.

Contemplative, Merritt lowered his binoculars, sighing in annoyance as he stroked his face. *Throw into the mix that the closer we get to the last known heading of* Australis *the worse the fucking weather gets... the more radio-electronic interference—faulty GPS signals, slow clocks, bad wireless connections. Adds up to a lot of irritating bullshit... Oh well—"Uneasy lies the head that wears a crown," as they say...*

Higgins had endured several of these storms, as powerful as any Merritt had ever encountered in his twenty-plus years as a sailor, in their efforts to find the *Australis*. Peering through his binoculars again as the mammoth destroyer heaved and fell like some vast roller coaster—lights flickering, deck rolling in the strong seas—the senior officer he vaguely made out what the ensign had seen: A shadowy triangular central mass situated among a scattering of large icebergs looming along the periphery of his vision like some ethereal vanguard of the *Flying Dutchman*. He frowned while adjusting the focus ring, his brow wrinkled in annoyance as he squinted past the thickening fog and billowing sea spray. *Christ, it's like something wants to keep us away...*

He glanced over at McConnell, his gray-haired scalp bristling. "You seeing this?"

McConnell worked to keep his footing as he peered through his binoculars. "Aye... *Some*thing. Appears man-made, sir, but hard to make out through the mist and—" A crackle from the headset around his neck interrupted him. Placing the speaker to his ear, he listened intently, then moved over to his station, his dark features pressed into a look of apprehension.

Merritt: "What's happening, McConnell?"

"Not—not sure, sir... There's a lot of static; I thought I heard... A *voice*. It was coming in on the same frequency as the last transmission—"

Continuing to monitor the gloom outside, Adams said, "*Definitely* something there, Commander. Looks to be a modest-sized vessel."

McConnell: "I've got something—putting up on speakers, sir. I have a radar reflection too. One small shape and a few larger masses; the larger areas *could* be land, but hard to say in this climate ... And I checked again—not on our maps."

A smoky haze of static filled the room, pushing back the sounds of the tempest for an instant: <<CH-CH-CH Gree! Mayday! [*blip, blip, blip*] Gree! CH-CH-*ay!* [*blip, blip, blip*]>>

More intense static. Then, garbled: "If you can hear my voice, please acknowledge! [*blip, blip, blip*] ... is not— [*blip, blip, blip*] My name is Christopher Faust, over. [*blip, blip, blip*]... urgent mes— [*blip, blip, blip*]... communicate! Repeat: This is—"

Silence. The wind howled in the sunless tumult outside the *Higgins*, sending chunks of ice and snow to shatter against the windows of the darkened bridge. Lightning seared again: closer, redder, like an eruption of stroboscopic tendrils cracking the black-ice sky into pieces. Distant thunder bellowed.

"McConnell, stay on that frequency, but keep monitoring the others; Adams, your thoughts?"

The young ensign was staring into the starless night, struggling to keep his equilibrium in the storm. "I... I believe it's *Australis*, sir. Who else would be this far from McMurdo? Granted, farther away than we expected her to be, but we heard the distress call... so we're obligated to check it out, Commander."

Merritt looked again, the stiff rubber eyecups of the Steiner chafing his eyelids: Illuminated by flashes of scarlet lightning, the triangular shape appeared to be a bow, with part of a mast attached as well; perhaps a half-submerged wreck, though it was too dim, too turbulent to make out anything definitive.

"Aye," the commander said. "Set a course for it."

II.

"Looks like we've found her, Commander. No one here, though." Ensign Adams released the button on his handheld as he stared into the blue-toned water, the white mast and bow of the sunken *Australis* thrusting up from the briny deep like the hand of a skeleton. The elements had relented since their post-midnight arrival; the ocean was almost peaceful.

At first light, Commander Merritt had deemed it safe enough to dispatch a small advance team of four men through the half-mile or so of chop between the moorage of the *Higgins* and the suspected wreck of the *Australis*. Though slightly overcast, the sun was evident, clear, though quite low on the horizon even now, at midday; it was urgent that they discern what was happening before night fell and the temperatures dropped.

"Roger that, Adams," McConnell replied. "Stand by."

As Adams and his crew of three awaited their next orders on the drifting rigid-hulled inflatable, he studied the *Australis*. It was spooky, surreal. The water here was so clear he could see far down into it, almost to the bridge of the research vessel. Straining, he swore he could see something... something large; a supple darkness—

"Adams, we have something near you, but not from the wreck, over."

Startled from his thoughts by McConnell's gruff drawl, Adams replied: "Roger that. What do you have?"

"Well... there's a signal coming from nearby. The co-ordinates are dodgy, as there seems to be some strange interference. Looks like it's coming from that mass I was explaining from the radar, though. Some seismic disturbances there. I got another signal a while ago like a voice too. See anything? Over."

"Actually, yeah; over to my left there's a big fog bank. Looks like about 800 or so feet away. Could it be from there? Over."

"That's about the proximity of the radar image, over."

Adams brought his binoculars up. As he peered through them, he thought he saw something large move in the mist on the horizon: *What the hell was* that?

"Roger, McConnell. I see something; request permission to investigate, over."

There was a long pause.

"Roger, Adams; weather's returning. Merritt says you've got an hour, over."

III.

"Let us go then, you and I,
When the evening is spread out against the sky—"
Like the Indianapolis at the bottom of the deep ...
Down to a dreamless sleep ...
Drifting,
Spiraling:

IV.

Back onboard the *Higgins*, Adams was shaken, dazed, as he reported what the search party had discovered: "So there *are* some islands, Commander." He looked from Merritt to McConnell as they stood in the infirmary, regarding the apparent sole survivor of the *Australis*: an unconscious man now lying on the sickbay table. "The radar image was correct... We found *Australis*, and there was something else... something deeper in the water, looked like it was poking around in the wreckage—"

"What? Like a seal? A shark or something? Or did you see a body?" Merritt asked, his voice edged.

"I-I can't say; it was some weird... *black*-looking shape, but iridescent too. Like oil on water. It seemed to be part of something else even larger... maybe it was just the water playing tricks on my eyes, or a part of the ship, but..." Adams looked to the floor. "Anyway, after we went through the fog, we all noted that the temperature was rising; it was becoming quite humid, too. I had to lose a jacket I got so warm. Then, as we disembarked onto this beach we landed on, we were accosted by these *giant*... flying bats or something, but with feathers. They were shrieking and carrying on. Sounded very human at times. Like a cat in heat. Our compasses were flipping out, and that's when one of my guys saw a helicopter blade half-buried in the sand. We formed a search line and walked for a mile or so—"

Commander Merritt's hands clenched. "No one authorized that, Adams! You should have radioed—"

"We *tried*, sir. The radios went dead right after we landed, and once we found the pieces of the helicopter... Respectfully, we weren't trying to get into trouble; we just wanted to see if there was anyone hurt—"

McConnell: "He's right, sir. The radios were unresponsive after the first forty-five minutes or so, and they were DOA back onboard."

After a silence, Commander Merritt nodded: "Carry on, Adams. Then what happened?"

"Well, we thought we heard screams—human screams—coming from somewhere up the beach, though the place has strange acoustics; the surf, the wind make it pretty noisy, not to mention those flying things squealing overhead, so it could have been coming from the dense vegetation toward the center of the island. Anyway, after about ten more minutes of walking, we ascended a small dune, and that's where the rest of the helicopter was." Adams swallowed, staring at the C.O. in trancelike, unblinking remembrance. He motioned toward the man on the bed. "We found him like this... Completely nude, crumpled up next to a bunch of half-frozen papers and the debris of the 'copter with the walkie-talkie in his hand. Only a few scratches on him from what we could see, just knocked-out. I'm... *amazed* he's alive," Adams said. His voice was quivering. "How... how could he be *alive*? In those temperatures... *Naked*? I mean it was warmer, but still plenty cold if you're exposed like that. And ... and the helicopter was *demolished*, like there was an accident or something. The bloody clothing next to him had a tag: *Faust*. That's the guy from the transmissions, right, McConnell?"

McConnell was gawking at the man in the infirmary bed, stunned, his hand covering his mouth. He shot a glance at Commander Merritt, whose red-eyed gaze was also fixed on the sleeping man, and nodded. "Tell him about the other thing you brought back, Adams."

Merritt broke away from his thoughts. "There was something else? What?"

Adams swallowed, his face suddenly ashen, and looked to the floor. Merritt looked again at McConnell, who took a deep breath.

"What did Adams bring back, McConnell? Another survivor? Where—"

"No, sir," Adams interrupted. "Not a survivor. It's in another lab; one of the medics is investigating it."

"Well let's go see, Adams," the commander said. He looked at McConnell. "I want to know the *second* this guy comes to."

McConnell nodded again. "Yes, sir."

V.

"Commander, have you heard the term 'globster' before?" Medic Aaron Randolph asked.

"Yes. Like sea monsters or something."

The medic smiled, thin blond hair falling over his forehead, freckled cheeks creasing at the corners of his eyes as he looked between the sullen Adams and his C.O. The ship was beginning to gently roll as night approached and a storm once more buffeted the *Higgins*. "That's *sort of* it, sir. Globsters are… kind of mysterious relics that wash up periodically. They can be hard to identify, as they have features of several different animals, or it *seems* like they do. Almost like the chimeras from Greek mythology. Some people even claim they're 'cryptids'—previously unknown or undocumented creatures, possibly related by era or locale, like the Loch Ness Monster, or Bigfoot. I mean, maybe they are, but it's doubtful; apocryphal accounts of plane wing gremlins, Chupacabras, and moth men make no sense, as they're generally too divergent from one another." Randolph paused, then added: "Of course, there are exceptions. They didn't think Giant Squids, okapis, coelacanths, or Komodo Dragons were real once either. Usually, though, it's a *lot* less interesting than that—they're just pieces of some animal, like that huge blue eyeball that washed up a couple of years back that they now think belonged to a dead marlin, or the badly decayed carcass of a big shark or whale—"

Adams looked up sharply, eyes wide. "That's no whale, Randy. Look again!"

The medic raised his hand: "I hear you. It's weird, alright! But stuff is starting to show up all over; things that were unknown before from the deep, or critters that normally never appear where they're found. Even mass strandings. Happened just recently in L.A.—one day a damn deep sea oarfish washed up, completely intact, then a few days later a barely-living Alaskan saber-toothed whale! They say it might be Global Warming or something, who knows? It's weird, though, and becoming more common. Not sure what *this* thing is; I checked it out under the 'scope, too. It's not like any other specimen we have onboard, that's for sure. The cryptozoologists would *love* it."

Merritt straightened up. "Can I see what you're talking about?"

"Absolutely, Commander. Right this way."

They walked to the rear of the room where the storage freezer and the other autopsy tools were stowed. The medic opened the locker door, pulled a covered tray from inside, and set it on the counter. The tray was about two feet long and over a foot wide; the white cloth covering the specimen barely concealed the bulging object underneath. The medic smiled at the C.O. and the ensign. "It's dense, heavy." He pulled the cloth away unceremoniously.

The thing on the tray was hard to comprehend; there was no

visual context for it. It was a drab gray, mottled with blooms of light pink. On one end, it was severed all the way through, the raw wound displaying its musculature and a core of bone. This side was slender, smooth; toward the other end of its length, there were what appeared to be scales that became an almost chitinous, hard appendage of some type, resembling a fixed-open claw. Within this structure, there was a softer retracted piece with what looked to be a suckered tentacle covered in miniature hooks. This black flesh was pliant, and the appendage seemed to be gently moving within.

Merritt's eyes widened. "Is that thing—"

The medic nodded. "Yes: It's moving. It's been moving since I got it."

Adams spoke at last: "It was moving around next to Faust on the beach. Pretty vigorously."

"Jesus. What the hell *is* it?" Merritt asked, stepping back in revulsion. "And that smell! Is that—"

"Yes," Randolph confirmed. "As it warms up, it starts emanating that strange odor... Like plastic burning."

The intercom interrupted them: "Commander Merritt, this is McConnell. Faust is awake, sir. Not said anything yet, but he woke up a little while ago."

The senior officer looked from Adams to Medic Randolph to the slowly writhing thing on the countertop. "Keep me posted on this, Randolph; I want to know what you find out about the microscopic results. Christ—gives me the fucking *creeps*. Let's go, Adams."

Merritt thumbed the button on the wall speaker: "Roger that, McConnell. On the way."

VI.

Drifting,
Spiraling:
The breath of a sigh,
Or the blink of an eye
Is all that it takes;
And then the dreamer wakes—

VII.

"Faust. My name is Christopher Faust," the man on the bed replied. His voice was weak, strangled.

Commander Merritt: "Were you with the *Australis* crew?"

Faust nodded; his gaze was distant, fixed on something just beyond the officer. Ensign Adams watched Merritt as he continued to question the man. "Where are the other members of your crew? Did they go inland?"

Faust nodded again. "Yes. Three... of them went to the center of the island. We started with nine. I was... the aviator." Faust's voice was curiously flat and atonal. He never made eye contact, just kept his gaze fixed straight ahead. "We... were attacked."

"'Attacked?'" Merritt shared a surprised look with Adams. "What do you mean? By whom?"

"Not whom—*what*."

"Okay, then," Adams said. "What?"

Faust slowly, mechanically, turned his head toward the ensign, his eyes staring forward. "By... the things in the air. The things from the sea."

There was a tense silence.

"Okay, Airman Faust," Merritt said at last, forcing a smile. "You've had a rough time. Let's reconvene this later, once you've been able to regain your strength."

Faust methodically turned to face Merritt again, features slack, rubbery, eyes unblinking.

"They're... alive on the *inside*, Commander. Three of them went to the center of the island."

Merritt nodded. "We'll see if we can—"

"And then," Faust interrupted, "the dreamer wakes."

Adams gasped, and the C.O.'s head snapped back in astonishment.

"What?" Merritt stammered, "What did you say, Faust?"

"The dreamer has *awakened*."

After a long and uncomfortable silence, Adams signaled Merritt to step out of the quarters.

"Let's go over and visit Randy again, sir," the ensign said as the two men moved away from the infirmary.

VIII.

"Wow. That's really *weird*," Medic Randolph said. "What does it mean? Is it from a book or something?"

Adams huffed. "Yeah, I'll say... it's from a weird dream *I've* been having—"

"And every time you nap or go to sleep," Merritt interjected, "this dream picks up at *exactly* the same place... Same strange feeling, same bizarre imagery, right?"

Adams stared at Merritt, his mouth hanging open. Finally: "Yes."

A cold sweat broke out on the C. O.'s body, yet he felt too warm. "I've been having it, too. Started around the time that we began looking for the *Australis*. Just shy of a week ago—"

"Oh shit, this is freaking me out, sir!" Adams exclaimed, plopping into a chair in Randolph's lab.

The medic stared at the two men who seemed suddenly unable to communicate. "Pretty strange. *Twilight Zone*-type stuff... Well, not to add *too* much more weird to it, sir, but I found something... *interesting* during the microscopic exam."

Merritt cleared his throat, rubbed his eyes, then turned his attention to Randolph. "Okay. What have you learned?"

"It's odd, I'll give you that, but just hear me out a minute..."

The medic sat down with the others, grabbed a pen and some paper and started writing and sketching. After a few moments, he began to explain his findings: "So this organism is... *unusual* physiologically. Perhaps you're familiar with the concept of the Hayflick Limit?"

Merritt shook his head.

"Well," the medic continued, "it's an observation in genetics. Basically, it's the idea that there are physical limits to the number of times a cell can divide... under certain conditions these limitations are able to be chemically or virally circumvented, avoiding the natural process of cellular suicide known as apoptosis. This thing not only looks to have solved this problem, but also has a 'workaround' for the shortening of telomeres as a creature ages. Conceptually, telomeres are the ends of genes that are worn down by cell division; imagine that they're like the little plastic caps on the tips of shoelaces that keep them from fraying. 'Younger' telomeres keep the genes viable. This is also the case with several cancers—that they can keep the telomeres 'young'—as a result, damage arises, in part, due to *unchecked* cellular division. Normally that's a good thing, as it would impact the length of the telomeres negatively, thus applying a kind of brake to out-of-control division—" Randolph drew some examples on the paper to assist the visualization; Merritt nodded for him to continue.

"Anyway, from what I can tell with this thing, there's very rapid, *controlled* cellular division, and an ability to deliberately allocate cell speciation. So in a way, these tissues have *characteristics* of a tumor, but without the need for a continuous—or in this instance *any*—blood supply, as they appear to take oxygen directly from the atmosphere; the integument acts as a porous gas exchange membrane, similar to the way insects breathe, but more complex. Sort of like an external lung." The medic glanced over to Adams who seemed to understand.

"So what does that mean?" Adams asked, leaning forward.

Medic Randolph tilted back in his chair and crossed his arms. "Not clear, but it looks like it makes these cells immortal. Not only that, but there's another strange element..." Randolph returned to the sketch paper. "See where I drew this? Here, and here?"

Adams and Merritt nodded their heads in understanding.

"It appears these cells are peculiar hybrids of some kind. They have aspects of genetic mosaicism, and are these little... *independent units*... they're like tiny mirrors of the larger organism—"

Merritt: "I'm not following."

Adams picked up the explanation: "What I think it means," he said as he glanced at Randolph, "is that *each* cell is a microcosm of the complete organism."

"Exactly: All of the material is there; each cell appears to have a pluripotent cellular reserve. It's not only immortal, like certain jellyfish, but *self-organizing*, completely contained within itself. And not only that," Randolph said, "but it seems that *every* cell is on some level ... *conscious* for lack of a better word—"

"What are you saying, Randolph?" Merritt asked, touching his temple as he struggled to understand.

"I'm saying, Commander, that the *cells* react not just as cells—meaning with respect to extreme heat, cold and some of the chemical agents I've applied to both the biopsy cultures and the entire appendage—but they cannot be 'killed' in the normal sense of the term; they regenerate, and relatively quickly. Not only that—they behave as though they have a type of 'collective awareness' and each can respond accordingly to the stimuli or circumstances as either A) a unified being, or B) as an autonomous *piece* of that organism, thus ensuring survival at *all* costs. They even seem to be able to absorb and replicate other proteins, which gives them the ability to... *become* that protein."

Adams laughed without humor. "Oh my *God*. You mean like that fucking '80s movie?"

Randolph looked surprised. "Yeah, actually. Quite protean. Just like that, or *Invasion of the Body Snatchers*. There are other examples in nature microscopically, and so on. Besides, this isn't quite the same. I seriously *doubt* this is an alien; it's probably just an evolutionary strategy. Most likely a viral thing, or at least started that way. Hell, turns out a shitload of our so-called 'junk DNA' is comprised of retroviruses that functionally seem to have no purpose now. Might've had some uses at one time, but those uses are genetically 'turned off', 'cause we don't need them due to the way we've evolved. Proof of that is the way our wounds heal; we have most of the same DNA as, say, a salamander, but they can regenerate arms and legs, and we can't. We just scar over."

Merritt's head was swimming. "So what did you do with the—"

"With the specimen?" Adams finished.

Randolph nodded toward the storage freezer. "In there; won't hurt it, but slows it down quite a bit. In fact, I noticed that the severed part is re-growing. Looks like it's trying the re-create the missing body."

"Shit! How do we rid of the fucking thing?" Merritt was genuinely alarmed.

Randolph assured him: "No worries, sir. It needs a *lot* of oxygen to facilitate this process. It's fairly immune to temperature extremes, but it can't stay submerged—kills the tissue in a matter of minutes based on my tests; of course, seems likely that a completely ... *integrated* organism might be able to overcome that problem. Could be multiple types of organisms, too: They reported other strange creatures there, right?" He paused, noting the concern on the C.O.'s features. "But with respect to this thing, Commander, don't be too worried—it takes a while to re-grow whole pieces. Probably a few days or more depending on size, maybe longer. The absorption trick is faster, but has similar limitations; I mean it's an 'organic machine' in a way, so while the duplicated components are nearly perfect, they occupy a state between being alive and dead. Besides," Randolph said, shrugging, "this is the find of a *lifetime*—we need to bring it back with us."

Before Merritt could mount a protest, the intercom sounded: McConnell.

"Commander, something... *interesting* is happening. Could you please report to the bridge?"

"What is it?" Merritt asked, pressing the switch.

"The ship near the island, the *Indianapolis* has—"

Adams gave a stunned look to Merritt: "Did you say *Indianapolis*, McConnell?" There was a pause.

"Sorry, sir. I'm tired, and I've been having this crazy dream... I mean the *Australis*—she's completely sunk now."

IX.

Equipped with sidearms, survival gear, and machetes, they returned to the island the next morning. Once on the beach, Faust stoically led Adams, Merritt, and three others into the forest at the center. McConnell had briefed them of increasing seismic activity during the past day, warning them to be mindful of possible tremors.

Overhead, huge bird-creatures the size of small cars swooped and pirouetted in the overcast sky; as the team was making its landing in the surf, Adams managed to photograph a bizarre, man-sized purple and red mega-crab exoskeleton that was drifting in a backwater near some crags. As was the previous case, compasses, radios, and GPS devices became unreliable.

Inside the canopy, the kaleidoscope of brilliantly-plumed flowers, lush plants, and fantastically odd-looking—even menacing—giant insects was overwhelming: The place was an explosion of noise, a jumble of odors, a riot of color. The weather had graced them with a fortunate reprieve.

"Christ, the biodiversity of this place is unbelievable. It's covered with all manner of independent ecosystems," Adams observed, slicing through the thorny undergrowth with his blade, face slicked with sweat. Merritt nodded in breathless agreement, but before he could speak, an awful shriek peeled through the tangled wilderness. It was human: female.

"Faust, you mentioned that *Australis* had a woman on board?" Merritt asked, wiping sweat away with his sleeve. They paused, quietly trying to ascertain the direction that the scream had come from.

"Yes." Faust replied, staring at Merritt, his face waxen, his demeanor indifferent. After another moment, he pointed. "That way."

X.

The breath of a sigh,
Or the blink of an eye
Is all that it takes;
And then the dreamer wakes—
"What if Earth
Be but the shadow of Heaven, and things therein?"

XI.

The explorers had reached an opening in the mega-flora, the evident remnants of a collapsed volcano caldera: It was hot, humid; the otherworldly antithesis of Antarctica. Even more incredibly, inside the caldera were the apparent ruins of a vast city, with indications of a long dead, yet obviously advanced, civilization. Merritt was in a state of mental shock as the team hacked away at more overgrowth: Caressing the intricate stone buildings, marveling at the complex etchings which scored the coarse rock edifices, some more than three stories tall, he was astonished that this place existed, and wondered about the people that had carved these stones. *How many other places are like this on Earth, just waiting to be uncovered?* The commander took note of the sky: It was getting dark, and he observed that, strangely, there were no animals or insects to be found in this area. The heavy air was still, musky, preternaturally quiet.

"Help... Help us!" It was a hushed, breathy cry from somewhere in the twilight.

Merritt: "Adams! Did you hear that?"

The rest of the search crew paused to listen. Once more: "Help..."

Deep in the interior, the landing party found her: Julia Murphy—former crewmember of the *Terra Australis Incognita*.

What was left of her, at least.

XII.

As the Moon's shadow eclipses the Sun,
So Man stumbles; and thus ends his run—

XIII.

Murphy was lying in a supine position, naked on the ground near one of the buildings: The dim light from the sky overpowered the brilliant light originating from large, ornate green and blue fungi covering the lower part of her torso and obliterating her legs. As they watched, the men could see the carnivorous fungus creeping across her skin, dissolving it and fueling their grim, heatless glow.

"Help me... Please help... " Her face was sweaty, her breath shallow, her dry lips cracked.

Even though he was horrified, Merritt felt compelled to act, and rushed past the stunned group to get near the stricken woman. "I'm Commander Scott Merritt, of the USS *Higgins*." Leaning closer to her, he swallowed back a stab of bile, fighting a surge of nausea at the sickly sweet odor coming from her mouth. His mind was racing as he suddenly yearned to be home with his family. He felt for this poor girl; she reminded him not only of his wife, but also of all the things he most cherished, that he was compelled to do anything to protect. She smiled wanly, then unleashed a blood-freezing scream of agony. Merritt's chest thundered in pity and terror.

"It... it chased us in here... " Julia's bony arms were shriveled, drawn into a pugilistic formation, Merritt noticed; he distantly remembered that as a sign of neurological damage: The fungus was aggressive—moving from the exposed viscera of her guts and over her chest by fractions of inches in just a few minutes.

"It chased us... into the city... then... Captain Roland slipped. That... that was him." She motioned with her head to a blackened knot of dehydrated shapes; even the bones had been dissolved by the fungus; the only thing remotely humanoid was its general size and form, and possibly a lump that resembled the jawless head of a lamprey. The ground rocked slightly, followed by a low rumble, not unlike thunder in the distance: a very minor quake. "Dr. Crowe tried to save him... but... it got him too."

"There were three of you?" Merritt asked, face softly illuminated by the surreal glow of the predatory fruiting bodies, as eerie and distressing as a corpse candle. Merritt suddenly understood why there were no other animals here: The area was overrun by the creeping fungi—dimly glowing all around as the daylight extinguished. The other patches were smaller; less recently fed he suspected, and the whole place was littered with similar black masses to the erstwhile Capt. Roland.

Other animals! Jesus, it's like this whole island is alive.

"My God…" Adams had made the same mental connection just then: "We have to *leave*, sir! It's trying to lure us in!"

"No!" Julia screamed. *"Save me!"* At that instant, her mouth exploded outward with slimy black mold, the lower portion of her face collapsing like a deflated mask, the eyeballs falling into the pulsating, radiant mass of mushrooms and bloody tissue.

Merritt screamed. He jumped backward in abject horror and panic as the fungus consumed the girl.

Too late.

XIV.

Thus ends his run—
"I should have been a pair of ragged claws
Scuttling across the floors of silent seas."

XV.

On the *Higgins*, McConnell was frustrated.

He had not been able to raise anyone for hours, and now the party was stranded on the island for the night. Even though they had been lucky with the weather most of the day—no way that could hold much longer—the seismic readings had spiked recently. He felt a certain amount of dread that a major event was likely in the immediate future. Something about the whole scenario deeply disturbed him, but he was hard-pressed to articulate exactly what it was; the sooner they abandoned this godforsaken place, the better he would feel. It reminded him of when he was working on the blowout after the *Deepwater Horizon* disaster in the Gulf of Mexico, not far from his hometown of New Orleans. The name of the well prospect had been Macondo, just like the fictional town created by Gabriel

García Márquez in his books. McConnell recalled that those had been nightmarish times, almost as surreal as the events in some of Márquez's works, as though the Earth was finally rebelling against the insult of humans overreaching their assumed dominion. BP, Transocean, and Halliburton covered up a lot, but there were things he had seen that still sickened him: trapped sea turtles burned alive; birds drowning because they were too heavy to fly away due to the thick crude slicking their bodies; massive, undocumented beachings as animals tried to escape the toxic sludge of oil, methane, and chemical dispersant. There had been other things; rumors of something else that had been discovered in the blowout, barely held in check by the final cap of the well. Some said it could never be capped permanently, and it was a matter of time before the fissures on the seafloor created by the disaster fractured to a point that whatever was there would become active again.

Adding to this anxiety, McConnell was exhausted; the strange dreams had been intensifying during the past two days the *Higgins* had been anchored near the uncharted atoll.

"Commander Merritt, Ensign Adams, come in. Over." Static, a little radio interference. All freqs.

McConnell was homesick too. They were scheduled for some leave after this last deployment researching low-frequency sonar, and he was glad to be done with it; the heartbreaking damage to the whales and their hearing was obvious when the dead ones floated to the surface. Who knew what else it did to the fragile marine environment, but they had documented some things, from devastating ecosystems to destabilizing underwater superstructures. *Where did it all end? Not with massive underwater blowouts, apparently, or man-made earthquakes in the Midwest caused by hydraulic fracking, or the murder of animals caused by human intervention in their environments...* He felt it was all so destructive, unnatural, evil.

"This is McConnell. Do you read, Adams? Over."

XVI.

Faust led the way out of the ruins; along with Commander Merritt, the horrific fungus had claimed two other men. Finally, on the beach, as faintly bioluminescent waves lapped the windswept shore, hissing into the dark sand, Adams could see the lights of the

Higgins off in the frigid distance. His walkie-talkie was useless; luckily their flashlights still worked for the time being. The ground shook again, adding to the tension on the beach.

"Great! We're trapped here on this insane fucking *rock* until morning..." Adams lamented, looking from the silent Faust to the other man, his breath trailing into the void. The man was a young enlisted that he vaguely recognized, but could not place by name. "And you are?"

"Seaman Recruit Anderson, sir." The man was visibly upset, but also seemed relieved to be on the strand, even in the extreme cold of the pre-dawn. "Never seen nothing like that back home in North Carolina, sir. Whatever had that girl... It was *bad*. Something *real bad*."

Adams nodded in a feeble attempt at reassurance, turning to face the *Higgins* out at sea, mentally struggling to figure out what to do next. "Yes, it sure—"

Abruptly, Faust tackled Adams from the rear, slamming him to the ground. The two thrashed on the damp earth while the stunned Anderson looked on, his light starkly flaring over the men writhing on the black sand. As they fought, Faust gained the upper hand, biting into Adams's cheek and savagely tearing a meaty chunk of flesh from the ensign's face, laying bare teeth, gums, bone. Adams was too panicked to think or feel—he reacted by unsheathing his machete and swinging wildly, yelling into the cold, dry night air...

The heavy blade found its mark, and cleanly separated Faust's arm from his body: He never screamed or made a sound, but in the cool LED illumination of Anderson's flashlight, a strange, acrid black smoke poured forcefully from both ends of the bloodless stump. Faust's mouth twisted in a silent mockery of pain; already the severed arm was crawling away in the surf, the end bulging with new growth, as the stump on his body began to display the withered approximation of a regenerated appendage, covered in mucus and red gore. Overcome by the bizarre tableau, Anderson and Adams screamed in unified revulsion.

Faust, bloodied and determined, came at them, his half-formed arm quickly developing into a grisly, formidably hooked caricature of a human limb. Then his mouth opened, splitting past the natural hinge of his jaw as a great beaked face—its knobby flesh translucent all the way to an eyeless skull tufted by a delicate lattice of pinfeathers matted with opalescent slime—erupted from the gaping, bloody maw that had been Christopher Faust, but was no longer. The same vaporous black smoke spewed from his destroyed facial orifices, obscuring the flashlight beam.

As the creature closed the distance between the stunned sailors, the entire island unexpectedly shifted... half-sinking into the deep, flooding the beach and creating an enormous wave as the morning sun seeped redly above the horizon.

It was beginning.

XVII.

"I should have been a pair of ragged claws
Scuttling across the floors of silent seas."
A pause—
A revelation—
A comprehension—
"The other shape,
If shape it might be call'd that shape had none
Distinguishable in member, joint, or limb;
Or substance might be call'd that shadow seem'd,
For each seem'd either—black it stood as night,
Fierce as ten furies, terrible as hell,
And shook a dreadful dart. What seem'd his head
The likeness of a kingly crown had on."

XVIII.

"Shit!"

McConnell felt the shockwave on the *Higgins* just as he was about to drift off to sleep. It rolled past the ship, causing it to lurch sideways in the water. Looking from his porthole, he could see the breaking dawn just clear the horizon, touching the clouds with fire. *Where are the islands?* Then he saw... *it*, and had to rub his bleary eyes in disbelief.

It started as a soft rolling on the water; then an object more than a mile across thrust up from the sea, perhaps a couple of hundred feet from the USS *Higgins*. The shape dwarfing the destroyer was vast; it seemed to sparkle from within as though some swallowed, ancient-future galaxy shone through its ebon, sea-drenched skin. In another eternal instant, the great being—dripping with kelp and seawater, glimmering in the vivid dawn like some unearthly, newborn titan—reared up to its full, multi-storied height.

McConnell's bladder voided unconsciously when he realized it was alive, and many thoughts crossed his mind: *Was this Satan? Or maybe an angel... Mother said that angels were fearsome creatures, not these little winged babies... Perhaps this was God itself?*

Gripping the window, his knuckles taut as he stared at the dreadful leviathan, McConnell's mind began to disengage. Somewhere, far away, it seemed, the sound of his ragged screams deafened him, as his overwhelmed consciousness tried to understand this being, to grasp the purpose of its hideous beauty. On the misty horizon, he noticed another giant rising up; this one was slightly different, but just as enormous... distantly, there was yet another on the skyline... and then another... They seemed to pull the very light from the firmament, gradually enrobed by wispy fringes of nightfall—as though their presence created a void in the fabric of life itself. As he watched, a great vortex began swirling in the ocean around the behemoth, slowly opening up and swallowing the destroyer... It was at that moment he realized something had changed in the world, and before the icy sting of Antarctic saltwater filled his nose and mouth, McConnell realized how lucky he was—indeed everyone aboard the doomed *Higgins* was—to be spared the horrors yet to come.

The great thing howled and his brain jellied, his ears bled, but the last thing McConnell saw before his consciousness was snuffed by the incomprehensible and his corneas stiffened from the freezing cold of the sea rushing in to fill him—to crush him, to wipe him from the memory of humankind—was the baleful sun blotted out by the extension of terrible, massive wings.

RESISTANT
Tori Eldridge

Kallie ignored the grasping hands and contorted faces as she hurried down the corridor, grateful for the level-three biosafety gear that insulated her from their misery. To them, she was another hooded white suit with goggles and mask. To her, they were overwhelming.

She focused her gaze straight ahead, trying to ignore the pleas for outlawed drugs. Everyone claimed to understand the prohibitions until it applied to them.

And these days, Kallie thought, it always applied to them.

A hand grabbed her arm and yanked her back to a gurney.

"Please, help me. Can't you see?"

She did. The welting rash and lesions had disfigured what might have been a handsome face. Syphilis. Such an easy disease to cure in her grandparents' day now delivered a death sentence. She shook her head and pried his swollen fingers from the sleeve of her coverall.

Her attending physician had warned the first-year residents about succumbing to pity and the repercussions of breaking the law. Not only would they lose their medical license, they'd serve a minimum of ten years in prison and get fined three times the amount of their school loans, which in her case, would indenture her parents to the government for the rest of their lives. And these punishments didn't even begin to address the ramifications to humanity. So while Kallie's heart ached for this doomed man, she would leave him for the hospital orderlies. No antibiotic Hail Mary to stave off the inevitable; just a curtained slot in the Palliative Care Ward where he would live out the rest of his miserable existence.

Or until he requested physician-assisted suicide and signed the release for a lethal dose of secobarbital.

"Someone will come for you soon." She hurried away before he could ask any more from her. "Damn," she muttered, sniffing and wishing for the hundredth time she could touch her face without the risk of spreading deadly pathogens. "Save the ones you can, Kallie. Save the ones you can."

No more distractions. Grandpa's forgetfulness had delayed the family carpool by twenty minutes and Kallie had been making up time ever since she entered the suit room of the hospital. She ran her hand up the front of her neck, checking for the umpteenth time that she had zipped the coverall to the chin and properly secured the cup-shaped N100 particulate mask over her nose and mouth.

The respiratory mask was designed to filter 99.97 percent of any germs she might encounter in the ER triage. Not a hundred percent, but then neither was the PAPR hood she was required to wear in the ER's airborne transmission wing. While many of her colleagues wore the level-four security hood even in the lower risk wings of the ER, Kallie preferred the comfort, visibility, and humanity she gained by wearing only the required mask and goggles: Suffering patients needed to see a caring physician, not a hazmat worker. Besides, the protection was almost identical.

Provided the mask fit.

Kallie sighed, steaming the lower half of her face. Just last week, a triage nurse with an improperly fitted mask had died after a child with influenza coughed in her face. The deadly strain killed the nurse in thirty hours. Kallie shook her head with regret. The paramedics should have recognized the extreme hazard and wheeled the girl directly to the airborne transmission wing. Instead they brought her to triage. Now a compassionate nurse with an ill-fitted mask was dead.

All because of a flu.

Kallie clenched her hands, frustrated by the injustice. Her grandfather claimed he had caught influenza dozens of times when he was young with rarely more treatment than rest, juice, and chicken soup. When that didn't work, his pediatrician had prescribed an antiviral. To a child! If that weren't hard enough to fathom, Grandpa said his parents used to get annual flu shots at the grocery store. Kallie could hardly imagine a world where death could be avoided so easily. Then again, the drugs and vaccines that had saved Grandpa and his parents from the flu had doomed the rest of humanity to uber-virulent, deadly-toxic superbugs.

How was she supposed to feel about that? Ashamed that her own relative had contributed to the problem? Or grateful he had lived to have children and grandchildren? After all, without Kallie, Dr. Raje would have no one to berate.

Kallie slipped through the open door and took a place behind her fellow residents, wishing for once she wasn't five-feet-ten.

Dr. Raje's face wrinkled like a stewed prune when he saw her. "Nice of you to grace us with your presence, Dr. Anderson. We were just discussing options for this patient's patellar fracture. Dr. Holmes believes we should cast it and send him to the second-floor general ward. Dr. Kwok suggests surgery and admittance to the third-floor infection ward. Perhaps you'd like to share your wisdom on the topic."

Kallie frowned. The patient, Eddie Spinks, had shattered his kneecap, and the chances of a comminuted fracture healing on its own in a cast were slim to none. More likely, he would suffer chronic pain and lifelong disability. And then there was the floating fragment to consider: Not only would the displaced bones knit improperly in a cast, the fragment would likely cause a deadly infection. On the other hand, cutting him open would almost certainly kill him.

Kallie took a breath and delivered a careful response. "Assuming he survived, the patient would have a better chance of full recovery with the surgery. Casting the knee is slightly less risky, but it would probably cripple him. I think the patient should be presented with the risk/reward statistics for both procedures then allowed to make his own decision."

Dr. Raje snorted. "And the hospital? What about the risks to us?"

Kallie bowed her head. Now that mankind had entered the era of antimicrobial resistance, doctors made decisions based on hospital liability and global responsibility. The patient had no say. She knew this. She just didn't accept it. Kallie had become a doctor to cure patients, not protect hospitals. And while she cared about the future of humanity, she didn't believe all the doomsday predictions and cautionary restrictions shoveled into the news.

What happened to the cool futuristic notions of the past? The hovercrafts and space elevators to the Moon and Mars? The body scanners that could detect illness in seconds? The nanotechnology and medical breakthroughs that were supposed to make disease obsolete?

Kallie stifled a snort of derision. Money for those fantastic advancements had been consumed by humanity's fight for existence.

Dr. Raje dropped the patient's chart into the slot at the foot of the bed with a decisive clank. He had given up waiting for Kallie's answer, if indeed he ever expected one. As Kallie watched her fellow residents follow Dr. Raje to the next bed, she peeked at the chart for the verdict: The fractured patella would be cast.

Kallie sighed again.

Sighing was becoming a regular occurrence and one her mother feared would harm her matchmaking score. Kallie didn't care. So what if disgruntled suitors marked her down a couple of stars? She didn't crave motherhood, and she had no desire to leave the people she loved to join some stranger's family. Kallie would rather never experience the supposed joys of sex than have her actions governed by another tribe's hierarchy.

All for the sake of safety.

Everything about her life felt controlled and monitored; and she hated it. Kallie didn't need the government, the Global Health Association, or anyone else telling her what to do. She knew how infectious diseases spread and, unlike the general population, could easily test any suitors for hostile microbes or genetic incompatibility—after all, her best friend worked in CADLab, California's most advanced diagnostic laboratory. But that wasn't how society worked. Children grew up in the shelter of their family compounds, attended virtual schools, and played with germ-safe siblings. When the hormones kicked in, suitable matches were found through online services and the young women—or sometimes teenage girls—were married off into other families while carefully chosen brides were brought in for the young men.

Civilization hadn't boldly expanded to the stars; it had shrunken into fearful tribes.

The patient on the ER triage table shifted then groaned. Patellar fractures were painful. Without surgery, Eddie Spinks would likely be moved to the palliative care floor along with the man dying from syphilis and every other terminally infected or contaminated patient.

The seventh floor was so crowded, the hospital had patients bedded in slots like cattle waiting for slaughter, which is exactly what they were. What difference did it make if Ebola—the cure for which had been discovered and discarded decades ago when the virus became resistant—ripped through the ward? It would be a blessing.

The hospital hazmat team could clear the corpses and sterilize the entire floor by morning. She knew: She'd seen it done.

"Hey, doc. What they gonna to do with me?"

Eddie Spinks was thirty-four—only five years older than Kallie—strong, athletic, probably the main support for his clan. He had crashed his motorcycle in the rain while hauling a dinette set harnessed to his back.

She patted his good ankle and forced a smile. "They're going to take good care of you."

"Yeah? Don't sound like it. I heard what you said about being crippled and all. Think I'd rather get cut open." He paused, waiting for a different verdict. None came. "Yeah. Figured as much. Thing is, my kin ain't strong enough to fetch the groceries. And now that guy run me over and bust up Jacob's bike… " He let that thought drift unfinished. "Heck, they don't even know I'm here."

Kallie checked the chart. "I'd call, but I don't see a number."

Eddie scoffed then flinched as the action jolted his knee. "We don't got a phone."

Kallie nodded with understanding. If his family lived below technology level, they also wouldn't have a computer, let alone a monitor wall like the one in her family's media room where her cousins attended school. How had Eddie gotten an education? From his kin? She doubted Ma and Pa had done a very good job.

"Where do you live?"

Eddie shrugged, carefully this time so as not to jostle the knee. "What difference it make? Not like anyone's gonna drive to Hidden Springs."

"Where's Hidden Springs?"

He gave her a look that said she'd just proved his point.

Kallie glanced at her residency team to make sure her absence hadn't been noted.

"How about a neighbor? Is there someone I could call who could run the message over to your folks?"

He shook his head. "None that got a phone. Besides, who would take the risk? I mean, it's not like my kin's sick or nothin'. But you never know, right?"

Kallie nodded. His neighbors were probably just like hers: keeping to themselves, terrified of germs, donning masks and clothes that covered every inch of skin no matter how hot the weather.

Except in Kallie's neighborhood, people could order what they needed online and have those deliveries left on stoops, where they could be sterilized before being brought into homes. Eddie's tribe couldn't do that.

She slid Eddie's chart back into the slot.

"What about Jacob? He'll want to know what happened to his bike, won't he?"

Eddie grunted. "Blast Jacob to hell. Him and his damn ideas. Why else that truck run me into the wall?"

"I thought you were in an accident. If this was hit and run, we have to call the police."

"I ain't callin' no police. Besides, Jacob worked for the government. If they're trying to kill him, cops ain't gonna do nothin' for me except let them know they got the wrong guy."

"What are you talking about? And who is this Jacob?"

Eddie snorted. "He could teach you a thing or two about infections—you and that uppity doctor."

Kalie grit her teeth. "Is that so? Well then I guess it's too bad he isn't here to help you."

"Nah. Jacob's smart, but he ain't no doctor. Used to work in a lab with germs and rats. Won't tell me doing what. Gotta be something top secret, though. Otherwise, why would someone try and kill him?"

"Why are you so sure someone was trying to kill him? Maybe the driver didn't see your bike. Ever thought of that?"

Eddie snorted louder. "I had a table strapped to my back. You tellin' me a driver couldn't see me? No. Someone mistook me for Jacob sure as shit. And now I'm gonna die." He shook his head. "Dumb bad luck."

Kallie sighed, wishing she had followed the rest of her team. Hadn't Dr. Raje warned her about engaging patients in conversation? Only every other day.

"You're not going to die, Mr. Spinks; but I'll call someone better equipped to talk you through these fears you're experiencing."

"I don't want no shrink. What I need is help for my kin."

Kallie gazed longingly at her team, who had moved on to a patient Kallie recognized from six months ago—an African-American boy with osteosarcoma. Since there were only a few palliative options to consider, her team wouldn't linger over his chart. Treating cancer had become a thing of the past. You either beat it, or you didn't. The Global Health Association had long since banned the use of cell-killing chemotherapy and radiation treatments that often led to skin infections. Doctors still performed surgeries on occasion but only the ones with the lowest risk of infection, and never on or near bacterial-rich gastric organs. No. After rejecting Eddie's relatively low-risk knee surgery, a conservative doctor like Patel would never approve pelvic surgery for a patient with such a dismal chance of survival. All of this meant Kallie could afford another minute with Eddie Spinks.

"You said you're the only one strong enough to do grocery runs; why does it take strength? Doesn't your family have a car?"

"Nope."

Kallie stifled another sigh. She should have known better than to ask. If Eddie's family lived below the technology level, they wouldn't be able to afford their one government-allotted car.

"How about mass transit? I know it's risky, but the UV blasts at the doors really do help; and the side effects are minimal compared to the disinfectants they used to use."

Eddie shook his head. "Pop built our place next to a river in the San Gabriel Wilderness after the government stopped funding the parks. Not too many folks live out there; survivalists mostly." He chuckled. "Guess everyone's a survivalist now."

Kallie smiled. "Some more than others. I'm still a city girl."

"Yeah. Can't see you packin' your gear down the river bank. Probably fall in and mess up that nice white suit."

Kallie pinched her lips into an annoyed grin. Bad enough she had to stuff herself into these sausage suits every morning without some hick patient making fun of her.

"Okay," she said, with an edge in her voice. "Time for me to go."

***

As much as she tried, Kallie couldn't get Eddie Spinks out of her head. Even when the paramedics rolled in the dying firefighter and she pressed her gloved hand against his gashed belly to stanch the blood, thoughts of Eddie lingered. Or more accurately—thoughts of Jacob.

What did the former government man know about infections that Kallie and Dr. Raje did not?

"Have you got it, Dr. Anderson?" asked Dr. Raje.

"Yes," Kallie said, pinching the ruptured intestine. "Give me a clamp."

The next twenty minutes passed with focused attention, relieving Kallie's mind of nagging questions. They returned when she dumped the contaminated gloves.

What did Jacob know? What kind of work did he do for the government? Was he a fabrication of a psychotic mind? Was Eddie Spinks an attention-grabbing liar?

Kallie snapped on a clean pair of gloves. She had another thirty minutes before the end of her shift; then she'd pay Mr. Spinks another visit—and order a psych evaluation for the morning.

***

As it turned out, Kallie's next task took her across the hall from the ER room Eddie shared with the osteosarcoma boy and a construction worker who had severed his hand.

Kallie glanced at their room while she gave her sleeping patient a cursory inspection. The woman had arrived screaming from a virulent urinary tract infection. Dr. Raje had ordered a morphine drip to spare her—and everyone else in the ER—from her anguish. Would Dr. Raje do the same for Eddie when his infection set in? No. By then, Eddie Spinks would have become someone else's problem.

Kallie released the woman's limp wrist and glanced at the clock. Visiting hours had ended. A straggler ambled out of the room across the hall. A construction worker checking up on his buddy? The uncle of the dying boy? Certainly, no friend of Eddie's. No one knew he was here, which reminded her that someone had to contact his family.

Kallie gritted her teeth. If she wanted it done, she'd have to do it herself.

"Hello, Mr. Spinks. How are you feeling?" she asked, from the foot of the bed.

He was dozing. Had Dr. Raje already put him on a drip? Couldn't have. No way an infection could have set in that fast. Just in case, she checked the IV rack for a morphine bag. Nothing other than saline.

"Eddie? It's Dr. Anderson. I need to ask you a few questions."

She jostled his arm. "Eddie? Can you hear me?"

She put a hand on his chest, leaned her cheek over his nose and mouth, and shouted for a nurse.

Five minutes later, she called the time of death.

***

Kallie planted her feet and glared at her family.

"It's not a big deal," she said. "I need to help a patient, that's all."

Her grandfather blew snot into his handkerchief and wiped his nose vigorously. "Not a big deal? Jeremy, talk some sense into your daughter."

Kallie's father nodded. "Grandpa's right. Since when do residents make house calls?"

"This is a special situation, Dad. The family doesn't even know this man's been hospitalized. They have no phone, no neighbors, and as of yesterday, no vehicle. They must be worried sick. Someone has to tell them."

Kallie wasn't about to mention that the patient had already died or that she found the circumstances of his death to be highly suspicious. Her family was alarmed enough as it was.

"But why you?" her mother asked.

"Why not me? Why not anyone? That's the problem with our society: Everyone's locked in their fear."

Grandpa slapped a palm on the table. "We take care of our own, young lady."

"And that's precisely my point. We've become a clannish, frightened society that doesn't give a damn about anyone else." She held up her hand to forego any further argument. "I became a doctor to help people. I won't let Eddie's family die in isolation. Someone has to help or they're not going to make it."

Her mom gasped. "I thought you were just going to break the news about your patient. You're not going to let any of these people in our car, are you? What if they're carrying a virus? What if they have bacteria clinging to their clothes?"

Kallie waved a hand impatiently. "No, of course not. But I could fetch some groceries, or take a message to a friend."

Or find Jacob.

That was the real reason Kallie wanted the van; she needed to know if Jacob was a real person or the delusion of a mentally disturbed man. Because if he did exist, and if he had worked in a government lab, and if he did know more about infections than Kallie or Dr. Raje or any of the other attending physicians at LA Memorial, then Jacob could either substantiate or refute Kallie's suspicions.

But first, she needed the van.

"I won't let anyone inside, Mom. I promise. But if they have a trailer, I'm going to hitch it to the van and move them to an in-law tribe."

Her father grunted. "An in-law tribe won't accept them, and you know it. Once a daughter marries, she separates from her birth family and joins her husband's family forever. That's the only way to stay safe. The germs have to be contained. Each tribe takes care of its own—period, end of story."

Kallie cringed to hear her grandfather's expression come out of her father's mouth. But that's what happened when generations were confined together for life. The diversity boom from the turn of the millennium had reverted into a homogenizing trend where online matchmaking sites chose potential mates based on the woman's predicted compatibility with her potential husband's tribe. The practice was based on the assumption that household harmony rose in direct relation to points of commonality. To this end, algorithms matched couples according to similarities—race, genes, intelligence, personality, religion, even hobbies. So while couples like Kallie's grandparents had come from different heritages and backgrounds, their descendants had become, and would continue to become, more alike with every carefully selected marriage. Even now, just two generations later, everyone in the Anderson family, including Kallie's sister-in-laws, were determined, intelligent people with hazel eyes, straight cinnamon-colored hair, broad shoulders, narrow hips, and long legs. All the women topped five-feet-ten. All the men ranged from six-one to six-four.

Kallie's dad heaved a sigh that sounded annoyingly similar to her own.

"How did you get so headstrong?" he asked.

Kallie snorted, followed by an identical snort from her grandpa, dad, mom, brothers, sisters-in-laws, three nephews, and two nieces until the entire family was laughing at the absurdity of the question. Then the merriment died away, like a wave receding from the shore, and the family was serious once again.

Kallie's father put a hand on her shoulder. "You'll be careful, won't you? Keep your doors locked and wear your level-four gear?"

Kallie shook her head. "I can't do that, I'll overheat. But I'll bring the hood in case I have to enter the house."

He frowned. "Not good enough."

"Dad, I'm not going to drive all that way in full gear. It's overkill. But I'll follow all standard precautions: I'll cover up, wear a mask and gloves, and keep a yard of distance between me and anyone I meet. Okay? I'll be fine. Promise."

Grandpa blew another nose-full of snot and grumbled something about foolishness and respect.

Mom gave her a hug. "Be careful."

Kallie kissed her cheek. "I will. Try not to worry."

As if that were even possible. Worry was an Anderson family trait.

***

It took Kallie two doubt-filled hours to drive out of Los Angeles and into the sparse, desert mountains of the San Gabriel Wilderness. Eddie's records listed the Hidden Springs Campsite as his address. As promised, it lay in the middle of nowhere.

She stepped out of the van, locked the doors, and clamped a boot onto the front wheel for good measure. The nearest anything was twenty-miles away. The last time Kallie had walked that far, was—well—never.

She left her biosafety gear in the van and opted for a long-sleeve cotton blouse, jeans, and a pair of jogging shoes. And because her parents hadn't raised a total fool, she had stuffed a pair of latex gloves and a particle respiratory mask in her back pockets. Although the make-shift gear didn't match her promise, Kallie felt certain the protection would suffice.

Charred disks dotted the plateau, reminding her of the camp songs Grandpa used to sing when she was a little girl. She had felt so close to him then, building blanket tents in the living room and warming her hands around a pile of rolled up red shirts. Grandpa painted his Boy Scouting adventures so vividly she'd wake the next morning with the scent of pine trees and the sticky feel of sap on her fingers. Each month she'd beg him to take her to the mountains; and each month he'd build another campsite out of blankets and rolled up shirts.

"No one camps outdoors anymore, Kallie-girl," he'd always say. "Were better off in our living room."

While it was true that most folks hid in the safety of their family compounds and sterile work environments, a courageous few headed to open spaces every chance they got. Kallie tried to convince her family to do the same, citing the health benefits of fresh air and exercise, but they refused to believe.

"Those articles are decades old," her father had said. "You can't believe those old wives' tales. Doctors know better now."

"But I am a doctor!"

"You're a resident. Don't get ahead of yourself."

Remembering his comment made her as angry now as it had that day. She couldn't understand how people as intelligent as her family could buy into such hysteria. Sure, the news was full of stories about doomed people infecting others out of spite, and communes in the wilderness where the infected gathered to live out the rest of their miserable days; but come on. Anyone with half a brain should be able to see that people dying of infectious diseases were like everyone else: a mix of good and bad, frightened and brave. And yet, despite their intelligence, Kallie's family, like the majority of healthy people, adamantly believed the doomed were plotting to infect the world.

Kallie had never seen any statistics or news footage to confirm the existence of these alleged communes; and the infected patients she had encountered were no worse than any other terrified, selfish citizen. Everyone in the world wanted to live. Everyone in the world was afraid to die. It was as simple as that.

Unfortunately, no one in her family shared the same opinion. Her mother was the worst, telling Kallie she was silly to think the government would stop funding national parks if the outdoors were truly good for people's health. Having mother call her silly stung worse than any of the condescending and dismissive comments made by her father and brothers. Women were supposed to support each other not tear each other down. So much for sisterhood.

Like a dog drying itself from a bath, Kallie shook away the thoughts and descended into the ravine. According to Eddie, his pop had built their homestead along the river. The glorified creek below, winding its way through the mountains, was the only water in sight. Kallie intended to follow it until she found the Spinks or ran out of sunlight.

Eddie's parting jab echoed in her mind: *"Can't see you packin' your gear down the river bank. Probably fall in and mess up that nice white suit."*

Not going to happen.

After forty minutes of clumsy rock jumping and mud sliding, Kallie found the settlement in a clearing between the river and the mountain—along with two barking, charging beasts.

"Oh my God," she said, dashing for a boulder. The mutts changed their course to intercept. "Help," she yelled. "Can you hear me? Call off your dogs!"

She leaped onto the side and scrambled up the face while the feral creatures lunged at her feet. Once safe on the top, Kallie waved at the cabins. "Hello? Can you hear me? Eddie sent me!" She looked down at the yellow-brown dogs yapping and scratching at the rock. "It's okay. I'm a friend. Really."

A gun fired, the dogs yelped, and a man shouted for them to heel. Kallie raised her hands over her head as the mutts raced to their master, a wizened man with a crippled leg.

"What you doing here, girl? You don't belong."

Kallie nodded. She surely didn't. "Eddie had an accident. He said you didn't have a phone, so I came out to tell you. He crashed the motorcycle."

The man stopped and slumped over his rifle, shaking his head and muttering to himself. After a moment he straightened his crooked back and motioned her off the rock with the muzzle of the gun.

"Come on down. Them pups won't hurt you."

Kallie eyed the snarling dogs. "You sure about that? They look kind of wild."

The man smiled and shushed his pets. "They got some coyote mixed in, but they do what I tell 'em."

She pointed to the gear hanging from her pocket. "I'm just going to put on my mask and gloves, okay?"

He nodded. "Suit yourself."

The man had no such protection. With his wide brimmed hat and overstretched tank—sagging to expose an equally sagging chest—he seemed more concerned about getting sunstroke than contracting germs.

Once she had the protective equipment securely fitted, she climbed down from the boulder. The mongrels stayed beside their master.

"So," said the man. "How's my boy?" His voice trembled.

Kallie understood. Even the slightest cut could become infected. She wished that was all she had to report. "He fractured his knee," she said, keeping her voice professional and dispassionate.

"They gon' operate?"

She shook her head. "I'm deeply sorry, Mr. Spinks. He didn't make it."

He raised the gun. "What you tellin' me? My boy's dead?"

Kallie held up her hands and tried to remain calm. "It wasn't a clean break. A truck ran him down. Crushed his leg between his bike and a wall." Her voice trembled. "I don't know what happened. He just—died."

"What you mean 'he just died?' Ain't nobody just die lessen somethin' or somebody kill him."

"I know. You're right. That's why I'm here. I'm a doctor. I was Eddie's doctor," she added, inanely. "Look, I want to ask you some questions."

Mr. Spinks shook his head and spit. "What I got to tell you? You the one takin' care of my boy. You tell me why he died."

"Sure. Just put away the gun, okay? Then we'll talk."

Mr. Spinks stared at Kallie for a long time. Then he lowered the rifle, hawked, and spit again.

"Thank you."

Mr. Spinks jutted his chin. "Well? Say your piece."

Kallie nodded and took a fortifying breath, praying the man wouldn't change his mind and shoot her. "Eddie believed the driver of the truck hit him on purpose because he thought Eddie was someone named Jacob. Do you know Jacob? Is he a neighbor?"

When Mr. Spinks didn't respond, she continued a little faster. "Eddie said he worked in a government lab and knew about infections. That he worked on top secret experiments with germs and rats. Do you know who I'm talking about? Does Jacob live around here?"

Mr. Spinks fingered the trigger. "What you want with Jacob?"

"So you do know him," she said, nearly laughing with relief. "That's great. Where can I find him?"

An elderly woman stood at the porch while a couple of women nearer to Kallie's mother's age approached with four girls following behind. Not one of them wore long sleeves, masks, or gloves.

"Get back in the house, Sue. This ain't no concern of yours."

The woman stopped and hugged her girls. "This have somethin' to do with Ed?"

Mr. Spinks raised his rifle and pointed it at Kallie. "Do as I say.

I'll be in once this doctor is on her way." He spat the word "doctor" as if it was the foulest thing he had ever been forced to say.

"Please. I know you're angry," said Kallie. "But if Jacob has information about fighting infections, wouldn't you want me to know?" She glanced at his family. "For your kids?"

"Ain't nothing wrong with my kids."

"There wasn't anything wrong with Eddie, either. Until there was."

Mr. Spinks glared at Kallie, who glared back defiantly. Neither spoke. Neither flinched. Finally, he huffed then pointed the barrel up the river.

"Back that way couple hundred paces. Through the gap in the rocks."

Kallie nodded and backed away. When she felt the soft soil of the river bank give beneath her shoes, she ran.

***

Kallie approached the cabin with caution, ready to bolt up a tree at the first sign of dogs. So far, all was quiet. Jacob had nestled his home in a grove of alders and pines, and since he had used the same woods to build his cabin, it blended perfectly. A less determined person would never have found it.

Not for the first time, Kallie wondered about her judgment. It was one thing to mistrust society from the comfort and protection of her home and hospital; it was quite another to hunt for trouble in the wilderness. What if Jacob had something worse than snarling dogs and a loaded rifle?

"Then I'm screwed," she muttered.

Guilt over losing her patient and an exalted sense of personal responsibility had set her on this path; stubbornness wouldn't let her leave it.

She took a couple more steps, thought better of it, and stopped a few yards short. While the laughable distance wouldn't keep her safe from a psycho redneck murderer, those few yards made her feel a teeny bit more secure.

"Hello? Is anyone home?"

A gruff voice spoke from behind. "Who's asking?"

She yelped and whirled to see who had startled her. He was a big man—broader and more muscular than any of her brothers—with bushy brows and ill-cropped facial hair. His sleeves were short and his collar unbuttoned to the chest. He wore black-rimmed glasses with powerful prescriptions that magnified an accusing glare. A short-barrel shotgun rested at his hip, aimed at her belly.

Kallie raised her hands, realizing too late that the gloves and mask made her look like a government health investigator. Somehow, she didn't think this man would appreciate those sorts of people.

"I'm a doctor. Eddie's father told me where to find you."

"Hm. And why would he do that?"

"Because Eddie died last night."

Instead of shock or gruff dismissal, the man loomed over her, like a buzzard inspecting a dying mouse. "Of natural causes?"

Kallie shook her head. "I don't think so. He came in with a fractured patella. Said a guy in a truck plowed into him because he thought Eddie was you."

The man bit his lip and shook his head so violently Kallie feared he might be having a seizure. Then he blasted out a gust of air and shook his head some more.

"Goddamnit! God damn them all to hell. Sons of bitches want a piece of me?" He glared up at the sky and yelled. "You want a piece of me? You sons of—" he peered back at Kallie, as if remembering she was there. "What do you want?" He shoved the stubby barrel at her stomach. "Start talking, or I'll blast a hole through your belly so big… What are you after? Why are you here? Who are you?"

He fired his questions in ever-loudening bursts, causing Kallie to stagger, heart pounding, hot breath steaming her mask.

"Nothing," she gasped. "I mean… I just want to know what's going on. Eddie said you used to work in a government lab and that you knew all sorts of secrets regarding infections. I don't want to cause any trouble. Honest. I'm just a doctor looking for answers."

He grunted a bitter laugh. "An honest doctor? That's a good one. Follow it up with the collective good and evil drugs and you got yourself a comedy routine." He lowered the barrel and walked toward her, chuckling at his own joke and muttering about arrogant assheads. "Go home. I don't have time for your ignorance."

Kallie's jaw dropped. "Excuse me?" She had enough of being dismissed, first by her attending physician and then by her parents. She wasn't about to get dismissed by a shaggy-faced, hulking, middle-aged lab rat.

"I'm not ignorant, and I'm sure as hell not a liar. And I'm not going home after driving all this way and hiking into bum-fuck nowhere without the truth." She tore off her mask and planted her fists on her hips.

To hell with germs. She wanted him to quake in her fury.

Instead he laughed.

"This isn't funny," she said.

He glared at her with dark predatory eyes. "No. It isn't." Then as if to prove his disdain for her and any germs she might be carrying, he headed on his way, passing so close the hairs on his arms brushed against the sleeve of her shirt.

Kallie froze, paralyzed by the thought of deadly germs crawling up her sleeve. Over her collar. Up her neck. Into her mouth. Her nose. Her eyes.

"Wait," she said, jolting herself out of the horrifying vision. "Why do you hate doctors?"

He turned around and adjusted his eyeglass as if to better inspect a curious bug. "Why did you risk contamination? Your family couldn't have been pleased to have you abscond with their one government-allotted car, not to mention having their daughter communing with disease-ridden rednecks in—How did you put it? Bum-fuck nowhere?" He chortled. "That's actually pretty good. Never mind. You want to know what I know?" He tossed his head and walked away. "Come and get it."

When he reached his cabin, he left the door open.

Kallie stood mute as indignation warred with doubt. This man, whom she assumed to be Jacob, offended her deeply. And yet, she wanted him to approve of her actions and appreciate her motives. She wanted him to acknowledge that she was one of the good guys. That she had sacrificed time and money and risked her life to come out here in the pursuit of truth. But how could she explain what she didn't fully understand?

She stuffed the mask and gloves in her pockets. She had come this far; she'd be damned if she'd run back home without answers.

***

The cabin's shutters stood open to bring in the light and the breeze, making the space seem larger and more welcoming than she expected. Jacob propped his shotgun in the corner of the kitchen area and fetched two blue-speckled cups, which he filled with coffee from a matching metal pot on a wood-burning stove.

"Milk's too hard to keep around here. Don't use it. Don't want it."

Kallie nodded. "Black's fine."

He stepped over the bench in front of a plank table and sat, gesturing for her to do the same on the opposite side. "My name's Jacob Roszak, but I guess you already know that."

"Kallie Anderson."

He sipped his coffee. "So why are you sitting in a stranger's cabin, drinking his coffee from a possibly germ-infected cup?"

She raised her chin and glared down her nose. "Why did you invite an unprotected stranger into your home?" She took a long, deliberate sip.

His mouth twitched into something close to a grin. "How'd they kill Eddie?"

"They?"

Jacob waved a hand. "Stop wasting my time, and answer the question."

Kallie shook her head. "I think it was a *him*. I saw a man leave Eddie's room just before I went in." She shivered despite the heat. "Something about him bothered me. Anyway, I don't know how, or even if he did it; and since my request for an autopsy and toxicology report was denied, I never will."

"Doesn't matter. Eddie's dead. I'm not. They'll keep coming. Sons of bitches will always keep coming. The question is: Why do you care?"

Kallie stared into his harsh dark eyes. Who was he to challenge her? A rogue chemist? A medical researcher gone off the deep end? A burnt-out government worker hiding from the big bad world? She faced her challenges. She worked in the trenches, day after day, risking her life to save others. Why did she care?

"Because I'm a doctor. It's what I do. And I want to know why you're not worried about contamination."

Jacob snorted. "Never said I wasn't worried. Bacteria, viruses, fungi, parasites—every microbe known to man is mutating faster than a hammerhead viroid. Anyone with half a cell in his brain would be terrified."

"You don't look it."

"Well, I am. Just not of you. You're too full of yourself to be a health risk."

"I'm full of myself?"

He flapped his hand in the air, as if her sarcasm was of no consequence. Then he swung his legs over the bench and paced through the kitchen and living areas, muttering about virulent strains and resistant superbugs. When he returned, he straddled the bench beside her and thrust his face uncomfortably close to hers. "Can you handle the truth?" he asked.

"What truth?"

He exhaled with frustration and rubbed his sloppily cropped hair, like he was trying to rid it of lice. Then he grabbed her by both arms and twisted her torso so she would face him squarely. "Have you ever felt like your world is closing in on you? That your freedoms are getting stripped away?"

Kallie glanced at his bare hands on the sleeves of her blouse and tried not to think about those crawling germs. "Well, sure. Hasn't everyone?"

"No. They're too scared to notice or too ignorant to object."

Kallie shrugged her arms out of his grip. "That's the second time you've mentioned ignorance. What is it you think you know that I don't?"

"Finally," he said, flinging up his hands and clenching his fists. "Something intelligent." He laced his hairy fingers, rested his meaty forearms on his thighs, and peered at Kallie. "I was a medical research scientist for the Gildenberg Consortium. Do you know who they are?" When Kallie shook her head, he mimicked her. "Of course you don't. They're an exclusive international group of the most influential people of our time: world leaders, politicians, billionaires, experts in science, finance, industry, media—any expertise deemed essential by the consortium to govern civilization and control the world."

Kallie shifted to put more distance between them. "Oh my God. You're a conspiracy nut."

"It's not conspiracy if you have proof."

"What proof?"

"An antibiotic against the most virulent strain of staff infection and an antiviral for the flu that just wiped out a hamlet in Upstate New York."

"That's impossible."

"Is it?" Jacob scooted closer. "Do you know why all the countries agreed to follow the advice of the Global Health Association? Because members of the Gildenberg Consortium hold influential positions—sometimes the highest positions—in every major government in the world."

Kallie shrugged. "What does that have to do with anything?"

Jacob frowned—and made a noise that implied he might have overestimated her intelligence—before stating the obvious. "Control and power. The easiest way to control a population is to isolate its factions and convince them to self-restrict. And the most efficient way to get a population to self-restrict is to prove a credible threat. Control the narrative, and make sure the faction leaders are rewarded by the loss of their community's freedom."

"This isn't the Middle East. Our country doesn't have factions."

"Of course it does. The patriarchal family tribes."

Kallie stared at him in shock. "My grandfather is not working with the government."

"Not willingly. But answer me this: Would your grandfather still be in control if you were allowed to live anywhere you wanted and marry whomever you wished?"

"You're crazy."

Jacob chuckled. "Maybe. But not about this. Women's rights have been deteriorating ever since our world leaders declared a global state of emergency in 2021, and POTUS announced his revolutionary Five Year Plan. You're too young to know, but at that time, our government offered huge tax credits and major discounts for early adapters who fell in line with the new living and transportation restrictions. Why do you think they did that?" When Kallie didn't respond, he answered for her. "Because it was in the best interest of the government—and the Gildenberg Consortium that runs it—to have everyone sell off their individual homes and cars so families could join together in large, easy-to-manage compounds."

"That's not the reason," she said, feeling more confident. "The government was trying to keep people from infecting each other. Everyone knows germs spread fastest in a crowd. It made sense to limit public interaction and avoid high concentrations of people. If we didn't live with family, we'd probably die of loneliness. So you're wrong, Jacob. Tribal living benefits Americans, and our government spent billions to help us do it."

Jacob stared back, dumbfounded. "You really believe that shit, don't you?"

His astonishment unsettled her. "Well, sure."

"And what about the cars? Do you agree with the allotment of one vehicle to every tribe? How's that working for you?"

Kallie shrugged. "It's hard, sure; but it's not my place to agree or not."

Jacob leapt from the bench and loomed over her, eyes blazing with rage.

"The hell it isn't! This is exactly what I'm talking about."

He threw up his hands and marched through the cabin, preaching to every seat and space as if they were occupied by members of a particularly thick-headed congregation. "Those sons of bitches turned our mass transit into goddamn death chambers, spraying passengers like cattle in a slaughterhouse, dousing them with UV radiation. And when those who could afford it went back to their cars and gridlocked traffic, as any intelligent person could have predicted, what did our wise and compassionate leaders do? Did they increase carpool lanes? Improve filtration systems in trains? No. They recalled the cars, destroyed the majority, and redistributed one vehicle per family tribe."

He circled his hand in an all-encompassing gesture as he stalked through his kitchen then stopped on the other side of the table. "They made traveling so untenable that we, as a society, chose to work, shop, play, and study at home." He planted his hands on the table and glared at Kallie. "They manipulated us into self-incarceration, and you won't question the government? Bullshit!" he yelled, hammering his fist on the wood. "You're a doctor. Caring is what you do."

Kallie flinched as her own words hit her in the face.

Much as she wanted to deny it, she feared Jacob was right. She was full of herself and hopelessly naive. Sure, she might argue with her parents about the unreasonableness of their fears and the ridiculous restrictions they heaped onto their already restricted lives; but it never occurred to her to challenge the legitimacy government law. After all, the president's Five Year Plan went into effect nineteen years before she was born. She had lived her entire life subjugated by the restrictions and hazardous practices Jacob had described.

"You're seeing it now, aren't you?" Jacob said, stepping over the bench to sit.

Kallie tilted her head, somewhere between a nod and a shake. "I don't know. We do seem to be feeding our own fear. But no one's forcing us to stay indoors and cling to people who look, act, and think like we do. And as far as I know, the government never said we had to send our girls away to other families or replace dating with computer algorithms." She shrugged and shook her head, apologetically. "I'm sorry, Jacob. I get what you're saying about the tribes. And men definitely have the power. I just don't buy into this global conspiracy. We did this to ourselves."

He heaved a sigh so loud even Kallie's grandfather would have been impressed.

"You're underestimating the reach and influence of the Gildenberg Consortium. Who do you think manufactured all the antimicrobials that caused the pandemic of 2021? Who do you think fueled hysteria and manipulated social reform? Who do you think defined a crisis so eloquently they convinced a global super power to buy into their fully tested, fully functioning solutions? And not just our country: Those sons of bitches hijacked the whole God damn world."

Now it was Kallie's turn to stand and pace. "This is crazy. Antimicrobial Resistance is science. Even Alexander Fleming acknowledged the dangers of penicillin soon after he discovered it. You can't blame the Gildenberg Consortium for the Post-Antimicrobial Era."

"Bullshit! Who do you think determines so called scientific fact? Every medical reality you think you know has been fed to you by experts and officials governed by them."

Kallie stared agape. "You're delusional."

Jacob didn't bother to answer; he just stood up and walked out of the room. A minute later, he returned from his bedroom with two security boxes. He kept one in front of him and pushed the other across the table for her.

"What's this?" Kallie asked, sitting back on the bench.

Jacob reached over and opened the box in front of her. A hundred tiny bottles lined up in five color-coordinated rows. Jacob placed his finger on the first bottle in each row as he explained their contents. "Antibacterial, antifungal, antiparasitic, antiviral for influenza, and an antiviral for chickenpox."

Kallie shook her head. "Impossible. We've exhausted every

antimicrobial known to science, and every new discovery has met with immediate pathogen mutation. These bottles might contain what you say, but they won't cure anything."

Jacob opened the box nearest to him and turned it to face her. "Test them."

Kallie stared at the vials, color-coordinated to match the alleged medications. Each of the five colors was marked with the most recent strains of a different horrifying disease. Kallie leaned back, instinctively trying to put distance between herself and the vials.

"You're mad."

"No," he said. "I'm a research scientist tired of watching the world go to hell."

Kallie looked from her box to his and back again. The virulent staff infection labeled on the orange-capped vial had infected nineteen patients, six nurses, and two doctors before the infectious disease team had isolated the contamination. All those infected died within a week to a month of contraction. She didn't want to consider the pandemic that could arise from the contents of the vial with the blue cap.

She closed her eyes. "Okay," she said, opening them again when she felt brave enough to continue. "Supposing everything you've said is true, how did you get these vials out of your lab? There must have been security. If the Gildenberg Consortium has even a quarter of the power you suggest, why are you still alive?"

Jacob smirked. "Who says I'm alive? It took three years to replicate and smuggle what you see in these boxes, followed by a very public and very thorough death. Unfortunately, it took so long that three of those cures no longer work with the current mutated strains of fungi, parasite, and chickenpox. That's why we need to act immediately."

Kallie gasped. "We? I don't know what you're planning, but I'm not doing anything with you. Or with those. I'm a doctor. I'm sworn to—"

"Kill? Because that's what you're doing, you and your chickenshit colleagues. Blaming your failures on antibacterial resistant infections when the truth is you've given up the damn fight. While you're sentencing poor saps like Eddie Spink to death, privileged people all around the world are getting cured. Clinical researchers in consortium-funded labs, like the one where I used to work, are generating new drugs every week for consortium-funded doctors to administer in astronomically expensive multi-drug blasts designed to confound even the quickest mutating pathogens. A process, by the way, that was only made possible because of the forty-eight-year global ban against using antimicrobials. While the rest of the world has been suffering and dying for the greater good, these selfish pricks have been shooting up and having a God damn party." Jacob jabbed his finger into the wood. "The Gildenberg Consortium is dividing humanity into masters and slaves—and every one of us is helping them do it."

As outlandish as it sounded, everything Jacob said rang true.

"Why are you telling me this?"

"Do you believe in coincidences? I don't. You wandered onto my property because I need you."

"Need me? What for?"

"I'm going to lock up the National News Corporation using an advanced sealant, stolen from another consortium-funded lab by a recently murdered friend of mine. Then I'm going to gas the studio with a fast-acting, lethal strain of influenza. When people start to die, I'll let them know where in the studio I hid the cure, along with the level-four restricted syringes that you will supply. The NNC will televise their exclusive and highly dramatic story, along with my carefully crafted statement describing the facts I have just shared with you. They won't care that the use and manufacturing of antivirals are outlawed, nor will they cling to their propaganda-inspired belief that they won't work. They will inject themselves with the drugs because they'll want to live. By the time rescue teams break into the studio, the influenza will have been arrested and my statements will have been proved."

Kallie stared in horror. "No. Absolutely not. I won't help you, and your plan wouldn't work even if I did. You said it yourself, that consortium will make you out to be a bioterrorist nut-job. They'll make everyone think it was a hoax."

He shook his head. "Not everyone. People all over the world will start to question and resist. They'll stop blindly submitting to government restrictions and demand a vote. Women will stop allowing and contributing to their own subjugation. The patriarchal family tribes will deteriorate. Doctors and scientists will dare to experiment again with drugs and treatments and discover the truth.

The Gildenberg Consortium will fail. I'll be dead, of course—that's inevitable—but my actions might save humanity." He leaned forward and fixed her with an uncompromising gaze. "How many lives will you save with your bogus excuse for medicine?"

***

One week later, Kallie stood at the door of CADLab working up the courage to either enter or run like hell. Inside her pocket she fondled two rolls of mints, a lipstick, and a round, stubby marker. They clicked together like ticking bombs. She pulled her hand away. What was she thinking? The contents of the vial hidden inside one of those harmless items could start an epidemic.

Or could it?

She had tallied the pros and cons and compared them, ad nauseam, followed by a long and serious discussion with Amy Lee over a sterilized cup of coffee at the dispenser shop across from the lab. In the end, they had agreed to take the risk. Amy, like Kallie, needed to know.

They had to know the truth.

Kallie hit the call button and was buzzed through the security door and metal detector to reception, where Fred, a medical university graduate and aspiring researcher, asked for her identification. While they had met on several occasions, CADLab policy required Fred to scan her driver's license. Kallie's name would be entered into the records. Anyone who checked would know she had come to visit Amy.

"Identification?" Fred asked again.

Kallie shivered. If Amy got caught analyzing the contents of these bottles, they'd both get thrown in prison without a trial.

"Sorry, Fred. I spaced out for a sec." She took out her wallet and handed him the card. "Here you go."

Fred scanned the license, returned it, and buzzed Kallie through the next door.

"Go on in. I'll let her know you're here."

At the end of the office-lined corridor, Kallie saw yet another security door, this one programmed with a palm-reading. The door opened, and a curvy Asian in a long white coat emerged. Aside from the straight hair braided to the middle of her narrow shoulders, Amy didn't resemble Kallie in any physical way. Her stubbornness, on the other hand, rivaled any Anderson.

Amy gestured to a cushioned arm chair and took a seat behind her desk. "How've you been, Kal? It feels like forever since I've seen you."

Not true, of course; but the casual conversation that ensued gave Kallie a chance to surreptitiously stuff the mints, lipstick, and marker between the cushion and the side of her chair. After she left, Amy would find a reason to straighten up and pocket the items. In this way she could sneak the vials into her lab without raising suspicions. CADLab screened their researches. The small cylindrical items Kallie had brought into the facility, while unremarkable for a visitor, would have raised flags for Amy.

***

Seven agonizing days passed before Kallie received a call from Amy asking her to meet at the coffee shop. During that time, Kallie had not returned to the San Gabriel Wilderness, and since Jacob Roszak didn't have a telephone, she had not spoken to the man who would might possibly become humanity's savior. Or one of the worst bioterrorists of the new millennium. That verdict depended on whether the two antimicrobials secreted in the lipstick and marker were effective against the respective bacteria and virus hidden in the two rolls of mints.

Savior or terrorist?

Kallie had been so eager to hear the results she had walked five miles rather than risk carpool delays with the family van. Now she was on her second cup of coffee. Without taking her eyes off the CADLab building, she pulled the lid off her sanitized cup, leaned in for a sip, then put the cup down. She couldn't stand it any longer. She had to call.

Amy answered on the second ring. "Hi Kallie. I'm heading for the door. Be out in a sec."

The door opened. Amy stepped out of the lab. Kallie raised a hand to wave through the window. A second later, the world exploded.

The detonation shook Kallie off her chair and shattered the shop's front window, spraying her with shards of glass. She felt her chest heave with a scream but was too deaf to hear the sound. Her head throbbed. Blood dripped in her eye. She staggered to the door. People screamed and shouted as they raced into the street to see what had happened. Some of them, like Kallie, bled from wounds. In the hysteria, Kallie searched for Amy, praying what she had seen hadn't actually occurred—that somehow, Amy had been knocked away by the explosion instead of blasted into pulp.

Fire leapt to nearby buildings, adding to the panic. Kallie rubbed the grit from her eyes and peered through the smoke. She couldn't find Amy, but she did see two brawny men in black paramilitary uniforms cutting through the panicked crowd and heading straight toward her. Fear gripped her gut. They had to be first responders here to help the injured or put out the fire. They couldn't be after her.

Why would anyone be after her?

But even as she asked the question, she knew the answer—everything Jacob Roszak had told her was true.

Kallie ducked behind a couple of men in blue company caps and throat-to-boot coveralls, staring over the white cups of their respiratory masks in horrified amazement at the destruction across the street. She left them to it and ran, staying low, behind the row of curbside cars before sprinting into an alley. Bullets struck the corner building, chipping bits of brick and mortar—and with them, any lingering doubts she might have had.

Whoever had blown up the lab and murdered Amy was after her.

***

Three hours later, Kallie drove a stolen coupe into the Hidden Springs Campsite, where she pulled off the broken asphalt lot, drove over an eroded curb, and followed a rocky path deep into the trees. Later, she might come back and use branches to further hide the car from the campsite. For now, she just needed the dense pines to conceal the vehicle from roaming helicopters.

She had no delusions. Kallie knew her life, as she had always known it, was over. She couldn't go home. She couldn't endanger her friends. And she'd never become a full-fledged physician. But none of that mattered anymore.

She grabbed the box of level-four restricted syringes she had pilfered from the hospital storage room and stepped out of the car. She'd never save another hospital patient, but maybe, she could help Jacob save the world.

WHAT LIES WITHIN
Ed DeAngelis

Life in a caravan is a life full of freedom. But a life also filled with danger. Lots of danger. I mean I can't emphasize enough the amount of danger. This is the world I was born into, a ravaged world, brought to the brink of destruction by our forefathers. From the green fire and terrible chemicals, a new world emerged, deadlier, harsher. But humanity survived, its people splintered, some of them even altered from generations after generations exposed to radiation and strange chemicals.

The first chapter of my life had been spent in the deserts of the West, in a ruined city called Vegas. It was a life of solitude, my own family having died early, leaving me to fend for myself among the ruined wasteland that was Vegas. That all changed the day I encountered a tiny but fierce redhead, my love, my life, *Lily*. Of course when I first saw her, she had been just a cloaked figure sprinting toward the ruined building I called home. Its true name, given to it by the old generations, was the Excelsior. She was being chased by a pack of rad coyotes. The ensuing encounter, followed soon by a hasty escape from my previous home, I prefer not to dwell upon. For that is my past, and now Lily and her family, the caravan, is my life. And right now, that life is me desperately trying to remain on top of our caravan's ten motor rigs as we attempt to outrun a gang of Mek Boys who have just come roaring out of the thick woods on their own custom motor rigs.

"How the hell did I get here?" I cursed out loud to myself, although my voice was swallowed by the roar of the rig's engine I was currently atop, strapped onto the roof with some rope, leather straps, and a prayer. Sitting, and I use that word loosely, upon a padded cushion, which did little to comfort my now bruised ass as it was slammed down over and over onto the metal roof each time we ran over a bump. Which I was pretty convinced that was all this road was made up of: holes and bumps. Yanking my trusty rifle up, which is the only heirloom I had left from my long-deceased parents, I focused on trying to draw an unobstructed line on one of the quickly gaining Mek Boy rigs. Being a caravan, our rigs were burdened down with all kinds of scrap, supplies, and other things that we had picked up along our travels. So speed was not something we excelled at.

Mek Boys on the other hand… their rigs were their life. Rigs and raiding, these two R's embodied the lifestyle these people tribed by, although Mek Boys normally lived in, or closer to, cities—more sources of scrap and parts to upgrade, repair, or even create, new rigs. Normally they didn't just appear out of the woods. But that thought was for another time.

I finally managed to draw an unobstructed bead on one of the leading rigs' driver, a crazy bastard with long, spiked hair and a pair of old goggles, his face covered in a plethora of strange red markings—some kind of tribal or superstitious marking. It was a wildly known fact that Mek Boys thought red coloring made things go faster. But regardless of what it meant, it was time to end him. I breathed deeply, focusing on his chest, the largest target, pulled the trigger… right as we hit another bump and my rifle jerked.

"Shit!" I swore as my shot went wild. I quickly sighted the driver again. This time my attention was drawn away from my target by the deafening roar of newly arrived engines, shapes suddenly blurring past as well as in-between our own racing rigs. The leading blur trailed behind it a length of fiery red, like a red, avenging comet. Lily, my beloved, had arrived, and with her came her units of scouts riding their two-wheelers. My beloved and her hand-chosen scouts were not much for running, unless it was running at anyone or anything that threatened the caravan and their loved ones.

A swell of pity momentarily rose within me for the Mek Boys, but that quickly transitioned into anger upon seeing sparks shooting off the armored front of the two-wheelers as the metal front plates absorbed and deflected the incoming fire. Anger was quickly replaced by a thunderous rolling swell of rage when I beheld sparks shooting off Lily's two-wheeler.

I watched with barely contained rage as Lily swerved to move out of the firing arc of the Mek Boy who had stood up on the passenger's side of the oncoming rig to gain a better line of sight on her.

My rifle snapped up, and the bouncing and jumbling below me seemed almost forgotten as I zoomed in, my rage focused. I sighted my target, exhaled, and pulled the trigger. The bulging eyes, the frantic stumbling upon the face of the once firing Mek Boy confirmed that my aim had been true. The driver lay slumped, a hole blasted in the middle of his helmet, blood and gray matter already oozing out. The rig went haywire, wheels spun wildly, jerking the speeding coffin-on-wheels sharply to the left. Which brought the out-of-control rig right into the path of another approaching rig. The resulting explosion was satisfying to say the least.

"Shoot at my beloved... I don't think so," I spat off the rumbling rig.

My shot, and the resulting explosion, had bought the caravan time. The sudden loss of two rigs had the Mek Boys slowing down. They had most certainly not given up the chase; they just needed to reevaluate the amount of danger the caravan posed.

The blare of gunfire brought another Mek Boy rig to a screeching halt, smoke pouring from the engine. The scouts had brought down that one. They circled it now, pouring lead into the passengers, who leapt out of the smoking wreck.

I glanced around, assessing our own situation as best I could from my vantage point. We had not emerged from this skirmish unscathed. Two of our rigs showed visible damage. One, a small rusty box-like rig, belonged to Julius and his family, Zena his wife, Vigo his son. The other was our heavy, water-tank rig. I didn't remember who was currently on driving assignment for the tanker. They were both moving still, but smoke was rising from Julius's rig, and the tanker was limping with what I assumed was a popped tire. A loud thumping suddenly brought my attention to my own vehicle. The large hand of Lily's father, Angus, was slapping the top of our rig, he was roaring my name as well. "Jack! Jack!" Such measures were needed to garner my attention during any kind of chase, as the cacophony of sound the caravan created was overwhelming. I leaned down, tapping his hand to let him know I had noticed him.

"What's the situation, lad?" Angus's burly voice roared at almost equal volume as the engine.

I had to scream to make sure he heard me. "The Meks are backing down! Three of their rigs down! Julius's rig and water tank are both damaged, but they're keeping pace for now!"

Angus's response was drowned out with the addition of another engine. Lily's bike sped up next to ours. She looked up at Angus through her helmet. Her one hand left the bike handles and flashed quick, and at least to me, complex signs, a special form of hand symbols and movements they had apparently made up that conveyed meanings. I had not yet learned them. But I got enough of the meaning from the explosion of profanities that roared forth from Angus.

Bad news. Then again, in this world, once I left Las Vegas and my skeletal tower the Excelsior, I found that bad news was in fact everyday news. The world had survived the end-of-times only to find they now lived in the worst-of-times. The roar of Lily's bike's engine diminished as she slowed, falling behind to rejoin her scouts in guarding the flanks as well as the two damaged rigs. I banged the top of our rig, wondering what the concern beyond marauding bloodthirsty Mek Boys could provoke such a reaction.

Angus didn't need to see me or know what I wanted to know. "Road up ahead is blockaded, meant to trap us. Bastards were gonna corner us. Gonna have to take an unknown route, lad. Keep your wits about you and warn me if anything looks off," Angus called from below.

I suddenly wished I had not asked. The caravan had mapped a good amount of the main roads across this blasted land. It was almost a sacred parchment to our kind, showing all our secret routes and the knowledge we had gained along them. But for every route we had mapped, there were a hundred more unknown to us.

I had asked once about this and Angus's response had been simple. "Because if ye found what ye considered a safe route, ye don't damn stray from it."

We were now going to be forced to do so, or be trapped, by a whole tribe of now vengeful Mek Boys. Sighing, I lifted my one free hand to rub my temples softly. From bad to worse. All I wanted was to camp someplace where we didn't have to be afraid. So I could snuggle up to Lily and actually attempt to enjoy my new life with her.

The caravan began slowing, the roar of the engines diminishing only slightly. I gazed behind us and took note of the large dust cloud far behind us. Just far enough that I couldn't see the size of the trailing Mek Boys mob but could judge it was fairly large. They were following us, thinking they were herding us to our doom. Waiting for us to fall into their trap.

We had to keep them thinking that for as long as possible. If they knew that we knew that the road was blocked and were going to take another route, they would push the attack. This time, they would swarm us, worked into a frenzy by the death of their people, but mostly due to the destruction of their precious rigs. So, slowing down was a calculated risk, but it was one that we needed to take. The water tank rig was having to slow. I saw eventually as we slowed that indeed a tire was blown. One of the four back tires. Smoke was still drifting from Julius's rig, but not as much now. Either way would have to eventually stop. But for now, we pushed on.

Our new route came up faster than I expected, but to be honest I didn't really know what to expect. It could be the same type of road we were on, which was a cracked, deteriorating, pock-marked, grayish black stone. But as long as it got us someplace safer, I wouldn't complain. We were currently heading east, and under normal circumstances we would have remained going east till we hit the coast. I was excited for that. I had never seen an ocean until just over a year ago. To my surprise it had been only a few hours from where I lived. We now headed to what I was told was another brand-new ocean. I was excited to see it. But right now I needed to focus on the present, then an uncertain future.

The road ahead split, forming a cross shape. There was a path going south, and north—east as well—but we knew going east was no longer a possibility. It was Angus's call, as our rig lurched to the front of the line. And slowly he drifted toward the north exit. I knew we would eventually head north once we reached the ocean, traveling along the ocean. Now we had to take a forced detour and begin our northward travels much earlier than expected.

The wooded area quickly gave way to a barren wasteland littered with rusted rigs and remains of old dwellings. This sort of sudden geographical change was not unknown. To go from areas of land where plant growth seemed to flourish to barren plots, where not even a blade of grass was to be seen for miles, occurred often. One moment you're sweating under the blazing sun; drive a few miles, and you hit a dust storm that turns into a snowstorm. There were various reasons I had been told: poisons leaking into the water, strange blights that killed all plant life for miles before suddenly stopping, that even nature itself had gone mad from the damage inflicted upon the world. But whatever the truth was, nature continued to prosper, and its creations twisted by radiation and other strange chemicals were now fighting back. I long ago had heard a term used in reference to this phenomenon: Nature finds a way.

Well... fuck nature. Rad coyotes in the desert, mangy sore-infested creatures that, although cowardly, presented a danger when traveling in a pack, Grunters in the northwest. Grunters were something I thankfully had only encountered once. They were massive, hairless creatures, who I had been told were once called bears that roamed the woods. They killed all that they encountered except other Grunters. Damn things were big enough to knock down whole trees and had claws sharp enough to rip through a rig's door to get to the fresh meat that was the people inside. And despite their size, they moved with great stealth, only a soft grunting noise giving away their approach—and your most likely impending doom.

The list of rad animals I had run into since leaving Vegas was growing rapidly, each one deadly and hungry for any flesh it could find. Hell, even plants were affected. The areas we had just passed through a few days past had long, hanging vines that blended in with the regular plant life. But upon touching living flesh they would coil around whatever was touching them, and *bam!* yank your ass straight up into the thick foliage where you would be wrapped up nice and tight till you died. But that wasn't the end. Once you died, the vines would deposit your now rotting carcass by the roots.

I had started keeping a detailed log in an old, empty book Lily had given me. I thought it would be useful to have all the dangerous creatures we encountered and the ways around them, or the best ways to defeat them, written down. Angus and many of the caravan had loved the idea and had gone through great lengths to give me as much detail and information about all kinds of hazards and creatures. Sharing this information with the various people in the towns we stopped in for trading or resupplying gained our caravan a decent amount of goodwill.

Angus's banging the rigtop once more brought my attention down to him. This time he held the caravan's only magner. The device was wonderful. You placed both holes on your eyes and it allowed you to see *really* far away on the other end. This magner was broken. Some of the special glass was broken on the one side. But the other hole worked just fine.

I was confused why he wanted me to use it. My eyesight was fantastic, but I figured out why after a quick scan of the horizon. The dust cloud kicked up by the following Mek Boy rig hoard had vanished. Snatching up the magner, I peered through the one working hole, but even with the special view, I saw things in the distance. We had only been traveling an hour or so. I banged on the hood, and when Angus leaned his head out, I informed him of this. He quickly stuck his arm out and made a few signals. The rig behind use made two loud short beeps and the caravan began to slow and within a few moments came to a halt.

Angus hopped out, his thick red beard wild and unkempt like his daughter's hair. "Keep yer eyes sharp, lad. If ye see them coming, start a-shouting."

And with that he was off, the caravan stopping as the various families and workers jumped out to re-gas and see what damage was incurred during the raid and what could be done to fix the water rig and Julius's rig.

I sat watch for over an hour, until Marcus, one of the other drivers, came walking past. Curious to the current goings on, I waved him down. "So what's the status of the rigs?"

"Water rig is shot up, but nothing major." Marcus sighed. "Julius's rig is leaking oil. We got it patched up for now. But we will need to replace the damaged hose pretty soon. Julius was hit, bullet went right through the rig, but also right through his shoulder. Stubborn S.O.B. kept driving the whole time. He's lost a good amount of blood."

"Shit! Is he gonna be okay?" I interjected quickly.

Marcus nodded. "I think so. Zena got him all patched up and the bleeding stopped. But he ain't gonna be driving for a bit. The Wranglers cleared out a spot in the back of their rig. Zena is gonna drive until her husband recovers."

"All right. Hey, you know if we plan on camping here or pushing on?" I shifted toward Marcus, my legs swinging off the side of the rig.

"Angus seemed to be pushing everyone to move fast. So, I assume move on." Marcus began moving away, heading back to his own rig.

"Hey, you seen Lily?" I called out quickly.

Marcus turned his head back but continued walking, a small smirk appearing. "Yeah, she is doing what she does. Off with the rest of her crazy girls, seeing what lies ahead. But don't ya worry. She will be back soon enough, and I'm sure you can sneak off to get yourself a few kisses before we head out."

My cheeks grew hot, as if I had been under the bright sun for hours. I merely nodded, turning around. I raised the magner up, pretending to scout the horizon, now eager to end this conversation. I had grown up alone and was unused to talks about physical affections with others. But Marcus had been correct. Me and Lily rarely got to spend any alone time together. Having *alone time* was a rare and precious thing when you didn't have your own rig yet. Even more so when you belonged to such close-knit family. Eventually, when I proved my worthiness to my new family, I would get my own rig. For now, I rode in Lily's rig. Well, to be more accurate, her father's rig. Since she was my family, but I had no rig, I depended on the generosity of her father. Although that wasn't really an issue. Angus was a good man. I had been told by others that he was extremely pleased that his only daughter had finally chosen a man to become one with. And that "said man," a.k.a. me, would be joining the caravan, and thus keeping his precious Lily close to him.

I sat there for almost an hour awaiting our departure. The caravan members used every moment of that hour to perform all kinds of minor maintenance on their rigs. The last few moments before leaving were then used to refuel ourselves. I was given a portion of dried fruit and had my water flask refilled.

But since I was on watch, the only moment I was free to jump off the rig was to relieve myself. After that, it was back on up, strapped in, and watching the horizon to the south. The sun was growing a little lower in the sky, but we still had a few more hours of light. I spun to face the north as the sound of engines filled my ears. Lily and her scouts on their two wheelers had returned. I raised my magner to observe their movements, which would let me know if they were being pursued. But I could tell by their relaxed weaving maneuvers they were fine.

It was time to get moving. Exploration was the name of the game now. The final goal? Get back heading east on a route we knew. Exploration was a very dangerous thing in a wasteland already filled with danger.

***

We waited for only a few moments to listen to the scouting intel. Ahead about thirty minutes was a city, one that was most certainly not empty. Lily described a large amount of movement, as well as signs of life, smoke, noise, light, etc. The main question was whether this city was more friend than foe. Could be an uncharted free-town, at least for our caravan, but also could have been a Mek Boys' hub. Which was a distinct possibility and would have explained the Mek Boys in the middle of nowhere ambushing us. Hell, it could even be a whole tribe of Savages. Normally Savages roamed the Wilds, as they were a nomadic tribe. But from time to time they entered cities to scavenge for supplies or to take them from the poor people that lived there.

But not all was bad news. A little luck seemed to be with us. The road we were on not only ran through the city, but peeled off to the east and west around the city. We would be able to skirt the edge of the city before heading east again, back in the right direction after only after a few hours heading north. All in all not a bad detour. We just had to avoid detection.

Which of course didn't happen. We had moved slowly, the roar of our engines down to a dull rumble. Right as we made the curve onto the eastbound road I spotted an approaching greeting party speeding toward us, at least twenty rigs pouring out of the city. Banging on the roof, I gained Angus's attention. "Angus! We got company approaching from the west, *fast.*"

"Damnit! Keep an eye on 'em, Jack. If any of those bastards get close, ya put a bullet into them like ya did the Mek Boys!" Angus quickly flashed a hand signal to the rig next to us. It replied with three loud blares from its horn. With that, the chase was on. We kicked our rigs into high gear, now once again fleeing for our freedom, but most likely our lives. I watched with a small pang of worry as I watched Lily fall behind, her scouts following suit behind and alongside her, dropping into formation as they fell behind to guard our rear.

This chase lasted for hours. The sun began to sink behind the looming horizon. But strangely enough, our pursuers never seemed to take the offensive. They would speed up, only to slow down as our scouts spun around and fired upon them. If they had been wishing to waste our ammo, they should have done it more often or sent up more heavily armored rigs that could take the hits. But every time we launched an offensive they withdrew, keeping a good distance most of the time. Even with the magner I couldn't tell what their plan was.

I hoped we weren't being led to another trap like the one before. But our salvation came from a new and unexpected source.

The barren land we drove on, like before, was barren for miles upon miles. Small, scattered wrecked structures and rusted rig frames littered the side of the road. But beyond that, nothing, until suddenly on the horizon I beheld a flash of gold. The barren wasteland transformed from a sea of brown to a sea of yellow as we approached an endless field of strange, long, stalky plants. Row after row of them, as far as the eye could see. And in the middle was the long, and now small-looking, road. We passed through the plants, and I found they were indeed tall. Each stalk by my guess was at least seven to eight feet high. But this strange barrier seemed to drive off our pursuers, as they drew to a halt before entering the field of golden-yellow plants.

We drove for another hour, but night had fallen, and with the overcast we needed to stop. Those rigs that had working lights dared not use them except in emergencies. Since we no longer assumed we were being followed, we began to park, each rig knowing where he was expected to be. The road was wide enough for two cars to drive side by side, with the two-wheelers able to easily go between. We parked with two rigs on either side, their tires still barely on the old, crumbling, hole-filled road.

Angus's rig was parked in the front, wedged between two other rigs. The rear was taken up by the Wranglers rig, forming an area in the middle where we could be surrounded on all sides. We always attempted to form a circle-like formation. The caravaners used a term to describe this practice called "circling the wagons." I had no idea what the hell a wagon was. But it didn't really matter. I knew it was done for safety. Within moments of the caravan stopping, people had already begun setting up their bedrolls, tents, and various other things. Our little caravan was as busy as a hive of stiggers—stiggers being small little flying insects that made large flaky nests. And if disturbed, they swarmed out and bit the hell out of a person. Their bites were not painful, but they left terrible red welts that if one was unlucky could become infected.

After unstrapping myself and hopping off the rig, I stretched for a minute before my curiosity got the best of me. I wandered over to inspect the strange, endless rows of this stalky yellow plant. As I drew closer, I saw they seemed to have strange pods attached to them and scattered all around their bases. Reaching out, I almost touched one of the strange pods, but my common sense, as well as the memories of what plants were capable of, quickly had me snatching my hand back to my side where it belonged. A sweet chuckle filled my ears, one that I knew well and already made my heart beat quicker.

"Aye, my beloved, it is good for ye to be cautious. But yer okay. These be corn stalks. They are a food plant. Although..." She paused, her voice taking on a more cautious tone. "I have nay seen it in such a plentiful manner. Not harvested, just left here to grow and then rot. There be piles of it all over the ground. Who would be daft enough to allow so much food to be wasted."

"Who indeed, daughter, who indeed?"

Angus had snuck up on the both of us. The whole family was super stealthy. And that was impressive for a man who was almost six and a half feet tall and built like he was part Savage. "But that be not our concern, nor a blessing for us, for the corn be well beyond eating. Gather up the fallen parts. They will burn well and will supplement our dwindling wood supplies." He clasped an arm around both me and Lily, dragging us into a vise-like hug. He leaned down and placed a tender kiss on his daughter's head. "I'm glad yer safe, my sweet lil firefly." Firefly, a very personal term of endearment. "Yah did me and our family proud today."

"Da!" Lily cried out.

I watched in amusement and slight discomfort from the tight hug as one of the toughest warriors in the caravan cheeks grew a deep red as she squirmed like a caught animal.

Angus laughed softly before looking at me. "And don't think I will be forgetting you, lad. Ye did a good job today. I heard from the scouts how yer shot took down two rigs." He patted my back and leaned down toward me.

I closed my eyes, my body growing tense. *Oh Lord, please don't kiss me.*

Thankfully no kiss came, only a whisper that turned into a knowing chuckle. "Yah get a little hot under the collar when people be firing up my lil firefly. But that's good, means yer gonna protect her even if she be able to handle it herself." His voice took on a more solemn tone. "Ye always have to look out for yer wife. Even if yah think she can handle it, ye need to always be there, *always.*"

I looked up, but Angus was already turning away, his vise-like bear hug gone as she stalked back to the caravan. "He is talking about your mo—"

Lily raised her hand, stalling the end of my sentence. "Nay, Jack, ye know I won't be talking about her... not yet." She raised her head, those beautiful green eyes shimmering softly with barely withheld tears, a soft smile given. Turning, she bent down and scooped up a large pile of the old corn before carrying it back to the center of the caravan.

I spoke softly as she walked away, her large patchwork cloak swaying behind her. "Okay, baby, but one day I will need to know what happened to your mother." I knew she didn't hear me, but that was okay.

I turned to gather up my own supply of old corn lying on the ground, but froze as a wind brought soft whispers to my ears. Whispers from within the corn. I blinked and looked up. "Hello?"

I heard rustling, and my body tensed for a moment, every hair on my body suddenly standing straight up and a cold chill ran down my spine, but I quickly attempted to shake it off. "Just the wind brushing these plants together... just the wind." I hurried back, eager to be within the center of the circle where the flicker of firelight was already growing.

I sat now, finally able to relax. The sound of merriment filled our small caravan as we sat together, ate together, and celebrated another day ending with one another. There were many reasons we had to be merry, although our meal tonight was spare, more dried fruit with some dried meat. The company made it a feast as my beloved sat next to me, her slender but firm frame nestled into me, her infectious laughter filling the surrounding area.

But despite the warmth of my love at my side, something gnawed at me. The fire was blazing now, the corn burning well, but the light... it didn't reach as far as it should. *Shouldn't it illuminate more?* As I look around, everyone's faces seemed hidden by shadows, all but the beauty right next to me. Her pale, freckled beauty almost always shined. But everyone else... shouldn't I be able to see their faces more clearly? All I had had to drink was water, no alcohol. That was when I realized the fire didn't feel very warm at all. My brows furrowed as I shivered and pressed closer to Lily. She, as always, felt warm. And with her warmth I finally managed to drift off to sleep.

***

My dreams were dark that night: eyes in the corn, eyes that never blinked; whispers that I heard but didn't understand, spoken in a tongue I hoped I never did comprehend.

I awoke with those whispers fading in my mind, now only half remembered echoes. The sun had risen, and I lay curled up next to Lily, a blanket over us, as we lay in the open by the now dead fire. I was not the first to awaken. Zena, Julius's wife, was up along with their daughter. Julius had been propped up and they were changing his bandages.

I called out softly, "How's he doing, Zena?"

She turned, and a smile stretched too thinly upon her slender face. "Not well, Jack. The bleeding has stopped... but he has a fever now. We have a little elderflower, so I've made him some tea to help. But we don't have much more in stock. I hope we can find some, or something else once we get out of these..." Zena paused, looking around slowly, as if seeking something. "...creepy fields. They make me uneasy for some reason."

"I know what you mean, Zena." Slipping from my lover's warm embrace, I snuck to relieve myself behind one of the rigs before starting to pack things up. I wanted to get the hell out of here as soon as possible. My uneasiness had grown with Zena's acknowledgment that this place was indeed creepy.

It was only a matter of minutes before others arose and their movements awoke others, and within fifteen minutes the camp was busy once more. In thirty minutes, we were heading down the road, the movement comforting me. I opted to sit on the top of the rig this time. Sentries were not needed, but the fresh air and sun brought back glimpses of Vegas, sitting by the window, the warm sun and a steady breeze kissing my skin. I had few fond memories of Vegas, but that was one of them.

So lost was I within my own memories of the past that I didn't realize we had stopped till squealing brakes and a hard jerking stop shook me from my reverie. I looked around quickly, my heart skipping a beat, assuming something was wrong. But I quickly determined the cause for our stop. A motionless rig sat on the left side of the road some hundred yards ahead. It was a small rig. A small amount of paint left on its rusty frame showed that it had once been a bluish tint. But beyond the color, and the fact it still seemed to have some bags strapped to it, it seemed abandoned.

"All right, lads, we have come across this before. Be on the lookout for ambushers," Angus cried as he stepped out of the rig below me.

Our scouts, who had been in the lead, dismounted from their bike rigs. Lily, who was normally always in the lead, stayed behind as she motioned with a few jerks of her hands for her fellow scouts to move ahead. As they stalked closer, they all withdrew a small pistol, along with various types of one-handed close-combat objects from small scrap blades to actual blades, and even a spiked club.

Lily was busy retrieving her preferred method of combat when off the bike—her bow. I had seen her skill with it the first time we met in Vegas. She had placed an arrow straight through a rad coyote's glowing green eye, while she was flipping through the air. She was a deadeye with her bow, and as she nocked an arrow, she began to stalk forward.

A fleeting thought to bring my own rifle to bear crossed my mind. But unless something happened, I did not want to risk shooting through my new family. Only Lily with her bow had the accuracy not to be inconvenienced or worried by people between her and whatever her target was.

"Movement!" one of the scouts cried out, and as one the whole group dropped to one knee and raised their pistols. Even before that happened, Lily's bow was drawn and aimed at the bug.

"Whoever ye be, show yerself. No violence will be given if none is shown." Lily's confident voice was the one to call out. We waited, many gazing out among the corn, waiting for the sudden rush of ambushers.

The door of the rig creaked open, and instead of being greeted by an ambush, we were met by a pair of grimy oil-stained hands. "P-p-please d-don't fire."

The stuttering voice somehow matched the gangly figure that crawled forth from within the rig. He was a spindly man wearing worn, tattered, dirty blue-jean overalls, his chest exposed as well as his clearly showing ribs. He looked like he was half-starved to death. A ratty brown beard and mostly bald head accentuated his almost crazed features. He got to his knees, head lowered, arms raised, but even from a distance they could be seen shaking, almost struggling to remain upright.

"D-do you have any f-food? Or w-water." His raised arms lowered slightly, grasping one another in a desperate plea. *"Please."*

The scouts, glanced back at Lily, and Lily glanced back at Angus. I watched Angus think for a moment, but I knew him, and I knew the rules of our people... well, my adopted people. No violence had been given, no disrespect shown, no sense of an ambush, only a desperate man who was starving and thirsty. Angus finally nodded, and with that simple motion, guns and bows were lowered and people were already exiting their rigs. I guess it was time for an early lunch.

Zeek, as we soon found out was the man's name, sat around us and had almost been silent for the past fifteen minutes, well beyond his slurping and gulping as he drank and scarfed down all we offered him. Finally, after a loud belch, he slumped back against one of our rigs. He gazed up, those eyes brighter looking as he was finally refreshed.

"Yah all a group of Trekers?"

Trekers, as I had found out, was the name other people had given to us and those like us who braved the wilds of this ravaged land to bring knowledge, trade, and the almost lost art of hospitality to the various groups of survivors we encountered. They had a very strong sense of honor. Being hospitable was important to them. A Treker would rather starve and go thirsty than breach the code of hospitality. Of course, the same courtesy was expected in return from those welcomed into our camps.

Our camp had once taken in a young boy. He had claimed he was abandoned and starving. The real truth was his family sent him in to steal supplies. He would drop them off on the edge of the camp during the night so his family could pick them up. He was caught one night after suspicion rose. Angus personally broke one of his hands, and I mean smashed it up bad, as well as one of his feet, and left him there for his family to find. He had broken their code of hospitality and had incurred my family's wrath. I prayed this man had no such ill intentions in mind.

"Aye." Angus nodded in acknowledgement. "I'm Angus, head of our family. I officially welcome ye to our caravan."

"Never seen your caravan in town before... in fact how was it you are here? My people in Lankers would have never let someone go east through the corn fields." Zeek slowly put down his bowl, looking now with a strange intensity in his eyes toward Angus.

Angus rubbed the back of his head, riling up his own curly red locks that he had gifted to his daughter. "Ah, well about that, lad. We be on the run from some Mek Boys earlier in the day. We were traveling our known routes to the south, and the damned fools tried to ambush us. They blockaded the road east. Thankfully me daughter and her scouts discovered the trap. We were able to bypass it, but that took us north toward yer city of... Lankers?"

Zeek nodded.

"Well, we didn't be knowing if your people would be welcoming, or if the town be filled with Savages. So, we skirted the outskirts, attempting to get back eastward. When rigs emerged from yer city, we feared the worst and fled." Angus wiped his brow now, which had broken out with beads of sweat, something that happened when he realized he had, in hindsight, made a bad decision.

"They weren't coming out to get yah; they were coming out to warn yah." Zeek's confirmation of what we all had been starting to think brought out a cluster of groans and profanities among the group.

"Aye, I be seeing that now. Something seemed off to me when they didn't fire at us. Their quick retreats upon being fired upon were also baffling." Angus's voice was strained as he wrung his hands together.

I knew in Angus's mind he had wronged those people, and even though it was unknowing, had been rude toward those who had only wished to help him and the caravan, which he was responsible for. But his self-imposed guilt was stifled, as Angus was not a dull person.

"Why would they be wanting to stop us from going this way? What is past these fields that warrants such caution?"

"It's not what lies past the fields. It is *Those that dwell within* that are the problem." Zeek's voice had become a chilled whisper upon uttering the strange term, or name.

Silence reigned for a moment, as if that statement had somehow stolen the voices from all gathered. I found my voice first, but noticed that I felt cold inside, as if chilled from a strong wind that didn't exist. "Who, or what, are *Those that dwell within?*

"No one knows what they are. Or where they came from. But they and the fields have always been here as long as anyone can remember. They dwell among the corn, never leaving it. They always hunger, and they try to trap people by leaving things you want or need along the edges of the corn. If... if you take something, you are trapped here unless you pay for your freedom with a willing blood sacrifice. Otherwise, you will drive and drive. No matter how long you drive, the corn will never end. I… I am the last of my family. My wife, child, and I were traveling to a small fortified town on the other side of the corn. There is more living space out there, and the corn keeps the Savages, and all other hostile creatures away from us, at least from one side."

"Come on now." I crossed my arms, my eyebrows rising in obvious disbelief. "Ghosts and monsters don't exist, at least not the kind that can't be explained by rad poisoning or various chemical mutations. If there are some kind of people living in the corn, causing problems, they can be handled one way or another. Hell, let's just burn the corn. You all know how well it burns and how dry it is. Let's burn the fields down and just drive away. It will keep them occupied."

Zeek was already shaking his head, a now steady stream of tears falling. "That won't work. My wife, Sheila, and I tried this. We had stopped to relieve ourselves. We only took our eyes off of him for a second. But that was all they needed. He was too young to understand, only a few summers old."

Zeek reached down, fumbling with something inside the front pocket of his overalls. Slowly he withdrew a strange, round, colored object with a small loop of string sticking out of it. He held the item up and it slowly began to spin, more string coming out of it. The disc-shaped item spun, and it began to glow, beautiful colored lights flashing.

There were soft gasps, as well as other sounds from those around us, along with soft whispers wondering what it was.

Angus was the one who answered the crowd. "It be a child's toy. You wrap the string around it, and when you let it fall, it spins. It seems this one makes colorful flashes. So, you're saying since he picked this up, you were now trapped here, unable to leave?"

"We became desperate. Sheila grabbed Vigo and tossed him in the rig. But we deep down knew it was too late. After five hours of driving, we knew we were doomed. We blamed one another, screaming and fighting till we were out of gas. We knew not to expect any others, and even if they came, they could do nothing. If we joined their group and drove with them, they would be cursed as well."

Protests suddenly erupted, but Zeek quickly waved his hands. "I can sit with you, I can share drink and food with you, just not travel. Well, I can now, for you have taken from *Those that dwell within.*

"Finally, with a sudden, well, what we thought was inspiration, we decided, like you just did, to burn the corn. Siphoning what little gas we had left in our tank, we lit both sides of the fields on fire. It seemed to work like a charm. The fire spread rapidly, consuming the corn like some holy fire wiping away the evil that marked this land. It was just about this time we realized the smoke was growing thicker around us and we found it hard to breathe. We stumbled into our rig, covering Vigo in a blanket, and holding on to one another. The last thing I remember was hearing Vigo's and Sheila's coughing. Then I passed out. When I awoke…"

Zeek had paused, a fresh set of tears once more running down his cheeks. "When I awoke, Sheila was gone. The passenger's side door was open and there was a large bloody trail leading from the seat, across the road… and into the corn. They had taken her. I never knew they could leave the corn, but it seemed that our trespass against them, had allowed them an unknown freedom. They had taken her, and the corn…" Zeek gazed around, looking from one side of the road, to the other. "…was back, untouched by the flames that only a short while ago had consumed it."

Soft gasps filled the area as my family recoiled with fright at this tale. Off in the distance I heard a soft cry.

"Dear God, I can see the dried blood still on the road. He is telling the truth."

Lily was the next to speak, although her voice was filled with a mixture of emotions to such a degree that even I could not identify what she was exactly feeling. "Where be your son, Zeek? Where be Vigo?" Even her accent seemed stronger, her voice growing harder as she spoke.

Zeek shook his head slowly, lowering it in shame before raising an unsteady arm and pointing back toward his rig. "I… I wouldn't… I couldn't let them take him. Yah gotta understand. They took her, and I could stand hearing him cry out to me for his mother, then days later for water and food." Zeek's head rose and his eyes now seemed almost vacant. I made it quick… when he was sleeping. He didn't suffer; he didn't know. Just a quick jerk and a snap and he was gone.

"If I had been brave enough, I could have saved them. They require blood, willing blood freely given. That is their price for anything taken. One must walk into the corn, a willing sacrifice to *Those that dwell within*. If I had been brave enough, my wife and child would still be alive."

I reached out and gently pulled Angus back a little before whispering to him, "Angus, you're not actually believing this crazy? There might be something in the corn. Something had to drag his wife away, but there ain't no ghost people who dwell in the corn, that can't leave the corn, but then can leave the corn, but only when you burn the corn. Then they can leave to steal someone which then magically regrows the burned corn. It's ridiculous. Something killed his wife, maybe even his child, after they ran out of gas here. Combine that with starvation and thirst… anyone would break. I'm sure once he is able to sleep, drink, and eat more we will eventually be able to find out what truly happened." I released a loud breath, realizing my hushed rant had left me slightly breathless.

Angus just nodded and gave me a strange, almost sorrowful, look. He turned to everyone and raised his hands. The family quickly grew silent. "This be unexpected and unwanted news. But do not fear. You are my family and I, as always, will take care of you. For now, let us gas up Zeek's rig. He will join us as we test to see if this curse has truly befallen us. For three days we shall travel. If we are nay free of the corn fields, we shall then decide what be our next step."

And like that, the decision had been made. I knew better than to question Angus publicly, as even as his only daughter's husband it would force him to act against me and would bring shame upon Lily. Shrugging, I headed back to my rig and went to hop up and onto my padded and belted scouting seat on the top.

Angus grabbed me gently as I began to climb. "Nay, lad, I want ye in the rig with me. We need to be having a talk."

That was unusual. Unless weather was bad, I almost always rode on top. My days spent sitting up in a tower in Vegas surveying my surroundings had sharpened my eyes. I could detect the slightest difference in the horizon and spot movement most would miss.

As I made my way into the passenger's seat, I glanced in the back. Angus's rig was packed with a little bit of everything. It held his, Lily's, and even my own personal possessions. Along with food, gas, and most of the more precious trade goods we had, the larger rig was stuffed. Enough room had been made, so someone could go lie down behind the two seats in case the weather was bad and we needed to sleep inside. Angus jumped in right after I did, and within a few minutes—since we needed to gas up Zeek's rig—we were on the move.

Angus was oddly quiet for a while as he drove. The silence broke after perhaps half an hour. "Ye have been sheltered, lad. Your city, Vegas, it was protected from certain things. Sure, there were rad creatures, and various other tribes constantly warring for dominance, but ye need to understand. When this world almost died many, many years ago, many things did die, many things changed, as well as many things were born into this world. But there are things, far older things, that awoke when the lights of the world died. Magic kept those things at bay, the magic of the old world. Your city seemed like it was ruined, but below it that old magic still flowed. I knew this for a fact, so I seen it with me own eyes as we left. Your tower was a pillar of light. The light of the old world. The dark things that awoke in this world are driven away by that magic. It pushes them away almost, keeps them at bay."

"Angus, please, I'm no child," I interrupted, slightly irritated at the fact Angus was buying into this guy's craziness.

But just as quick as I had cut in, I was cut off. "Nay, lad, you listen to me. I, as well as the others, even Lily, have seen things, encountered things. Many terrible, some amazing. But all of them are not caused by radiation, or by mutations. I have even seen people who glow with a strange light, a greenish... witchlight. These people can summon forth powers normal people couldn't even imagine—conjuring terrors, or flames, or even healing terrible wounds in a matter of seconds. They are rare, but each trip across these tattered lands brings more and more stories of them, more encounters with them and encounters and stories of unknown things, terrible unexplained creatures and occurrences. Your city, because of the old-world magic that runs below it, was safe from these things. But you are with us now; you are part of me family. You need to know; you need to believe. Because believing, can save yer life. Disbelief will do nothing but keep you blind until it is too late." Angus gave me a rather long, slightly stern, sideways glance.

I met his eyes with my own steady and unflinching gaze. "I understand that sometimes things seem like they are magical. They seem like they have no possible explanation other than being caused by otherworldly entities, or mysterious spooks and creatures. But... I lived in a city where things that I did, things that I saw, that looked like magic. Or people who seemed like they could use magic were in reality scammers, people who wanted to control you or gain things from you. I made water appear high above the ground from apparently nowhere. I created fake light without a battery being seen or used." Your own daughter thought it was magic. She has told me so. But it wasn't.

I could see Angus was about to interrupt, his mouth already opening. "Let me finish. I understand that I have not seen everything in this world. Perhaps there are spooks, magic, and otherworldly creatures that have awoken. And for your safety, Lily's safety as well as the rest of the caravan's safety, I shall be cautious about anything I encounter that I am unsure about." I already did this, so this wouldn't be much of an issue for me, but I wanted to say something to placate Angus.

Angus nodded slightly. We continued driving in silence, which was fine by me. There was indeed a growing, gnawing worry inside of me as the corn fields continued undisturbed, mile after mile. Hour after hour.

***

We stopped for the night. The mood was somber. The corn still remained on all sides, and now it exuded a sense of malice so thick it weighed us down. Fires were kept low, using only small amounts of our dwindling wood supply. None dared to approach the corn and partake from the mounds of dried plants that lay around the stalks. As if that wasn't bad enough, Julius was getting worse. Zena tended to him, but his fever was growing and the caravan was out of any remedies to aid in his recovery. Things would be over soon. Zeek had mentioned there was a small settlement on the other side of the corn. That I remembered, and that statement of his I believed. Once we reached it we could barter for treatment for Julius, resupply, and be on our way with new knowledge of the area and two new towns to trade with.

Early next morning I became terribly aware that my worldly views on the supernatural might need to be reconsidered. I stared down, as did the rest of my group, at the signs of a campsite, one made in the middle of the road, one with a large, dried, bloody drag mark on the outskirts.

Our campsite, the one we had found Zeek at. The same site that we had left… two days ago.

The caravan was in an uproar. People were panicking. Angus was doing all he could to keep his people from losing it. Some of our clan claimed that they had not used any corn and thus were only cursed because they traveled with us. Others blamed Zeek, saying we only became trapped because he now traveled with us.

The caravan was on the verge of tearing itself apart, fueled by fear of endless days among the corn, of a slow death at the hands of thirst or starvation—all of this brought on by the fear of *Those that dwell within.*

I was not concerned for Zeek. No one would dare harm him. Such an atrocious act would be an affront of all we stood for. Any Treker would die before bringing harm unto a welcomed guest. At most, they might expel him from our group, making him travel alone. But if we were truly trapped, that wouldn't accomplish anything. We would just keep running into him, over and over and over again. People leaving was more of an issue, as no one was forced to stay with the family. Any who chose to leave would be allowed to, with whatever property was their own as well as a farewell gift of food and supplies. But once you leave, you may never return. And such a loss would be a terrible blow to our family.

Angus traveled from rig to rig, speaking to the families they belonged to. He was a physically imposing man, but he was gifted with a silver tongue. And within a few hours, tempers had calmed, although everyone was close to the breaking point. Fear, worry, and sorrow still filled the camp as we broke down for the night. Angus was meeting with the heads of the other families, trying to work out some kind of plan. I stood on the outskirts of the caravan, staring into the corn.

I heard the whispers again. But this time I wasn't so sure it was just the stalks rustling in the wind. I felt eyes upon me but saw nothing.

"Jack?" Lily's sweet voice broke the rustling whispers from within the corn.

I turned, the chill of this night banished by the nearness of Lily. "Yes, my lil firefly?" I smirked, responding to her with her father's, until recently, secret nickname.

Lily's beautiful green eyes narrowed. My greeting was returned to me in the form of a small but powerful fist being slammed into my arm.

I groaned, cradling my poor arm. "Damn baby, I think you broke it!" I chuckled.

"Ye be fine. Hush your crying and man up." She pressed up to me, placing a kiss on my cheek before leaning her body against mine. "You on guard duty?"

"Yeah, I won't be in bed till late. Moon still has…" I raised my hand bringing my four fingers together, and placed them next to the moon, my index finger barely touching its outline. Then flipped my hand once over, then once again. Each of my four fingers measured an amount of time. Once the moon reached a point in the sky equal to my tenth finger, I would be done. "Till just around here." I held my hand there for her to see.

I smiled at her and saw those lovely plump lips turn into a pout. "I hate these long trips. I want ye all to myself. I hope the town after this has rooms for rent. I want alone time with me man." She leaned in close, her warm breath tickling my neck. But just as quick as her breath had warmed me, my skin grew cold as she drew away, hips swaying in a terribly teasing manner as she headed back toward the inner ring of the caravan before heading to, then into, our rig.

The night was anything but quiet. The sounds of slumber filled my ears. The fire had all but died out, but that was okay. My night vision had fully kicked in, and with an almost full moon, I was able to see pretty well down the road. But it was not there that I was looking. It was within the corn. The wind had died down, but the soft indecipherable whispers continued. I nervously gripped my precious rifle, holding it tight. The whispers continued, their words just beyond comprehension. But I felt—I knew deep within myself—that I never wanted to hear what they were saying. For such knowledge was not meant for me.

The whispers were suddenly interrupted by a soft groan. Followed by a dragging-like sound. My mind instantly flashed to Zeek's story and the bloody drag mark. My rifle snapped up and I gazed around, swinging it back and forth, looking for the sound. Another soft groan filled the night. My heart began to race. Should I wake the caravan? Should I alert someone? Where the fuck was the other guard on post? How has he not heard that noise? Unless, he was the one groaning. Perhaps *Those that dwell within* had gotten him.

I moved quickly to the opposite side of the caravan, peering around a rig, I found the guard… sleeping, slumped against one of the rigs, gun in his hands. He was snoring softly.

"Shit." I was pissed but also relieved that he was alive but asleep. If we survived this… no, not if but when, I would inform Angus and let him deal with this issue. But for now, I needed to figure out where the groaning and scrapping had come from.

Heading back to my side of the caravan, I heard the faint groan once more. As I peered along the edge of the rig I had been guarding, I finally saw movement, something dark crawling slowly out from between two rigs about thirty feet ahead of me. It looked like a person. Hefting my rifle, I crept forward, staying low until I had closed the gap, raising my rifle. The groaning stopped and the crawling figure turned its head to look at me.

"Julius?" I mouthed the name softly as the figured revealed itself to me. "Julius, what the hell are you doing?"

His voice was weak, raspy. "Please help me, Jack. I—I don't have the strength." Julius shuddered, his body wracked with coughs, which he tried his best to muffle.

"Help you? Damnit, Julius, what are you doing out…?" Insight flooded my mind, and I knew what he was trying to do. Zeek had told us that the only way out was a willing blood sacrifice. *Those that dwell within* demanded a willing blood sacrifice. "You can't. What about Zena? What about Vigo?" I was angry. The growing volume of my voice was evidence of this.

"Please, keep your voice down." Julius was wheezing, struggling to speak complete sentences. "I'm dying…, Jack. My blood… is poisoned… from my… wound." Another rasping deep cough rattled poor Julius's body. "If those things… in the corn demand blood… let them… have mine. Hopefully, they will choke… on it. I… am willing to… do… this for my family, for all of… you. But I don't… have the strength. Please, lend me… some of yours. Help me walk to my… fate like… like a man. Not… crawl like a child." Julius was wheezing with each breath now, speaking was becoming more and more of a labor for him.

I tried to swallow the sudden large lump in my throat, but it just wouldn't go down. "Julius, there has to be another way. You just can't go in there. Who knows what will happen?"

"It is... the only way. I'm already dead. If... I die out here... it means nothing. But if I go in there..." He looked toward the corn. "It means everything! I... I won't let Zena or Vigo die... because I was too weak... like Zeek was." He gazed back from the corn up to me. "Lily, might die... Angus might die. If... I don't, go in... who will? Who... will die for this caravan? Please... help me to save everyone. Please, Jack, in the name of God, help me." His raised his arm, hand open, reaching out for mine.

God forgive me, but I took it. I put his arm around my body and helped him to his feet. And then I led him to the edge of the corn and let him go. For a moment, I thought he would fall. But I watched as Julius summoned up all that was left in him and slowly stumbled into the corn.

The whispers from within the corn grew louder, now chanting in a language I still didn't understand, and was grateful for that fact, as the words made my stomach twist, and my mind shuddered in revulsion. I shut my eyes tight, but the chant only went on for a few seconds.

When I opened them again, Julius was gone. I didn't even hear the rustle of corn from someone moving through it. Just silence, not even the whispers. I turned, tears in my eyes. I walked back into the caravan to wake Angus and let him know what had occurred.

***

Angus had quickly awoken the rest of the caravan. If Julius's sacrifice had indeed freed us, he was not willing to wait till morning to find out. Zena had remained quiet, her eyes red from tears as she now took over the position of head of her family. Somehow, I think she knew what he had planned. Perhaps he had told her. No one asked; no one wanted to know.

Zeek had chosen to stay. He was unsure if Julius's sacrifice had paid for him as well. He would not risk cursing us twice by traveling with us. He would wait an hour and then follow. If he was free, he would meet us on the outskirts of the corn fields.

Before we left, Angus walked over to Zeek, who was busy packing up his own rig. I watched as Angus placed an old revolver and a single bullet into Zeek's hand. "In case you can't get out, lad, don't let them take you."

Zeek just nodded, loaded the revolver, and jumped into his rig.

We drove for hours, the sun starting to creep into the sky, our hope dwindling. But the roar of Lily and her scouts flew back through the caravan, howls of joy erupting from them. They spun around, driving past us and pointing. Up ahead we saw in just a few minutes what had brought them such joy—the end of the corn fields. Just ahead of us they ended and were replaced by rolling hills covered with green grass and sparse trees and shrubs. Off in the far distance upon a prominent grass covered hill, civilization appeared. A small town, most likely the outpost Zeek had mentioned to us. But to me and I am sure others in our caravan it was the sign of our victory over the dark forces within the corn, a victory bought with blood, but a victory nonetheless.

As we exited the corn, I gave one last look back toward what could have been our prison and tomb, the seemingly unending fields of corn. I wished I hadn't. Dark figures stood among the stalks, watching us leave: dark shadowy figures with red glowing eyes, eyes that never blinked, eyes that always watched as we one by one left their domain. Those eyes looked hungry. They looked angry.

SHORTED
Patrick Freivald

Barry couldn't breathe.

He stumbled, dizzy, chest squeezed by a sudden, inexplicable panic. The world hazed from the bustle of a New York City crosswalk to red to black. A creeping, omnipresent dread brought him, shaking and sweating, to the asphalt. Legs bumped against him as the crowd skirted his fetal body, other seventy and eighty-year-olds rushing to and from jobs as meaningless as their lives.

He crawled on hands and knees toward the shoulder, desperate to get out of traffic before the light turned. The thought of tires crushing his bones and rupturing his organs brought a new wave of panic. Nobody would stop for a Short; he wouldn't have.

Once on the curb he sat back, squeezed his eyes shut against the flashes of sunlight on passing cars, hummed to himself to drown out the rustling shuffle of a million feet, like spiders casting webs across his brain. He forced himself to recall the Professional Development training for dealing with Shorts, a seminar the government required over thirty years earlier after the first chips failed: Shorts may become confused, anxious, irrational. Desperate. After decades with the regulation chip, they'll be at a loss what to do with a world they find suddenly strange and terrifying, and may become violent. Standing protocol: ignore them, get on with your business, and let the police deal with them.

The police!

They'd picked him up sixty years ago for stealing a car, a stupid act brought about by nothing more than boredom. Compassionate but firm, they'd brought him in and given him his chip, and everything had run like clockwork since. With his help they found—

My sister! He hadn't thought of Sasha since, his moods and concerns regulated by the neural implant. She had had brown hair like his, and blue eyes. She must have gone gray long ago, and would look just like their mother.

Mama! She couldn't still be alive, not after all this time.

Lying on the curb, he wept for her.

***

"Why did scientists seed the sky?" Miss Schotts surveyed the room before calling on Barry, to the disappointment of Jayden, who pouted and crossed her arms.

"To increase the albedo of the Earth!" A new word, learned only that day; Barry tasted it on his tongue. Al-bee-dough. A lumpy word, it sounded like a town in Arizona, or a disease that left huge warts all over your skin.

"That's right," his teacher said. "By upping the reflectivity of the upper atmosphere—making it shinier—climatologists like your dad are going to save us all from global warming."

Over the following months, as a way to teach percentages to Barry's fourth-grade class, Miss Schotts had incorporated the numbers into her lessons—0.7 increased to 0.76, an increase of 8.57%, made by dispersing reflective nanoparticles into the upper atmosphere. His pride at successful calculation—on paper but without a calculator—locked the numbers into his mind. They followed the results through the months, adjusting their figures on a paper chart Miss Schotts had pinned up next to the Smart Board. Barry got to adjust the chart every day at the beginning of class, his reward for being the son of the man who led the project that would save mankind.

He remembered her frown when 8.57% became 9.2%, her furrowed brow at 10.1%. When they hit 12.8% Barry leaped up onto the stool before the class bell had rung to add more construction paper to the chart, and almost slipped off at the coughing sob that had erupted from the teacher's throat. He turned, tacks in one hand, paper in the other, to find her curled up in her chair, shaking, face buried in her knees. She'd shrieked when Becky tried to comfort her and didn't stop until school security dragged her away—and Barry hadn't missed the wet streaks down the guard's cheeks, either.

***

On the curb, he kept his eyes squeezed shut and sobbed, unable to contain the anguish of never seeing again the loved ones he hadn't thought about in six decades, unable to process the nightmare world around him, billions of citizens acting out the death throes of human existence until their pointless bodies crumbled to dust. Those years flashed through his mind: punching a clock to shuffle countless

255

medical records for the National Health Board and pass them on to someone else, collecting a check of useless money to pay for an apartment where he sat and watched live feeds of other people doing the same kind of work on his giant television, marking off the days on his electronic calendar because the chip found time important enough to notice, jobs important enough to do. He'd exercised to stay in shape, and for a few decades read United Nations updates on the plight of countries who had refused chipping, until he realized they'd been sending the same, recycled updates for at least ten years.

Strong arms wrapped him, and he cried into them, muttering fractal despondencies into their unyielding embrace. They lifted him, set him down on a soft surface.

He opened his eyes when the world jerked. A van, the cab separated from the passenger compartment by a cage. Thick padding covered the floor and walls, the off-white color of clouds choked by smog. Sitting up, he steadied himself against the wall as the driver careened through the streets, barely glimpsed through the window of the passenger's compartment.

Her wizened face a mass of wrinkled, semi-transparent skin, gray hair tumbled in wondrous curls to spill across the padded shoulders of her police uniform. The police had to wear armor because Shorts could turn violent in a moment. The chipped had nothing to gain, but Shorts had nothing to lose; the difference in behavior couldn't be more stark, according to the sixty-something who'd given the lecture. He'd be dead by now too, his estate turned over to the government for caretaking.

Caretaking for what?

Barry shuddered, consumed by childhood memories no longer filtered through a dispassionate lens built of P-N junctions and microscopic solder joints.

***

His parents had pulled him out of school, taking Barry and Sasha into the mountains to a home Dad had bought "in case things went wrong." A log cabin on the surface, it had a basement six times bigger than the house, all of it given over to hydroponic gardens and rabbit cages. Sasha loved the garden, and loved watching wolves and deer and the occasional elk with their father's binoculars, especially the wolves. She worked without complaint but refused to kill rabbits for their meals; his father hadn't spared Barry that kindness. They home-schooled as winter set in early, early enough to bury crops in California under first inches of snow, then feet. People fled the mountains as the snow piled high, and their father's telescoping rods thrust solar panels ever higher in search of every spare watt.

In the Sierra Nevadas, February stretched into June, and the news spoke of famine, of ships ice-locked in New York Harbor, of a mass exodus toward the equator, of bodies piled a hundred high at closed borders. It spoke of hydroponics projects beyond a scale mankind had ever dreamed.

And it spoke of Nyloxx.

Recipients determined by anonymous lottery in the Western world, by fiat elsewhere, the drug would sterilize millions, take pressure off of dwindling resources and give the rest of the human race a fighting chance. A year became two as they ate rabbits and watched old TV shows and learned from books in Dad's library until the day Dad didn't come out of his study. Mom couldn't bring herself to look, and Sasha wouldn't do it, so Barry had put the revolver back in the hidden compartment in the bottom drawer, dragged the body outside where the snow could bury it, and cleaned up the mess—he'd killed and butchered enough rabbits by then that the blood hadn't bothered him, not all that much, and nothing had struggled under his hands as he broke its neck.

He only cried later, at night, biting on a finger so they couldn't hear him.

***

The back door opened to a blast of sunlight, snapping Barry from his reverie. Two blank-faced policemen flanked the driver. Salt-and-pepper hair, good muscle tone, they couldn't have been more than sixty-five. LGs—the last generation.

"Get down, please," one said.

He did, joints aching as he clambered over the bumper and trailer hitch onto the broken asphalt parking lot.

"What's going to happen to me?" It came out a blubbering mess, a tumor of worry unleashed across his mind in an orgy of unwanted emotion. Standing straight, he sniffled, wiped his nose with the back of his hand, and repeated himself in a calmer tone. "What's going to happen to me?"

"Do you understand that your regulator has failed?"

He nodded.

"And that the neural interfaces are too delicate? That once failed it cannot be repaired or replaced?"

Another nod.

"Do you understand that we cannot allow the de-chipped to live among the normal populace?"

He hesitated. For the first time he wondered why; but because he understood the fact, he nodded again.

"We have an area for the de-chipped. You'll not be allowed to leave, but as long as you don't try to escape or commit violence you'll be allowed to stay as long as you like. You'll enjoy all government services uninterrupted."

"Okay." He cast his eyes down and allowed the officers to lead him through the door. It closed behind him, and through the wall he heard the crunch of tires on gravel. He looked up.

Men and women sat at tables in an outdoor yard, watching ancient programs on televisions hung on the walls or talking in small groups. They ignored him, so he returned the favor to sit at an empty picnic table and wait for whatever would happen to happen.

He hadn't meant to cry, but he wiped tears from his eyes and shoved down memories of his family.

***

As ultraviolet light pulverized the nanoparticles and the snow melted, survivors drifted back to their homes or dug out from where they'd holed down. A billion people had died, and it would be another several years before crop levels could even hope to return to normal. Nyloxx in genetically-modified food had prevented millions of births, and would prevent billions more if all went to plan. A reduced population could, over time, be managed by the dwindling resources of an exhausted planet.

It took three years for things to return to normal, or a veneer of normal stretched over regret and loss. Barry and Sasha watched the renewed news broadcasts from the safety of their mountain refuge, Barry itching to get out of their icy tomb, Sasha already planning how best to help people. On their TV screen they watched the survivors go back to work and rebuild their lives as if they hadn't just dodged the apocalypse, as if they hadn't murdered and stolen their way through the Long Winter, as if they hadn't "done what they had to do" at the expense of anything and anyone that got in their way. Billions of monsters fell grateful into banality, seizing the opportunity to forget. Then, given the chance, these people elected the same politicians, who vowed greater oversight over the same scientists, who in turn said they were very sorry and vowed to be so much more careful in the future.

His mother enrolled them in private school, and booked them tennis and golf lessons, and went back to work at the charity, now overseeing the stunning number of orphans created by the savagery of the past half-decade. Barry read and learned and golfed—he had no aptitude for tennis, and no desire to gain one—and with the help of tutors and teachers climbed to the top ten percent of his class. Sasha volunteered at a refugee camp until the day she took a beating for being her father's daughter. They'd broken her nose and bruised her kidney, and six weeks later the sixteen-year-old girl went back, defiant and fearless in her search for a better humanity.

***

Wood creaked next to him.

"Hi, I'm Janice."

Barry opened his eyes to a face he could have recognized. Wizened, liver-spotted, with papery skin stretched too thin over a freckled skull sporting wisps of yellow-white hair. Her lips pulled back to expose her teeth, an awkward tic on the verge of hideous; it took him a moment to recognize a smile.

"Barry," he said, just able to choke out the word.

She reached out and grabbed his hand. Too stunned to react, he didn't pull away as she flipped it over and ran her fingers down his. Rheumy wetness rimmed her light green eyes.

"We've met, you know."

He shook his head. "When?"

"Last year, after a meeting with your boss. We shared an elevator, and I shorted on the way down. You left me there on my knees for the police."

He opened his mouth, closed it.

"You don't have to apologize. I rode that elevator for hours before they showed up. You had a lot of company."

"Then how do you remember me?"

"We were talking when it happened."

"I don't—" Only he did remember. She fell on him, screaming and crying, and he'd turned to face the doors. "I'm so sorry."

"You didn't know any better."

He closed his eyes. "But now I do. And I'm sorry."

***

Crawling under the façade of normalcy, one critical thing had changed.

Neonatal wards dwindled and died, their empty halls abandoned or repurposed to other ends. Even a five-year-old could do this math—Nyloxx administered to sixty percent of the population should have reduced new births by sixty percent, not a hundred.

As birthrates collapsed to zero, scientists far too like his father wrung their hands and tried to explain. Words like "systemic" and "persistent" did little to assuage a race faced with their self-caused extinction. Years of research caused eventual pregnancies. They rejoiced along with the rest of the world at the first pregnancy, and thousands more induced with drugs and in vitro fertilization. They cried together at her miscarriage. A second miscarriage followed, then thousands, then millions. In desperation, children carried to twenty-three weeks were extracted via C-section; none survived.

Smothered under the blanket of impending oblivion, many killed themselves, sometimes taking their families with them in poison or car crashes or hot, red shotgun blasts, sometimes slipping away alone under the embrace of opiates or narcotics. Some turned to God, reconciling their unanswered prayers with a just punishment mankind must have somehow deserved. For a few years art thrived, turning ever darker before collapsing under the inevitability of the end.

Many wandered, not bothering to bathe or work, shuffling from soup kitchen to park and back. Sasha stayed out later and later as their numbers grew, choking the streets and emptying factories, collapsing production and shifting ever more burden onto those few who would still provide for others. At Barry's behest, she gave it up, gnawing at the bit in their solitude, sullen rage spiked by occasional bouts of despondent impotence.

Drugs proved unreliable, for them or for anyone—antidepressants could help with day-to-day anxieties, but held no power over the hopelessness of a world that hadn't seen a live birth in five years. Neuroscientists had discovered a means to artificially suppress or stimulate the amygdala, hippocampus, and other parts of the brain to control emotional response, and the government offered the chip—in reality, a network of chips implanted throughout the brain—to anyone who wanted it. Results looked promising, and ever more people signed up until only a few holdouts in any given community refused the treatment.

It didn't take years for volunteer treatment to become mandatory. Unpredictable and violent, the un-chipped presented a danger to civilized society. They had to be treated for the good of all.

Back in their mountain retreat, his mother and Sasha worked with an underground movement to resist forced chipping. Uninterested in their politics and bored of always being cooped up, Barry had run down to the nearest town to score whatever booze he could dig up from the zoned-out chippers' basements, and stole a car to get home. He floored it when a cop drove up behind him and he went off the road and hit a telephone pole.

He remembered struggling against their professional insistence— and their handcuffs—up until the moment the needle went into his neck.

And he remembered calmly walking the calm-faced men in suits through how to get to their house, how to disable the security system, and where they were likely to find his mother and sister so that they might calm them too.

***

Janice shook her head, chewing and swallowing the bite of her apple before replying.

"No. If you try to escape they'll kill you. They call it 'aggressive noncompliance.' Nobody gets out of here except in a body bag."

"That's absurd," Barry said. Three weeks in "the yard" and he'd managed to go only the past two days without breaking down into hysterical sobbing more than once or twice. He didn't understand these people and their weary resignation; he just knew he had to find his sister.

"There's no such thing as absurd anymore."

"No, I guess not. But if Sasha's alive, I have to find her."

Janice smiled, and this time he recognized the beauty in it. Ninety-two years old, she'd been one of the last to give birth to a viable child, a son she'd had chipped at six years old because that's what you did to the un-chipped. He stayed with her until a heart attack took him on his sixty-second birthday ten years earlier; she grieved for him suddenly and passionately in an elevator a decade later.

"You can't know she's out there."

"No, but if she were chipped I'd have seen it. I've—I've got a good memory for numbers, always have. Her social security number never came across my desk. Not once, ever."

"It's a big world. You can't have seen them all."

"Two five four, seven six, three one five seven."

A grunt, possible acknowledgement that he'd pulled hers from his memory.

"I'm going home. I know how to get there. I just need to get out of here."

She pinned him with a hard stare. "Aggressive noncompliance."

"There has to be a way."

Her head dropped into her hands, rubbed her face before looking up at him, fingertips peeling down her eyelids into a gross caricature. "These people are emotionless. Don't you understand what that means?" Sitting up, she grabbed his hands and squeezed them. "They don't get bored or antsy or horny, they don't get distracted. They just guard us and eat and sleep until they die of old age. That's it. They have nothing better to do, because they don't want to do anything else."

"There has to be a way. What about the garbage?"

She quirked an eyebrow. "What do you mean?"

"The trash has to leave here somehow."

"Compactor. Messy."

Hopelessness squeezed his heart. "What, then? There has to be something."

She sighed, long and melodramatic, before letting go of his hands. "Let me talk to some people. There might be a way."

For the first time in his adult life, a glimmer of hope burned in his chest. He closed his eyes.

"Thank you."

***

The police had come back to him with a report: no sign of his family at the mountain hideout.

He gave them their old address, before the Long Winter, and their new address after, plus his mother's work and Sasha's old daycare provider. A thousand questions later they released him, sent him to training for his new job. He never got an update on them, and until he'd shorted it had never occurred to him to wonder.

***

Janice ate her canned spaghetti with gusto, slurping the pasta into her mouth to mash it apart with her dentures. Her companions, three men he'd only met in passing but who treated her with old fondness, ate theirs with similar flair. Barry looked down at the limp noodles and runny, pink sauce pooled beneath them, a tomato-and-vegetable-protein derivative he'd eaten countless times without complaint, and his stomach churned.

"You must be hungrier than I am." He pushed the plate away.

Janice pushed it back. "No, no. Eat it, and all of it. Now."

"I'm not hungry."

Her companions scowled. The shriveled, bald man to her left pushed up his thick glasses and stared down his nose at them both. "You didn't tell him, did you?"

"I didn't."

Barry twirled a bundle of soppy noodles onto his fork and shoved them into his mouth. "Told me what?" he said around the wad of pasta.

"We drugged your spaghetti."

He choked, then swallowed.

"What?"

She twirled up another bite. "Romeo and Juliet ploy. You want out, we're getting you out." Another forkful went into her mouth.

"So, I'm going into a coma?"

"For a day, maybe two. They never pay much attention to the bodies when they get a mass suicide. Just toss them into a tarpaulin and haul them to the dump. This was basically your idea, so chow down."

"My—mass suicide?" He brightened, and plowed through another forkful. "You're coming with me?"

She patted his hand. "No, dear. We're not coming with you. There's nothing for us out there. We're just..."

"The diversion," the bald man finished for her, slurping up the last noodle and wiping up the last of the sauce with his finger.

"What... what's in your pasta?"

"Ground peach and cherry pits. Should be lethal in... minutes."

A python constricted his chest, his breath staccato explosions that didn't draw in enough air. "You can't! It's—"

Janice coughed, covering her mouth with the back of her hand. Swooning, she fell against the man next to her.

"Wow. Fast." His eyes bugged out in alarm before he slumped

forward onto the table.

Barry tried to stand, spun, and landed face-down on the bench. He reached out across the table for Janice's limp hand, but lost consciousness before he touched it.

***

Darkness.

He fumbled for his light, touched cold flesh, recoiled.

Breath came in panicked jerks, and brought with it the sharp, throat-burning stench of bodily fluids and death. Woozy eddies drowned the world.

Squirming against the slick, stiffened meat of his companions, he lashed out against the thick, rubbery blanket that choked off air and light.

Fingers brushed metal. He followed the rough line, found the edge, and dug his fingernail into it. He gasped as the zipper parted, at the gust of warm, fetid air and the sudden pain in his finger. It pulsed, red in the dying sunlight, the nail pulled back and out of the flesh. He put it in his mouth, sucked on it, and moaned when he looked down, clenching his teeth around the top of his knuckle to muffle the sound.

Four bodies lay in the bag with him, naked flesh slicked with shit and vomit, faces twisted into agonized rictuses frozen in place by rigor mortis. Janice leered at the night sky, dead eyes glittering under the moonlight, toothless mouth a final indignity—the police had taken her dentures along with her clothes. Had his companions killed themselves for him, or had they used him as an excuse to end their wait? Did it matter? He scrambled for purchase, putting his arms on things he didn't want to think too hard about, and pushed, kicking with his legs to free his lower body from the tangle.

Old bones creaked. Withered muscles strained.

His leg came free with a wet sucking noise and he erupted from the bag. The world spun too much to stay on his hands and knees. Gasping, he collapsed face down on the heaped refuse. He wept, for the obvious, callous inevitability of it. The police had dropped their bodies in the dump with the rest of the garbage.

It took a while—minutes or hours, he didn't know—for the world to stop its relentless spin, settling into a queasy knot in his stomach.

He clambered down the mess, past old appliances and furniture,

264

the remains of entire houses and buildings dumped for lack of anything useful to do with them—reduce, reuse, recycle, save the planet, conserve fossil fuels; all of it had been rendered pointless by the Long Winter and the solution to it, Nyloxx, loose in the soil.

Goosebumps pricked at his skin; not the chill of winter, but a cool summer breeze across his wet, bare skin. Nose wrinkling at his own stench, he found an old throw pillow and tore off the cover, using the coarse fabric to wipe off the worst of the grime and moist decay.

He pulled a plaid dress shirt and newish jeans from an old dresser and elsewhere scored a pair of black leather dress shoes, but put none of it on. Creeping up under cover of heaped garbage, he tried the door to the trailer by the entrance and found it unlocked; in the age of the regulator, no one had a reason to steal. He let himself in, washed up as best he could in the bathroom sink, and put on the scavenged clothes.

A wraith stared out of the mirror. Gray hair wild, chin a riot of scruffy gray whiskers, eyes sunken and haunted. No one would mistake him for chipped, but he didn't have a razor or even a comb. He wet his hands and patted down his hair, called it good enough, and stumbled out into the night.

He followed the stark white streetlights to town, a mindless little village consisting of a cafeteria and three office buildings surrounded by largely automated farms, their GPS-controlled combines and auto-harvesters working in the dark to feed a dwindling populace. Nine cars sat on Main Street, and he had to laugh. An ancient Tesla XVII sat under a light, the streamlined four-seater an updated clone of the model he'd stolen six decades earlier.

A raucous noise echoed down the street, a ragged cry from a throat unused for laughter. He clamped his hand over his mouth. Hurrying before anyone investigated, he opened the door, slipped inside and hammered the button with his thumb. The lights clicked on and a navigation screen overlaid the windshield. He turned it off, preferring the dim quiet, and pulled out onto the road.

He'd never made the drive, and it had been a lifetime, but he knew it by heart. His headlights crawled up the mountain at thirty miles an hour—sick and weak from whatever the hell Janice had given him, he couldn't trust anything faster. The world still swam when he turned too fast, and with the human population shattered he expected a million deer to throw themselves in front of his car, but saw none.

He entertained the idea that Nyloxx hadn't poisoned them too. Maybe wolves had come back, kept the herds in check. Sasha had always loved wolves.

The road deteriorated as deciduous, temperate trees gave way to old-growth conifers, and he had to turn on the heater to keep the windows from fogging up. The dark swallowed him, and the rhythm of the wheels rocked him to a lullaby of night sounds. He shook his head to stay awake, rolled down the windows to let in the chill.

At long last he found the driveway, smothered with tall grass tamped down into a pair of overgrown packed-earth runnels. Twin silver lines marred the grass where someone had driven over it in the past few days, or at least since the last rain. He turned and eased down on the gas. The car rolled through with a hiss that increased and decreased in intensity with his speed, interrupted here and there by the sharp bang of a black-eyed Susan against the bumper. Mama had planted those flowers in their garden, the year after the snow melted; they'd spread, and now dotted wherever trees hadn't smothered. His mind failed him on how far he had to drive, but he knew the moment before the cabin came into view.

No lights shone in the windows, and moonlight scattered off of a roof that jarred with his recollection—slate gray tin instead of mottled brown shingles. The yard had disappeared under a wild green tangle, and the bannister leading up the front steps to the porch lay akimbo next to the disconnected, rotting porch swing.

His spark of hope flickered, dimming to match the vacant cabin.

He killed the car and got out, shutting the door with more authority than was necessary. If anyone lived here, he didn't want them surprised.

A reluctant shuffle dragged him up the creaking steps to the front door. Ajar, it creaked open to reveal the ruined remains of human habitation—a rotted-out couch showing springs and rat's nests; moldy plates piled next to the sink just visible through the kitchen door; the old, red-brick hearth blackened and littered with beer cans.

"Hello?" His voice rang out in the empty, soulless space. A fat raccoon darted from under the couch, bumbled two steps toward the door, then retreated into the kitchen without undue haste—it didn't fear him. And why should it? Why should any animal fear man anymore?

With no answer, he approached the bookcase against the far wall. Most of his father's collection had disappeared. A few had rotted to nothing. But *The Book of Daniel* by E.L. Doctorow stood tall and proud on the third shelf up, the sleeve on the hardcover defying the ravages of time except for a scuff on the spine betraying the aluminum underneath.

He grabbed the book with both hands, pushing in the top while pulling out the bottom. It gave. The bookcase popped away from the wall on silent hinges, betraying the ladder leading below.

The rich, earthy smell of a garden twisted his stomach. His mouth went to sandpaper at the thought of killing another rabbit, cutting around its neck and tearing off its skin moments after petting it and calling it a good girl. He gagged on the memory, sucking in air to displace it—sterile, cool, bleach with a sweet hint of lemon. Someone had cleaned, and recently.

He climbed down the two stories, knees aching with every rung, knuckles white as the vertigo ebbed and flowed. "Hello?" he called, halfway down, voice echoing through the tiny antechamber that led to the greenhouses. His feet hit the floor and he walked through the dark to the light switch, flicking it up with old confidence.

As the LEDs flashed on, figures rushed him. Stars exploded through his skull as they slammed him against the wall, pinning his arms and legs with their bodies.

A black woman in nurse's scrubs looked him up and down, and grunted. Her gray afro matched the wrinkled skin stretched over chubby cheeks, the softness in her face at odds with the murder in her eyes. "Shorted, did you?"

"Yes," he said, breath short and raspy through the fingers around his throat.

"It's Esther." She backed up, and his assailants let him go. He rubbed his wrists and stepped away from the wall.

"You know me?"

"Your name is Barry Esther. You must be, what, seventy-four?"

"Seventy-three."

"Seventy-three. I'm Annie, and I'm in charge here. Don't do anything impulsive."

"I won't," he said. "I'm just looking for my family." Her smirk could have meant anything. Hope soared, fragile and exposed. "Are they here?"

"Your mother passed not long after you were taken. Sasha called it a broken heart."

It had to be true, but knowing it stabbed an icicle through his chest. "A long time, then."

"A long time," Annie said. "We have some of her things in Sasha's desk."

"She's here?"

Annie jerked her head toward the door to the greenhouse. "Follow me."

It wasn't an answer, exactly.

One of his attackers, an old man over six and a half feet tall, opened the door into soft, warm light. Barry stepped around the huge man and gasped.

The greenhouse of his childhood shattered into memory, replaced by a hospital ward, two rows of fifty—no—sixty beds. Women lay in each, most of their bellies bulging to one degree or another. IVs trailed upward from needles piercing their arms; skinny legs stuck out from underneath hospital gowns. Gray and wrinkled, the youngest of them couldn't have been ten years his junior. And none of them looked enough like his sister to be an older version of her.

"What is this place?"

"The Nursery. Sasha founded it, not long after, you know. After. We knew each other from the food kitchen, you remember?" He nodded; she continued. "Twenty years in, she found me, shorted, administering what care I could to other Shorts. She offered me a chance to do something more."

Annie walked down the rows and he followed, waiting patiently as she passed kind words and greetings to each woman, touching hands and kissing foreheads, rubbing pregnant bellies and massaging swollen feet, until at last she stopped at a small desk set against the farthest wall. Above it sat a portrait, his family, smiling in happier times—he couldn't have been more than five. Barry leaned forward, knees turning to jelly, unable to think, to breathe. They got him settled into a chair and handed him the frame. With shaking hands he ran his fingers down the glass, leaned in and kissed it.

No psychic connection crackled from the smooth, cold surface. No mystic message whispered across time that everything would be all right. He wiped his eyes and looked down at the book, leather-clad with "Sasha Esther" emblazoned in peeling silver on the bottom-right corner. Setting down the photo he opened the diary, hands shaking.

The first page showed an old printed picture, ink faded with time. Sasha, a beautiful, vibrant woman, a mirror of their mother, leaning against a man as she cradled an infant, so tiny, too tiny, his head bulging over his right eye, his left drooping too low. A sad smile blossomed on her loving face. Underneath, it said, "Sasha, Bob, and Little Barry."

He read. With fertility drugs she'd conceived, birthing Barry during C-section at twenty-three weeks. He'd lived three days. Their next lived a week. The one after that miscarried fourteen weeks in, the next bled down her leg after only ten.

Through blurred eyes he found the nurse. "Where is she? Can I see her?"

The nurse nodded toward the desk, where a small purple vase rested against the wall. It had shattered and been repaired with gold, an old Japanese trick their father had loved, the beauty that came from broken things. Barry remembered it from Sasha's room, after their father had passed—she'd taken it as a memory of him, and kept flowers in it when she could find them. Now, a crude engraving near the bottom said SME, dated thirty years earlier. He ran his fingers down the smooth pottery, traced the letters.

"She's gone." Like everyone else. "So you put her on a desk?"

"I'm sorry," Annie said. "She wanted to rest with her children."

He swallowed. "What happened?"

"She carried her fifth to twenty-five weeks. We pulled her out, but your sister didn't survive. The baby made it nine days. We named her Ruth."

"Sasha was, what? Fifty-one years old?"

"About that."

"What was she doing having children?"

The nurse stepped back—he still didn't know her name—and gestured at the beds. "Do you see anyone here of childbearing age? Thousands of women have lain in these beds. Tens of thousands. We do what we can: fertility drugs, different donors, in vitro stabilization techniques, genetic engineering. We've had children survive ten days, even two weeks, with so few deformities, hell, you could almost think them normal. It's… progress."

"Have any lived? Beyond… beyond—"

"No. And it only gets worse as their mothers get older. But one of these days we might get lucky."

"Then why?"

She kneeled next to him and whispered into his ear. "What else are we to do?"

A noise escaped his lips that might have been a laugh, might have been a cry of despair.

Barry couldn't breathe.

He stumbled out of the chair, dizzy, chest squeezed by a sudden panic. The world hazed from red to black. Voices, stern and sharp, called out behind him. A door slammed, a bookcase creaked shut.

He came to at his father's desk, the wood pale and cracked after so many years of neglect. Sasha sat in front of him with her children, the purple and gold vase encasing all that remained of hope or joy, a beautiful lie that things can be repaired, made more beautiful. A million white lines crackled through the glaze, the truth of entropy made manifest on the vessel that contained the ashes of hope. His father's revolver rested cold in his hand, black metal marred with flecks of rust where pieces meshed, the faintest smell of gunpowder still lingering in the drawer that lay open at his knee.

He raised it, turned it over, ran his fingers down the dark curves. He cocked the hammer, and it slid back with little difficulty, latching into place with a faint click.

Outside, a wolf howled. Another answered, then another.

Tears melded the urn into the gun, the gun into the urn. Sasha had always liked wolves.

THERE IS NO... GOD
Lance Taubold

"Are we all in agreement, then?" the one called Adam asked.

"I am," the one called Cain said.

"I am as well," the one called Abel said.

"The final, corrupt world leader has taken control of the greatest of Earth's nations. It is only a matter of months, or perhaps hours, until the fatal decision is made setting earth on a disastrous course to perdition," Adam said.

"It has not all been bad," Eve said. "There have been many shining and glorious moments over the centuries."

"True," Adam readily agreed. "We can all recollect many fine civilizations and individuals. Some remarkable accomplishments and discoveries. Surprises and disappointments."

"But always two steps forward—"

"And one step back," Cain finished for Abel.

Adam added, "Even though we created them in our own image, then gave them the ability for diversification, evolution, the power of choice and reasoning, the corruptive—dare I say—evilness has won out in the end."

"It is a pity, as the majority of humans desire happiness and contentment," Eve said, shaking her head in regret.

"Then that is what they should have fought for," Cain rejoined.

"I agree with you, Cain. But happiness was not enough for everyone. Some strove for more." Adam walked around the large room, taking in the floating screens surrounding it. "The past century had the most advances in so many ways. Technology alone advanced tenfold. But not humanity, or goodness, generosity, altruism, love of fellow man or woman." He looked to Eve, sadness in his golden eyes.

Eve gave him a sad smile. "Yes, these past decades have shown us how selfish humans can be, how disconnected everyone has become with the advanced technology, each generation becoming more insular and uncaring. For so many, the Bible that we gave them has been forgotten or discounted."

"They will remember it now," Cain said, sad bitterness evident in his tone, hinting at the impending doom. "The Book of Revelation may have been somewhat hyperbolic, but its overall intent is true."

"Armageddon, the end of days, the Apocalypse," Abel muttered.

"It has finally come to this. Even your return, Cain, as the Christ, would not have enough of an effect. We have been given no choice." Adam's voice carried the solemnity of its meaning.

"But," Eve said, "we have agreed to uphold the final chapters of Revelation and to begin anew."

Adam nodded. "We have." Abel and Cain gave their silent assent.

Abel stood. "Yet we have not decided who the two will be—the next 'Adam and Eve.'"

"It will become apparent, I trust," Adam said. "Each of us has his tasks as the four horsemen."

They looked at one another. Determination came into each of their eyes.

Adam turned to Abel. "The Black Horse first. Pestilence."

"Let the Apocalypse begin."

***

Curtis Ralyea stared at the General Assembly and could not believe the words he had just heard. As ambassador to France, he had recently been having a difficult time—and that was putting it mildly. The Charlie Hebdo massacre had started the reign of terror in the country. And terrorist attacks had escalated from there. More and more fatalities each time. As ambassador, he had tried to reassure the French President that the new American president would be much more protective and offensive toward terrorists than the one from the former regime. And he had hoped it would be so.

But it hadn't been so. The new president was offensive all right. He had offended nearly every nation in the world—at least all but those who wanted something from him or could benefit in some way.

As a child, Curtis had always tried to do the right thing, help people. When he got older, he saw the situation of the planet and wanted to help bring about peace. He had no delusions that he could do it alone, but he wanted to be part of the effort to make it happen.

He had studied hard: world history, politics, socioeconomics, languages. He spoke seven languages fluently: Mandarin, Arabic and

Swahili, and had a command of four others. He had met all the right people, and all of that combined with his blond hair, blue eyes, square jaw, and a fit, but not overly muscular, physique had helped to make him the youngest US ambassador ever (at twenty-four and by three months) over Edward Rumsey Wing, the 1869 Minister to Ecuador. Now, at thirty-two, it had come to an end.

His ambition and hard work had paid off professionally, but personally, he was less than successful. He *knew* a multitude of people, but as for friends—let alone a girlfriend or boyfriend (he hadn't felt a strong inclination either way)—he had none. Yes, he could say it unequivocally: he had no friends. He liked people, but they usually disappointed him—make that they *always* disappointed him. He could always read the lust in men's and women's eyes: for his looks, his position. Just once, he wanted someone to see past the exterior, the superficial, to see him for who he was.

Perhaps he expected too much. The world had gotten too fast, too impersonal. It was all about immediate self-gratification. Thanks to technology, that had become simple.

Was he becoming cynical? He hoped not. He didn't want to be. He did believe in the essential goodness of man. His parents had been good people. He was sure there were others out there as well. His parents' generation had been more considerate, more patient, more optimistic. His generation, less so. And the one after—the millennials—the less said, the better.

Still, he would not give up hope, even if sometimes he felt like Diogenes looking for an honest man.

He listened to the Secretary General, try to quell the outrage in the vast hall—the protestations, the outright yelling. He noticed the quiet acceptance of some, and the smug, almost victorious countenances of the knowing few. He took it all in. His stomach lurched. He fought to keep the bile down. Could this really be happening?

The United Nations was no longer?

Was this the beginning of the End of Days?

***

Gatsby Langdon was Australian by birth, American by choice, cynical by nature. At 6'4" and weighing a solid 250 pounds, with dark hair and almost coal-black eyes, he was an imposing figure. He had invested wisely in real estate, and had seen the handwriting on the wall several years ago, in time to sell—and sell *big*. For all intents and purposes, at thirty-five, he was retired in his semi-opulent apartment overlooking Central Park and the Upper West Side. He could live well and do as he pleased, go where he wanted, be with most anyone he wanted. But in spite of all his ostensible cynicism, he held on to the smallest sort of optimism.

He'd come from a well-to-do family, never wanting for anything. He'd come to America when he was four. He had no "Strail" accent—unless he wanted one. Sometimes it was fun to turn it on, and men thought it was sexy… women too, but he didn't care. What he *did* care about was finding someone to love and love him in return. Clichéd, but true. But where? Granted he wasn't a barfly or a party-type guy, but he would have thought that in his business transactions and meetings over the years he would have found someone… but he hadn't even come close. Except for… except for the fact that he was a priest! Father Gordon. Father Rick, really. That's what Gatsby had called him. Father Rick had taught him about goodness, and faith, and hope. And if he really had to admit it, he wasn't a cynic by nature. Rick had taught him that too. Also, the belief that man is inherently good, and to believe in himself. And it had rung true to him.

After Father Rick had moved on, hopefully to greener pastures than the craziness of New York, Gatsby began to champion worthwhile causes and campaign for equal rights.

He stopped his woolgathering and his eyes focused on his wall screen in front of him: *CNN BREAKING NEWS*. He turned up the volume.

"By a two-thirds vote, the United Nations has been abolished." The commentator paused, as if not believing what his monitor was revealing.

"What?" Gatsby yelled aloud. "This is insanity!"

He sat in front of the television for the next couple of hours, listening, uncomprehending… crying.

"Father Rick, where are you now? Where is God now? Is this the beginning of the end?" Gatsby asked to the heavens.

There was no response.

***

Anna Wycoff awoke and stretched. *This is going to be a good day,* she thought, and rubbed the sleep from her eyes.

274

She could not have been more wrong.

Anna left her apartment building and stepped out onto West 30th Street.

It was May 1. The sun was shining, and she was starting her new job at the United Nations. Well, not actually at the UN, but working as personal assistant to Curtis Ralyea, the incredibly handsome ambassador to France.

Her job would require her to travel with him, and she loved to travel. There was an important meeting today at the UN of the General Assembly. All were required to attend, as an impending announcement was to be made. She was still trying to remember the pronunciation of the Secretary General's name. For some reason, she kept reversing letters. Maybe she could call him by his first name. She smiled to herself. And *maybe* she'd never even get to meet him. Ah well, the important name to her was Curtis Ralyea, her boss.

Her father, being very well connected, had gotten her the interview. She had studied hard and had graduated top of her class from Vassar. She spoke fluent French and had studied abroad for a year and a half. She had the knowledge and the skills, now she needed to put them into practice.

She approached the magnificent on East 42nd Street and First Avenue. God, she loved New York, and this awe-inspiring building especially. She never tired of looking up and seeing all the flags waving in the breeze: Europe, Asia, South America, Africa... the whole world unified... joined together in one place.

She let out a deep sigh of pleasure.

And now she was part of it. Making the world a better and more peaceful place. She knew if she said her thoughts aloud they would come off as grandiose or pompous, or deluded, but it was how she felt. World peace was her goal.

She wasn't sure how long the meeting was to last today, but she didn't care. She would spend her time walking around, exploring, admiring, getting accustomed to the place, and thanking God that she was now a part of this world.

She had gotten her clearance, credentials, and badge and was free to "explore." Curtis had told her she was welcome to sit at the back of the Assembly and could listen to what the various world ambassadors had to say. There were earbuds available so that she could listen, and the different languages would be translated for her.

With earbuds firmly in place, she entered the massive hall.

From the back of the hall, she looked around, trying to spot her boss. She scanned the ambassadors, some dressed in their native garb, all seeming to be slightly energized. Had she missed something? Most were engaged in animated conversations with one or more of their fellow ambassadors. Then the Secretary General arrived at the podium. Everyone took their seats and an eerie hush came over the Assembly. Yet the electricity in the air remained.

The Secretary General began to speak in his accented English. His tone was the most solemn she had ever heard.

Anna listened, stupefied. She heard the words issue forth, her ears hearing, her mind unbelieving.

It *couldn't* be!

Her life. The UN. The world. The future. Was it all over?

***

Curtis filed out of the Assembly. Numb. His fellow ambassadors—well, not anymore—they were all just men and women now. No more ambassadors. No more embassies. What would he do now? Oh, my God! What would the *world* do now? There were too many despots and oligarchs in power, each wanting to be its own entity, thinking they could fight terrorism on their own and be independent from the rest of the world. That they didn't need the help and support of other nations. What were they thinking? *Delusional.* This was more than a disaster. It was a global catastrophe!

He heard a faint voice. "Mr. Ralyea? Mr. Ralyea!" He looked to the left. Up against the wall, through the crowd, he could see her. The face familiar. He tried to recall... Anna! His new assistant. He remembered; he was to meet her after the assembly. She looked... forlorn. Lost.

He worked his way through the sea of people. "Anna."

She threw herself into his arms. His natural instinct was to embrace her. He did. He felt her body trembling, shoulders heaving.

"Mr. Ralyea... Curtis... what's happening?" she mumbled into his chest between sobs.

"I'm not sure, Anna. Everything will be all right."

All right? Who was he kidding? Everything would *never* be all right again.

He had to get them out of the melee. "Come with me." He took her hand and led her forcefully through the crowd. He could hear the multitude now, the cacophony deafening. Shouts. Crying. It was chaos.

Chaos.

The world was chaos.

***

Gatsby walked into the small innocuous bar on Second Avenue. It was dark. A handful of people was all he could see. It *was* two o'clock in the afternoon. It shouldn't be packed. He went to the bar.

"Hey, Gatsby, how ya been? Haven't seen you for a while. Lookin' good, as always."

"Busy. How've you been, Cory? Double Johnny Black and soda, please."

"You know me. Work. Gym. I might compete." Cory brought his arms up and posed, flexing his over-large biceps in his one-size-too-small T-shirt.

"You've got the guns. Good luck." Gatsby grabbed his drink from the bar, handed Cory a credit card. "Run a tab."

"You got it, my man. Any time you wanna hit the gym with me, or whatever... You still got my number, right?"

"I do."

"Sweet." He leaned over the bar. "Love to see ya again."

One drunken night.

"Me too. I've got to do a little work now," Gatsby said. He pulled out his phone, indicating working on it, and wandered off to the far corner of the bar where he saw a vacant booth with no one else around. He needed to think.

"Gotcha, Gatsby. I'll make sure nobody bothers you."

Gatsby noticed the other four male patrons were all at the bar. Two of them were enrapt in the *BREAKING NEWS* about the UN folding displayed on the television behind the bar. The other two were enrapt in each other.

As Gatsby sat, he heard the door open. He turned and saw a pretty woman and a very good-looking man walk in. He took in the fit form of the man and wondered if they were a couple. It seemed a little odd for them to be here—in the middle of the afternoon—like he was. Both were well-dressed. A business lunch? In a gay bar? He turned back in his booth and slid all the way in, his back to the room. The tall, wooden booths were just high enough to hide him from view.

He felt his booth move slightly and realized the couple had sat right behind him.

"...was a good choice." He heard the woman say.

"Please, call me Curtis," the man said. "I have a couple of friends who like this place. Pleasant and low-key. You can have a conversation here. Anna, we need to figure out the future. The announcement—or rather pronouncement—by the Secretary General is cataclysmic."

Interesting, Gatsby thought. *Who are these two?* He took a sip, then realized he was empty. He got out of the booth. When he stood, the two stopped talking. His eyes met Curtis's and he smiled. Curtis returned the smile.

Over the next hour and half, and three more Johnny Blacks and sodas, Gatsby listened—eavesdropped would be more appropriate, he guessed—to the two and began to plan his future while the couple discussed the "fate of the world."

His "liquid courage" finally spurred him to say something. He stood. "Excuse me, I'm sorry for interrupting. My name is Gatsby Langdon. I shouldn't have been eavesdropping, I know—"

"I thought I recognized you," Anna cut him off. "You're the real estate tycoon."

Gatsby smiled at her. "Guilty. As I said, I couldn't help overhearing you discussing today's disaster at the UN. I know many influential people in politics and I have not even heard a whisper of this happening."

Gatsby could see Curtis sizing him up, deciding whether to speak.

And before he did, Anna broke in again, "My name is Anna Wycoff. This is Curtis Ralyea. This is—was—my first day on the job for Curtis. I was to be his personal assistant. How do you think *I* feel?" She knocked back the last third of what appeared to be a martini. "Oh, my God," she said. "That sounded so selfish. I'm not like that. *Really.* It's the liquor. I'm a nice person. *I am.* I am so mortified. Forgive me?"

Gatsby gave a laugh, in spite of the situation. "Nothing to forgive," he said to the back of Anna's head, which was now face down on the table.

She raised it and looked at him. "Thank you for being so gracious. Curtis, I'm sorry. Well, if I hadn't already lost my job, I guess that would have done it."

Now Curtis laughed out loud. Gatsby noted he looked even more handsome when he smiled.

The ice seemed to be broken now, and Curtis, after wiping his eyes, said, "Anna, you're not fired and you still have a job as my assistant. I will, perhaps, need you more than ever." Anna gave a weak smile. "And you, Mr. Langdon—"

"Gatsby."

"—Gatsby, would you care to join us?"

"Thank you, Curtis. I would." He slid into the booth next to Anna. As he did, he motioned to Cory to bring another round.

***

Several hours and several drinks later, the three were still in deep discussion. The bar had gotten appreciably more crowded as the evening arrived. They had ignored all around them.

"We know North Korea is a smoldering volcano. China has its own agenda. As does Israel. Russia with the new Cold War that seems to be heating up. *Our* president is a loose cannon. Even England wants to keep things close to the vest.

The men nodded.

Anna continued, "And none of these so-called leaders are willing to recognize the truly evil force in the Mideast. The terrorists and their puppets *will* destroy all that is good."

Curtis joined in. "Their sphere of influence is vast. Nowhere is safe from them. I've been over there and seen their unspeakable power firsthand." He blocked a memory of torture and beheading from his mind. "Europe has never been more divided. They are all running scared, doing nothing, waiting for the next shooting, or explosion, or bombing to happen." He took a long drink, catching the eye of the unnervingly handsome and charismatic man across from him. He would be a fool to deny there was a definite attraction on both their parts. Yet there was also an underlying sexual vibe from Anna as well. The whole situation was preposterous. A giant anachronism amid global crisis.

The three glanced around, now, as the decibel level had risen. Every eye was glued to the four televisions over the bar. All the men—and the smattering of women—seemed to be huddled close together. One mass. Then Curtis began to notice the faces. Some were crying openly. Others had their faces buried in their partners' chests. Still others only stared, mouths agape.

279

Curtis looked at the nearest screen and saw *BREAKING NEWS: Widespread outbreak spreading across Asia into Europe.*

The images flashed over the screen: Hospitals flooded with mobs of people, people in the streets literally dropping like flies. Curtis heard someone say, "Turn it up."

The crowd grew eerily silent and the reporter's voice issued from the screen:

"*...plague of epic proportions has swept across Asia, leaving hundreds of thousands, possibly millions, dead. The source of the outbreak is as of yet unknown, as is the actual nature of this rampant, impossibly-fast-spreading disease. People in all Asian and European nations have been ordered to stay inside and avoid contact with anyone outside their homes. It has not been determined if the disease is airborne or not. The CDC and other global disease centers will be working around the clock to bring us information. Travel has been suspended to and from the affected countries, but all travel has been highly discouraged at this point. This all coming on the heels of today's announcement abolishing the United Nations...*"

"Oh, my God!" Anna said and covered her mouth in horror. With her other hand she clutched Gatsby's arm. "What is happening to the planet?"

Gatsby spoke, "We need to leave. Now. My apartment is close. We'll be safe there."

"Safe?" Anna asked. "Safe from what?"

"I-I-" Gatsby stuttered. "I don't know why I said that. It just came out. But—"

"You're right. We need to go," Curtis said and got up, a little unsteadily, from the booth. In spite of all the liquor he'd consumed, his mind was surprisingly clear. The dire pronouncements must have sobered him. He looked at Gatsby, who also appeared to have sobered fast. He was adroitly helping Anna from the booth, snatching up her purse and slinging it over her shoulder.

The crowd paid no attention as they made their way to the door. "Wait outside. I'll close out," Gatsby said, wending his way to the bar.

They stepped out into the warm spring night, but Curtis still felt chilled to his bones. Gatsby joined them. "This way," he said. "My car and driver are over here to the left."

Curtis noticed the sleek black limo and wondered when Gatsby had called... or if he'd been there all the time. In any case, he was grateful they were able to escape so rapidly and easily.

The silent driver held the door open for the three and they climbed in.

***

It had been a week since the outbreak. And "outbreak" had been a massive understatement. Hundreds of millions, possibly billions, had died worldwide—intense headaches, leading to bleeding from facial orifices, followed by brain aneurysms.

Not pretty.

The areas most affected were the third-world countries, where tribes and groups were completely obliterated, seemingly based on proximity to one another... almost as if it were planned.

***

"Abel, your planned attack was quite successful, having eliminated the masses of underprivileged and largely unthought-of population," Adam said.

Abel nodded, his face grim. Cain and Eve held his hands, knowing how difficult it had been for him, while at the same time dreading their own ineluctable "rides."

Adam approached Abel and kissed him lightly on the mouth. "It had to be done."

"I know," Abel replied softly, then rose and embraced Adam, kissing him again. "Thank you."

Cain and Eve's eyes held tears of compassion. They silently reached for one another. Cain spoke after several moments had passed. "War is fomenting worldwide, as we knew it would. The stronger nations are using the pestilential devastation to their advantage, to prey on the weakened states and overtake them."

"You must prevent them from using nuclear tactics, Cain," Eve admonished, squeezing his hand hard. "We do not want them to destroy our planet."

"I have prepared for this, Eve." He squeezed back.

"Then," Adam said, "it is the time for the ride of the Red Horse."

***

"We've been here for *weeks*," Anna said. "So many nations annihilated... I don't see how I can ever recover from this. And now with wars breaking out everywhere..." Her tears flowed.

Gatsby had his arm around her and let her sob, get it out. The three of them had shared many a tear over the last weeks. Curtis and

281

he had used their contacts to see if they could learn where the outbreak had come from or who had caused it. No one knew.

What they did discover, though, was that Russia, China, North Korea, the Mideast (Israel and Iran, largely), and the United States had planned to use the plague to their own purposes. They were all gathering their arms and forces to, well, conquer what was left of the world.

Curtis spoke, "The Mideast will be the biggest massacre of all, you both realize. Israel thinks they'll win; Iran thinks they will. The Saudis think they will… and what about the terrorist contingent? They're everywhere. Those sneaky, suicidal bastards will just infiltrate them all, as they already have, and wipe them out from within. I mean, why do they care? Kill 'em all! They're going to heaven with two thousand virgins, or whatever!"

"Curtis, please, calm down. It hasn't happened yet. Come here."

Curtis got up from the chair, opposite the large, brown leather sofa where Gatsby sat with Anna. Gatsby had an inviting arm open to him and he sat within it. Gatsby hugged him close.

"My dear friend, you are such a good man… You are both *good* people."

Anna sniffled.

Curtis choked out a "right."

Gatsby continued, "You *are*. Don't forget that. When the world returns from its insanity and everything settles we will…" He stopped, and started to chuckle. Curtis and Anna looked up at him.

When Gatsby had their full attention, he sang in a decent baritone, *"We'll pick ourselves up, dust ourselves off, and start all over again…"*

They both stared at him as if he'd lost his mind.

"What?" he said off their looks. "You know I'm gay. I like musicals. And I thought we could use some levity in this…" He lowered his voice. "…darkest of times."

They both still stared until, at last, Curtis cracked a smile, followed by Anna. Then both broke out into full-throated laughter. Gatsby joined them.

Curtis, drying his eyes, recovered first. "If we can still laugh, maybe there is hope."

"That's my boy," Gatsby said and kissed his cheek.

"Hey…" Anna said.

"And... my girl," Gatsby kissed her as well.

They all looked from one to the other.

Gatsby knew they all felt it. He was sure they could hear his heart beating faster. He could. Where could this go? *Why now? Dear God, why now?* He knew Anna and Curtis were attracted to each other. And he was certainly attracted to Curtis. But Anna had also worked her way into his heart. Funny how tragedy could draw people together. But here they were.

Anna said, "Gatsby, what are we going to do? I mean, we can't stay here forever."

"She's right, Gats," (the new pet moniker Curtis had dubbed him with) "we have to go to our... our homes."

Gatsby was prepared for this. "Go home to what? To whom? You're both single, alone in the city, no families... like me."

Neither responded. He knew they couldn't. Then his capper: "And I love you both. You're my family. We need to stick through this *together*. And not to be too much of a wet blanket, but the truth is the truth, for however long we have..."

Again there was silence.

Then, in common acquiescence, Anna and Curtis slumped into Gatsby and held on.

***

The Russian army attacked first, choosing Europe as its war zone to start. He swept through the weakened continent—army ants over a cow's carcass.

China followed closely, sweeping through Southeast Asia and into his real goal: India. While most of India's billion-plus population had been wiped out by the plague, the land mass was something China had always coveted. And after conquering those lands, they planned to impress those populations to help him devour Indonesia... then on to Australia.

This, of course, unbeknownst to the North Koreans, was also their goal as well: South Korea, Mongolia, the South Pacific,... Australia.

The Red Horse's game plan was quite canny. And he knew his players. The American President was his favorite. With his megalomania, he knew exactly what the President would do.

And he did.

The President split his fronts and attacked Canada and Mexico at once. Then, using the Canadian forces, he would combine them with the Mexican troops and drive his forces down through Central and South America to Cape Horn. Canada, for some reason, after being devastated by the plague, seemed unable to recover or move on, losing their Prime Minister and all but one cabinet minister. It was primed for the US's picking. And the "wall" that the government had decided to build on Mexico's border with the US, having been held up with red tape, proved to be a blessing in disguise. Now they could move as freely into Mexico as the illegal immigrants had moved into the United States.

The Mideast and Africa would take care of themselves. The terrorist groups had infiltrated all of the major countries and the genocide of the "Infidels" would be child's play.

The Red Horse's ride was done.

***

"Not to get political," Anna said, "But to call our President a 'loose cannon' may have been the understatement of the century. He basically annexed Canada and Mexico folded their cards almost before he started."

The plague seemed to have ended on its own, for some inexplicable reason, Curtis thought. And now here the three of them were together, still at Gatsby's. And it was a foregone conclusion that they would remain here until... Until what? The end of the world? Could it really be so?

After weeks of cogitation and deciphering, (Curtis had secretly been studying the Book of Revelation and its different translations.) he could hold his thoughts no longer. "And not to get religious or Biblical, but you both may or may not know about the Four Horsemen of the Apocalypse in the Book of Revelation—"

"I'm familiar," Gatsby said dryly.

"Me too," Anna added.

"Sorry," Curtis recanted. "I grew up religious. Wasn't sure about you two. Anyway, I've been researching what the Book says. The first two horses are Pestilence and War. And the whole thing about the Anti-Christ arising from the Mideast... What if the terrorist faction is the Anti-Christ? The Bible doesn't really say that it's a man. I think the real evil—infestation, if you will—is that and has been for quite some time. An evil virus slowly poisoning humanity."

"Hmm." Anna looked at him, taking a long swallow of her

Cabernet. "I studied the Bible in college and I see where you're getting this, but what about the other signs? The Seven Seals? etc." She sucked in a sharp breath.

"What is it?" Gatsby asked.

"This may be stretching things, but, The Seven Seals could be seven S-E-A-L-S?" She spelled out. "Just a thought," Anna said.

"Yes! The Special Forces guys! I like your thinking, Anna," Gatsby said, tongue firmly implanted in cheek.

"You are joking, aren't you?" Curtis narrowed his eyes at her.

"Yes. Maybe. Who knows?" Anna shrugged and sipped her wine.

"All right, you two wannabe conspiracy theorists, I have actually *tried* to interpret these Biblical references, but I haven't found any *real* corollaries to—"

"Perhaps they were merely add-ons, if you will." He smiled ironically at Curtis. "Seriously speaking now, prophecies of doom to frighten the poor masses into being righteous. After all, what are a mere Four Horsemen and an Anti-Christ compared to the addition of Seven Seals, Seven Trumpets, Seven Bowls, the Lamb of God, the Whore of Babylon, Satan's Doom...? It's all so dramatic and foreboding. What poor soul wouldn't be frightened into submissiveness by all that?"

Curtis heard the sarcasm in his voice, but at the same time wondered if he was that far off the mark. Mark... of the Devil? Another harbinger? He felt himself smile wryly.

"I amuse you?" Gatsby asked.

"No... I mean, yes, you do amuse me, and I'm glad you are having fun with it, but I think your allegations may have a ring of truth. When the Bible—Revelation—was written by John, the world—the Mideast, coincidentally—was mostly peasants and menial laborers. They needed guidance and laws, and hope. What if..." He sighed in exasperation. "I think I'm *more* confused now than I was before I postulated my theory."

"Ah, my handsome friend, your theories are as good as, and probably better than, any."

"I agree with Gatsby, Curtis." Anna had finished her wine and was pouring more for the three of them. "And the more I think about it, the more I think you're on to something. The big problem is, though, is there anything we can do about it? Other than watch it all play out from our ivory tower in the sky. Mind you, it is a *fabulous* ivory tower." She raised her glass to Gatsby and drank. "And there are no two other people I would want to spend the last days of Earth with."

"Hear, hear," the men toasted back.

After a large gulp, Curtis said, "My head hurts… and it's not from the wine. In fact, I intend to drink a lot more of it—that is if you've left any, Anna." He held out his glass to her. "If you would be so kind. And Famine is the next horsey up."

Anna raised the bottle for him. "Horsey?" She drained the last of the bottle into his glass. "No famine here," she mumbled, and shook the empty bottle.

"I'll get another." Gatsby took the empty bottle from her.

"My prince," Curtis and Anna said together. They froze, expressions puzzled. Then all three laughed.

**

"Have you thought of where the new Eden, new Jerusalem, will be?" Eve asked Adam.

"Several areas have possibilities," Adam responded.

"I don't think it should be in the Mideast," Cain said.

"Nor I," Abel added. "Maybe an island, or Australia. Tasmania."

"I was thinking somewhere in the United States. Of course, all areas will have new names," Adam said. "I'm fond of the West Coast."

"San Diego has the best climate," Cain volunteered.

Eve nodded. "And an ocean breeze as well." She glanced at Abel. "And not as many dangerous animals for our chosen couple."

"Only suggestions," Abel said, holding his hands up in defense. "San Diego is nice."

"Very well, then," Adam said. "San Diego will be the new Eden."

"Eos. For dawn. A new beginning." She looked to the other three for acceptance. They nodded.

"But who will be the two to begin the world anew?" Abel asked, not to anyone in particular.

Adam turned to Eve. "After your ride as Famine, we will look to those who remain, then start making the most important of decisions."

They all felt the weight of the decision.

Who would they choose?

**

As they watched the fate of the world unfold before them on the cold, dispassionate television screen, the three new friends shared everything they thought. There was no reason to hide anything. Who would care? They were their own world now.

The love between them was palpable, Anna observed. Did she love Curtis? Undoubtedly. Did she love Gatsby? How could she not? Both were handsome, with Curtis's boyish, blond, good looks, and Gatsby with his dark looks and bad-boy air. She didn't realize how wonderful it could be to have two such devoted, loyal, and honest friends like them. Ironic that here at the end of times she would find such happiness. And she had. If she had lost either of them to plague, or the famine that had now begun—as predicted—she wouldn't want to live. As extreme as that sounded, it was how she felt. She looked at the two men engrossed in the television, and smiled.

Gatsby said, "It's like watching a live game of Risk. The US has North and South America; Russia has Europe and part of Asia, over to Kamchatka; North Korea has parts of eastern Asia, the South Pacific and half of Australia; China the bulk of Asia, including India and the other half of Australia; and finally the mysterious terrorist faction, with no discernable leader, conquered the Mideast and all of Africa. It's crazy!"

"And now they're after one another," Curtis said. "Add to that the worldwide crop failure..."

"The Black Horse, Famine." Anna's tone held all the weight of the expected inevitable. "How long can the fighting last without food to feed the troops?"

"I have a question that for some odd reason no one has addressed." Gatsby stood up to look at the two when he said this. "Why has no one dropped one dreaded nuke?"

Anna and Curtis looked at one another, shrugged.

Anna spoke first. "They're afraid of destroying the world?" Her voice went up an octave on the last word. She looked to Curtis for help.

"Don't look at me for an explanation. I gave up on rationality months ago. Maybe they're animal lovers?" He looked at the screen and the ubiquitous *BREAKING NEWS* banner. "It seems Famine is doing her job well."

"How do you know Famine's a *she?*" Anna said, almost

defensively.

Curtis cocked his head. "I don't know. It just came out. Sorry, didn't mean to offend."

"None taken," she said. "Just curious. But strangely… I agree; I think Famine's a *she*."

"Curiouser and curiouser." Gatsby raised one eyebrow. "Famine—feminine? They do *sound* similar."

"Ah, perceptive, Gats. You're more than a wealthy, pretty face."

"Are you trying to make me blush, Mr. Ambassador?" Gatsby asked, still standing.

Curtis stood up next to him—his face mere inches from Gatsby's. He wet his lips, saying, "It seems I have."

Anna laughed softly, feeling the underlying tension between them. They were two of the most beautiful men she had ever seen. But it was their souls that made them so beautiful. Oh sure, outwardly they were movie-star handsome, but they both had such pure, loving spirits. She found herself saying aloud, "You're both so beautiful."

Wordlessly, Gatsby reached for her and pulled her to them, then said, "You two have made my life… and for that I will be forever grateful."

Anna saw the tears in his eyes.

"I *do* believe we have been blessed as well," Curtis murmured. Anna saw his tears reflected there, then realized her own eyes had welled up.

Gatsby swallowed hard before saying, "This will go on record as the poorest taste for a pun of all time, but… all I can say is: Till death do we part."

They both pushed him hard onto the couch.

***

Eve sat between Cain and Abel, while they waited for Adam, discussing the remaining meager population left and the possibilities for their new "Adam and Eve."

"There is a man in France that has the qualities we are looking for," Abel said.

"There is a woman in New Zealand—"

"Ahem." Adam entered.

"Adam," Eve started, "we have our choices made."

"As do I," Adam returned. "There will only be two chosen, as you know. Two to begin our new Eos. Let us carefully review our candidates."

Cain said, "I feel quite strongly about my choices. I don't see how we can come to an accord."

Adam smiled gently. "It will all come right, and as it should be. We will be in perfect agreement before Earth beholds the Pale Horse."

***

As bizarrely wonderful as their unpredictable meeting had been, the three couldn't have been more grateful for one another.

Gatsby sat silent, watching his two beloved companions, both silent as well. They stared at the enormous screen. There was one news station that still aired, and even that one now only aired sporadically, a few die-hard (*poor choice of words*, he thought) dedicated reporters, doing what they loved to the bitter end. Or in his, and Anna's and Curtis's case, the bitter *sweet* end.

He smiled at them, content. Yes. Content. He couldn't remember ever feeling so content. Dare he say happy? Well, to himself he could.

They all knew the days were numbered, and then they would be no more. The Pale Horse would come and take the remaining with it.

"Contemplating the secrets of the universe, my friend?" Curtis pulled him from his reverie.

"Something like that. I was thinking how ironic that the world leaders set out to conquer a doomed world... instead of enjoying their last days. Pathetic, really. And... I wasn't going to say this, but why the hell not? I'm happy. I know Death, literally, is near, yet your love—yes, love, because what we have is so much more than friendship—has brought me to a place that I never thought could exist. You and Anna have given me what we all strive for: a life fulfilled by people who unconditionally love you. What more could I ask?"

"More time?" Anna said wryly. She got up and moved to the overstuffed chair where Gatsby sat. She plopped down on one arm; Curtis mirrored her on the other side. They both put their arms around him.

Gatsby could feel the love radiate from them. "Yes, more time would be nice."

"I have an idea," Anna said. "Let's turn off the TV for good and play some games. Maybe pop on some CDs from your extensive collection of musicals and sing along."

Gatsby felt his eyes burn. "I think that's the best idea I've heard for a long time."

"I second it." Curtis gave him a hug, leaned over, grabbed the remote, and clocked the television off. Under his breath, he said, "It's not like we don't know the ending."

"Gallows humor. That's the spirit," Gatsby said and clapped Curtis on the back. He got up and headed to a wall cabinet.

Curtis raced by him and grabbed the cabinet door. "I get to pick the show."

"And *I* get to pick the game," Anna said from another corner of the great room where she was opening a large door.

"How did you know where the games are?" Gatsby asked.

"After all this time, did you think we wouldn't snoop a little? Please. I even know where you hide your sex toys." She gave a little giggle.

Indignant, Gatsby said as he strode over to her. "I *don't* have sex toys."

"I know." She smiled coyly. "But you're so cute when you get riled."

"True," Curtis said, crossing the room to them. He produced two CDs. "*Camelot* or *Brigadoon*? I'm feeling a Lerner and Lowe mood. I thought about *On a Clear Day*—"

"That's Lerner and *Lane*," Gatsby corrected.

"I actually knew that, my musical maven. I was checking you." Curtis poked him in the side. "But I do like that show too."

"Touché," Gatsby said. "*Camelot* first?"

"Done." Curtis walked over to the state-of-the-art sound system, fiddled with it a bit, and soon the overture was playing, resounding throughout the room from the cleverly concealed speakers.

"Monopoly?" Anna asked.

"Not against the real estate mogul here." Curtis said, and gave Gatsby another poke in the ribs.

"Risk?"

"Too ironic." This time Gatsby poked Curtis back.

"Life?"

"The same," the two men said together, and attempted to poke one another again. They laughed.

"Behave, boys," Anna gave them a mock severe look.

They returned the same mock contrite looks.

All three laughed.

"Trivial Pursuit?" Anna continued.

The men nodded their approval.

"All right, then." Anna pulled the blue box from a shelf. "Just remember four-point-oh from Vassar..." She let the threat linger in the air.

"Bring it on, girl," Curtis said.

Gatsby moved to the bar. "I think martinis all around."

"You read my mind," Curtis said, sitting at the large coffee table and slipping off his shoes. "I need to be comfortable for this," he said off Anna's quizzical look.

"Absolutely," she said and slipped her own shoes off as well.

Gatsby set a large tray with a glass pitcher and three martini glasses on the table. Each glass sported two olives. He poured.

They raised their glasses.

Anna said, "To you both. Thank you for everything."

Curtis said, "To the finest people I have ever met."

Gatsby's throat closed. He felt his eyes filling. "To love."

"To love," the three said.

***

"As I said, Cain," Adam began, "we would all completely concur with our choices."

"Yes, they're perfect," Cain said. He held Abel's hand and squeezed it.

"Yes, perfect," Abel added and squeezed Cain's hand in return.

"I believe the woman is an even better choice than the one we had originally thought of. Eve," Eve said. She gave Adam a small hug. "are you ready to finish this, Adam?"

"I am. The final ride of the Pale Horse."

***

The world came to an end.

***

Then... the beginning...

***

They awoke on the beach, stirring slowly, rubbing their eyes.

They were naked, but not embarrassed.

They stared at one another, puzzlement in their eyes as they tried to remember.

They stood and brushed the sand from their bodies.

"Where are we?" Anna asked, looking around her.

"I don't know, but it's warm and beautiful. Idyllic," Curtis answered her.

"Yes, it is," she said. "Calm and serene."

They looked inland, but they saw nothing but land and trees.

"My guess is Coronado… San Diego area. I was here many times, when it was inhabited," Gatsby said as he rose and began brushing himself off.

"What do you think this means?" Anna asked.

"I think it means we've been given a second chance," Curtis said. His head slowly nodded, knowingly.

"I do too." Gatsby moved between his two fellow survivors. "I don't know how, or why us—why we've been chosen. But I *do* know I thank God for this inexplicable opportunity."

He took both of their hands.

"Let's make sure we get it right this time."

THE WRONG KIND OF RENAISSANCE
Lee Lawless

"It seems, more and more, that the world is a race between education and catastrophe."
-H.G. Wells

Chapter One - The Curriculum
NEW BEDFORD, MASSACHUSETTS
Valentine's Day, 2027

I can't fucking believe they're squaring off with swords in my bar. I mean, I *can* believe it (bullets are worth their weight in gold, and Manny's not going to risk hurting his capable, valuable hands by pummeling this guy to death), but this is the shit that usually goes down at the pirate spots down by the docks, not the private-bar second floor of my Officer's Club.

Oddly apt, Manny's foe is clutching an old US Army officer's dress sword, though he doesn't look like he's ever had training with it, or any other weapon for that matter. He clutches the sword two-handed even though it's clearly a one-handed saber. Light on his toes, Manny's noting how his foe is bent forward, like he's maybe gonna take a baseball-style swing. Manny's drawn his Spanish sword, forged from fine Toledo craftsmanship, its startlingly gorgeous blade gleaming in the lustrous lamplight. *Exquisito, si,* though I'd never seen him use it as more than a fashion accessory.

I can't kick them outside. I can't let them downstairs. Captain Arturo's crew are everywhere, and one or both of these guys will be shanghaied before I can make it down the back stairway.

I can't let either of these guys out of my sight, actually until our little payment issue is resolved. So I'm left with the only option, unsavory as it might be to my sensibilities, to my fine dark-wooden bar, my masterpieces on the walls, my exceptional leather furniture.

I've gotta let them fight it out.

The resonant undercurrent notion of *you're in a lot of trouble* was a theme that had played through my mind many times, like an earworm song that you couldn't shake and just had to sing along to, like it or not. I mentally hummed its malignant melody in the background of my main thought, another frequent strain that, for better or for worse, harmonized with the original theme.

I thought what I always thought when two, or more of the 6,000-odd known remaining humans of the region undertook armed battle against each other.

Someone's really gonna get their feelings hurt.

***

Look, I know it sounds crazy, but nowadays, we look out for each other. Even me, though I'm one of the surliest sweethearts you'll ever meet. I just don't like being unnecessarily too mean to people. We'd already had so much of it. Six years' worth of dealing with the fallout, both literal and every level of metaphorical.

Six years ago, on an event we now referred to as A-Day, an electromagnetic pulse weapon had gone off in low earth orbit, somewhere over an otherwise-unremarkable expanse of Kansas. It had been enough to wipe the year 2021 straight backward, about a century and a half previous. The ensuing droughts, famines, disease, and general barbarity of our (dear departed) civilization made it seem like we'd gone much further back, at least for a good year there after the end.

But like all bad ends, it was the chance for fruitful new beginnings. The slate wasn't clean, per se, but a lot of us were determined to not lose the lesson, despite losing basically everything else we were used to.

It was a weird Renaissance, but some of us tried to make it work.

Like artists reusing a canvas to create a fresh masterpiece over an inspiringly inept attempt, we rebuilt. The going wasn't easy. At several points, nuclear weapons had been thrown around in a spiteful free-for-all, a final "fuck you" from superpowers and terrorists alike, all determined to bring everyone else down with them. The nukes had ironically been one of the few things that had been treasurably well protected, ensconced in suitcases or silos with Faraday cages shielding them from any sort of circuitry malfunction that would stop them from seeing through their eventual missions of mayhem.

The snow had only stopped falling gray this year.

So it was a hard, long enough time after the collapse (six years after the EMP blast, five after nukes sealed the remaining deals, three and a half after humanity had eaten or beaten most of our fellow risen apes into extinction) that we started feeling secure enough in our survivor status to actually take tally of things.

That was where my job came in. I run Trooley's Tourist Tavern, same name as the place I had in NYC, *R.I.P.* Except this one is on Union Street in New Bedford, former whaling capital of the world and current cradle of resuscitated civilization. Not the only hive of humanity remaining, but by most standards, one of the best. Amidst that, my spot has become a de facto trading post for, well, basically everything. Whatever's left from everywhere.

Overall, America is ironically back the way it started, populated with tightly insular, judicious (if not judgmental) enclaves nestled into the northeast coast. Below that, the climate had bullied its way down the border, causing flooding and tsunamis on a scale that would have been singularly deadly on its own. We still caught pieces of it, but had been lucky that the south (now nearly fiction, as far as we knew) had taken the brunt of the hits. Judging by the scant communications we had with the rest of the world, we figured they hadn't fared too much better either, after all was said and done. Still, at least the initial war/famine/pestilence/death toll had already relieved hundreds of millions of the burden of dying slow. But nowadays, we had decided that starving or dying of exposure was no way to go for the other survivors, and here in town we made sure all the folks who flocked to our streets and shores, at the bare minimum, wouldn't have to worry about those things anymore.

That's the cool thing about the end of the world. We hit rock bottom, and then started to rebuild with much better intents than most of us had ever had before. You can tell the difference, because this time, we genuinely give a fuck about each other, and for the most part, we're happy.

Yeah, some days I barely believe it myself. But then I wake up on the third floor of my big-ass bar, in my penthouse loft that overlooks the ocean, all the way out to the horizon. I smoke a giant homegrown joint straight into my face, maybe slap some handsome soldier or sailor or the hot hockey coach on the ass, then go downstairs with him into my beautiful bar for breakfast. Delivered from my local buddies/handymen/trading partners the Rockeros, of course. (Here at Trooley's, we don't keep a lot of food on hand to serve, it attracts pirates like bears in the wild. While we're all mostly decent these days, a person with an empty belly can also be a person with an empty conscience.) Sometimes I'll let Santi, my awesome Argentine barman, run the place for the afternoon. I'll ride my bike out to the beach and just lay there, listening to the waves draw over the smooth little rocks of the shore, lapping lavishly like the earth is applauding me for still existing.

Not today though. Today I was busy.

While the creation of a new and improved civilization valued a lot of fresh ideas and attempts at things like updated policy and hardier technology, plenty of old-old things still had value. That was why I was sitting upstairs at the Officer's Club, the private bar I'd appointed to the second floor of Trooley's, polishing a bag of Greek drachmas, shiny survivors from some other, older apocalypse. The Greeks still had a fair shipping consortium afloat, and got off on trading with this stuff, and god (Zeus?) knows they had enough of it lying around, even just historically. When one of their freighters pulled into port yesterday, they'd forked me these for a round of weed-mead and few barrels of the local hemp oil (which all the diesel boats are running on now, usually in conjunction with solar cells.) I'm not some serious historian or anything, but the nature of my work makes it necessary to have more than a functioning knowledge of what might be valuable. The drachmas were a good enough trade for the booze and the fuel.

As usual, I'd have preferred music (musicians, instruments, records, whatever), or exotic libations, or even literature (reading at the bar had become cool again, thanks to the EMP blast killing all those little devices we used to hunch over for happiness), but as far as old-school silver coins go, these were pretty cool. Not nearly enough to buy University Admission, but pretty cool. I polished them with a focused reverie, pausing intermittently to take small sips of my precious coffee (real, not instant), the beans of which I'd traded a Portuguese sailor six boxes of bullets for. Downstairs, I heard the echoes of Santi singing along to REO Speedwagon's *Take It On The Run* as he readied the main bar for the day.

The fervent footfalls up the stairs, accompanied by the cheery clatter of an armful of silver bracelets, meant my morning meditation was at an end.

"Reliiiiiiii!" Joy exhorted, her preteen shriek equal parts enthusiastic and obnoxious. "Is Rudy here?" She skipped across the room, her ridiculous excess of jewelry a-clanking. That was the funny thing about "valuables", nowadays. Some of the ones that had been in excess have now deflated to the level of junk jewelry. A ten-year-old could have an armful of Tiffany silver and diamonds, but it might not buy a cup of coffee in a place that'd sell you a slave in exchange for some sugar packets.

My kid cousin, Joy, took this opportune depreciation to a somewhat hilarious extreme, trying for all of (the remainder of) the world to be as fancy as any debutante back in the day. Not only was she constantly laden with silver, diamonds, rare opals, and other gems and treasures, she also wore a full face of makeup, every single day, the sort of princess-play that looked weirdly cute combined with her usual utilitarian uniform of combat boots, jeans, and a hacked-up Patriots hoodie.

I can't really disparage her accoutrement choices. Though I save my good jewelry for special occasions, I own a variety of completely real Rolexes that I wear flippantly, and have been known to trade them for things like Stones records. Hey, treasure is what you treasure.

"Good morning to you too, monkeyface," I told the glittering, tittering Joy. "No, Captain Brough has not graced us with his presence yet."

"Shoulda guessed. You'd be tryin' ta smooch him if he was. Whatcha got?" She plunked down next to me at the bar, her eyes agleam at the shining coins.

"Ancient arcade tokens."

"What's an arcade?"

This happens more often than I mean for it to. I reference something from the not-distant (though apparently very distant) past without realizing that Joy has grown up in a completely different realm than the one that any previous kids had.

"We used to have big rooms full of video games. It was something fun to do. Kids then couldn't shoot real guns as often as you can, not kids in cities at least."

"Sounds boring."

I didn't offer a rebuttal. Best she never worry about what she missed back then. If it's one good thing the apocalypse did, it was foster a sense of renewed enjoyment of simpler things. Particularly for kids, which still seems amazing to me, given that as a two-year-old, Joy had known how to flip through an iPad to get to gaming apps. Although the bar kept a stash of all the great analog games, which were played by young folks and less-young alike, the old computerized conditioning was long gone, and a healthy respect for outdoor adventures had taken its place.

Sometimes, too much so.

"Guess what?" Joy piped up through a stolen sip of my coffee. "I saw Robbo's raiders!"

"You know Captain Arturo would cut your tongue out for not addressing him properly?"

"One was a kid!" she barreled on, the threat not deterring her in the slightest. "He was playing piano on the deck at Las Diablas and they were all cheering for him! Do you think they'll try to trade him?"

"Not here they won't. Captain Arturo knows we don't traffic humans. Anyway, The University doesn't need any pirate kids. They need people that're gonna use their skills and smarts to help the world." *What's left of it, anyway.*

"He's really good, though," she continued. "Like, crazy good. Like that Doors band guy. Or Chopin."

Of all the loot I've scored and hoarded in my bartender/barterer life as of late, I have to tell you, I'm probably most proud of the record stash. It takes up so much room in the sub-basement that upstairs we need three-ring binders like karaoke books full of the titles, if you want to buy, trade, or spin something. It's a diverse and vast archive of everything from 45s to 72s, with various vacuum-tube devices around rigged to spin and amplify them. Joy's quite the little crate-digger, I've seen her select some serious gems from stashes that get slapped up for trade. Of course, it only figures though, given her mentors. Between me and Santi blasting everything from Aerosmith to Zeppelin on the regular, with classical, reggae, ska, punk, metal, and jazz, if tipped well for it, Joy knew her stuff.

Oh also, The University housed every living legend of music we could find. That helped her education too. A few of them were slated to perform at the bar tonight, as usual for Fridays.

"How d'you know he's good?" I challenged. "The hell Li let you inside Las Diablas."

"I heard the music all the way down the block, so I rode down the side street and looked over the fence. The kid didn't look so good. He was playing like crazy though, Reli, you shoulda seen it."

Fucking figured. My kid cousin, sneaking off to pirate bars while I'm supposed to be teaching her how to run a reputable establishment. How the hell did I end up setting such a bad example? I used to be so much worse than this, and I became at least a little better (I think.) But that didn't matter at the moment.

"Robbo was bragging they made him play for ten hours last night. The kid looked it too…"

I tossed the last drachma into its bag.

"All that music and chatter in Spanish and you still heard that?"

Joy scowled, "Your boring-ass lessons actually work. You should be proud."

"Well, it's not nearly as fun as hanging out with pirates, that's for sure."

Joy changed tack, appealing to what she somehow knew was a soft spot for me, although I never mention anything about it.

"Rudy's a privateer, though," she said proudly.

I sighed. "I know he says that all the time, but 'privateer' is just a fancy word for 'pirate.' Just because your dad said Ru… *Captain Brough* could liberate stuff from all over the place and keep it safe at The University doesn't mean he's not a pirate."

"Does that make my dad the pirate king?"

Sort of, I was tempted to say, but thought better of it. Martin O'Daye, a.k.a. Joy's father, a.k.a. The Admiral, a.k.a. The Chancellor, a.k.a. my uncle Marty, had built an actual empire out of what remained from about fifty other major ones. He ran The University, which folks far and wide knew to be the safest, healthiest, smartest live-in educational facility in the Northeast.

Although now, in all honesty, it was probably the best place *anywhere* to live, work, learn, and otherwise cooperate to survive.

Uncle Marty had been a merchant seaman before quitting the open ocean to teach geometry at a nice prep school outside Boston. He'd worked his way up the administrative ladder, but hated the politics and eventually took to teaching at the former University of Massachusetts at Dartmouth, now known simply as The University. A remarkable campus built in the Brutalist style of layered, formerly-"futuristic" looking assemblages of concrete, the school had survived the worst of everything and still stood in its Stonehenge-styled circle, nestled neatly on acres of land that his students had carefully coerced into becoming arable. Other students had learned engineering, or oceanography, or medicine, or any number of useful skills from a worldwide array of professors who had survived and who'd made their way to this educational enclave.

But Uncle Marty, for all his former maritime badassery and genuine genius at running an institution of higher education, values one particular skill over anything, and a lot of people are surprised to find it's the last one they expect.

Sure, when everything had first gone wrong, the people we needed to collect were farmers. Hunters. Doctors. Soldiers. The usual complement of survivalist types. Many had found their way to The University, and had been welcomed for either offering these skills or offering to learn them in exchange for labor that aided the school and community. But now that a rough rendition of society was back in place, Uncle Marty valued keeping the civility in civilization more than anything.

Which was why, stashed in one of the great and mysterious Brutalist buildings of The University, ensconced in near-nukeproof concrete halls and tunnels, my Uncle Marty, former geometry teacher extraordinaire, had amassed a collection of art and antiquities that rivaled the greatest museums the world had ever seen.

And yeah. More than a little bit of piracy had been involved in the collection thereof.

Well, *privateering*.

No one could deny that it was a safe and smart move. The world's great museums had been located near-uniformly in the world's greatest cities, all of which were lucky if they still had enough infrastructure left to house roaches. Quietly and carefully, missions had been launched over the course of the last few years to "reconnoiter, respond, and recover" some of the greatest works of art the former world had ever seen, and the current world might otherwise have never seen again be it due to weather, elements, animals, and decay (general or societal). Were some of them part of previously-private collections? Probably. Were those collection's owners still alive? Probably not. If they were, they were welcome to come take up their claim with uncle (Chancellor, Admiral) Marty.

No one had yet contested any of the holdings.

So, judging by the number of wide-eyed travelers that came through New Bedford every day from both land and sea, even among the mere million human beings we'd estimated to be the remaining population worldwide, word had clearly gotten out about this. For better or for worse, the care of the value (and the value of the care) had made The University a near-heavenly haven. Although we tended well to those who arrived in town, the schooling, living conditions, food, medicine, and just sheer fucking *possibility* of The University made it a beacon of benevolence.

It didn't even inspire the pirates to heist The University's collection so much as contribute to it, in exchange for an interesting array of things. The most valuable of those things was, of course, to be formally inducted into the esteemed ranks of the student body. To somehow, by superb skill or knowledge or treasure or humanitarian heroics, be worthy of gaining Admission.

The University was currently operating at maximum capacity, and it was no small deal deciding who earned a coveted class placement when one opened up.

Thus, thanks to my proximity both genetic and geographic, I didn't just sling local beer and weed-mead for a living. Trooley's Tourist Tavern was also a default admissions office.

"If you asked my dad nicely, you think he'd he give the kid Admission?" Joy entreated.

"You know The University's full," I admonished. "Until they finish the new expansion, it's already busting at the seams." This was an understatement. People were willing to sleep in the dorms' halls and ride bikes or horses or hempoline-converted vehicles from neighboring towns miles away, maybe just to catch a single lecture hall class. Still others were happy to put in a day's work that could be exchanged for feast-caliber food and drink at their well-kept cafeteria. As for medicine, The University had an astonishing record of patient satisfaction for an institution that was basically operating with the same equipment as one would have had in the middle of the last century.

"Ask him for me too, Reli," Manny lilted, cruising in with a bag of his famous burritos hanging from one ornately-tattooed arm. "No, actually, don't ask him. I love my starving artist lifestyle, and if I survived the apocalypse without learning math, I don't need to learn it now."

"Starving, my concave moon-tanned ass. Thanks for the burritos, dude."

"No problemo," Manny smiled, his bright white teeth lighting up his caramel-colored face. Like Joy, Manny prided himself on maintaining a height of fashion in these apocalypse-afterparty times. His well-greased Elvis haircut with its studiously-placed forelock, pegged dark jeans, inexplicably shiny patent leather boots, and tight black T-shirt give him a charming throwback look that would have made him cool in any decade over basically the whole last century. But the sheathed Spanish sword hanging from his bondage belt, copious sharp silver skull rings, and .38 caliber bullets worn in his ear gauges make it known that for all the flash, he was still always ready for a fight. Or at least, that's the image he put up.

He nodded at the bag of drachmas. "Hey, what's with the subway tokens? We goin' to Rockaway Beach?"

"Hah. I wish," I smirked. "It just wouldn't be the same in a radiation-proof suit, would it?"

"Hell, I'd wear one of those at Coney Island, even before shit went down!"

We laughed. Manny pulled out a detailed drawing and unfolded it before me.

"Speaking of the old stomps, check this out."

The sketch was a somewhat architectural one, a diagram of a bench. It looked for all the world like an old New York subway bench, one of the wooden ones, except Manny's design had it made from all sorts of compressed layers of things.

"You remember these?" he asked.

"You remember Manhattan?" I laughed. "Of course! You making this?"

Joy, accustomed to wrenching my attention back when she wanted it, grabbed a drachma from the bag. "Heads or tails?" she asked.

"Tails," Manny told her. Joy smiled affirmatively as it landed in her palm. "Yeah," he told me. "If I can borrow some of your tools. I got the basic frame down, but I wanna sand it better."

"That's cool," I said. "Look at you, being all tribute-y to the public services of yore! Or is this a prank? Did you build it out of crushed train parts or something?"

He winked. "Prank, public service, same thing."

Joy flipped the coin high in the air. "Heads or tails?"

"Heads," Manny and I said at the same time. Joy dropped the drachma, which rolled under one of the plush leather library chairs.

"Same thing?" I joked to Manny. "That's not what the judge said on your, what was it? TWELVE counts of Transporting Instruments of Graffiti and Defacement of Public Property?"

"The man's always tryin' ta crush my art. That subway tunnel never looked better, and you know it."

I did know it. Though I hadn't been tagging walls and dodging train cars for the greater artistic good like Manny had, being trapped deep underground in the Manhattan subway on A-Day is one of the only reasons I was still here. But that doesn't matter right now.

"Have Santi take you down to the vault," I told Manny. "I gotta get to the Community Coalition meeting. Joy, up and at 'em."

Joy crawled out from under the library chair, clutching the drachma. "It was tails." She clambered back over to the bar next to Manny. "Can I see your drawing?"

"Keep it," Manny said, pushing her the paper. "Joy, girl, you show your daddy that sketch. He'll want one of them bitches... excuse me, one of my lovely *benches*... up in his office lobby, like, yesterday, *mi amor.*"

Manny kissed Joy on the head and she hopped off the barstool, grabbing his hand to lead him downstairs. I hefted the bag of burritos, one of the many marvels that materialized from Manny's workshop down by the docks, and made sure all the oil lamps were extinguished before I headed downstairs too.

The burritos are a sideline. I knew Manny and his crew (a gang of similarly-sharp Latino punks locally known as the Rockeros) fucked with gambling, and drugs of a spicier variety than the kindbud we already had fields of, and likely lines to other stuff that I really didn't want to be party to. I knew this because they'd fucked with these things since we'd been buddies in New York. For all the forever ago, some things are remarkably intransient. But even if their worst habits had survived the apocalypse, their best had as well. Manny and the Rockeros were still some of my best friends.

As for my other friends, we had business to attend to.

***

Chapter 2 – The State of The Union Street

Hatred is a science of mixology. A shot of skullduggery here, a dash of duplicity there. Its flavors can be strong, bitter, acidic, or many other varietals, but racial or national hatred is particularly unsavory. It used to be popularly served on the masters' tabs, to make sure that the oppressed have reasons to bicker amongst themselves, rather than rise up against the real problem. This convoluted concoction suppressed useful, productive, necessary violence and misdirected it against our often otherwise attack-unworthy fellow humans.

The tree of liberty needed to be watered with the blood of tyrants, but for a while there at the end, we were all just sipping some strange brew that exsanguinated our fellow man.

Fortunately, the flavors of hate soon turned sour. It got poured straight down the drain, for the most part, when we learned the hard way that we really all were in this together, for better or for worse.

I mean, the world had already been through enough, humanity in particular. Like I said, I don't really like hurting anyone's feelings unduly. Quite the opposite, actually.

It's weird to say, but the apocalypse was an awesome aphrodisiac.

As we gathered around the first floor's horseshoe-shaped main bar for our weekly Community Coalition meeting, it was clear that the absent privateer Captain Rudy Brough was probably taking significant advantage of that fact. I didn't want to think about it. I didn't want to think about him nestled in some rickety Victorian brothel across town, or some University grad's stony school flat, or the bunkhouse at one of the farm breweries, snuggled up with some honey who helped farm the honey that was made exclusively from cannabis-pollinating bees. That same honey (the bee puke, not the theoretical girl) was used in an ancient Gaelic alcohol recipe we affectionately called "weed-mead." Next to the endless barrels of hemp oil the local farms produced as fuel, weed-mead was our greatest export.

No, I wasn't going to think about where he was right now, Captain Rudy Brough, the self-styled privateer and commander of the cannabis-carting corsair, the *U.S.S. Pot Yacht*. On A-Day, he'd escaped Manhattan, driving an older grocery delivery truck, where he'd been safely ensconced in the refrigerated back when things went wrong. A series of odd adventures later, the dude who'd been kicked out of the Navy in the '90s for smoking weed was now in charge of distributing some of the finest ganj products to ever float the East

Coast. His adorable ass had just gotten into town last night, and while I didn't necessarily begrudge him some R&R, we had business to attend to.

The other members of the Community Coalition were already present, sipping tea and munching their own Manny-made breakfast burritos. With Rudy currently absent, that left us with a favorite few locals who, in my opinion, actually ran everything in this town that wasn't directly University-affiliated.

"Morning Reli," said Officer Rick, a former State Trooper who had survived A-Day's fallout thanks to locking himself and some of his squad in an old subterranean jail cell beneath Boston. While the rule of law here was still lackadaisical, Officer Rick and his men would still "patrol and control" where needed, which saved the rest of us a lot of trouble. "You hear the pirates are in town?"

"It's Valentine's Day," reasoned Li, the owner of the Las Diablas pirate bar/brothel down the street. "Robbo and his raiders deserve love too."

"Let 'em find some mermaids to rape," Officer Rick sneered. He'd had run-ins with Robbo (known properly as the pirate Captain Roberto Arturo) and the raiders more than once, but a rough armistice was usually reached on major holidays, if only so the raiders could party in peace.

"My girls all seem to love them," Li countered. "Captain Arturo and his men are free to trade their treasure with me." Li always maintained an ultimate chill, one of a number of reasons we made good allies despite technically being business competitors. As a fellow former New York bartender who'd been stocking bottles in a sub-basement cooler on A-Day, she had only noticed her generally-candlelit bar's whole block had gone dark once she stepped outside for a smoke. She'd simply, coolly, loaded her touring bike with all the good bottles and cash she could carry off that fated, formerly treasured island. A stunning Chinese girl who favored intricately-wrought silk outfits in avant-garde styles, her appreciation for art rivaled my own. Her appreciation for danger exceeded it.

"Sure, but does he have some kid with him?" I asked Li. "Should we be worried there?"

Li's face became a caricature mask of excitement. "I couldn't wait to tell you! He's INCREDIBLE! Reli, this kid Pablo is amazing. You gotta hear him. I know you don't want Robbo in here, but you gotta let this kid at the piano. You'll see."

"Maybe later," I said. "There's a lot to get handled before the show tonight, and I've gotta check in with The Admiral too. Which brings us to our next point. As we all know, a slot for Admissions has opened up, thanks to one of the football team graciously heading north to serve with the Mass National Guard helping refugees in Boston. Coach Tony, who are our candidates?"

The final member of our community cabal, Coach Tony, a.k.a. Tony Toast, had been flipping through a large binder of papers on the bar, and his striking blue eyes blasted the room like stadium floodlights.

"We have a number of valuable candidates," he said. "I have profiles on each of them for your perusal, but the Chancellor has made it clear he'd like the spot filled by the end of next week. There are several major candidates I'd like to bring your attention to..."

Tony goes off all analytically, his former hotshot business-bro side showing. He'd been having a swank multi-martini lunch in the vault of a retrofitted Manhattan bank-turned-fancy restaurant when A-Day went down. To his credit, he'd made sure his private sailboat got the entire party of twenty people off the darkened island. You'd think he'd have taken up some esoteric hobby now, like numismatics or something, but he's actually reconnected a lot with his Masshole roots. He's the hockey coach for the University team, who plays against the brewery teams, the stray Canadians who've been trickling down in furry tribal swaths, or once a whole squad of Russian submariners who'd docked down the harbor when their navigation system tanked. That had been a surprise for everyone involved. Everyone had assumed at least one other superpower had anti-EMP equipped nav gear. Not so much, it turned out. They sold off their dud supplies for scrap in the port, just before the game, and gave us a lot of friendly hell for ending the world before they'd had a chance to. The school team beat them 4-2. Tony had been really proud of that.

We called him "Tony Toast" since he's just scorchingly handsome, and in keeping with the theme of many survivors, loves wearing nice clothes. His are mostly dressy versions of casual outfits like you'd wear if you were slumming it in the Hamptons, or sometimes really posh handmade suits for when he's coaching a game, but I'd be lying if I said he didn't look his very best absolutely nude–a gameplan we ran every now and then. I couldn't lust after a pirate (sorry, *privateer*) like Rudy forever, especially when he apparently always had other pretty priorities in port.

Tony finished listing some qualities of various candidates, but it was clear he was saving the best for last. He handed the binder of bios around the bar.

"Do any of you guys recognize these images or that insignia?"

Li and Officer Rick passed, eyebrows raised and shoulders shrugged.

But when the file got to me, I forgot to breathe.

The images were copious in their coverage and perspectives. Some were close-ups of terrain, some analytically distant, some with numerical markings and charts in the margins. The most interesting were clearly thermal readouts, infrared heat signature maps clearly taken from outside the atmosphere, from low earth orbit if not higher.

The small, winged design sketched out in the dossier sent an almost tangible electric pulse through my mind.

The sketch was of the former United States Army's official insignia for an astronaut.

***

Chapter Three – Admissions

The old rotary phone rang and Joy, who'd been sitting at the far end of the bar painting her nails, jumped up to grab it.

"Trooley's Tourist Tavern. You loot it, we scoot it!"

I glared at Joy. Her goofy phone pickups were going to hit the wrong ears someday and cause me some proper hell. We weren't some fencing operation. This was a reputable establishment. Well, reputable as one could be, these days.

"HI!" the enthusiastic/obnoxious shriek returned. I knew the caller must be Rudy. I returned to addressing the business meeting that he should have been physically present for.

"Tony, where the hell did you get this?"

"The guy got into town three days ago. Says he was working at Harvard as an engineering professor but that it's a mess up there. He claims there's talk of an overarching plan for inland expansion, something called Operation Glades. Lotta folks are heading west or further north to Maine. Not New Hampshire, that nuke plant meltdown fucked up a lot. But in Boston, people are evacuating their asses off, the flooding's getting really bad, and there's too many rumors General Zhao's gonna arrive to finish things off. The panic is real."

"But Zhao's a specter," Li piped up. "Why would he come here from China just to screw with Boston? Especially Harvard? They're a shadow of what they used to be."

"Boston's got a lot of history and artifacts still," I reminded her. It was true, especially among some of the older, well-defended areas of the town that hadn't been as abused by the ravages of time and turmoil. "Harvard has an awesome archive too…"

"Maybe not for long," Officer Rick said seriously. "My guys up there tell me your astro-bro might be right about Zhao. Folks are spooked, for sure. Even if they're not spooked, I'm hearin' the same stuff about Maine. Lots of land, clean water, someone's even mouthing off about reopening a ski mountain. Look, no one up there wants to admit defeat, Bostonians are the original American revolutionaries. Some of them will stay there until the city's underwater. That said, if folks are evacuating Harvard, we need to make a smaht move."

Rick's accent often came out when he was stressed. Dropping that one "r" in "smaht" was a statement unto itself.

"Alright," I said. "We can't worry about Zhao yet. We need to focus on what's in front of us. Tony, these documents are as genuine as I can figure. I think we've got a spaceman on our hands. If I'm reading these thermal images correctly, it's a report of all the bombing events worldwide. I know some of those satellites and receiving stations, especially the ones communicating with the big labs, are pulse-proofed. They would have survived the EMP, it's just that most of the Earthbound end that wasn't able to pick up all the data. Except this guy apparently did, from somewhere."

I shuffled the images again, handing a few back around. The damage was astonishing, worse than anyone would have thought. Bright red and orange heat-signatures bloomed around the globe.

And we'd *already* thought it was literally the worst thing ever. Now we knew for certain that it was somehow even worse. The fallout would still be falling over many of these areas.

"Australia's done for," Li noted. "Antarctica too."

The thermal map of Antarctica looked like multicolored swiss cheese. Massive swaths of what should have been ice were entirely the wrong hue, bright yellow or red instead of blue.

"That explains a lot of the flooding," Tony said somberly. "I wonder how much longer we've got."

"We're based on better bedrock," I reminded him. "Boston is half landfill."

Still... The University was far enough inland that there wouldn't be any damage, but as for the rest of us, we were not more than a solid Tom Brady toss from the Atlantic. The subterranean shanghai tunnels beneath my bar made it less than a five-minute walk to the docks. Trooley's, and indeed a huge swath of Union Street, could be done for if a few more glacier chunks decided to stir themselves into our mix.

Focus. Remember what we're valuing right now.

"Where is this guy, Tony?"

"I got him a temporary bunk by one of the hydroponic vegetable farms. He seems to know a lot about the process, even with our rudimentary setups. Says he can streamline things, help improve the power sources, all sorts of stuff." Tony chuckled, his smile flashing with a nice bit of optimism. "Reli, he said he's the former commander of the space station."

I looked at the military insignia sketched on the page. It was a silver pair of wings, with a shield bearing an ascending star and rocket contrail in the middle. A faker would probably have slapped the circular NASA "meatball" on their bio, or created some scientific-sounding gobbledygook that no one else could decode, but I'd always loved astronauts. This all looked authentic.

Social media is not something I miss, not by a long shot, but I remembered having been "friends" with quite a few spacefarers back in the day, if only to follow their adventures through their astonishing pictures and video. I asked our astronaut's name. Tony told me. I explained that, at least visually, I could confirm who he was.

"Joy, when did Rudy say he was getting here?" I asked.

"ASAP," she replied.

As soon as he pleases. To be fair, he'd been at sea for the last two months, and he'd have had no idea we had an Admissions slot open, or that we were discussing new candidates. Still, his opinion was important to our group when he could offer it, and I wanted him here. *Fine, alright, maybe not even just necessarily for his opinion.*

"If we're in agreement that this guy is our pick, I can go swing past the hydro farm and bring our guy to the campus. Li, find me this mini-Mozart and he can come too, at least for a physical. Reli, you and Rudy can meet me there once that lazy stoner surfaces."

Tony collected the thermal images, though I took a lingering final look at them. Australia and Antarctica were straight fucked. Ditto much of Africa, and a uniquely unsettling preponderance of Asia, including the Orient, the subcontinent, and most of Russia. We'd known from the trading boats that Europe had taken some hard hits, but these showed exactly where. Basically only small patches of non-bombed area remained. One of images depicting the area from space didn't show very many lights at all, where once much of the continent had appeared a luminous diamond from above.

Speaking with their traders, you'd never have guessed how bad it was. Europe, as usual, was still keeping a stiff upper lip, and like us had also conquered themselves back into a sense of community. We traded with ships from Ireland, Spain, Germany, France, Portugal, Greece, Britain, and some of the Scandinavian nations too, and while most mentioned things were bad, it was clear that they were playing up their perseverance.

We (the human We, or in this case, the rather inhuman We) really had demolished damn near everything.

"Hah," Officer Rick noted as he handed the images back to Tony. "Look at the fucking Mid-East. Nighty night, sandbox."

We openly laughed. Who fucking cared about the Middle East. Of course no one could really prove it, but it was more than speculated about who'd hit the light switch six years ago. About how reports of an Arabian space program had all been a front for the EMP satellite. About how American military bases in the region were on high alert for weeks beforehand. About how some faction group of militant morons had tried to claim responsibility on the internet, before realizing they'd self-censored their victory tirade by tanking America's entire computer-based infrastructure.

They got to revel in their long-term Luddite lifestyle now. Good riddance. We had better things to do.

The phone rang again. Joy grabbed it and met my side-eye gaze as she chirped, "Trooley's Tourist Tavern! You clip it, we flip it!" Immediately, however, her smile dropped. "Yessir," she said seriously. "Yessir. I'll tell her. Thank you, sir." She hung up. "Your astronaut just talked his way into a chat with The Admiral. He wants the whole intel file immediately."

"Well, looks like our choice has been made," Li noted. "Shall we adjourn?"

We all rose, shaking hands and clapping backs. Made promises to reconvene here for the show this evening. It was sure to be a good one, hell, with the musicians we'd spent time rescuing, our weekly jam sessions are better than nearly any stadium show you'd have seen back in the day.

Tony gave me a quick kiss as he left. "Happy Valentine's Day. I know you're probably all excited that Rudy's back, but…"

"We'll talk later tonight," I promised him, replying with another kiss in turn.

He flashed that winning smile, the one that'd sealed countless huge business deals back in the day, and I was more than a little happy he was as enthusiastic about seeing me. I stared unapologetically at his athletic ass as he left, his designer jeans proving their old thousand-dollar price tag's worth of quality even now, amidst all this anarchy.

I was so distracted that it took me a second to recoil when a tall, gangly man stepped into the bar's doorway in front of me. Rambo, our badass bouncer, wasn't in until the evening, and my hand instinctively fell to the ball-bearing sap at my side.

The guy's gray eyes gleamed and glared as he leaned in, feeling too close to me. I stepped back and yelled for Santi.

"Please," he implored. "My name's Harold. I don't want any trouble. I have something you really might want."

"Trading hours commence on Monday," I stated stoically.

"Please," he intoned. He was wearing a rough-looking pea coat and dress-blue uniform pants that looked too big on his skinny frame. He swung an architect's blueprint tube off of his shoulder just as I sensed Santi appearing behind me, an Easton aluminum bat no doubt in his left hand. I subtly leaned left to accommodate anything that might ensue. Santi liked fighting lefty, which added an element of surprise towards the dudes who always expected him to draw or punch from the right.

"I know you know how to obtain Admission," this guy Harold said, his voice somewhat hoarse. Maybe from the nasty February weather, maybe from yelling. Maybe both. Maybe worse. "I know it's not easy to get. But please, hear me out."

"Why?" Santi spat, his Argentinian accent adding a veil of vehemence.

"I was with the National Guard's nuclear cleanup crew," the guy said. "I've just come from New York City."

***

Chapter Four – Starry Fight

In one of the collections of papers in the basement I have the final copies of the New York Times. Also the Post and Daily News too, but the Times one was my favorite. So stoic. So like the Grey Lady, to calmly explain that a terrorist attack of unknown but strongly speculated origin had taken place.

The kicker is the format. The Grey Lady had been reduced to a blue-inked one-pager that even the crummiest punk-rock 'zine scenesters would have derided. But to me, that gritty, charred slice of regular office paper shows me all the beauty of total commitment, a captain going down with his ship.

I dunno. I wasn't *old*-old when it all went down (I'm still not, though I damn well feel it some days) but I was old enough to remember what it was like before all the technology ran all the things. I knew that final edition of the Times, that smudgy purple-print "Dear John" to humanity, had been typed up on a manual typewriter. Someone at the office must have had one, maybe as a prank gift or an ostentatious "real journalist" piece of desk setting. It didn't care about the lack of electricity. The hastily-aligned borders and blue residue of the ink could only mean one thing: it was cranked off, by hand, on some old mimeograph machine that must have been dug out of the depths of a basement or storage locker.

But it existed. It told its story. Even if all the news that was fit to print was little more than a few breathless rumors, some hints for hauling out, and the final, friendly headline of "GOOD NIGHT AND GOOD LUCK", it existed.

Kind of funny, that we'd spent time from the dawn of the printing press safeguarding first editions of various books as the height of value. Now, for some items, it was their LAST edition that was the only thing that mattered.

Oh well. It existed. It told its story. Survival in and of itself is a kind of value, never let anyone (or yourself) tell you otherwise.

What Harold was doing appeared to be an issue of survival.

I let him inside and he wasted no time sitting down at the bar and undoing the cap on his blueprint tube. Santi watched him suspiciously, as though the tube was filled with anthrax or explosives or something, and the gingerly way Harold handled it did indeed make it seem like the object inside was of dangerous value.

"I was part of a cleanup crew on the East Side," Harold explained, rubbing his hands together for warmth as he readied to show us his prize. "Hundreds of mansions, penthouses, all that old money. There was stuff to be saved. I'd heard how important it was to you guys. I wanted to help. God knows no one on that forsaken island cares."

I studied his pale pallor, his obvious anxiety, his thinning buzzcut. I wondered if the radiation maybe didn't hit him harder than he thought. I knew the National Guard tried to conscript a lot of help in the A-Day aftermath, but this guy just didn't fit the bill somehow.

Still, a part of me wanted all the news from New York that he could express, even if they were exaggerated or secondhand. The truth can set you free, but stories can set you safe.

Not that any of us were really safe, anymore, but I did want to hear his tale.

"The Met went into lockdown, there was no breaching the security doors," he explained, referring to the Metropolitan Museum of Art. No surprise there, that castle of creativity was one of the most heavily-guarded institutions in the world, EMP blast or no.

"But," he continued, "there's a lot of glass on the ground floor of the Museum of Modern Art. We got in there pretty easy."

"Who's we?" I asked. He named a battalion I made note of to double-check with Officer Rick. Santi repeated it, apparently aware of their existence from elsewhere, and offered the guy a semi-serious salute, which Harold crisply returned. Oddly enough, I was beginning to believe this guy.

But believe him or not, what followed was going to require verification.

From the blueprint tube, possible-guardsman Harold pulled out a rolled canvas. It was smallish, but when he unfurled it, its simple elegance radiated out at us, mesmerizing as a masterpiece.

Sitting on my bar, surrounded by walls covered with random art and imagery from nearly every location humanity had previously inhabited, a little luminous in the sunlight seeping in from the front windows, was Vincent Van Gogh's "Starry Night."

And though there was no possible way Harold could have known this, he'd rescued Uncle Marty's all-time favorite painting.

Santi and I stood there, staring, scrutinizing, and speculating. Harold wore an impassive look that partially said he's completed his mission, and partially said he wanted compensation for doing so.

There's no way he could have known it was Uncle Marty's favorite. But this? If this was real, it'd mean Admission. Astronaut or no astronaut.

This was the actual definition of priceless.

"Well," I said. "I need to take this downstairs and examine it under better lighting. Of course, you're welcome to join me."

"Lead the way," Harold replied. I nodded to Santi, who was already in working position behind the bar, and touched the sap at my side to silently show I'd be safe.

We walked back through the room that used to be a kitchen (now a glorified storage space for easily-traded items). I kicked up an unobtrusive floor panel in the back.

A stairway descended into darkness. Harold suddenly looked nonplussed. I hit a generator-fed light switch, one of the few bits of precious electricity we'd been able to reconfigure in the last few years, and led him into the flickering underground.

The basement of the bar is the same size as the main room, an expanse nearly as big as a regulation basketball court. It's filled with supplies, a major archive of art, treasures for trade or University installment, and a good amount of storage for stuff belonging to sailors who are currently at sea. But that wasn't the room we were going to. Through another padlocked door, we wound through a deeper section of the underground, now inside the centuries-old shanghai tunnels that pirates used to drag press-ganged captives through en route to the docks.

One more padlocked door, this one steel. Behind it, the stone sub-basement stairs were cold as the grave, the corridor spooky-silent as we approached one of several steel doors similar to the first. I was one of a very few people who knew how to navigate down here, by design. I ushered Harold into a room not much larger than a big closet and shut the door with a thud.

"Wait here."

I left through a side door and in the sub-basement's darkened main chamber, I rearranged a few things, rolling a large rack toward the antechamber's thick observation window. Using a flashlight, I briefly examined Harold's canvas again. Back in the small antechamber with Harold, I pulled the black curtain from the observation window and hit the lights. Even though the retro-fixed technology wasn't quite there yet, even to the elite echelon of traders I brought down there, the effect itself was still pretty impressive.

But not as impressive as to what it illuminated.

As the still-evolving lights buzzed and flickered their way to life, I noted Harold's face reflected in the clear bulletproof plastic of the observation panel. In the space of a few seconds, he registered a spectrum of emotions, from horror to amazement to utter unbelievability.

The horror was that I was holding a gun to his head.

The amazement was that just beyond a few inches of bolted-on bulletproof window, on one of a number of large rolling racks which I'd long ago hired Manny to craft from old industrial piping, there were five exact, gorgeous, very nearly perfect copies of Van Gogh's formerly one-and-only "Starry Night", and they had sealed Harold's death warrant.

***

Also nestled amongst the treasures in the basement is my brig.

Yeah, I have a brig. What? I need it. Precisely for people like Harold, who was now occupying it most morosely.

I'd added his copy of "Starry Night" to my collection. It really was quite a good fake.

"Now Harold," I said calmly through the thick steel bars of the single cell. "I'm not saying you're a forger. I'm just saying that this is an extremely interesting painting, and that the pirates' penalty for trying to pass forgeries is death."

"But you're not a pirate," he countered.

"No, I'm not. But you are. There's not an army in the world that salutes left-handed."

I'd watched upstairs when Santi had cleanly caught him. It was a simple test, Santi throwing his lefty salute at suspicious soldiers or sailors, and only real ones knew to call him out on it.

"Now, we have two problems. Number one, I've studied the REAL one enough to know that that painting is a forgery, and that's a punishable offense. But that's not the *interesting* problem."

Harold stared stonily.

"The *interesting* problem is who the forger could actually be. It could be you, but I don't think it is. I think you got that by hook or by crook from someone else, and I'm *interested* to learn who that someone might be. Because, I must say, they are very talented. Now, I know there are Chinese artists who can spin these things out, made to order. Down to the brushstroke. Could you be working with them?"

Harold didn't reply, though it seemed like he wanted to.

"Because I've heard the Chinese are ramping up to hit some major places around here. Could you be working for them? Flooding the market? Infiltrating to learn our operational secrets here? If that's true, I'm sorry to say, you've seen nothing of the extent of our empire."

This was true. Apart from the numerous, rather esoteric treasures I kept on the bar's walls, and my decent but diverse archive here downstairs, all the major collections were at The University.

"Now, I don't like hurting people's feelings, let alone killing them," I continued. "Especially not over art. But I can't let you stay here." I let that sentence hang, as Harold hanged his head. "I work with all the dockmasters," I continued. "If you were to give me some strong intelligence, perhaps I could set you up on a decent ship's crew…"

"Please no. There's beasts in the sea."

The way he said it took me aback, first mentally and then physically as I stopped short and leaned my head back to scrutinize his face. His eyes, suddenly steely and hard, betrayed no fear, but rather staunch, almost fear-inducing certainty.

"You can't be a sailor?" I asked.

"Please. *Please* no."

Images of Moby Dick, Cthulhu, all the great and grievous thalassophobia-inducing creatures swam and slunk through the brine of my mind. Fukushima had emptied into the ocean, Indian River too. That other one on the beach in New Hampshire. Probably loads more too, by now. It wasn't at all out of the scope of speculation to think that maybe a bad reaction had occurred with organic life somewhere in the murky deep, and what prowled the depths was not happy about it.

Maybe resigning Harold to such a fate with such a creature was justice in itself for all this. I took a moment to seriously ponder my reply, when I heard a distinct sound.

Footsteps bounding down the stone stairs.

Bracelets clanking as hands unlocked a padlock.

"Reli!" Joy admonished, her eyes wide at Harold in the brig.

"Not now. Go back upstairs."

"Reliiii," Joy whined. "For real. Come up!"

"Stop it. I'm serious."

"Me too," Joy exhorted. "Rudy's here."

***

Chapter Five – The Chancellor's List

He was wearing a ridiculous tri-cornered hat that he had looted out of some historical collection or theatre somewhere, because of course he was. He even wore a cravat and one of those brass-button tailcoats like you'd see in an oil painting of some noble seafarer, although most of those old paintings wouldn't include a guy rocking Rudy's bushy beard, thick silver earrings, and murals of tattoos. But Jesus, he even had the knee socks. Playing privateer for all he could.

It irked me how adorable it all was.

He was sitting at the bar sipping a snifter of our best weed-mead, dealing out poker hands with Joy and Santi, using my drachmas as chips. When he saw me he stood and, ridiculous as it was, doffed his tricorner hat and bowed to me.

Who the hell pulls that sort of shit? Some former New York hipster playing privateer, that's who.

My chest felt a little expansive as he again stood upright and came in for a hug.

"How's it going, darlin'? How was the meeting?"

"Important." I hustled behind the bar, grabbing my jacket, gloves and Mohawk-knit ski hat. "We need to get to The University."

"Aren't you going to ask me how the ocean was?"

"You made it back. I assume the ocean was equitable."

"Indeed. I brought back a plethora of pleasantries. Don't we have a moment to…"

"No. Joy, suit up." I threw her her own winter gear from behind the bar.

Rudy swirled the liquor languorously in his snifter, watching amusedly as we completed our braving-the-outdoors ministrations. Winter, nuclear or otherwise, was goddamn cold around here. I yanked my ski hat down over my ears.

"Santi, I'll be back with the band in a few hours. Hold down the fort?"

"*Si, hermana.*"

Rudy quaffed his weed-mead. "Always a pleasure, Senor Santiago. See you a little later." Rudy reached under the bar's edge and removed a hilariously huge greatcoat made of several large, furry animals, including what appeared to be most of a bear.

"Trading with the Canadians, I see?" I asked as we headed for the door.

"Among others. They do like our beer though, which is great, because for some Frenchy reason they still have exceptional chocolate in Montreal up for trade. Those snow-Frogs keep it real."

Rudy had a carriage parked outside, a black hansom fit for six passengers. Four well-kept horses pawed the lightly snowy ground, their harnesses jingling softly.

Reading my sugar-rimmed thoughts, Rudy continued, "Don't worry, of course I brought you some. Down here you'd be lucky to catch a stale Hershey bar." He opened the carriage door for Joy to clamber in.

"What's a Hershey bar?" she asked innocently.

Rudy looked at me with mock consternation. "Reli, what the hell are you teaching this child?"

He shut the door. We climbed onto the driver's bench, me riding shotgun.

"Oh, you know, just math, accounting, business, science, history, English, Spanish, and probably now sex ed, if you can't keep your damn cabin boy away from her."

"Robbo's cabin boy. You know I only keep fur-children on my boat."

That was an understatement. Rudy sidelined in rescuing all manner of abandoned (or wild) animals, from the mundane to the inappropriately exotic. The local zoo still had a giraffe he'd drunkenly hijacked from some theme park in pre-flooded Florida and hauled up the coast. That had been one hilarious docking day at the port.

He lightly jogged the reins, made smooching sounds at the horses, and without a moment's pause they carted us up the street.

"If you guys are hanging out today, keep her away from the actual pirates, please," I requested. "Last thing I need is for The Admiral's daughter to stowaway and end up getting pitched overboard halfway across the Goddamn Atlantic."

"They wouldn't throw her overboard," Rudy reasoned. "She's good collateral."

"Don't you think of shanghai'ing her, either, no matter how much she begs you."

"I'm a privateer, not a pirate. I don't shanghai. I *impress*."

I wish you'd impress me. The thought leapt to my mind nigh-unbidden. *Sexually or seafaringly. Hell, both. I don't want to run a crummy pirate-prone trading post of a bar forever. I'd be one hell of a first mate…*

I reined my thoughts in, wary that they'd somehow leap out into obviousness across my face.

Values. I needed to remember them. We had too much here, and too much at stake, for something as transient and distracting as my dumb feelings to get in the way.

"Speaking of impressing, I have someone in the brig that could use a dose of salty air," I told him.

"Oh really?"

As we trotted through town, the shiny black carriage turning the townsfolk's heads, I summarized the events of the morning. Rudy's solution, as I'd suspected, was a brutally efficient one.

"I'll talk to Robbo tonight. Better yet, I'll get one of the Rockeros to talk to him, he trusts them more with shit like that. He'll wonder why I didn't want the guy."

"You're seriously saying I should just foist this guy Harold on a pirate? Legit, sell him into slavery?"

"Robbo might take him off your hands for cheap. He lost a bunch of guys in a firefight somewhere off Cuba. Ask him for a Picasso or something, you know he'd rather offload all that Spanish stuff safely anyway. If it can't be fired, fucked, or food, he probably doesn't want it."

"I'll think about it. Let's see what The Admiral says."

We rode in silence down the old highway towards The University. If it were summer, we'd have taken the beach route, with the billions of stars raining down on the rocky shore, their radiance completely undeterred by human light pollution any longer. But it was cold and getting windier, and I tucked my face into my long scarf until we pulled onto the Ring Road around the famous concrete campus.

Idly, I wondered if the astronaut commander would know how to get the school's impressively large telescope back in working order.

Might as well still enjoy dreaming about other worlds, now that we'd fucking wrecked this one.

***

Uncle Marty (sorry, *The Admiral*) had an office in the main campus center building, though it was an unobtrusive one, tucked up a strange set of stairs off of the auditorium. The walls, some thirty feet high with only one small sideways window at the top, were filled up with his favorite acquisitions. The highest parts of the wall featured huge medieval tapestries, while a little lower, there were some larger classic masterpieces. An El Greco, a Dali, a Monet, a Cezanne. Below that, there was an array of vintage weapons, swords and shields and helms and lances, not so high that they're out of arm's reach. Around eye-level were more paintings, as well as carefully-compiled curio cabinets of sculptures, glassworks, silver, and ancient stone statues.

The Admiral admired it all.

What he didn't admire was tardiness, inefficiency, indecision, and problems that should have been solved long before they were presented to him. After he'd pored once again over the folder of space-based images, he sat back in his regal, intricately-carved wooden throne of an office chair. He stared over his slim silver-rimmed glasses at me, his sea-green eyes roiling and short, spiky white hair standing at attention.

"I can't take them both, and I can't reject a kid who's being held in servitude. What do you propose we do about this, Reli?"

"Sir, if it's possible to continue to allow the commander to stay in the hydro lab…"

"I'm not making one of our greatest Americans live like an underfunded grad student. We'll find him a room on campus, somehow. What I'm concerned with is how we can integrate him into the system, organize classes and classrooms for him, obtain enough supplies to escalate the science he wants. It's not just him, Reli. It's everything he stands for. We're never going to reach the level of greatness he was a part of. Not even if he helps us to try harder to get there."

"It's just different, sir," I mumbled. "It's still very decent."

"'Very decent' might be fine for you and I, but it's not normal enough when a ten-year-old child is living among bloodthirsty pirates."

"I could trade for him, sir. There's enough gunpowder and fuel to spare…"

"We are NOT abetting piracy. It's bad enough I gave Captain Brough a letter of marque and now he's traipsing selling pot and stealing camels."

"It was a giraffe, sir."

"I don't care. We need to figure out a way to get that kid off Captain Arturo's boat without aiding his armory OR having half the town burned to the ground by angry Spanish marauders."

I took a deep breath and explained Rudy's idea about enslaving (no, *trading*) Harold.

"He's of no use," The Admiral said. "Even if he did do the painting, neither I nor Captain Arturo wants someone who can forge 'Starry Night'. I want someone who can help us rebuild our entire goddamn society. I don't care what the raiders want, as long as it doesn't involve intervening with us."

On that point, I needed to raise another question. "What about the intel on the Chinese? You think there's anything to it?"

"If it is, we'll find out soon enough. I'm sending Rudy to Boston to get to the bottom of things."

Something inside my chest suddenly felt sticky. "Sir, doesn't Captain Brough have to…"

"He'll sail north and verify if there are new Maine encampments and farms, first. He can offload a holdful of beer barrels between there and Boston and have plenty of room for cargo on the return trip. If there are refugees or artifacts he wants to recover en route home, we'll be ready."

If *he returns home. If the Chinese haven't overrun Boston looking for goods and gold.*

But I couldn't stand there in front of one of the most important men left in the world and defy his orders. Then I'd never get a letter of marque, or sail with anyone who had one.

"But if this Harold guy is right, shouldn't we use him to gather more intel?"

The Admiral gave me an almost bored glare. "You know as well as I do that if he was somehow close enough to get Chinese intel, they know he's here right now. He's burned." The Admiral continued to examine the documents from the astronaut commander, the Harold issue no longer pressing. Glancing briefly up at me, he stated with finality, "Tell this Harold his service is of no interest. His collateral is no good with me." He looked down over his glasses. "Take whatever compensation you require from him."

The unspoken "even if that compensation IS him" didn't hang dreadfully in the air. It was just a fact. I'd either have to kill Harold, have him killed, or slave-trade with actual pirates who I'd just as soon not court the dubious graces of.

This was my problem now. The Admiral had more important ones to deal with.

As I was mentally calculating how valuable an apparently, non-military, non-navy, non-reality-oriented weirdo like Harold would be toward a seasoned, mean, murder-prone pirate crew, a strange soundtrack permeated the room.

It seemed like it must certainly be in my head, but when The Admiral looked up at me quizzically, I realized he could hear it too.

A piano sonata. Bach, maybe. It'd been a while since I'd caught any orchestras.

The music was only mildly muffled by the tall concrete walls, but the intercoms of course hadn't worked since A-Day. The Admiral, straightforward as ever, solved the mystery by opening the office door off to the side of his desk.

I'd known the door was there, but often forgot, thanks to it being obscured by an elegant medieval unicorn tapestry, one of a few that were nice enough to deserve eye-level status. The moment the tapestry was pushed aside and the door was opened, the music floated in fancifully.

Uncle Marty, The Admiral, gave me a stern but intrigued look, as though this were part of some surprise party prank on both of us, and I better not have been in on it.

We walked out onto the small balcony that overlooked the cavernous concrete main auditorium. Back in the day, the room had seen the likes of The Clash, Bob Dylan, Henry Rollins, and probably thousands of theater productions. Now, it served mostly for major University meetings.

Not today though.

Onstage, lit by military-grade floodlights that had been rescued from an underground nuke bunker somewhere, a kid (who I assumed must be Pablo) was absolutely shredding the sonata.

Sitting next to him on the bench, utterly rapt, was Joy.

The only person in the audience was the astronaut. He still looked surprisingly like the same guy who'd graced the cover of TIME magazine and newspapers nationwide when he'd returned from an important, lengthy space mission. Even from my perch on the balcony, thanks to the glow of the massive lights onstage, I could tell his stoic face was entrenched in a tsunami of tears. He wasn't angry though. He was enraptured.

Stock-still, unwillingly to even breathe lest we somehow disrupt the fantastic flow of the music, The Admiral and I just stood there on the balcony. Like two sailors high in a crow's nest who've just spotted land but are still trying to suss out if it's a mirage or not, we let the sound transport us, sailing ever further into what could be the promise of a marvelous new world.

The astronaut felt the same, I could just tell. He was wearing the look I remembered he'd worn on the news when he first was retrieved from his space capsule. A look of wonder, of fulfillment, of knowledge and survival thanks to teamwork from all that was great in mankind. Yes, the heroic astronaut and former commander of the space station, a man who'd gazed at everything our entire earth could offer, and there he was, reduced to tears by a child and a few harmonious frequencies.

His value to history and the future stopped dead in its tracks for one critical, heartwrenching moment of the present.

I didn't envy the Admiral the choice he was going to have to make, figuring out a way to somehow protect both the best of our past and the best of our future.

***

Chapter Six – Impressions

Rudy and I made the rounds of the musicians' dorm, laughing and drinking through the incessant clouds of smoke and hail of sounds produced therein. I knew we couldn't linger too long (hell, I can hang in that dorm all day every day, and have been known to lose significant amounts of time there) so we quickly rallied the six band members who were performing that evening. (I won't tell you their names, but you've heard of them. One of them, long ago, had jokingly been referred to as the likeliest human candidate to survive the apocalypse, and I gotta tell you, we're all really happy that he did.)

After dropping them off at the bar and abetting their setup, Rudy went to go talk to the Rockeros about me talking to Robbo. He was probably also talking to the Rockeros about all manner of other illicit business, but I didn't intervene. *Not my circus, not my pirate-ass monkeys.*

Harold was still in the brig. It was safest, really. For now.

I busied myself making sure the bar's guests, now filtering in for pre-show drinks, were feeling well and welcome. I tacked up all the new pictures and posts on my Placebook Wall, an analog version of an old social media favorite, formerly accessible via a little device that'd fit in your hand, but which now runs about twenty feet along the back left wall of Trooley's. It was a nice way for people with paper "profiles" to leave messages, pictures, replies and promises for those whose ships or overland convoys might not find them in the same place too often. Today it was filled with love notes.

The crowd hadn't really arrived yet, so Santi had the bar well in hand. Couples canoodled in the lamplight, sipping weed-mead or one of the many fine local craft beers, ciders or sparkling wines. The old vacuum-tube jukebox was blasting funky 45 records, I was engaged in a hearty round of pool with two of the musicians and one of Officer Rick's troopers, and everything seemed copacetic.

But when Rudy and Manny came in, I could tell by the looks on their faces that they were up to something.

We convened upstairs in the Officer's Club immediately. I'd decided to keep it closed for the evening, as the main bar could easily accommodate most crowds, and anyway we had business to discuss.

"We're sticking to HIS story," Manny explained. "You said the guy tried to sell it that he was on a cleanup crew in NYC? Sweet. Hold him to that. Robbo will send some crimps to boost him real quick."

"I can't walk the guy out the front door, though. Too much chance he'll straight flee. And I can't let a band of Robbo's raiders saunter into my sub-basement."

"Seal the sub-basement doors, let them use the regular old shanghai tunnel. The one you use for keg transport to the docks," Rudy said.

"Set him free here, in the bar, once it gets real crowded," Manny added. "Leave the tunnel to the vault open in the kitchen. Wham-bam-hot-damn, homeboy's gonna be scrubbin' decks by sun-up."

"What does Robbo think I'm asking for in return?"

"That's the beauty of it," Manny said. "You don't gotta worry you sold the dude out. I'm just gonna tell Robbo you caught some

THE WRONG KIND OF RENAISSANCE – LEE LAWLESS

asshole who tried to boost something off the bar's collection, you didn't have the heart to kill his ass, and you're setting him free up in here after you use him for some hard labor."

"As opposed to using our boy Manuel Laborrrrr for it," Rudy joked, rolling the "r" at the end of his mean nickname for Manny.

It wasn't a good plan, but it was definitely a plan. There was one major issue.

"I'm not letting Robbo in here. If the raiders act decently, they can boost him out from the bar like you say, but Robbo's too much of a liability." I didn't need to elaborate on the fact that if Captain Roberto Arturo learned too much of the floorplan here, he'd eventually come back and loot us lock-fucking-stock. Art was an armistice, maybe, but my considerable cache of everything from firearms to Fentanyl was something else.

"Problem solved," said Rudy. "Time to rock the boat."

***

Rudy's ship, the *U.S.S. Pot Yacht*, was corsair-style craft that, like its revolutionary brethren of the original Massachusetts Navy, flew under a flag bearing a green pine tree against a white background with "AN APPEAL TO HEAVEN" as its motto in black. The pine tree on this particular flag bore more than a passing resemblance to a cannabis plant, but hey, to each their own appeal to heaven.

The lower decks were filled with an ingenious array of cannabis grow-bins, fed from solar panel-powered LED lights (reclaimed from inside a metal warehouse that had served as an impromptu Faraday cage on A-Day) and desalination tanks. One storage hold was full of dried and packaged buds, while kegs of weed-mead and local beer also served as good ballast. The main quarters were decorated in a comfortable, chill style, with a few cozy couches serving as communal chairs.

Robbo was not sitting in any of them. He and two of his confederates were standing militarily upright, hands on sword pommels, ready to parley or pounce.

I'd only seen Captain Roberto Arturo a few times before, and always from afar. Once or twice through a spyglass on my roof, just to make sure he wasn't making any trouble when docking or leaving port. From that distance, he'd appeared very handsome, his dark Spanish complexion, shadowy scruff, and sumptuous, chin-length brown hair giving him an exotic appeal. He favored wearing all black, in a classically piratical style, and it most certainly suited his tall, sinewy frame. His musculature made him appear relaxed, but I was certain at any point he could lunge and make a kebab out of Rudy, Manny, and I, all in one fell stab. Close up, his brown eyes appeared hard and black, wily and creepy-calm at the same time. His facial expression was just *dark*.

Not moody dark. Like, something-left-a-mark dark. Sure, we'd all had our fair share of hard times these last few years, but goddamned if we didn't most all just collectively agree to suck it up, hauling happy-hellishly hard, our bootstrap-clenching teeth gnashed into smiles.

I guess that made it even the more startling when someone still genuinely appeared *haunted*.

Robbo had, at some point, quite clearly been wronged.

I just hoped his countenance wasn't so sour thanks to him already deducing my plan.

Like a knife cutting through a sail as a means of marauding in an old pirate movie, Robbo cut to the chase.

"Where is Pablo?" he asked in accented but effective English. "He was not to leave my men's sight. I allowed Li to have him sent to your University for medical treatment she claimed he required. But my men were turned away at the gate, and now, we are owed."

Rudy and Manny shifted uncomfortably. The real pirate in this bunch had already commandeered the conversation.

"I'll make sure he's back in your *care* tonight," I said evenly. "Pablo needed fairly significant attention. In the meantime, I understand you've discussed another transaction with my colleagues here?"

"Yes," Robbo sneered. "We will take out your trash. Congratulations on having a community so caring, you are willing to throw whole human beings to the mercy of pirates if you do not consider them useful enough."

I wasn't about to fight. I strongly wanted to return to the bar.

Never mind that I had no goddamn clue where the hell Pablo could possibly be.

"Have him working in the main bar by midnight," Robbo decreed. "The loading tunnel will remain unobstructed and unlocked at both ends, if you value us not breaking in through your front door to obtain our mark."

"That's fine," I said.

"Pablo will be there as well. He will enter the tunnel and travel through it first, to ensure its safety for us. My men will follow. You will not draw attention nor action against us." He paused and offered a smile that felt ghastly, despite his undoubtable good looks. "If you fail to meet any of these requirements, my men and I will raze your bar to the ground."

"I understand."

Robbo turned to Rudy, throwing him a small sack of what sounded like heavy coins. "We will take one barrel of your mead. You are not to follow us anywhere near New York City on this recovery mission. If I find out you have done so, we will shell your ship into a modern art masterpiece, installed at the bottom of the ocean."

Rudy clapped his hands. "Cool, so we're all in agreement! Great! Let's get you boys that keg. Reli, Manny, guess there's some *pressing* issues to attend to?"

"Yes," I said, hoping for all the world that Robbo couldn't hear my heart thunking through my chest at this range. I extended my hand toward him to seal the deal. Robbo stared at it flatly.

Figures. Pirates don't have honor. They don't shake on things. Ugh, how are you still such a fuck-up, even after everything in the whole rest of the world has been fucked up already?

His inscrutable black eyes fixed on mine, Robbo reached down, grasped my hand, and raised it to his lips. I felt dirty, but oddly, wildly excited. He could probably see my pulse thunking through the veins in my wrist. But I didn't draw away.

Roberto Arturo, the pirate captain who'd just kissed my hand like the most aristocratic gentleman ever, barked an order in Spanish to his men and strode out of the room. Rudy ushered us out, then followed.

I asked Manny to come with me back to the bar. I needed someone to keep an eye on Harold, who was about to be released quite literally into the wild.

***

There was no way around it. We had to give the kid back if we wanted to avoid certain doom. We couldn't just kidnap a pirate kid, even if he was being forced to play piano for ten hours a night.

Uncle Marty seemed to have known that from the get-go.

Without mentioning my further plans for Harold, I got Uncle Marty to agree to have Pablo delivered to the bar. I hadn't exactly been lying to Robbo. Pablo had indeed been medically vetted at The University that day, and found to have only a slight head cold accounting for his ill appearance. But the doctors had found no trace of any serious abuse, and as such, it behooved us to let him go.

My kind of raising the bar did not involve watching the razing of my bar.

Joy had inevitably begged her way onto the carriage bearing Pablo to us. The two of them now sat together in one of the plush leather armchairs in the Officer's Club, listening to the music waft up from downstairs, their heads leaned together as though their minds were left and right stereo speakers playing the same song.

Downstairs, the crowd was rocking out to the band scorching it up onstage. The old tube amps they used were stalwartly smashing out the sound, the weed-mead and beer were flowing, people were dancing, and no one had a clue that I was about to have a man in my basement prison kidnapped into pirate slavery.

Robbo had done a good job of hiding his confederates. I had no idea which of the generally well-dressed, decently-groomed folks in the crowd were his crimps. I decided to wait until very near to midnight to release Harold into the crowd.

When I unlocked him from the basement and told him he was free to go, he definitely didn't believe me. I maybe sold it too hard, telling him no hard feelings, and hey, to go have a drink at the bar on me. I was keeping his painting, but thanks for the heads-up on the creepy creatures in the sea, whatever the horrific hell he'd meant by that.

Everything seemed to be working as well as possible for this crazy situation. Until Harold spotted Manny.

Manny had done a good job of discreetly dancing in the crowd while keeping his eye on Harold, but like I said, the kid was sharp. He stood out. And for reasons I didn't understand at that exact moment, Harold decided to chase him.

Manny knew we had to keep Harold trapped. He also knew he couldn't send him through the shanghai tunnel first. The deal had been for Pablo to preclude him. So Manny did the only other thing he could think of, which actually had seemed like a decent idea for about thirty seconds.

He chased him upstairs to the Officer's Club.

And that's where all hell broke loose.

***

Chapter Seven – Expulsion

In all the old dystopia stories, there'd be zombies everywhere, or mutant marauders or whatever, but we never used to figure that after the end of things, for the most part, we'd actually all be pretty chill. But I was a fool to think an inexplicable pact to be reasonable somehow just flourished organically out of the still-irradiated soil. I thought we'd recognized the value of safety, and the safety of value, but everyone's definitions of both of those things vary too vastly.

Upstairs, Harold immediately began yelling that he should kill Manny for what he'd done. Harold had been the first one to draw, as it were, having wrenched one of the old officers' sabers off the wall. Manny calmly drew his own weapon, but didn't counter Harold's ranting.

I demanded that Joy take Pablo downstairs into the ex-kitchen where the basement tunnel trapdoor was, but told her not to go into the tunnels. When I turned back after ensuring the two were gone, Manny and Harold were taking swings at each other. It wasn't pretty, nor was it cool. I yelled repeatedly at both of them to stop.

As both huffed for breath, weapons still at the ready, Harold growled, "You fucking traitor. You sold me the fuck out."

"You owed me, *maricon*," Manny growled. "You owed me bigtime. You chose your punishment. You did what you wanted to."

The blades clashed again. Harold got clipped fairly badly on his non-dominant shoulder, the blood seeping into his dark peacoat. He turned to me, bereft.

"I didn't forge the painting," he huffed loudly at me. "HE did! HE forced me to try to pass it off on you!"

And though I saw rage and sadness on Manny's face as he looked at me imploringly, I suddenly realized this was the truth.

***

"MARICON!" Manny curses again, rushing Harold vehemently. Harold uses this outburst to carefully sidestep him and swipe the saber severely through Manny's midsection. In horror, Manny drops to the ground, his tight T-shirt revealing a nigh-vivisectional slash across his belly.

Harold withdraws. "Tell her," he screams, "Tell her the truth!"

"I'm so sorry, Reli," Manny gasps, his eyes rolling uncontrollably with the pain. "I just wanted to see if my art was good enough. I thought I could get it past you." He coughs, and a sickening slippery sound follows. "I thought The Admiral would give me Admission if he saw what I could do," he wheezes. "I thought he could have me redo any of the old paintings that got lost, so we could have them. So we could all have them." A macabre moan escapes his rapidly-paling lips. "I begged Santi to let me look at all the other copies, so I could get it perfect. I told him keep it secret, it was a gift for a girl. Don't be mad at him. I was so close. So close."

I have no idea what to say, but I know I need to say something fast. The glow is fading from Manny's dying form.

"It was beautiful, Manny," I say, smoothing his now-mussed Elvis hairdo into its proper iconic arrangement. "It was beautiful. If Santi hadn't tricked Harold with the lefty salute, I would have thought your painting was genuine. It was perfect, Manny. *It was perfect.*"

His radiant smile appears once more as the rest of the light leaves his body.

The pirates who didn't look at all like pirates are standing in the doorway, swords drawn from sheaths hanging astride their nice khakis. Harold stares at them, clearly too unstable to take on more contenders.

"Captain Arturo says you're coming with us," one of them snarls.

Harold's eyes go horrifically wide as he lets out a feral scream.

"NO! YOU'RE WRONG! THERE'S BEASTS IN THE SEA! DEMONS! NO! YOU CAN'T TAKE ME!"

The pirates approach, very much intending to ignore the rantings of this crazy man.

A man so crazy that, as the Robbo's nattily-attired raiders draw near, he lifts the saber and stabs himself through the stomach, seppuku-style.

As he collapses, he murmurs softly, but still defiantly, "*Not the sea.*"

The pleasant-looking pirates survey the carnage for a second, sternly warn me against following them, and dash back downstairs.

***

I wait all of twenty seconds before giving chase. The music downstairs has drowned out the mayhem above. I dash to the back of the main bar and through the swinging doors.

There's no one in the kitchen.

Not Rudy, not Robbo's raiders, not Joy, not Pablo, not anyone.

There's only one small, shiny object sitting on the closed trapdoor.

A drachma, tails up.

***

When I run up the stairs, taking them two at a time to my rooftop observation deck, I can just make out the dark outline of Robbo's black freighter pulling out of the its dock in the harbor.

***

Chapter Eight – Rocking The Renaissance

My autopilot reaction is to dash back down to the docks, but I don't want to chance the tunnels in case the pirates have left traps or other terrors in their wake. I shove through the whole goddamned romance-celebrating crowd at the front of the bar, running straight into Tony Toast, who's dancing with some other girl. I don't even pause to ponder if I care. Hauling ass on foot down the snowy street, I dash haphazardly into Las Diablas, where Li is laughing and pouring shots for some scruffy-looking men and their attendant floozies at the bar.

"Have you seen anyone?" I gasp. "Joy? Rudy? Pablo?"

"No," she says cautiously, then confidently, "Something's wrong."

"Yeah," I wheeze. "I lost…" I was going to name who, then realize I've already explained myself.

"I'll tell you if I see any of them," Li replies reasonably. "By the way, I think Tony Toast wanted to hang out with you tonight, he was looking for you…"

"I'll spank him later. Thanks." I dash outside and toward the docks once more.

The U.S.S. *Pot Yacht* is dark, but it's still there. The crew's all off, partying in town, and the dockmasters all know I'm not a threat to security. I jump aboard.

Rudy is unharmed but bound and gagged, lying on the floor of the main bay, which has been cleanly liberated of every single barrel of weed-mead and every bale of bud they'd had.

The whirring of small generator engines and hydrobubblers tells me that they left him all the grow rigs though, which seems nice, although they probably now intend on finding him again after the

331

next harvest.

Well, what the hell else do you expect from pirates?

The first thing I do when I remove the gag is ask where Joy is. Rudy coughs and nods at his sleeping quarters, and sure enough, there she is. Also unharmed but similarly bound, the pirates at least let her sit on the bed.

I remove her gag and ask if she's okay. She's missing a few of her nicer diamond bracelets. *Goddamn fucking pirates.*

"I gave them to Pablo," she quickly explains, sensing my ire. "To remember me, since I said I couldn't go with them."

"They ASKED if you wanted to go with them? Like, politely?"

"Yeah."

Just as I'm pondering calling her out on this outrageous lie, Rudy staggers to his feet and stumbles in.

"It's true," he confirms. "They asked if she wanted to go learn how to be a real pirate instead of a fakeass, excuse me, *fakebutt* like me, because look how dumb I was to get robbed like this. They said to be careful who she trusted. She said she trusted *you*, and no smelly pirates could tell her not to."

I shake my head. "Seriously?"

"Seriously. Then she asked if Pablo could stay, because they were friends and she liked his music. They laughed their ass… their rear ends off at that." Rudy sighs and rubs his neck. "Then they blindfolded me and knocked me out."

"What happened then?" I ask Joy.

"Pablo said he wanted to stay too," Joy sniffled. "He said he liked it here, and that all the people were really nice, and the piano in the school was really nice, and that I was his best friend yet. He said he'd jump off the boat if they tried to take him away. But now he's not here." She's still sniffling, trying not to cry, but a trickle of tears is exposed in her melting mascara. "And you're gonna be mad at me."

"No, sweetie, no. I'm not mad at you."

"You're gonna be," Joy repeats. "Robbo's raiders made me open up the sub-basement when they ran out through the tunnels with us. There were only two of them with us, but they forced me to bring them a bunch of stuff. They were scared to go inside, because they thought there were traps. I gave them a lot of stuff, Reli."

Fuck. Fuck. *Fuck.*

"There's one okay thing, though," Joy said.

There is NO okay part of this situation, except the fact you're still alive, I wanted to scream at her, but bit my tongue. I cross my arms and raise my eyebrows, awaiting her reply.

"I only opened the room with all the fakes in it. I gave them a bunch of those. Sorry, but I had to give them the good ones. But they're just a bunch of smelly pirates. At least with the good fakes, they probably won't know the difference. Even if they did dress up and pretend to be nice."

***

Officer Rick is waiting at the top of the trapdoor when we get back from the boat, via the tunnels this time. I hadn't wanted to enlist him in the search for Rudy and Joy, but of course he'd gotten suspicious when Li told him how worried I'd been.

I take him upstairs to survey the crime scene while Rudy takes Joy and the musicians back to campus. Santi knows something's wrong, but I wait until the last guests are gone before explaining the story to him. I don't mention anything about how I know he let Manny use all the forgeries for references. He doesn't need any of this trouble on his mind.

I just really hate hurting peoples' feelings. It used to serve me so well in the service industry. Guess that, like so many other things, needs updating.

Earlier today, I thought I'd be pretty mad if I wasn't falling asleep next to Rudy, but now I just want to crash.

The value of not doing anything at all is sometimes inestimably important.

***

The next morning, in The Admiral's office, I'm explaining everything. Well, explaining what I can. I still have a LOT of questions.

"Why can't we pursue Robbo? I don't care he threatened us, he also took half of this quarter's harvest! Can't Rudy retaliate somehow?"

"Even if I did know the answer to that, telling you would be a tremendous security breach. You're on Robbo's raiders' radar too, now. Don't make yourself more of a target."

I genuinely wonder how the hell Robbo got away with all that loot in such a short time.

It dawns on me, in the same place that dawn still always breaks in the US.

"Rudy's helping him, isn't he? Are they convoying to Maine? Robbo with the product in a better-armed boat, and Rudy ready to pick up more supplies?" I go for broke. "He was gone all morning yesterday. Planning, repacking probably. They tied him up to make it look good, so he won't lose face in town or with me, and now he'll give the appearance of a mission north while Robbo goes south, but they'll re-meet somewhere else. Since, if the Chinese are coming, we can't openly support pirates, but we need them to do all the shit we're not up for. And you can't tell me, because if I let it slip, every pirate and privateer left will be gunning for both of them as traitors!" I yell my astonished accusations with authority, although I know I'm probably not getting answers anyway. But I want to see the Admiral's reaction. I've bartended long enough to know how easily people will let secrets slip if they secretly want them to be known.

"Operation Glades is real, isn't it? There's another base up there, isn't there? Is it ours?"

"Don't ask me questions whose answers jeopardize even more lives than your own," the Admiral snaps, then cools. "Run the bar, run it right, don't run off, and you might find out some answers for yourself sometime. The *correct* way."

I push my luck. Fuck it, I've shoved it uphill this far.

"Can you at least tell me if there really is a ski mountain?"

The Admiral stares at me sternly, his countenance revealing nothing.

"When I have time to focus on rebuilding *recreational athletic facilities*, on top of running an institution of higher education, a community collective that nurtures six thousand souls, and amassing an artistic archive unparalleled in any era of humanity, I assure you, Aurelia, you can pull the first pint in the base lodge."

I'm almost assuaged by this, but now my mind's humming like a generator. A distressing thought comes to light. "If Robbo's helping Rudy and working under his letter of marque, Rudy could get hanged for piracy if they're caught by authorities in another city…"

The Admiral, clearly finished with my malarkey, cuts me off.

"Captain Arturo's whereabouts are presently unknown," he clips. "Captain Brough is slated to return around St. Patrick's Day. Perhaps by then you'll have enough fortifications and organization secured to be able to entrust the bar to someone long enough to undertake a recovery mission of your own. Though that remains a point of *strong* speculation."

That's it. There isn't any use arguing. All I can do is fix what I've allowed to go wrong.

If only more people got such a chance, ever. I still considered myself lucky.

St. Patrick's Day it was, then. I'd be ready.

Who was I kidding. Uncle Marty was never going to let me leave. I was never getting out of Union Street, pirates or no pirates. Privateers or no privateers.

But I can be better. I can keep trying. And that's worth all of the rebirth you can endure.

"Thanks, Uncle Marty. See ya."

As I leave, the distinct sound of piano notes coalescing (Bach, maybe Beethoven, I dunno) seeps through the concrete walls, the music as tenacious as radioactivity, and just as luminous in the right conditions.

Humming some superb sonata, which I'm sure someday soon I'll learn all about, I step out into the slight swirls of snow, watching the whiteness grace the ground, each flake never knowing if it'll end up as part of an avalanche or an oil painting, but bidden to work together all the same. The sun, though it could kill them, makes them sparkle.

In the distance, around the Ring Road perimeter of the campus, the former commander of the International Space Station is riding his bicycle to class.

And maybe, just a little bit beneath where the snow's melted off the ground, I see some green blades of grass fighting their way upward, embraced by the dirt but reaching toward the sun.

NOBODY STARVES
Ron Goulart

The straight falling rain blurred the glass wall of the cubicle and Arlen Lembeck could not see any of the billboards that dotted this sector of Greater Los Angeles. Or maybe it was his eyesight. He'd been docked a 100 calories for missing punch-in last Tuesday and he had the feeling his new eating program was affecting his vision. He leaned back in his chair until the headrest was a half inch from the headrest of his cubicle chief and picked up the ear trumpet that fed into Secretary Central.

The quota of subliminal outdoor billboard slogans for Cubicle 97 of the Greater Los Angeles Subliminal Outdoor Bureau was twenty-five this week. Going over quota could mean ten more calories a day and a membership card in one of the new Venusian import warehouses. Lembeck didn't understand Venusian imports but Edith was still upset about the calorie cut and something like this might boost her feelings.

Though he was thirty-four and only a Class B 14, Lembeck was a good slogan man. The *Cubicles 90-100 Newsletter* had mentioned him twice in the last month.

"Touching," said Burns Smollet, the cubicle chief.

"Sorry," said Lembeck. Accidentally his chair had ticked against his chief's.

Smollet was only a week past his thirty-first birthday. He was a B10 and had been for six months. Of course he'd been given credit for his Propaganda Corps Reserve time. Edith was not up on protocol and Smollet's age and rank bothered her. Smollet was a pretty fair slogan man, though.

A small pink card slapped out of the *In* slot and landed face down next to Lembeck's left hand. Absently, like a confident card player, Lembeck turned the punch card over. "Report 8:45 tomorrow (the twenty-fifth) for Termination Processing," it read. "Wing 6 of the Pre-Termination Board, Hollywood & Vine, Greater Los Angeles,

Sector 28. Thank you for the interest you've shown."

Lembeck swallowed. "They can't fire me on a Wednesday," he said.

"There was a memo to that effect last month," said Smollet. "Are they?"

Lembeck held up the pink card. "I have to turn in all my cards, food and everything, and go back to the Employment Complex." He had been with the Outdoor Bureau for seven years, since before his marriage.

"No sweat," said Smollet. "They'll fix you up in no time. And after all, these days, nobody starves."

That was a nice slogan. "Thanks for reminding me," said Lembeck. "You're right."

"Now that that's settled," said Smollet, "let's get going on the quota. I'm going to have a hell of a time breaking in a new man and not slowing the stride of Cubicle 97."

The other two men in the cubicle looked up and nodded sympathetically at Lembeck. Then everybody got going on the slogans.

***

The Pre-Termination Board was fully automated so it wasn't as embarrassing as it might have been. The last time Lembeck had been here, seven years ago, they'd had fac-human androids. Now everything looked like a machine. Except the doorman who, in keeping with an old robotics tradition, was made in the image of a proper English butler.

Waiting in the Card Surrendering Room foyer, Lembeck let himself loosen up a little. He stretched his legs and made fists of his hands a few times. Edith had taken it all pretty well. The Power Bureau had jumped the gun and cut everything off but Edith had rounded up some candles and they'd had a pretty romantic dinner. The pantry outlet had scrambled at midnight and nothing would come out but garbage so they'd skipped their midnight wafers. Edith was confident that the Employment Complex would do something nice for him this time.

Holding hands in the candlelit dining cubicle they'd even suggested to each other that someone had had Lembeck fired so that he could be switched to a better job. It did seem a possibility.

Edith had not had an Employment Card since four years ago

when the clinical android at her office had decided she was pregnant. Their live doctor had disagreed but by that time the card was cancelled and the waiting list for married women in Edith's age and rank group was closed until such a time as conditions shifted. That was all right. Lembeck had never had a bad deal from the Employment Complex.

***

Things got disturbing over on Sunset in the Post-Termination Board offices. The big Temporary Food Card machine was making an odd whirring sound. Finally it said, "Lembeck, Lembeck, Arlen, Arlen."

"Yes, sir?" Lembeck said, watching the bright gray machine. It was ten feet high and ten feet wide and, as he watched, the little brass plate with the manufacturer's name popped off and the four little zuber screws pinged on the imitation floor.

"Lembeck, Lembeck, Lembeck, Arlen, Arlen, Arlen," said the Food Card machine.

"Yes, I'm right here. I was told to check with you people before I went over to the Employment Complex. So that I could have a Temporary Food Card until I am put through Pre-Indoctrination by my new place of employment. And then I have to get all my other cards here, too, and see somebody about getting my parking receipt validated."

"Lemlen Arbeck Becklem Lenlem Beckbeck Lenlen Ararar," said the machine.

"Arlen Lembeck," corrected Lembeck.

Two more zuber screws popped out from some unseen place. "Follow the red line and your processing will continue."

A throbbing scarlet line, six inches wide, appeared on the floor and snaked like downhill water for a door in the far wall. Once through it Lembeck found himself outside on Sunset Boulevard.

"It'll be okay," he told himself. He put his timevox to his ear and it told him it was sixteen minutes from his appointment at the Employment Complex. And that was way down on Spring Street in Sector 54. He would have to come back to Post-Termination later. He reminded himself to ask somebody at Employment Complex about it.

***

It was the first time he'd seen an android cry. This one was in Re-

Placement and looked something like an A10 with extra calorie allotments. Lembeck asked, "Nothing?"

"Look," said the android, holding a sheaf of graphs up to Lembeck. It sniffed quietly. "Though less than human, Mr. Lembeck, I pride myself on having more than a human share of compassion." Its wide unwrinkled head shook from side to side, deflecting the course of the tears. "Your aptitude tests are depressing."

"Couldn't I take new tests? After all, those were done seven years ago when I was still a young man in my twenties."

"No, no," said the android, smoothing the graphs out on the desk. "These were made just today."

"When? I've only been here twelve minutes."

"That revolving door you came through is no ordinary revolving door." The android nodded. "Take my word for it, Mr. Lembeck, if there's one thing we know about you with a certainty it's your aptitudes."

"There must be something."

"You see," said the android, "the demand for ceramics is so small at present. Most authorities seem to agree that the Venusian imports are ceramic in nature. The balance of import and local products and the surplus storage factors involved in the output of Greater Los Angeles make chances pretty slim for anyone in the ceramics line."

"But I'm a slogan writer. I was a B14 in Subliminal Outdoor," said Lembeck. "I'm not a ceramicist. My job classification card will show that."

"The cards in your case are still processing over in Sector 28," said the android. "Besides the aptitude figures show that you're a ceramicist. You may feel some inclinations in other directions but we can't honestly put you into a new job where you'll be unhappy and frustrated."

"I was happy for seven years as a slogan writer."

"As you say, though, you entered that line at an early unformed age. Now, wiser and more mature, your real strengths and weaknesses shine through. You can be sure we'll keep you on file. Venusian imports may be only a fad."

"Isn't there some temporary job?"

"You wouldn't be happy in an uncertain situation like that."

"Well," said Lembeck, "there's a problem in that I didn't get any temporary food cards and lodging cards and all the rest of the cards when I was at Post-Termination. Something went wrong and then it was late and I had to rush over here. I even had to pay for my own parking."

"I don't believe," said the android, "that anything can have gone wrong. If you wish to make another appointment to see Post-Termination I can get you the forms to fill out."

"Fine. Could I get another appointment today?"

"You can't even *get* the forms until next week."

"And the new job?"

"Possibly toward the spring if current trends remain constant."

"What do my wife and I do till then? See, we don't have any food cards at all. She doesn't work at present and I had to surrender all my cards at Pre-Termination. So if..."

"Mr. Lembeck," interrupted the android, "let me assure you. Nobody starves. I would suggest, considering the personal nature of your problem, that you consult the Therapy Wing over at Welfare Hub. They're out by the beach over in Sector 24. It's a pleasant drive out there since the rain's let up."

"Thanks," said Lembeck, standing up.

"Would you mind leaving by the side door? If you go back through the revolving door that'll produce another aptitude test. One more like this will depress me even more."

Lembeck used the side door.

***

Therapy was closed for alterations and the Information Booth in the Welfare Hub's Alternate Lobby suggested that Lembeck try the Motor Club of Southern California.

"The Motor Club?"

"Oops, oops," said the booth. "Sorry, Mr. Lembeck. Correcting. With your problem you had best see the Abraham Lincoln, Etc. Handout Kitchen in Sector 54, down on Central Street. They'll give you a food bundle and a good word until you get on your feet again."

"Thank you."

"No trouble. They have lots of road maps."

***

All the androids at the Abraham Lincoln, Etc. Handout Kitchen had beards. According to a sign in the Waiting Room today's special was veal wafers.

"Welcome, son," said a whiskered android. "In the name of

340

Abraham Lincoln, Theodore Roosevelt, Warren Gamaliel Harding, Barry Goldwater and 17 Latter-Day Great Americans let me welcome you." He handed Lembeck a nine by twelve punch hole sheet of blue paper and a pen, which was chained to his wrist. "Sign that and your package of nourishing food will be handed to you with the sincere best wishes of a group of citizens who, although they are too proud to let themselves sink down to poverty and too energetic not to rise to A rank, nevertheless take pity on those unfortunates who are lazy and indigent and, in many cases, just don't want to work for their bread or, as is the case today, veal wafers."

Lembeck read the paper over. "This says I swear under threat of criminal prosecution that I have never cadged a meal from the Abraham Lincoln, Etc. Handout Kitchen before and won't ever come whining back here again,"

"It's our way of teaching you to do and dare, risk and rise, stand and deliver," said the android. "Sign by the little X's."

Lembeck hadn't eaten since the night before and it was now nearly dusk. He signed.

***

Two days later Lembeck had to divorce his wife. He and Edith still loved each other. In fact, the candlelight suppers had brought them closer together. But the Real Estate Council had evicted them from their two-room apartment on the twenty-sixth floor of the Zanuck-Sahara Building and before Edith could move back in with her mother she had to be legally divorced from Lembeck. Living with her mother seemed to be the only way to get immediate food for Edith, The Abraham Lincoln, Etc. Handout Kitchen must have circulated Lembeck's name on their daily ne'er-do-well lists. When he went to a Food Dole Shelter two IBM machines blacked his eye and tossed him out. The Post-Termination Board gave him an appointment a month hence for a pre-interview to reconsider his request for a Temporary Food Card. The only thing that had come off smoothly and quickly was the divorce.

After that Edith was able to sneak food to Lembeck once a day. Her mother, though, was on a Pensioner's Low Calorie Food Allotment and even with an Incompetent Dependent Food Card in the offing for Edith there wasn't much chance of a lot of food coming out of the pantry outlet at Edith's mother's.

From an unemployed TV writer, with whom he had been ejected

from a Down-But-Not-Out One Night Sleep Hostel, Lembeck learned that the Adopt A Misfit Center might help him.

"You mean I can get a job with them?"

"No," said the ex-TV writer, guiding Lembeck into a thin slit of an alley that was policed by an android cop with a defective tube that made him night blind. "Here. We can sleep here tonight."

"I've been sleeping in my car," said Lembeck, settling down on some weeds, "but the Great Los Angeles Credit Authority took it back a couple days ago. Because I missed my regular $38.01 payment. If I'd had my savings account I could have done something. It turns out I forgot to send in my monthly statements saying that I wasn't planning to withdraw the money. They've been taking out a service charge of eight dollars and so the savings are gone."

"You're going to be perfect for the Adopt A Misfit Center."

"But not for a job?"

"No. Childless couples go there to adopt whatever they want. Not everyone wants a troublesome little kid. There are those who prefer maturity. When I was on top I adopted six 50-year-old men just to bounce my ideas off of. Those days we had a big six room place in the Benedict Canyon sector of Greater LA."

"Somebody would want to adopt a thirty-four-year-old ex-slogan writer?"

"Maybe," said the ex-writer, leaning back against the slick wall of the building. "Me, they didn't want. Ex-TV-writers depress people."

"I'll make an appointment," said Lembeck.

That night he dreamt of wafers.

***

The day before Lembeck visited the Adopt A Misfit Center an A2 couple from the Palm Springs sector of Greater Los Angeles had come in and adopted a 43-year-old ceramicist. That meant there would be a 30-day waiting period before Lembeck's application could be considered. The lobby of the Misfit Center did give him a cup of near-coffee and two donut wafers and that took care of the food problem for another day. That was Tuesday.

On Wednesday Lembeck got by on the food Edith slipped him. Thursday an A5 dropped a 20 calorie coupon in Lembeck's hand in front of a Martian style foodmart and Lembeck went in and had twenty calories worth of something thick and light blue. He now weighed fifteen pounds less than his usual one hundred fifty and his beard had filled out. The rest of the week he tried making the rounds of Termination Boards and welfare outlets again in hope of getting an earlier appointment. All he got was a small red punch card listing him as a Chronic Malcontent. He had to carry the card with him at all times or pay a fine.

On Sunday, Lembeck found the All-Purpose Automatic Religious Center. It had never occurred to him to turn to the church for help but as he was walking by the bright silver building in the derelict sector of Greater Los Angeles, a strong aroma of hot soup drifted out over the gold turnstiles and Lembeck was compelled to go inside.

There were, surprisingly considering the strong food scents inside, only two other people in the great vaulted room. An old C rating derelict in frayed gray sports clothes and an attractive blond girl of about twenty. The girl had on a clean pair of faded denim pants and a pale tartan shirt. The sniffling C rating derelict was sitting in front of the Buddhist display and the girl knelt before an automatic religious android whose denomination Lembeck couldn't place.

The smell of soup, and possibly a meat course, was strong in the big shadow-ceilinged room. Lembeck couldn't locate its source. He picked a friendly looking scarlet robed android and pushed the "On" button.

"What is life without a purpose, without a goal?" Asked the android in a warm rich voice.

"Could you tell me where the dining room is?"

"What is life without a goal? I will tell you, my son. A hollow shell."

"I didn't eat yesterday. I thought, noticing the aroma, that I might be able to arrange for a meal here."

"Those of us who have fallen from the main currents of Greater Los Angeles Society need goals, too. And though it is truly said that nobody starves in this day and age, nevertheless a certain hunger can grow up."

"That's right," agreed Lembeck.

"A two-year hitch with the Martian Reclamation And Roadway Corps provides you with a goal, a purpose and three minimum calorie requirement meals each and every day," said the android. "When I have finished my sermon an application blank will issue from the slot marked goal. Sign it and put it back in the slot. This time tomorrow you will be en route to the red planet on a fine ship

343

where meals of great warmth and nourishment are served at regular hours. Sign, my son."

"I don't want to go to Mars. I have an ex-wife down by the ocean. I just want something to eat until I get a job."

"Life is nice when you have a purpose," said the android and clicked off.

An application form dropped out into Lembeck's hand.

"Don't," said a voice at his side.

It was the blond girl. "Ma'am?"

"The other guy's too far gone for us, but you might do. Want to join?"

"Join what?"

"Tell you outside," she said. "Come on."

"I don't want to go to Mars."

"Neither do we."

"Couldn't I see somebody about a bowl of soup?"

"There's no food here."

"The smell."

"It's a chemical substance they feed into blowers," she said, nodding her head at the ceiling.

Lembeck went outside with the girl.

***

Sawtelle was a tall grizzle-whiskered man, thin in his khaki coat and pants. He handed Lembeck a half a vegetable wafer and a real piece of near-cheese. The food caught a pleasant glow from the camp fire. "I have a hundred in my group so far," Sawtelle said. "Dotted all over the Sierra Madres here." He pointed at the 100 million lights of Greater Los Angeles fanning away far below. "Misfits and unemployables. We don't eat well. But we do, with our raids and our experimental gardens, manage to eat without taking charity."

The blond girl, her name was Margery McCracklin, was one of Sawtelle's recruiters. She was sitting quietly across the cave.

Lembeck, watching her as he ate, noticed that her wrists were narrow and sharp, her ankles, too. It had taken them a long time to climb up here into the mountains to Sawtelle's temporary encampment. "You steal food and supplies?" Lembeck asked. He broke the piece of cheese into four sections, making each one last four bites.

"Yes," said Sawtelle. "Only from the A class and the top half of

344

the B's. Those who have well above the minimum."

"I have an ex-wife," said Lembeck. "If I joined you would I be able to see her?"

"I have an ex-wife, too," said Sawtelle. "Margery has an ex-child. We all try to pay visits and give over what food we can."

Lembeck ran his tongue over his teeth. "I hate to hurt my job chances."

Margery laughed. "You'll probably never get called back in. Once you get edged out of the system you seldom get back."

"It has nothing to do with you," said Sawtelle. "With an almost 100% automatic employment and welfare system in Greater Los Angeles little kinks are bound to show up now and then."

"I'll never work again?"

"That's what," said Margery, hunching toward the small fire, "has happened to most of us. If you get another chance with them they need never know about this part of your life."

"They usually only check for an actual conviction record," said Sawtelle. "You could be given a criminal inclinations aptitude test. You could get caught." He cut himself a hunk of near-cheese from the piece in his jacket pocket.

"All right," said Lembeck. "What the hell. Okay."

Margery smiled at him.

***

An A class housewife in a four-room ranch style house in the Pasadena sector of Greater Los Angeles shot Margery dead on the third food raid Lembeck went on.

Lembeck kept running, a package of turkey wafers under his coat. There was no doubt that Margery was gone. The blaster pistol had lit up the night long enough for him to see her die over his shoulder.

At dawn he was well into the mountains. But where Sawtelle was he had no idea. Margery had been his partner on all his missions and, since Lembeck was still breaking in, Margery had been entrusted with the pattern of campsite shifts.

Day came on and Lembeck opened the package of wafers and ate two, chewing and swallowing fast as he climbed. His stomach made unsettled sounds and he stopped finally and ate a whole handful of the turkey wafers.

The brush was thick and there were clusters of trees up here. Lembeck had trouble breathing and he knew that he must have climbed higher than he had realized. He made it over a rise and found a narrow path leading down into a slight cup-like clearing. This would be a good place to rest.

He sat on a mossy rock and ate another handful of wafers and then the box was empty. Lembeck dropped it between his feet. That was wrong. He decided to hide the empty box.

Off to his right a thick growth of thorny bushes tangled together over a crevice. He went over to stuff the empty wafer carton in there. His hand and arm got scratched as he slid the box in through the thorns. He cocked his wrist to fling the box away. But the box hit against something solid. Lembeck shoved both hands in and forced the bushes aside. He saw a door handle.

"Well, let's see now," he said. He twisted one arm up to guard his face and head and then pushed through the bushes. He caught the handle and turned it. A door opened in and he fell forward and onto a slanting corridor. His hand still on the handle, he looked at the door. A small plate on it read: "Nuclear Emergency Food Storehouse No. Twenty. Stocked by the Pasadena Chamber of Commerce, May, 1991."

Lembeck left the door open and moved down the corridor. When he hit the end of the incline, lights went on in the room beyond. "It's stayed in working order all these years," he said.

The room was bigger than the apartment he and Edith had had and it seemed to be surrounded by other rooms. On shelves on two walls there were packages of preserved foods and in the room's center there was something labeled "Safe Water Well." Another room had smoked meats, the real stuff, and bottles of wine and brandy and whiskey. There were packages and containers of foods Lembeck had only heard of. Besides all that there were shelves of old-fashioned food wafers. And all of the food was still edible. The labels testified that it had been preserved in ways that would make it last until an emergency made its use necessary. There had been no emergency since 1991, not the kind the Pasadena Chamber of Commerce had been thinking about.

In all there were five big rooms, each filled with food and assorted drink, including two still functioning wells. Lembeck laughed as he made glancing inventories of the storehouse. He knew exactly what he would do now. That religious android had been right. When you had a purpose, life was okay.

Lembeck took a look around the main room and then ran up the ramp corridor to the outer door.

He slammed the door shut and ran back inside.

He started to eat.

Discover new and exciting works by 13Thirty Books at
www.13thirtybooks.com

Made in United States
North Haven, CT
27 December 2022